D1575964

One Plus One

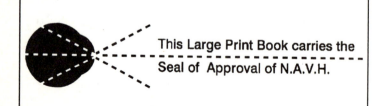

This Large Print Book carries the
Seal of Approval of N.A.V.H.

ONE PLUS ONE

JOJO MOYES

THORNDIKE PRESS
A part of Gale, Cengage Learning

GALE
CENGAGE Learning·

Farmington Hills, Mich • San Francisco • New York • Waterville, Maine
Meriden, Conn • Mason, Ohio • Chicago

GALE
CENGAGE Learning·

Copyright © 2014 by JoJo's Mojo Limited.
Thorndike Press, a part of Gale, Cengage Learning.

ALL RIGHTS RESERVED

Thorndike Press® Large Print Core.
The text of this Large Print edition is unabridged.
Other aspects of the book may vary from the original edition.
Set in 16 pt. Plantin.

LIBRARY OF CONGRESS CIP DATA ON FILE.
CATALOGUING IN PUBLICATION FOR THIS BOOK
IS AVAILABLE FROM THE LIBRARY OF CONGRESS

ISBN-13: 978-1-4104-6671-6 (hardcover)
ISBN-10: 1-4104-6671-X (hardcover)

Published in 2014 by arrangement with Pamela Dorman Books, an imprint of Viking, a member of Penguin Group (USA) LLC, a Penguin Random House Company

Printed in the United States of America
1 2 3 4 5 6 7 18 17 16 15 14

To Charles

ACKNOWLEDGMENTS

Thank you as ever to my amazing Penguin teams on both sides of the Atlantic. At Penguin UK I am in particular indebted to Louise Moore, Clare Bowron, Francesca Russell, and Elizabeth Smith, as well as Mari Evans and Viviane Basset. In the United States, thank you to Pamela Dorman, Kiki Koroshetz, Louise Braverman, Rebecca Lang, Annie Harris, and Carolyn Coleburn. Thank you, too, to all the lovely media escorts — Cindy Hamel Sellers, Carolyn Kretzer, Debb Flynn Hanrahan, Esther Levine, Larry Lewis, and Mary Gielow — who have spent so much time with me over there this year. In Germany, thank you to Katharina Dornhofer, Marcus Gaertner, and Grusche Junker and all the team at Rowohlt for your wonderful work.

At Curtis Brown, thank you yet again to my indefatigable agent Sheila Crowley, and to Rebecca Ritchie, Katie McGowan,

Sophie Harris, Rachel Clements, and Alice Lutyens, as well as Jessica Cooper, Kat Buckle, Sven van Damme, and of course Jonny Geller.

Thank you to Robin Oliver and Jane Foran for advice on insider-trading law. I have had to skew the legal procedure slightly to fit the plot, so any errors or anomalies are entirely my own.

More generally, thank you to Pia Printz, Damian Barr, Alex Heminsley, Polly Samson, David Gilmour, Cathy Runciman, Jess Ruston, and Emma Freud, as well as the gang at Writersblock, for excellent narrative interruptions. Also for excessive levels of help, advice, and general loveliness, Ol Parker and Jonathan Harvey — thank you.

Thanks nearer home to Jackie Tearne, Chris Luckley, Claire Roweth, Vanessa Hollis, and Sue Donovan, without whom I couldn't have fit in the actual writing.

Thank you to Kieron and Sharon Smith and their daughter Tanzie, after whom the main character in this book was named in appreciation of their generous bid in a charity auction in aid of the Stepping Stones Down Syndrome Support Group.

And thanks to my parents — Jim Moyes, Lizzie and Brian Sanders — and, most important, Charles, Saskia, Harry, and Lockie, for being the point of it all.

Prologue:
Ed

Ed Nicholls was in the creatives' room drinking coffee with Ronan when Sidney walked in. A man he vaguely recognized stood behind him, another of the Suits.

"We've been looking for you," Sidney said.

"Well, you found us," Ed said.

"Not Ronan, you."

Ed studied them for a minute, then threw a red foam ball at the ceiling and caught it. He glanced sideways at Ronan. Investacorp had bought half shares in the company a full eighteen months ago, but Ed and Ronan still thought of them as the Suits. It was one of the kinder things they called them in private.

"Do you know a woman called Deanna Lewis?"

"Why?"

"Did you give her any information about the launch of the new software?"

"What?"

"It's a simple question."

Ed looked from one Suit to the other. The atmosphere was strangely charged. His stomach, a packed elevator, began a slow descent toward his feet. "We may have chatted about work. No specifics that I remember."

"Deanna Lewis?" said Ronan.

"You need to be clear about this, Ed. Did you give her any information about the launch of SFAX?"

"No. Maybe. What is this?"

"The police are downstairs searching your office, with two goons from the Financial Services Authority. Her brother has been arrested for insider trading. On the basis of information that you gave them about the launch of the software."

"Deanna Lewis? *Our* Deanna Lewis?" Ronan began to wipe his spectacles, a thing he did when he was feeling anxious.

"Her brother's hedge fund made two point six million dollars on the first day of trading. She alone cleared a hundred and ninety thousand on her personal account."

"Her brother's hedge fund?"

"I don't understand," Ronan said.

"I'll spell it out. Deanna Lewis is on record talking to her brother about the launch of SFAX. She says Ed here said it was going to be enormous. And guess what? Two days later her brother's fund is among the biggest purchasers of shares. What exactly did you tell her?"

Ronan stared at him. Ed struggled to gather his thoughts. When he swallowed, it was shamefully audible. Across the office the development team was peering over the tops of their cubicles. "I didn't tell her anything." He blinked. "I don't know. I might have said something. It's not like it was a state secret."

"It *was* a fucking state secret, Ed," Sidney said. "It's called insider trading. She told him you gave her dates, times. You told her the company was going to make a fortune."

"Then she's lying! Shooting her mouth off. We were just . . . having a thing."

"You wanted to bone the girl, so you shot your mouth off to impress her?"

"It wasn't like that."

"You had sex with Deanna Lewis?" Ed could feel Ronan's myopic gaze burning into him.

Sidney lifted his hands. "You need to call your lawyer."

"How can I be in trouble?" Ed asked. "It's not like I got any benefit from it. I didn't even know her brother had a hedge fund."

Sidney glanced behind him. The faces

suddenly found something interesting to look at on their desks. He lowered his voice. "You have to go now. They want to interview you at the police station."

"What? This is nuts. I've got a software meeting in twenty minutes. I'm not going to any police station."

"And obviously we're suspending you until we've got to the bottom of this."

Ed half laughed. "Are you kidding me? You can't suspend me. It's my company." He threw the foam ball up in the air and caught it, turning away from them. Nobody moved. "I'm not going. This is our company. Tell them, Ronan."

He looked at Ronan, but Ronan was staring fixedly at something on the floor. Ed looked at Sidney, who shook his head. Then he looked up at the two uniformed men who had appeared behind him, at his secretary, whose hand was covering her mouth, at the carpet path already opening up between him and the door, and the foam ball dropped silently onto the floor between his feet.

CHAPTER ONE:
JESS

Jess Thomas and Nathalie Benson slumped in the seats of their van, which was parked far enough away from Nathalie's house that they couldn't be seen from inside. Nathalie was smoking. She had given it up for the fourth time six weeks ago.

"Eighty pounds a week, guaranteed. And holiday pay." Nathalie let out a scream. "Bloody hell. I actually want to find the tart who left that earring and thump her for losing us our best job."

"Maybe she didn't know he was married."

"Oh, she knew." Before she'd met Dean, Nathalie had spent two years with a man who turned out to have not one but two families on the other side of Southampton. "No single man keeps color-coordinated scatter cushions on his bed."

"Neil Brewster does," Jess said.

"Neil Brewster's music collection is sixty-seven percent Judy Garland, thirty-three percent Pet Shop Boys."

They had cleaned together every weekday for four years, since back when the Beachfront Holiday Park was part paradise, part building site. Back when the developers promised local families access to the swimming pool and assured everyone that a large upmarket development would bring benefits to their little seaside town, instead of sucking out what remained of its life. The faded moniker, BENSON & THOMAS CLEANING, was stenciled on the side of their white van. Nathalie had added underneath: A BIT DIRTY? CAN WE HELP? until Jess pointed out that for two whole months half the calls they had received had nothing to do with cleaning.

Nearly all their jobs were in the Beachfront development now. Hardly anybody in town had the money — or the inclination — to hire a cleaner, except for the doctors, the solicitor, and the odd client like Mrs. Humphrey, whose arthritis had stopped her from doing it herself. It was a good job on the one hand. You could work for yourself, organize your own hours, pick and choose your clients for the most part. The downside, weirdly, was not the crappy clients (and there always was at least one crappy client) or that scrubbing someone else's toilet somehow left you feeling like you were one step lower on a ladder than you had planned to be. Jess didn't mind pulling lumps of hair out of other people's plug-holes or the fact that most people who rented holiday homes seemed to feel obliged to live like pigs for a week.

What she didn't like was that you ended up finding out much more about other people's lives than you really wanted to.

Jess could have told you about Mrs. Eldridge's secret shopping habit: the de-signer shoe receipts she stuffed into the bathroom bin, and the bags of unworn clothes in her wardrobe, the tags still firmly attached. She could tell you that Lena Thompson had been trying for a baby for four years and used two pregnancy tests a month (rumor had it she left her tights on). She could tell you that Mr. Mitchell in the big house behind the church earned a six-figure salary (he left his pay slips on the hall table; Nathalie swore he did it deliberately) and that his daughter smoked secretly in the bathroom.

If she was so inclined, Jess could have named the women who went out looking immaculate — hair faultless, nails polished, lightly spritzed with expensive scent — who thought nothing of leaving soiled knickers

17

in full view on the floor. Or the teenage boys whose stiff towels she didn't want to pick up without a pair of tongs. There were the couples who spent every night in separate beds, the wives insisting brightly when they asked her to change the spare-room sheets that they'd had an "awful lot of guests lately," the lavatories that required a gas mask and a HAZCHEM warning.

And then every once in a while you got a nice client like Lisa Ritter and popped over to vacuum her floors and came away with a diamond earring and a whole load of knowledge you could really have done without.

"It's probably my daughter's, from when she came home last time," Lisa Ritter had said, her voice quivering slightly with the effort as she held it in her hand. "She's got a pair just like it."

"Of course," Jess said. "It probably got kicked into your bedroom. Or carried in on someone's shoe. We knew it would be something like that. I'm sorry. If I had known it wasn't yours, I would never have bothered you with it." And she knew right then, as Mrs. Ritter turned away from her, that that would be it. People didn't thank you for bringing bad news to their doors.

At the end of the road a padded toddler toppled gently onto the ground like a felled tree and, after a brief silence, started wailing. Its mother, her two armloads of shopping bags perfectly balanced, stood and stared in mute dismay.

"Look, you heard what she said the other week — Lisa Ritter would get rid of her hairdresser before she'd get rid of us."

Nathalie made the face that said Jess would look on the bright side of a nuclear apocalypse. "Before she got rid of 'the cleaners.' That's different. She won't care whether it's us or Speedicleanz or Maids with Mops." Nathalie shook her head. "Nope. To her, from now on, we'll always be the cleaners who know the truth about her cheating husband. It matters to women like her. They're all about appearances, aren't they?"

The mother put down her bags and stooped to pick up the toddler. Jess put her bare feet up on the dashboard and let her face fall into her hands. "Bugger it. How are we going to make up that money, Nat?"

"That house was immaculate. It was basically a twice-a-week polishing job." Nathalie stared out the window.

"And she always paid on time."

Jess kept seeing that diamond earring. Why hadn't they just ignored it? It would have actually been better if one of them had simply stolen it. "Okay, so she's going to cancel us. Let's change the subject, Nat. I can't afford to cry before my pub shift."

"So, did Marty ring this week?"

"I didn't mean change the subject to *that*."

"Well, did he?"

Jess sighed. "Yup."

"Did he say why he didn't ring the week before?" Nathalie shoved Jess's feet off the dashboard.

"Nope." Jess could feel her staring. "And no, he didn't send any money."

"Oh, come *on*. You've got to get the Child Support Agency onto him. You can't carry on like this. He should send money for his own kids."

It was an old argument. "He's . . . he's still not right," Jess said. "I can't put more pressure on him. He hasn't got a job yet."

"Well, you're going to need that money now. Until we get another job like Lisa Ritter's. How's Nicky?"

"I went round to Jason Fisher's house to talk to his mum."

"You're joking. She scares the pants off me. Did she say she'd get him to leave Nicky alone?"

"Something like that."

Nathalie kept her eyes on Jess and dropped her chin two inches.

"She told me if I set foot on her doorstep once more she'd batter me halfway to next Wednesday. Me and my . . . what was it? . . . me and my 'freakazoid kids.' " Jess pulled down the passenger mirror and checked her hair, pulling it back into a ponytail. "Oh, and then she told me her Jason wouldn't hurt a fly."

"Typical."

"It's fine. I had Norman with me. And, bless him, he took an enormous dump next to their Toyota and somehow I forgot I had a plastic bag in my pocket."

Jess put her feet back up.

Nathalie pushed them down again and mopped the dashboard with a wet wipe. "Seriously, though, Jess. How long has Marty been gone? Two years? You're young. You can't wait around for him to sort himself out. You've got to get back on the horse," Nathalie said with a grimace.

"Get back on the horse. Nice."

"Liam Stubbs fancies you. You could totally ride that."

"Any certified pair of X chromosomes could ride Liam Stubbs." Jess closed the window. "I'm better off reading a book. Besides, I think the kids have had enough upheaval in their lives without playing Meet Your New Uncle. Right?" She looked up,

21

wrinkled her nose at the sky. "I've got to get the tea on, and then I've got to get ready for the pub. I'll do a quick ring-round before I go, see if any of the clients want any extras doing. And you never know, she might not cancel us."

Nathalie lowered her window and blew out a long trail of smoke. "Sure, Dorothy. And our next job is going to be cleaning the Emerald City at the end of the Yellow Brick Road."

Number 14 Seacole Avenue was filled with the sound of distant explosions. Tanzie had calculated recently that, since he'd turned sixteen, Nicky had spent 88 percent of his spare time in his bedroom. Jess could hardly blame him.

Jess dropped her cleaning crate in the hall, hung up her jacket, made her way upstairs, feeling the familiar faint dismay at the threadbare state of the carpet, and pushed at his door. He was wearing a set of head-phones and shooting somebody; the smell of weed was strong enough to make her reel.

"Nicky," she said, and someone exploded in a hail of bullets. "Nicky." She walked over to him and pulled his headphones off, so that he turned, his expression briefly be-mused, like someone hauled from sleep.

"Hard at work, then?"

"Study break."

She picked up an ashtray and held it toward him. "I thought I told you."

"It's from last night. Couldn't sleep."

"Not in the house, Nicky." There was no point telling him not at all. They all did it around here. She told herself she was lucky he had only started at fifteen.

"Is Tanzie back yet?" She stooped to pick up stray socks and mugs from the floor.

"No. Oh. The school rang after lunch."

"What?"

He typed something into the computer, then turned to face her. "I don't know. Something about school."

She lifted a lock of that dyed black hair, and there it was: a fresh mark on his cheekbone. He ducked away. "Are you okay?"

He shrugged, looked away from her.

"Did they come after you again?"

"I'm fine."

"Why didn't you call me?"

"No credit on my phone." He leaned back and fired a virtual grenade. The screen exploded into a ball of flame. He replaced his headphones and went back to the screen.

Nicky had come to live with Jess full-time eight years previously. He was Marty's son

23

by Della, a woman he'd dated briefly in his teens. Nicky had arrived silent and wary, his limbs thin and elongated, his appetite raging. His mother had fallen in with a new crowd, finally disappearing somewhere in the Midlands with a man called Big Al, who never looked anyone in the eye and clutched an ever-present can of Tennent's Extra in his oversized fist. Nicky had been found sleeping in the locker rooms at school, and when the social workers called again, Jess had said he could come to them. "Just what you need," Nathalie had said. "Another mouth to feed."

"He's my stepson."

"You've met him twice in four years. And you're not even twenty."

"Well, that's how families are these days."

Afterward, she sometimes wondered whether that had been the final straw; the thing that had caused Marty to abdicate responsibility for his family altogether. But Nicky was a good kid, under all the raven hair and eyeliner. He was sweet to Tanzie, and on his good days he talked and laughed and allowed Jess the occasional awkward hug, and she was glad of him, even if it sometimes felt as if she had basically acquired one more person to feel anxious about.

She stepped out into the garden with the phone and took a deep breath. "Um . . . hello? It's Jessica Thomas here. I had a message to call."

A pause.

"Is Tanzie . . . ? Is . . . is everything all right?"

"Everything's fine. Sorry. I should have said. It's Mr. Tsvangarai here, Tanzie's maths teacher."

"Oh." She pictured him: a tall man in a gray suit. Face like a funeral director.

"I wanted to talk to you because a few weeks ago I had a very interesting discussion with a former colleague of mine who works for St. Anne's."

"St. Anne's?" Jess frowned. "The private school?"

"Yes. They have a scholarship program for children who are exceptionally gifted in maths. And as you know, we had already earmarked Tanzie as gifted and talented."

"Because she's good at maths."

"Better than good. Well, we gave her the qualifying exam paper to sit last week. I don't know if she mentioned it? I sent a letter home, but I wasn't sure you saw it."

Jess squinted at a seagull in the sky. A few gardens along, Terry Blackstone had started singing along to a radio. He had been known to do the full Rod Stewart if he thought nobody was looking.

"We got the results back this morning. And she has done well. Extremely well. Mrs. Thomas, if you're agreeable, they would like to interview her for a subsidized place."

She found herself parroting him. "A subsidized place?"

"For certain children of exceptional ability St. Anne's will forgo a significant proportion of the school fees. It means that Tanzie would get a top-class education. She has an extraordinary numerical ability, Mrs. Thomas. I do think this could be a great opportunity for her."

"St. Anne's? But . . . she'd need to get a bus across town. She'd need all the uniforms and kits. She — she wouldn't know anyone."

"She'd make friends. But these are just details, Mrs. Thomas. Let's wait and see what the school comes up with. Tanzie is a talented girl." He paused. When she didn't say anything, he lowered his voice: "I have been teaching maths for almost twenty-two years, Mrs. Thomas. And I have never met a child who grasped mathematical concepts as well as she does. I believe she is actually exceeding the point where I have anything to teach her. Algorithms, probability, prime numbers —"

"Okay. This is where you lose me, Mr. Tsvangarai."

He chuckled. "I'll be in touch."

She put down the phone and sat heavily on the white plastic garden chair that had grown a fine sheen of emerald moss. She stared at nothing, in through the window at the curtains that Marty had always thought were too bright, at the red plastic tricycle she had never got round to getting rid of, at next door's cigarette butts sprinkled like confetti on her path, at the rotten boards in the fence the dog insisted on sticking his head through. And despite what Nathalie referred to as her frankly misguided optimism, Jess found her eyes had filled unexpectedly with tears.

There were lots of awful things about the father of your children leaving: the money issues, the suppressed anger on behalf of your children, the way most of your coupled-up friends now treated you as if you were some kind of potential husband stealer. But worse than that, worse than the endless, bloody exhausting financial and energy-sapping struggle, was that being a parent on your own when you were totally out of your depth was actually the loneliest place on earth.

27

CHAPTER TWO:
TANZIE

Twenty-six cars sat in the car park at St. Anne's. Two rows of thirteen shiny four-wheel-drives faced each other, sliding in and out of the spaces at an average angle of 41 degrees before the next in line moved in.

Tanzie watched them as she and Mum crossed the road from the bus stop, the drivers talking illegally into phones or mouthing at bug-eyed blond babies in the rear seats. Mum lifted her chin and fiddled with her house keys in her free hand, as if they were actually her car keys and she and Tanzie just happened to have parked somewhere nearby. Mum kept glancing behind her. Tanzie guessed she was worried she was going to bump into one of her cleaning clients, who would ask what she was doing there.

Tanzie had never been inside St. Anne's, although she'd passed it on the bus at least ten times because the National Health Service dentist was on this road. From the outside, there was just an endless hedge, trimmed to exactly 90 degrees (she wondered if the gardener used a protractor), and big trees where the branches hung low, sweeping out across the playing fields as if they were there to shelter the children below.

The children at St. Anne's did not swing bags at each other's heads or back each other against the wall to steal lunch money. There were no weary-sounding teachers herding the teenagers into classrooms. The girls had not rolled their skirts six times over at the waistband. Not a single person was smoking. Her mother gave her hand a little squeeze. Tanzie wished she didn't look so nervous. "It's nice, isn't it, Mum?"

She nodded. "Yes." It came out as a squeak.

"Mr. Tsvangarai told me that every single one of their sixth-formers who did maths got A or A starred. That's good, isn't it?"

"Amazing."

Tanzie pulled a bit at Mum's hand so they could get to the headmaster's office faster. "Do you think Norman will miss me when I'm doing the long days?"

"The long days."

"St. Anne's doesn't finish till six. And there's maths club on Tuesdays and Thursdays — I'd definitely want to do that."

Her mother glanced at her. She looked really tired. She was always tired these days. She put on one of those smiles that wasn't really a smile at all, and they went in.

"Hello, Mrs. Thomas. Hello, Costanza. It's very good to meet you. Do sit down."

The headmaster's study had a high ceiling with white plaster rosettes every twenty centimeters, and tiny rosebuds exactly halfway between them. The room was stuffed with old furniture and through a large bay window a man on a ride-on mower traveled slowly up and down a cricket pitch. On a small table somebody had laid out a tray of coffee and biscuits. You could tell they were homemade. Mum used to make the same kind before Dad left.

Tanzie sat down on the edge of the sofa and gazed at the two men opposite. The one with the mustache smiled like the nurse did before she gave you an injection. Mum had pulled her bag onto her lap and Tanzie could see her holding her hand over the corner Norman had chewed. Her leg was jiggling.

"This is Mr. Cruikshank. He's the head of maths. And I'm Mr. Daly. I've been head here for the past two years."

Tanzie looked up from her biscuit.

30

"Do you do chords?"

"We do," Mr. Cruikshank said.

"And probability?"

"That, too."

Mr. Cruikshank leaned forward. "We've been looking at your test results. And we think, Costanza, that you should sit your GCSE in maths next year and get it out of the way. Because I think you'd rather enjoy the A-level problems."

She looked at him. "Have you got actual papers?"

"I've got some next door. Would you like to see them?"

She couldn't believe he was asking. She thought briefly of saying "Well, duh," like Nicky would. But she just nodded.

Mr. Daly handed Mum a coffee. "I won't beat around the bush, Mrs. Thomas. You are well aware that your daughter has an exceptional ability. We have only seen scores like hers once before and that was from a pupil who went on to be a fellow at Trinity."

He went on and on so much that Tanzie tuned out a little: ". . . for a very select group of pupils who have a demonstrably unusual ability, we have created a new equal-access scholarship." *Blah, blah, blah.* "It would offer a child who might not otherwise get the advantages of a school like this the chance to fulfill their potential in . . ." *Blah, blah.* "While we are very keen to see how far Costanza could go in the field of maths, we would also want to make sure that she was well rounded in other parts of her student life. We have a full sporting and musical curriculum." *Blah, blah, blah . . .* "Numerate children are often also able in languages . . ." *Blah, blah* ". . . and drama — that's often very popular with girls of her age."

"I only really like maths," she told him. "And dogs."

"Well, we don't have much in the way of dogs, but we'd certainly offer you lots of opportunities to stretch yourself mathematically. But I think you might be surprised by what else you enjoy. Do you play any instruments?"

She shook her head.

"Any languages?"

The room went a bit quiet.

"Other interests?"

"We go swimming on Fridays," Mum said.

"We haven't been swimming since Dad left."

Mum smiled, but it went a bit wonky. "We have, Tanzie."

"Once. May the thirteenth. But now you work on Fridays."

Mr. Cruikshank left the room, and re-appeared a moment later with his papers. She stuffed the last biscuit into her mouth, then got up and went to sit next to him. He had a whole pile of them. Stuff she hadn't even started yet!

She began going through the pages with him, showing him what she had done and what she hadn't, and in the background she could hear Mum and the headmaster's voices rumbling away.

It sounded like it was going all right. Tanzie let her attention travel to what was on the page. "Yes," Mr. Cruikshank was saying quietly, his finger on the page. "But the curious feature of renewal processes is that, if we wait some predetermined time and then observe how large the renewal interval containing it is, we should expect it to be typically larger than a renewal interval of average size."

She knew about this! "So the monkeys would take longer to type Macbeth?"

"That's it." He smiled. "I wasn't sure you'd have covered any renewal theory."

"I haven't, really. But Mr. Tsvangarai told me about it once and I looked it up on the Internet. I liked the whole monkey thing." She flicked through the papers. The numbers sang to her. She could feel her brain humming and she knew she had to go to this school. "Mum," she said. She didn't usually interrupt, but she was too excited and forgot her manners. "Do you think we could get some of these problems?"

Mr. Daly looked over. He didn't seem to mind about the missing manners. "Mr. Cruikshank, have we any spares?"

"You can take these."

He handed them over! Just like that! Outside a bell rang and she could hear children walking past the office window, their shoes crunching on the gravel.

"So . . . what happens next?" Mum asked.

"Well, we'd like to offer Costanza . . . Tanzie . . . a scholarship." Mr. Daly lifted a glossy folder from the table. "Here's our prospectus and the relevant documentation. The scholarship covers ninety percent of the fees. It's the most generous scholarship this school has ever offered. Usually fifty percent is our maximum, given the extensive waiting list of pupils hoping to come here." He held out the plate toward Tanzie. Somehow they had filled it with new biscuits. This really was the greatest school ever.

"Ninety percent," Mum said. She put her biscuit back on her saucer.

"I do appreciate that there is still a considerable financial commitment involved. And

34

there would also be uniform and travel costs, and any extras she might want, like music or school trips. But I would like to stress that this is an incredible opportunity." He leaned forward. "We would love to have you here, Tanzie. Your maths teacher says you're a joy to work with."

"I like school," she said, reaching for another biscuit. "I know lots of my friends think it's boring. But I prefer school to home."

They all laughed awkwardly.

"Not because of you, Mum," she said, and helped herself to another biscuit. "But my mum does have to work a lot."

Everyone went quiet.

"We all do, these days," said Mr. Cruikshank.

"Well," Mr. Daly said, "it's a lot for you to think about. And I'm sure you have other questions for us. But why don't you finish your coffee, and then I'll get one of our pupils to show you around the rest of the school? Then you can discuss this between yourselves."

Tanzie was in the garden throwing a ball for Norman. She was determined that one day he would fetch it and bring it back. She had read somewhere that repetition increased the probability of an animal learning how to do something by a factor of four. She wasn't sure Norman could count, though.

They'd got Norman from the animal shelter after Dad left and Mum stayed awake for eleven nights in a row worrying that they would be murdered in their beds once everyone realized he'd gone. Brilliant with kids, a fantastic guard dog, the rescue center said. Mum kept saying, "But he's so big."

"Even more of a deterrent," they said with cheery smiles. "And did we mention he's brilliant with kids?"

Two years on, Mum said Norman was basically an enormous eating and crapping machine. He drooled on cushions and howled in his sleep, plodded around the house shedding hair and leaving evil smells behind him. Mum said the rescue center had been right: nobody would break into their house for fear Norman would gas them to death.

She had given up trying to ban him from Tanzie's bedroom. When Tanzie woke up in the morning, he was always stretched across three quarters of the bed, hairy legs across her bedsheet, leaving her shivering under a tiny corner of duvet. Mum used to mutter about hairs and hygiene, but Tanzie didn't mind.

They'd got Nicky when she was two. Tanzie went to bed one night and when she woke, he was in the spare room and Mum just said he would be staying and he was her brother. Tanzie had once asked him what he thought their shared genetic material was, and he'd said, "The weird loser gene." She thought he might have been joking, but she didn't know enough about genetics to check.

She was rinsing her hands under the outside tap when she heard them talking. Nicky's window was open and their voices floated out into the garden.

"Did you pay that water bill?" Nicky said.

"No. I haven't had a chance to get to the post office."

"It says it's a final reminder."

"I know it's a final reminder." Mum was snappy, like she always was when she talked about money. There was a pause. Norman picked up the ball and dropped it near her feet. It lay there, slimy and disgusting.

"Sorry, Nicky. I . . . just need to get this conversation out of the way. I'll sort it out tomorrow morning. I promise. You want to speak to your dad?"

Tanzie knew what the answer would be.

Nicky never wanted to talk to Dad anymore.

"Hey."

Tanzie moved right under the window and stood really still. She could hear Dad's voice on Skype, tense.

"Everything all right?" She wondered if he thought that something bad had happened. Perhaps if he thought Tanzie had leukemia, he might come back. She had watched a TV film once where the girl's parents divorced and then got back together because she got leukemia. She didn't actually want leukemia, though, because needles made her pass out and she had quite nice hair.

"Everything's fine," Mum said. She didn't tell him about Nicky getting battered.

"What's going on?"

A pause.

"Has your mum decorated?" Mum asked.

"What?"

"New wallpaper."

"Oh. That."

Grandma's house had new wallpaper? Tanzie felt weird. Dad and Grandma were living in a house that she might not recognize anymore. It had been 348 days since she last saw Dad. It was 433 days since she'd seen Grandma.

"I need to talk to you about Tanzie's schooling."

"Why? What's she done?"

"Nothing like that, Marty. She's been offered a scholarship to St. Anne's."

"St. Anne's?"

"They think her maths is off the scale."

"St. Anne's." He said it like he couldn't believe it. "I mean, I knew she was bright but . . ."

He sounded really pleased. She pressed her back against the wall and went up on tippy-toes to hear better. Perhaps he'd come back if she was going to St. Anne's.

"Our little girl at the posh school, eh?" His voice had puffed up with pride. Tanzie could imagine him already working out what to tell his mates at the pub. Except he couldn't go to the pub. Because he always told Mum he had no money to enjoy himself. "So what's the problem?"

"Well . . . it's a big scholarship. But it doesn't cover everything."

"Meaning what?"

"Meaning we'd still have to find five hundred pounds a term. And the uniform. And the registration fee of five hundred pounds."

The silence went on for so long Tanzie wondered if the computer had crashed.

"They said once we've been there a year we can apply for a hardship fee. Some bursary or something where, if you're a deserving case, they can give you extra. But basically we need to find the best part of two grand to get her through the first year."

And then Dad laughed. He actually laughed. "You're joking, right?"

"No, I am not joking."

"How am I meant to find two grand, Jess?"

"I just thought I'd —"

"I've not even got a proper job yet. There's nothing going on round here. I'm . . . I'm only just getting back on my feet. I'm sorry, babe, but there's no way."

"Can't your mum help? She might have some savings. Can I talk to her?"

"No. She's . . . out. And I don't want you tapping her for money. She's got worries enough as it is."

"I'm not tapping her for money, Marty. I thought she might want to help her only grandchildren."

"They're not her only grandchildren anymore. Elena had a little boy."

Tanzie stood very still.

"I didn't even know Elena was pregnant."

"Yeah, I meant to tell you."

Tanzie had a baby cousin. And she hadn't even known. Norman flopped down at her feet. He looked at her with his big brown eyes, then rolled over slowly with a groan, as if it were really, really hard work just lying on the floor.

"Well . . . what if we sell the Rolls?"

"I can't sell the Rolls. I'm going to start the weddings business up again."

"It's been rusting in our garage for the best part of two years."

"I know. And I'll come and get it. I just haven't got anywhere to store it safely up here."

The voices had that edge now. Their conversations often ended this way. She heard Mum take a deep breath. "Can you at least think about it, Marty? She really wants to go to this place. Really, really wants to go. When the maths teacher spoke to her, her whole face lit up like I haven't seen since —"

"Since I left."

"I didn't mean it like that."

"So it's all my fault."

"No, it's not all your fault, Marty. But I'm not going to sit here and pretend that you going has been a barrel of laughs for them. Tanzie doesn't understand why you don't visit her. She doesn't understand why she hardly gets to see you anymore."

"I can't afford the fares, Jess. You know that. There's no point you going on and on at me. I've been ill."

41

"I know you've been ill."

"She can come and see me anytime. I told you. Send them both at half term."

"I can't. They're too young to travel all that way alone. And I can't afford the fares for all of us."

"And I suppose that's my fault, too."

"Oh, for Christ's sake."

Tanzie dug her nails into the soft parts of her hands. Norman kept looking at her, waiting.

"I don't want to argue with you, Marty," Mum said, and her voice was low and careful, like when a teacher is trying to explain something to you that you should already know. "I just want you to think about whether there is any way at all you could contribute to this. It would change Tanzie's life. It would mean she never has to struggle in the way that . . . we struggle."

"You can't say that."

"What do you mean?"

"Don't you watch the news, Jess? All the graduates are out of work. It doesn't matter what education you get. She's still going to struggle." He paused. "No. There's no point us going further into hock just for this. Of course these schools are going to tell you it's all special, and she's special, and her life chances are going to be amazing if she goes, et cetera, et cetera. That's what they do."

Mum didn't say anything.

"No, if she's bright like they say she is, she'll make her own way. She'll have to go to McArthur's like everyone else."

"Like the little bastards who spend all their time working out how to bash Nicky's face in. And the girls who wear four inches of makeup and won't do PE in case they break a nail. She won't fit in there, Marty. She just won't."

"Now you sound like a snob."

"No, I sound like someone who accepts that her daughter is a little bit different. And might need a school that embraces it."

"Can't do it, Jess. I'm sorry." He sounded distracted now, as if he'd heard something in the distance. "Look. I've got to go. Get her to Skype me Sunday."

There was a long silence.

Tanzie counted to fourteen.

She heard the door open and Nicky's voice: "That went well, then."

Tanzie leaned over and finally rubbed Norman's tummy. She closed her eyes so she didn't see the tear that plopped onto Norman.

"Have we done any lottery tickets lately?"

"No."

That silence lasted nine seconds. Then

Mum's voice echoed into the still air: "Well, I think maybe we'd better start."

Chapter Three:
Ed

Deanna Lewis. Maybe not the prettiest girl, but definitely the one who scored highest on Ed and Ronan's campuswide Girls You'd Give One Without Having to Drink a Fourth Pint First points system. As if she'd look at either of them.

She'd barely registered him the whole three years of university, apart from that time when it was raining and she was at the station and asked him for a lift back to the halls in his Mini. He had been so tongue-tied the whole time she was in the passenger seat that he had said barely a word, except a vaguely strangled "No worries" when he let her out at the other end. And those two words somehow managed to cover three octaves. She had stooped to peel the empty crisps packet from the sole of her boot, dropping it delicately back into the foot-well, before shutting the door.

If Ed had it bad, Ronan had it worse. His

love had weighed him down like a cartoon dumbbell. He wrote her poetry, sent anonymous flowers on Valentine's Day, smiled at her in the dinner queue and tried not to look crushed when she failed to notice. And after they had graduated, set up their company, and swapped thinking about women for thinking about software — until software became the thing they actually preferred thinking about — Deanna Lewis gently morphed into a college reminiscence. "Oh . . . Deanna Lewis," they would say to each other, their eyes distant, like they could see her floating in slo-mo above the other drinkers' heads at the pub.

And then, three months ago, some six months after Lara had left, taking with her the apartment in Rome, half the contents of his stock portfolio, and what remained of Ed's appetite for relationships, Deanna Lewis friended him on Facebook. She had been based in New York for a couple of years, but was coming back and wanted to catch up with some of her old friends from uni. Did he remember Reena? And Sam? Was he around for a drink at all?

Afterward, he was ashamed that he hadn't told Ronan. Ronan was busy with the new software upgrade, he told himself. It had taken him ages to get Deanna out of his system. He was in the early stages of dating that girl from the not-for-profit soup place. But the truth was, Ed hadn't had a date in forever, and a bit of him wanted Deanna Lewis to see what he had become since the company was sold a year ago.

Because money, it turned out, bought you someone to sort out your clothes, skin, hair, body. And Ed Nicholls no longer looked like the tongue-tied geek in the Mini. He wore no obvious signs of wealth, but he knew that, at thirty-three, he carried it like an invisible scent around him.

They met at a bar in Soho. She apologized: Reena had blown them off at the last minute. She had a baby. She lifted a faintly mocking eyebrow as she said this. Sam, he realized long afterward, never showed. She didn't ask about Ronan.

He couldn't stop staring at her. She looked just the same, but better. She had dark hair that bounced on her shoulders like a shampoo advert. She was nicer than he remembered, more human. Perhaps even golden girls were brought down to earth a little once they were out of the confines of university. She laughed at all his jokes. He could sense her surprise that he was not the person she remembered. And it made him feel good.

They parted after a couple of hours. He wasn't really expecting to hear from her again, but she called two days later. This time they went to a club and he danced with her, and when she lifted her hands above her head, he had to focus really hard not to picture her pinned to a bed. She was just out of a relationship, she explained, over the third or fourth drink. The breakup had been awful. She was not sure she wanted to be involved in anything serious. He made all the right noises. He told her about Lara, his ex-wife, and how she had said her work was always going to be her first love, and that she had to leave him to save her sanity.

"Bit melodramatic," Deanna said.

"She's Italian. And an actress. Everything with her is melodramatic."

"Was," she corrected him. She kept her eyes on his as she said it. She watched his mouth as he spoke, which was oddly distracting. He told her about the company: the first trial versions he and Ronan had created in his bedroom, the software glitches, the meetings with a media tycoon who had flown them to Texas in his private jet and sworn at them when they refused his buyout offer.

He told her of the day they'd gone public, when he had sat on the edge of his bath watching the share price go up and up on his phone and begun to shake as he grasped just how much his whole life was about to change.

"You're that wealthy?"

"I do okay." He was aware that he was this close to sounding like a dick. "Well . . . I was doing better until I got divorced, obviously . . . I do okay. You know, I'm not really interested in the money." He shrugged. "I just like doing what I do. I like the company. I like having ideas and translating them into things that actually work for people."

"But you sold it?"

"It was getting too big, and I was told that if we did, the guys in suits could handle all the financial stuff. I was never interested in that side of things. I just own a lot of shares." He stared at her. "You have really nice hair." He had no idea why on earth he said this.

She'd kissed him in the taxi. Deanna Lewis had slowly turned his face to hers with a slim, perfectly manicured hand and kissed him. Even though it was more than twelve years since they were at university — twelve years in which Ed Nicholls had been briefly married to a model/actress/whatever — some little voice in his head kept saying: Deanna Lewis is kissing me. And she wasn't just kissing him: she hitched up her skirt and slid a long, slim leg over him — apparently oblivious to the taxi driver — pressed into him, and slid her hands up his shirt until he couldn't speak or think. And when they got to his flat, his words came out thick and stupid, and he not only didn't wait for the change but didn't even check what was in the wad of notes he handed the driver.

The sex was great. Oh, God, it was good. She had porn moves, for Christ's sake. With Lara, in the last months, sex had felt like she was granting him some kind of favor — dependent on some set of rules that only she seemed to understand: whether he had paid her enough attention or spent enough time with her or taken her out to dinner or understood how he'd hurt her feelings.

When Deanna Lewis looked at him naked, her eyes seemed to light up from inside with a kind of hunger. Oh, God. Deanna Lewis.

She arrived again on Friday night. She had worn these crazy knickers with ribbons at the sides that you could pull undone so that they slid slowly down her thighs like a ripple of water. She rolled a joint afterward, and he didn't normally smoke but he had felt his head spin pleasurably, had rested his fingers in her silky hair and felt for the first time since Lara left like life was actually pretty good.

And then she said: "I told my parents about us."

He was having trouble focusing. "Your parents?"

"You don't mind, do you? It's just been so good . . . feeling like . . . I belong in something again, you know?"

Ed found himself staring at a point on the ceiling. *It's okay,* he told himself. *Lots of people tell their parents stuff. Even after two weeks.*

"I've been so depressed. And now I just feel" — she beamed at him — "happy. Like madly happy. Like I wake up and I'm thinking about you. Like everything's going to be okay."

His mouth felt oddly dry. He wasn't sure if it was the joint. "Depressed?" he said.

"I'm okay now. I mean, my folks were really good. After the last episode they took me to the doctor and got me on the right meds. They do apparently lower your inhibitions, but I can't say that anyone's complained! Ha ha ha ha!"

He handed her the joint.

"I just feel things very intensely, you know? My psychiatrist says I'm exceptionally sensitive. Some people bounce through life. I'm just not one of those people.

Sometimes I read about an animal dying or a child being murdered somewhere in another country, and I will literally cry all day. Literally. I was like this at college, too. Don't you remember?"

"No."

She rested her hand on his cock. Suddenly Ed felt fairly certain it was not going to spring to life.

She looked up at him. Her hair was half over her face and she blew at it. "It's such a bummer losing your job and your home. You have no idea what it's like to be really broke." She gazed at him as if weighing up how much to tell him. "I mean properly broke."

"What . . . what do you mean?"

"Well . . . like I owe my ex a load of money, but I've told him I can't pay him. I have too much on my credit card right now. And he still keeps ringing me, going on and on about it. It's very stressful. He doesn't understand how stressed I get."

"How much are you talking about?"

She told him. And as his jaw dropped, she said, "And don't offer to lend it to me. I wouldn't take money from my boyfriend. But it's a nightmare."

Ed tried not to think about the significance of her use of the word "boyfriend."

52

He glanced down at her and saw her lower lip tremble. He swallowed. "Um . . . are you okay?"

Her smile was too swift, too wide. "I'm good! Thanks to you, I'm really fine now." She ran a finger along his chest. "Anyway. It's been heaven going out for nice dinners without wondering how I can afford it." She kissed one of his nipples.

That night she slept with one arm slung over him. Ed lay wide awake, wishing he could ring Ronan.

She came back the following Friday, and the Friday after that. She didn't pick up on his hints about things he had to do at the weekend. Her father had given her the money for them to have a meal. "He says it's such a relief to see me happy again."

He had a cold, he told her, as she came skipping across the road from the Tube station. Probably best not to kiss him.

"I don't mind. What's yours is mine," she said, and attached herself to his face for a full twenty seconds.

They ate at the local pizza place. He had started to feel a vague, reflexive panic at the sight of her. She had "feelings" about things all the time. The sight of a red bus made her happy, the sight of a wilted plant in a café window made her vaguely weepy. She was too much of everything. She was sometimes so busy talking that she forgot to eat with her mouth closed. At his apartment she peed with the bathroom door open. It sounded like a visiting horse was relieving itself.

He wasn't ready for this. Ed wanted to be on his own in the apartment. He wanted the silence, the order of his normal routine. He couldn't believe he had ever been lonely.

That night he had told her he didn't want to have sex. "I'm really tired."

"I'm sure I could wake you up . . ." She had begun to burrow her way down the duvet. There followed a tussle that might have been funny in other circumstances: her mouth poised to plug onto his genitals, him desperately hauling her up by the armpits.

"Really, Deanna. Not . . . not now."

"We can snuggle, then. Now I know you don't just want me for my body!" She pulled his arm around her and emitted a little whimper of pleasure, like a small animal.

Ed Nicholls lay there, wide-eyed, in the dark. He took a breath.

"So . . . Deanna . . . um . . . next weekend I have to go away for business."

"Anywhere nice?" She ran her finger

speculatively along his thigh.

"Um . . . Geneva."

"Ooh, nice! Shall I stow away in your case? I could be there waiting for you in your hotel room. Soothe your troubled brow." She reached out a finger and stroked his forehead. It was all he could do not to flinch.

"Really? That's nice. But it's not that kind of trip."

"You're so lucky. I love traveling. If I wasn't so broke, I'd be back on a plane in an instant."

"You would?"

"It's my passion. I love being a free spirit, going where the whim takes me." She leaned over, extracted a cigarette from the packet on the bedside table, and lit it.

He had lain there for a bit, thinking. "Do you own any stocks and shares?"

She rolled off him and lay back against her pillow. "Don't suggest I bet on the stock market, Ed. I haven't got enough left to gamble with it."

It was out before he really knew what he was saying. "It's not a gamble."

"What isn't?"

"We've got a thing coming out. In a couple of weeks. It's going to be a game changer."

"A thing?"

"I can't really tell you too much. But we've been working on it for a while. It's going to push our stock way up. Our business guys are all over it."

She was silent beside him.

"I mean, I know we haven't talked a lot about work, but this is going to make a serious amount of money."

She didn't sound convinced. "You're asking me to bet my last few pounds on something I don't even know the name of?"

"You don't need to know the name of it. You just need to buy some shares in my company." He shifted onto his side. "Look, you raise a few thousand pounds, and I guarantee you'll have enough to pay off your ex-boyfriend within two weeks. And then you'll be free! And you can do whatever you want! Go traveling the world!"

There was a long silence.

"Is this how you make money, Ed Nicholls? You take women to bed and then get them to buy thousands of pounds' worth of your shares?"

"No, it's —"

She turned over and he saw she was joking. She traced the side of his face. "You're so sweet to me. And it's a lovely thought. But I don't have thousands of pounds lying

56

around just now."

The words came out of his mouth even before he knew what he was saying. "I'll lend it to you. If it makes you money, you pay me back. If it doesn't, then it's my own fault for giving you dud advice."

She started laughing and stopped when she realized he wasn't joking.

"You'd do that for me?"

Ed shrugged. "Honestly? Five grand doesn't really make a big difference to me right now." *And I'd pay ten times that if it meant you would leave.*

Her eyes widened. "Whoa. That is the sweetest thing anyone's ever done for me."

"Oh . . . I doubt that."

Before she left the next morning he wrote her a check. She had been tying her hair up in a clip, making faces at herself in his hall mirror. She smelled vaguely of apples. "Leave the name blank," she said, when she realized what he was doing. "I'll get my brother to do it for me. He's good at all this stocks and shares stuff. What am I buying again?"

"Seriously?"

"I can't help it. I can't think straight when I'm near you." She slid her hand down his boxers. "I'll pay you back as soon as possible. I promise."

"Whatever. Just . . . just don't say anything to anyone about it, yes?"

His faux cheer bounced off the apartment walls, smothering the warning voice in his head.

Ed answered almost all of her e-mails afterward. He said it was good to have spent time with someone who understood how weird it was just to have got out of a serious relationship, how important it was to spend time by yourself. Her replies were short, noncommittal. Oddly, she said nothing specific about the product launch or that the stock had gone through the roof. She should have made more than £100,000. Perhaps she had lost the check. Perhaps she was backpacking in Guadeloupe. Every time he thought about what he had told her, his stomach lurched. So he tried not to think about it.

He changed his mobile-phone number, telling himself it was an accident that he forgot to let her know. Eventually her e-mails trailed off. Two months passed. He and Ronan went out and moaned about the Suits; Ed listened to him as he weighed the pros and cons of the not-for-profit soup girl and felt like he'd learned a valuable lesson. Or dodged a bullet. He wasn't sure which.

And then, two weeks after the SFAX launch, he had been lying down in the creatives' room, idly throwing a foam ball at the ceiling and listening to Ronan talk about the best way to solve a glitch in the payment software, when Sidney, the finance director, had walked in and Ed had suddenly understood that there were far worse problems you could create for yourself than overly clingy girlfriends.

"Ed?"

"What?"

A short pause.

"That's how you answer a phone call? Seriously? At what age exactly are you going to acquire some social skills?"

"Hi, Gemma." Ed sighed, swung his leg over the bed so that he was seated.

"You said you were going to call. A week ago. So I thought, you know, that you must be trapped under a large piece of furniture."

He looked around the bedroom. At the suit jacket that hung over the chair. At the clock, which told him it was a quarter past seven. He rubbed the back of his neck. "Yeah. Well. Things came up."

"I called your work earlier. They said you were at home. Are you ill?"

"No, I'm not ill, just . . . working on

something."

"So does that mean you'll have some time to come and see Dad?"

He closed his eyes. "I'm kind of busy right now."

Her silence was weighty. He pictured his sister at the other end of the line, her jaw set.

"He's asking for you. He's been asking for you for ages."

"I will come, Gem. Just . . . I'm . . . I have some stuff to sort out."

"We all have stuff to sort out. Call him, okay? Even if you can't actually get into one of your eighteen luxury cars to visit. Call him. He's been moved to Victoria Ward. They'll pass the phone to him if you call."

"Two cars. But okay."

He thought she was about to ring off, but she didn't. He heard a small sigh.

"I'm pretty tired, Ed. My supervisors are not being very helpful about me taking time off. So I'm having to go up there every weekend. Mum's just about holding it together. I could really, really do with a bit of backup here."

He felt a pang of guilt. His sister was not a complainer. "I've told you I'll try to get there."

"You said that last week. Look, you could

drive there in four hours."

"I'm not in London."

"Where are you?"

He looked out of the window at the darkening sky. "The south coast."

"You're on holiday?"

"Not holiday. It's complicated."

"It can't be that complicated. You have zero commitments."

"Yeah. Thanks for reminding me."

"Oh, come on. It's your company. You get to make the rules, right? Just grant yourself an extra two weeks' holiday."

Another long silence.

"You're being weird."

Ed took a deep breath before he spoke. "I'll sort something out. I promise."

"And ring Mum."

"I will."

There was a click as the line went dead.

Ed stared at the phone for a moment, then dialed his lawyer's office. The phone went straight through to the answering machine.

The investigating officers had pulled out every drawer in the apartment. They hadn't tossed it all out, like they did in the movies, but had gone through it methodically, wearing gloves, checking between the folds of T-shirts, going through every file. Both his laptops had been removed, his memory sticks, and his two phones. He had had to sign for it all, as if this were being done for his own benefit. "Get out of town, Ed," his lawyer had told him. "Just go and try not to think too much. I'll call you if I need you to come in."

They had searched this place, too, apparently. There was so little stuff here it had taken them less than an hour.

Ed looked around him at the bedroom of the holiday home, at the crisp Belgian linen duvet that the cleaners had put on that morning, at the drawers that held an emergency wardrobe of jeans, pants, socks, and T-shirts.

Sidney had also told him to leave. "If this gets out, you're seriously going to fuck with our share price."

Ronan hadn't spoken to him since the day the police had come to the office.

He stared at the phone. Other than Gemma, there was really no one he could talk to without having to explain what had happened. Everyone he knew was in tech anyway, and with the exception of Ronan, he wasn't sure how many of these people would qualify as actual friends. He stared at the wall. He thought about the fact that during the last week he had driven up and down to London four times just because, without work, he hadn't known what to do with himself. He thought back to the previous evening when he had been so angry, with Deanna Lewis, with Sidney, with what the fuck had happened to his life, that he had hurled an entire bottle of white wine at the wall and smashed it. He thought about the likelihood of that happening again if he was left to his own devices.

There was nothing else for it. He shouldered his way into his jacket, picked a fob of keys from the locked cupboard beside the back door, and headed out to the car.

CHAPTER FOUR:
JESS

There had always been something a bit different about Tanzie. At a year old she would line up her blocks in rows or organize them into patterns, and then pull certain blocks away, making new shapes. By the time she was two she was obsessed with numbers. Before she even started school she had worked her way through the local bookshop's collection of math workbooks for years two, three, four, and five. She would tell Jess that multiplication was "just another way of doing addition." At six she could explain the meaning of "tessellate."

Marty didn't like it. It made him uncomfortable. But then anything that wasn't "normal" made Marty uncomfortable. It was still the thing that made Tanzie happy, just sitting there, plowing through problems that none of them could begin to understand. Marty's mother, on the rare occasions that she visited, used to call Tanzie a swot. She would say it like it wasn't a very nice thing to be.

"So what are you going to do?"

"There's nothing I can do right now."

"Wouldn't it feel weird, her mixing with all the private-school kids?"

"I don't know. Yes. But that would be our problem. Not hers."

"What if she grows away from you? What if she falls in with a posh lot and gets embarrassed by her background? I'm just saying. I think you could mess her up. I think she could lose sight of where she comes from."

Jess looked over at Nathalie, who was driving. "She comes from the Shitty Estate of Doom, Nat. I would be quite happy for her to lose sight of that."

Something weird had happened since Jess had told Nathalie about the interview. It was as if she had taken it personally. All morning she had gone on and on about how her children were happy at the local school, about how glad she was that they were "normal," how it didn't do for a child to be "different."

Tanzie, meanwhile, was more excited than she had been in months. Her scores had been 100 percent in maths and 99 percent

65

in nonverbal reasoning. (She was actually annoyed by the missing 1 percent.) Mr. Tsvangarai, ringing to tell her, said there might be other sources of funding. Details, he kept saying. Jess couldn't help thinking that people who thought money was a "detail" were the kind who had never really had to worry about it.

"And you know she'd have to wear that prissy uniform," Nathalie said, as they pulled up at Beachfront.

"She won't be wearing a prissy uniform," Jess responded irritably.

"Then she'll get teased for not being like the rest of them."

"She won't be wearing a prissy uniform because she won't be bloody going. I haven't got a hope of sending her, Nathalie. Okay?"

Jess got out of the car, slammed the door, and walked ahead so that she didn't have to listen to anything else.

It was only the locals who called Beachfront the "holiday park"; the developers called it a "destination resort." Because this was not a holiday park like the Sea Bright caravan park on the top of the hill, a chaotic jumble of wind-battered mobile homes and seasonal lean-to tents. This was a spotless array of architect-designed "living spaces" set among

66

carefully manicured paths. There was a sports club, a spa, tennis courts, a huge pool complex, a handful of overpriced boutiques, and a small grocery store so that residents did not have to venture into the scrappier confines of the town.

Tuesdays, Thursdays, and Fridays, Benson & Thomas cleaned the two three-bedroom rental properties that overlooked the clubhouse, then moved on to the newer properties: six glass-fronted modernist houses that stood on the chalk cliff above the sea.

Mr. Nicholls kept a spotless Audi in his driveway that they had never seen move. His sister came once with two small children and a gray-looking husband (they left the place immaculately clean). Mr. Nicholls himself rarely visited, and had never, in the year they'd been cleaning the place, used either the kitchen or the laundry room. Jess made extra cash doing his towels and sheets, laundering and ironing them weekly for guests who never came.

It was a vast house; its slate floors echoed, its living areas were covered with great expanses of sea-grass matting, and there was an expensive sound system wired into the walls. The glass frontages gazed out onto the wide blue arc of the horizon. But there were no photographs on the walls or suggestions of any kind of actual life. Nathalie always said that even when he came, it was as if he were camping there. There must have been women — Nathalie once found a lipstick in the bathroom, and last year they had discovered a pair of tiny lacy knickers under the bed (La Perla) and a bikini top — but there was little to suggest anything else about him.

"He's here," muttered Nathalie.

As they closed the front door, a man's voice echoed down the corridor, loud and angry. Nathalie pulled a face. "Cleaners," she called. He didn't respond.

The argument continued the whole time it took to clean the kitchen. He had used one mug, and the bin held two empty takeaway cartons. There was broken glass in the corner by the fridge, small green splinters, as if someone had picked up the larger pieces but couldn't be bothered with the rest. And there was wine up the walls. Jess washed them down carefully. She and Nathalie worked in silence, speaking in murmurs, trying to pretend they couldn't hear him.

Jess moved on to the dining room, dusted the picture frames with a soft cloth, tilting the odd one a centimeter or two to show they'd been done. Outside on the deck sat an empty bottle of Jack Daniel's with one glass; she picked them up and brought them inside. She thought about Nicky, who had returned from school the previous day with a cut ear, the knees of his trousers scuffed with dirt. He shrugged off any attempt to talk about it. His preferred life now consisted of people on the other side of a screen; boys Jess had never met and never would, people he called SK8RBOI and TERM-N-ATOR, who shot and disemboweled each other for fun. Who could blame him? His real life seemed to be the actual war zone.

Ever since the interview Jess had lain awake, doing calculations in her head, adding and subtracting in a way that would have made Tanzie laugh. She mentally sold her belongings, ran through lists of every single person she might be able to borrow money from. But the only people likely to offer Jess money were the sharks who circled the neighborhood with their hidden four-figure interest rates. She had seen neighbors borrow from those friendly reps who turned suddenly gimlet-eyed. And again and again she came back to Marty's words. Was McArthur's really so bad? Some children did well there. There was no reason why Tanzie shouldn't be one of them if she kept out of the way of the troublemakers.

The hard truth of it was there like a brick wall: Jess was going to have to tell her daughter that she couldn't make it add up. Jess Thomas, the woman who always found a way through, who spent her life telling the kids that it would All Work Out, couldn't make it work out.

She hauled the vacuum cleaner down the hallway, wincing as it bumped against her shin, and knocked on the door to see if Mr. Nicholls wanted his office cleaned. There was silence, and as she knocked again he yelled suddenly, "Yes, I'm well aware of that, Sidney. You've said so fifteen times, but it doesn't mean —"

It was too late: she had pushed the door half open. Jess began to apologize, but with barely a glance the man held up a palm, as if she were some kind of a dog — *stay* — then leaned forward and slammed the door in her face. The sound reverberated around the house.

Jess stood there, shocked into immobility, her skin prickling with embarrassment.

"I told you," Nathalie said, as she scrubbed furiously at the guest bathroom a few minutes later. "Those private schools don't teach them any manners."

Forty minutes later, Jess gathered Mr. Nicholls's immaculate white towels and sheets into her holdall, stuffing them in with more force than was strictly necessary. She walked downstairs and placed the bag next to the cleaning crate in the hall. Nathalie was polishing the doorknobs. It was one of her things. She couldn't bear fingerprints on taps or doorknobs.

"Mr. Nicholls, we're going now."

He was standing in the kitchen, just staring out through the window at the sea, one hand on the top of his head like he'd forgotten it was there. He had dark hair and was wearing those glasses that are supposed to be trendy but just make you look like you've dressed up as Woody Allen. He had a lean, athletic build, but wore a suit like a twelve-year-old forced to go to a christening.

"Mr. Nicholls."

He shook his head slightly, then sighed and walked down the hallway. "Right," he said distractedly. He kept glancing down at the screen of his mobile phone. "Thanks."

They waited.

"Um, we'd like our money, please," Jess said.

Nathalie finished polishing, and folded and unfolded the cloth. She hated money conversations.

"I thought the management company paid you."

"They haven't paid us in three weeks. And there's never anyone in the office. If you want us to continue we need to be up to date."

He scrabbled around in his pockets, pulled out a wallet. "Right. What do I owe you?"

"Thirty times three weeks. And three weeks of laundry."

He looked up, one eyebrow raised.

"We left a message on your phone, last week."

He shook his head, as if he couldn't be expected to remember such things. "How much is that?"

"One hundred and thirty-five all together."

He flicked through the notes. "I don't have that much cash. Look, I'll give you sixty and get them to send you a check for the rest. Okay?"

On another occasion Jess would have said yes. On another occasion she would have let it go. It wasn't as if he were going to rip them off, after all. But she was suddenly sick of wealthy people who never paid on time, who assumed that because seventy-five pounds was nothing to them, it must be nothing to her, too. She was sick of clients who thought she meant so little that they could slam a door in her face without so much as an apology.

"No," she said, and her voice was oddly clear. "I need the money now, please."

He met her eye for the first time. Behind her Nathalie rubbed manically at a door-knob. "I have bills that need paying. And the people who send them won't let me put off paying week after week."

He took off his glasses and frowned at her, as if she were being particularly difficult. It made her dislike him even more.

"I'll have to look upstairs," he said, disappearing. They stood in uncomfortable silence as they heard drawers being shut emphatically, the clash of hangers in a wardrobe. Finally he came back with a handful of notes.

He peeled off some without looking at Jess and handed them over. She was about to say something — something about how he didn't have to behave like an utter dickhead, about how life went that little bit more smoothly when people treated each other like human beings, something that would no doubt make Nathalie rub half the door handle away with anxiety. But just as she opened her mouth to speak, his phone rang. Without a word, Mr. Nicholls spun away from her and was striding down the hallway to answer it.

"What's that in Norman's basket?"

"Nothing."

Jess was unpacking the groceries, hauling items out of the bags with one eye on the clock. She had a three-hour shift at the Feathers and just over an hour to make tea and get changed. She shoved two cans to the back of the shelves, hiding them behind the cereal packets. She was sick of the supermarket's cheery "value" label.

Nicky stooped and tugged at the piece of fabric so that the dog reluctantly got to his feet. "It's a white towel. Jess, it's an expensive one. Norman's got hair all over it. And dribble." He held it up between two fingers.

"I'm going to wash it later." She didn't look at him.

"Is it Dad's?"

"No, it is not your dad's."

"I don't understand —"

"It's just making me feel better, okay? Can you put that stuff over there in the freezer?"

He slouched against the kitchen units. "Shona Bryant was teasing Tanzie at the bus stop. Because of her clothes."

"What about her clothes?" Jess turned to Nicky, a can of tomatoes in her hand.

"Because you make them. All the sequins you put on them."

"Tanzie likes shiny stuff. Anyway, how does she know I make them?"

"She asked Tanzie where they came from and Tanzie just told her. You know what she's like."

He took a package of cornflakes from Jess and put it on the shelf. "Shona Bryant's the one who said our house was weird because we had too many books."

"Well Shona Bryant's an idiot."

He leaned down to stroke Norman. "Oh. And we got a reminder from the electric company."

Jess let out a small sigh. "How much?"

He walked over to the pile of papers on the sideboard and flicked through. "Comes to more than two hundred altogether."

She took out a packet of cereal. "I'll sort it out."

Nicky opened the fridge door. "You should sell the car."

"I can't sell it. It's your dad's only asset." Sometimes Jess wasn't entirely sure why she kept defending her husband. "He'll sort it out when he's back on his feet. Now, go on upstairs. I've got someone coming." She could see her walking up the back path.

"We're buying stuff off Aileen Trent?" Nicky watched her open the gate and close it carefully behind her.

Jess couldn't hide the way her cheeks colored. "Just this once."

He stared at her. "You said we had no money."

"Look, it's to take Tanzie's mind off the school thing when I have to tell her." Jess had made her decision on the way home. The whole idea was ridiculous. They could barely keep their heads above water as it was. There was no point even trying to entertain it.

He kept staring at her. "But Aileen Trent. You said —"

"And you're the one who just told me Tanzie was getting bullied because of her clothes. Sometimes, Nicky . . ." Jess threw her hands into the air. "Sometimes the ends justify the means."

Nicky's look lasted longer than she felt entirely comfortable with. And then he went upstairs.

"So I've brought a lovely selection of things for the discerning young lady. You know they all love their designer labels. And I took the liberty of bringing a few sequinned things, as I know your Tanzie's a bit of a magpie."

Aileen's "shop" voice was formal, with overly precise diction. It was quite odd, emerging as it did, from someone Jess had seen regularly ejected by force from the King's Arms public house. She sat cross-legged on the floor, reached into her black holdall, pulled out a selection of clothes, and laid them carefully on the carpet.

"There's a Hollister top here. They're all into Hollister, the girls. Shocking expensive in the shops. I've got some more designer stuff in my other bag, although you did say you didn't require high end. Oh, and two sugars, if you're making one."

Aileen did a weekly round of the neighborhood. Jess had always issued a firm thanks-but-no-thanks. Everyone knew where Aileen got her knockdown bargains with the tags still on.

But that was before.

She picked up the layered tops, one with glittery stripes, the other a soft rose. She could already see Tanzie in them. "How much?"

"Ten for the top, five for the T-shirt, and twenty for the trainers. You can see from the tag they retail for eighty-five. That's a serious discount."

"I can't do that much."

"Well, as you're a new client, I can do you an introductory bonus." Aileen held up her notebook, squinting at the figures. "You take the three items and I'll let you have the jeans, too. For goodwill." She smiled, her skin waxy. "Thirty-five pounds for a whole outfit, including footwear. And this month only I'm throwing in a little bracelet. You won't get those prices at T. J. Maxx."

Jess stared at the clothes laid out on the floor. She wanted to see Tanzie smiling. She wanted her to feel that life held the potential for unexpected happy things. She wanted her to have something to feel good about when she gave her the news.

"Hold on."

She walked through to the kitchen, pulled the cocoa tin from the cupboard where she kept the electricity money. She counted out the coins and dropped them into Aileen's clammy palm before she could think about what she was doing.

"Pleasure doing business with you," Aileen said, folding the remaining clothes and placing them carefully in the bin bag. "I'll be back in two weeks. Anything you want in the meantime, you know where to find me."

"I think this will be it, thanks."

She gave Jess a knowing look. *They all say that, love.*

Nicky kept his eyes on the computer when Jess walked in.

"Nathalie's going to bring Tanzie back after maths club. Are you going to be okay here by yourself?"

"Sure."

"No smoking."

"Mm."

"You going to do some studying?"

"Sure."

Sometimes Jess fantasized about the kind of mother she could be if she weren't always working. She would bake cakes, smile more, stand over them while they did their homework. She would do the things they wanted her to do, instead of always answering:

Sorry, love, I just have to get the supper on.

After I've put this wash on.

I've got to go, sweetie. Tell me when I get back from my shift.

She gazed at him, his unreadable expression, and she had a weird sense of foreboding. "Don't forget to walk Norman. But don't go round near the off-license."

"As if."

"And don't spend the whole evening on

the computer." She hoicked up the back of his jeans. "And pull your pants up before I can't help myself and give you the world's biggest wedgie."

He turned and she glimpsed his brief smile. As Jess walked out of his room, she realized she couldn't remember the last time she'd seen it.

CHAPTER FIVE: NICKY

My dad is such an arsehole.

CHAPTER SIX:
JESS

The Feathers public house sat between the library (closed since January) and the Happy Plaice fish-and-chip shop, and inside it was possible to believe it was still 1989. Des, the landlord, had never been seen in anything but faded tour T-shirts, jeans, and, if it was cold, a blouson leather jacket. On a quiet night, if you were unlucky, he would explain in excruciating detail the merits of a Fender Stratocaster against a Rickenbacker 330 or recite with a poet's reverence all the words to "Money for Nothing."

The Feathers was not smart, in the way that the Beachfront bars were smart, and it did not serve fresh seafood or fine wines and family-friendly menus catering to screaming children. It served various kinds of dead animal with chips, and it scoffed at the word "salad." There was nothing more adventurous than Tom Petty on the jukebox and a battered dartboard on the wall.

But it was a formula that worked. The Feathers was that rare thing in a seaside town: busy all year-round.

"Is Roxanne here?" Jess started putting out the bags of potato chips as Des emerged from the cellar, where he had been tying on a fresh barrel of real ale.

"Nah. She's doing something with her mother." He thought for a minute. "Healing. No, fortune-telling. Psychiatrist. Psychologist."

"Spiritualist?"

"The one where they tell you stuff you already know and you're meant to look impressed."

"Psychic."

"Thirty pounds a ticket, they're paying, to sit there with a glass of cheap white wine and shout, 'Yes!' when someone asks did someone in the audience have a relative whose name began with *J*." He stooped, slamming the cellar door shut with a grunt. "I could predict a few things, Jess. And I won't charge you thirty pounds for it. I predict that so-called spiritualist is sitting at home right now, rubbing his hands and thinking, *What a bunch of Muppets.*"

Jess hauled the tray of clean glasses out of the dishwasher and began stacking them on the shelves above the bar.

"Do you believe all that old bollocks?"

"No."

"Course you don't. You're a sensible girl. I don't know what to say to her sometimes. Her mother's the worst. She reckons she's got her own guardian angel. An angel." He mimicked her, looking at his own shoulder and tapping it. "She reckons it protects her. Didn't protect her from spending all her compensation on the shopping channels, did it? You'd think that angel would have had a word. 'Here, Maureen. You really don't want that luxury ironing-board cover with a picture of a dog on it. Really, love. Put a bit into your pension instead.' "

Miserable as Jess felt, she couldn't help but laugh.

"You're early." Des looked pointedly at his watch.

"Shoe emergency." Chelsea slung her handbag under the bar, then fixed her hair. "I got chatting online to one of my dates," she said to Jess, as if Des weren't there. "He's absolutely gorgeous."

All Chelsea's Internet dates were gorgeous. Until she met them.

"David, his name is. He's looking for someone who likes cooking, cleaning, and ironing. And the odd trip out."

"To the supermarket?" Des asked.

Chelsea ignored him. She picked up a dishcloth and began drying glasses. "You want to get yourself on there, Jess. Get out and about a bit instead of moldering in here with this lot of droopy old ball sacks."

"Less of the old, you," Des said.

The football was on, which meant that Des put out free crisps and cheese cubes, and, if he was feeling particularly generous, mini sausage rolls. Jess had taken home the leftover cubes, with Des's blessing, to make macaroni and cheese until Nathalie had told her the statistic for how many men actually washed their hands after going to the loo.

The bar filled, the match started, the evening passed without note; she poured pints in the commentary gaps and thought, yet again, about money. The end of June, the school had said. If she didn't register by then, that was it. She was so deep in thought that she almost didn't hear Des until he dumped a bowl of potato puffs on the bar beside her. "I meant to tell you. Next week we've got a new till coming. It's one of those where all you have to do is touch the screen."

She turned away from the optics. "A new till? Why?"

"That one is older than I am. And not all the barmaids can add up as well as you, Jess.

The last time Chelsea was on by herself, I cashed up and we were eleven quid out. Ask her to add up a double gin, a pint of Webster's, and a packet of dry-roasted and her eyes cross. We've got to move with the times." He ran his hand across an imaginary screen. "Digital accuracy. You'll love it. You won't have to use your brain at all. Just like Chelsea."

"Can't I just stick with this? I'm hopeless with computers."

"We're going to do staff training. Half a day. Unpaid, I'm afraid. I've got a bloke coming."

"Unpaid?"

"Just tap-tap-swipe on a screen. It'll be like *Minority Report*. But without the bald people. Mind you, we'll still have Pete. *Pete!*"

Liam Stubbs came in at a quarter past nine. Jess had her back to the bar and he leaned over it and murmured "Hey, hot stuff" into her ear.

She didn't turn round. "Oh. You again."

"There's a welcome. Pint of Stella, please, Jess." He glanced around the bar, then said, "And whatever else you have on offer."

"We have some very nice dry-roasted peanuts."

"I was thinking of something a bit . . . wetter."

"I'll get you that pint, then."

"Still playing hard to get, eh?"

She had known Liam since school. He was one of those men who would break your heart into tiny pieces if you let him; the kind of blue-eyed, smart-mouthed boy who ignored you all the way through years ten and eleven, laughed you into bed when you lost your braces and grew your hair, then gave you nothing more than a cheery wave and a wink forever after. His hair was chestnut brown, his cheekbones high and lightly tanned. He drove a taxi at night and ran a flower stall in the market on Fridays, and whenever she passed, he would whisper, "You. Me. Behind the dahlias, now," just seriously enough to make her miss her stride. His wife had left him about the same time Marty had departed. ("A little matter of serial infidelity. Some women are so picky.") And six months ago, after one of Des's after-hours specials, they had ended up in the ladies' loo with his hands up her shirt and Jess walking round wearing a lopsided smile for days.

She was taking the empty cardboard crisps boxes out to the bins when Liam appeared at the back gate. He walked up to her so that she had to back against the wall of the pub garden. The entire length of his body was just inches from hers and he said softly, "I can't stop thinking about you." He held his cigarette hand well away from her. He was a gentleman like that.

"I bet you say that to all the girls."

"I like watching you move around that bar. Half the time I'm watching the football, and half the time I'm imagining bending you over it."

"Who says romance is dead?"

God, he smelled good. Jess wriggled a bit, trying to get herself out from under him before she did something she'd regret. Being near Liam Stubbs sparked bits of her to life that she had forgotten existed.

"So let me romance you. Let me take you out. You and me. A proper date. Come on, Jess. Let's make a go of it."

Jess pulled back from him. "What?"

"You heard."

She stared. "You want us to have a relationship?"

"You say it like it's a dirty word."

She slid out from under him, glancing toward the back door. "I've got to get back to the bar, Liam."

"Why won't you go out with me?" He took a step closer. "You know it would be great . . ." His voice had dropped to a whisper.

"And I also know I have two kids and two jobs and you spend your whole life in your car and it would take about three weeks for you and me to be bickering on a sofa about whose turn it was to take the rubbish out." She smiled sweetly at him. "And then we would lose the heart-stopping romance of exchanges like this forever."

He picked up a lock of her hair and let it slide through his fingers. His voice was a soft growl. "So cynical. You're going to break my heart, Jess Thomas."

"And you're going to get me fired."

"I take it this means a quickie's out of the question?"

She extricated herself and made her way toward the back door, trying to make the color subside from her cheeks. Then she stopped. "Hey, Liam."

He looked up from stubbing his cigarette out.

"You don't want to lend me five hundred quid, do you?"

"If I had it, babe, you could have it." He blew a kiss as she went inside.

She was walking around the bar to pick up empties, her cheeks still pink, when she saw him. She actually did a double take. He was sitting in the corner alone, and there were three finished pint glasses in front of him.

He had changed into Converse trainers, jeans, and a T-shirt; he sat staring at his mobile phone, flicking at the screen and occasionally glancing up when everyone cheered a goal. As Jess watched, he raised a beer and downed it in one long, thirsty gulp. He probably thought that in his jeans he blended in, but he had "out of towner" written all over him. Too much money. The kind of studied scruffiness that only comes with expense. As he glanced toward the bar, she turned away swiftly, feeling her mood darken.

"Just popping downstairs for some more snacks," she said to Chelsea, and made for the cellar. "Ugh," she muttered under her breath. "Ugh. Ugh. Ugh." When she re-emerged, he had a fresh pint and barely looked up from his phone.

The evening stretched. Chelsea discussed her Internet options, Mr. Nicholls drank a few more pints, and Jess disappeared whenever he got up to the bar — and tried not to meet Liam's eye. By ten to eleven, the pub was down to a handful of stragglers — the usual offenders, Des called them. Chelsea put on her coat.

"Where are you going?"

Chelsea stooped to apply her lipstick in the mirror behind the optics. "Des said I could leave a bit early." She pursed her lips. "Date."

"Date? Who goes on a date at this time of night?"

"It's a date at David's house. It's all right," she said, as Jess stared at her. "My sister's coming, too. He said it would be nice with the three of us."

"Chels, have you ever heard the expression 'booty call'?"

"What?"

Jess looked at her for a minute. "Nothing. Just . . . have a nice time."

She was loading the dishwasher when he appeared at the bar. His eyes were half closed and he swayed gently, as if he were about to embark on some free-form dance.

"Pint, please."

She shoved another two glasses to the back of the wire rack. "We're not serving anymore. It's gone eleven."

He looked up at the clock. His voice slurred. "It's one minute to."

"You've had enough."

He blinked slowly, stared at her. His short dark hair was sticking up slightly on one side. "Who are you to tell me I've had enough?"

"The person who serves the drinks. That's usually how it works." Jess held his gaze. "You don't even recognize me, do you?"

"Should I?"

She stared at him a moment longer. "Hold on." She let herself out from behind the bar, walked over to the swing door, and, as he stood there, bemused, she opened it and let it swing back in her face, lifting a hand and opening her mouth as if to say something.

She opened the door again and stood there in front of him. "Recognize me now?"

He blinked. "Are you . . . did I see you yesterday?"

"The cleaner. Yes."

He ran a hand through his hair. "Ah. The whole door thing. I was just . . . having a tricky conversation."

" 'Not now, thanks' tends to work just as well, I find."

"Point taken." He leaned on the bar. Jess tried to keep a straight face when his elbow slipped off.

"So that's an apology, is it?"

He peered at her blearily. "Sorry. I'm really, really, really sorry. Very sorry, O Bar Lady. Now can I have a drink?"

"No. It's gone eleven."

"Only because you kept me talking."

"I haven't got time to sit here while you nurse another pint."

"Give me a shot, then. Come on. I need another drink. Give me a shot of vodka. Here. You can keep the change." He slammed a twenty on the bar. The impact reverberated through the rest of him so that his head whiplashed back slightly. "Just one. Actually, make it a double. It'll take me all of two seconds to down it. One second."

"No. You've had enough."

Des's voice broke in from the kitchen. "Oh, for Christ's sake, Jess, give him a drink."

Jess stood for a moment, her jaw rigid, then turned and poured two measures into a glass. She rang up the money, then silently placed his change on the bar. He downed the vodka, swallowing audibly as he put the glass down, and turned away, staggering slightly.

"You forgot your change."

"Keep it."

"I don't want it."

"Put it in your charity box, then."

She gathered it up and shoved it at his hand. "Des's charity of choice is the Des Harris Holiday in Memphis Fund," she said. "Really. Just take your money."

He blinked at her, and took two unbalanced steps to the side as she opened the door for him. It was then she noticed what he had just pulled from his pocket. And the super-shiny Audi in the car park.

"You're not driving home."

"I'm fine." He batted away her protest, dropping his keys. "There aren't any cars around here at night anyway."

"You can't drive."

"We're in the middle of nowhere, in case you haven't noticed." He gestured at the sky. "I'm miles away from everything, and stuck here, in the middle of fucking nowhere." He leaned forward, and his breath was a blast of alcohol. "I'll go very, very, slowly."

He was so drunk that peeling the keys from his hand was embarrassingly easy. "No," she said, turning back to the bar. "I won't be responsible for you having an accident. Go back inside, and I'll call you a taxi."

"Give me my keys."

"No."

"You're stealing my keys."

"I'm saving you from a driving ban." She held them aloft, and turned back toward the bar.

"Oh, for crissakes," he said. He made it sound as if she were the last in a long line of irritations. It made her want to kick him.

"I'll get you a taxi. Just . . . just sit there. I'll give you your keys back once you're safely inside it."

She texted Liam from her phone in the back hall.

Does this mean I get lucky? he replied.

If you like them hairy. And male.

She walked back outside and Mr. Nicholls was gone. His car was still there. She called him twice, wondering if he'd headed off to a bush to relieve himself, then glanced down and there he was, fast asleep on the outside bench.

She thought, briefly, about leaving him there. But it was chilly, and the sea mists were unpredictable, and he would likely wake up without his wallet.

"I'm not taking that," Liam said through the driver's window when his taxi pulled into the car park.

"He's fine. He's just asleep. I can tell you where he's got to go."

"Nuh-uh. Last sleeper I had woke up and vomited all down my new seat covers. Then somehow perked up enough to do a runner."

"He lives on Beachfront. He's hardly going to do a runner." She glanced down at her watch. "Oh, come on, Liam. It's late. I just want to get home."

"Then leave him. Sorry, Jess."

"Okay. How about I stay in the car while you drop him off? If he's ill, I'll clean it up. Then you can drop me home. He can pay." She picked up Mr. Nicholls's change from where he had dropped it on the ground beside the bench and sifted through it. "Thirteen pounds should do it, yes?"

He pulled a face. "Ah, Jess. Don't make it hard for me."

"Please, Liam." She smiled. She placed a hand on his arm. "Pretty please."

He gazed down the road. "All right."

She lowered her head to Mr. Nicholls's sleeping face, then straightened and nodded. "He says that's fine."

Liam shook his head. The flirtatious air of earlier had evaporated.

"Oh, come on, Liam. Help me get him in. I need to go home."

Mr. Nicholls lay with his head on her lap, like a sick child. She didn't know where to put her hands. She held them across the back of the rear seat, and spent the whole journey praying that he wouldn't be sick. Every time he groaned, or shifted, she wound down a window, or leaned across to check his face. Don't you dare, she told him silently. Just don't you dare. They were two minutes from the holiday park when her phone buzzed. It was Belinda, her neighbor. She squinted at the illuminated screen: *Boys have been after your Nicky again. Got him outside the chip shop. Nigel's taken him to hospital.*

A large, cold weight landed on her chest. *On my way,* she typed.

Nigel says he'll stay with him till you're there. I'll stay here with Tanzie.

Thanks, Belinda. I'll be as quick as I can.

Mr. Nicholls shifted and let out an elongated snore. She stared at him, at his expensive haircut and his too-blue jeans, and was suddenly furious. She might have been home by now if it weren't for him. It would have been her walking the dog, not Nicky.

"Here we are."

Jess directed him to Mr. Nicholls's house, and they dragged him in between them, his arms slung over their shoulders, Jess's knees buckling a little under his surprising weight. He stirred a little when they reached his front door, and she fumbled through his keys, trying to find the right one, before she decided it would be easier to use her own.

"Where do you want him?" said Liam, puffing.

"Sofa. I'm not lugging him upstairs."

She pushed him briskly into the recovery position. She took his glasses off, threw a nearby jacket over him, and dropped his keys on the side table that she had polished earlier that day.

And then she felt able to speak the words: "Liam, can you drop me at the hospital? Nicky's had an accident."

The car sped through the empty lanes in silence. Her mind was racing. She was afraid of what she might find. How badly was he hurt? Had Tanzie seen any of it? And then, under the fear, the stupid, mundane stuff, like, Will I be hours at the hospital? A taxi from there would be at least fifteen pounds.

"You want me to wait?" asked Liam, when he pulled up at A and E.

She was running across the tarmac before he had even stopped the car.

He was in a side cubicle. When the nurse showed her in through the curtain, Nigel rose from his plastic chair, his kind, doughy face taut with anxiety. Nicky was turned away, his cheekbone covered with a dressing and the beginnings of a black eye leaking color into the socket above it. A temporary bandage snaked its way around his hairline.

It was all she could do not to let out a sob.

"They're going to stitch it. But they want to keep him in. Check for fractures and whatnot." Nigel looked awkward. "He didn't want me to call the police." He gestured in the general direction of outside. "If you're all right, I'll be getting back to Belinda. It's late . . ."

Jess whispered her thanks, and moved over to Nicky. She placed her hand on the blanket, where his shoulder was.

"Tanzie's okay," he whispered, not looking at her.

"I know, sweetheart." She sat down on the plastic chair beside his bed. "What happened?"

He gave a faint shrug. Nicky never wanted to talk about it. What was the point, after all? Everyone knew the score. You looked like a freak, you got battered. You still looked like a freak, they still kept coming after you. That was the crushing, immovable logic of a small town.

And just for once, she didn't know what to say to him. She couldn't tell him it was all right, because it wasn't. She couldn't tell him the police would get the Fishers, because they never did. She couldn't tell him that things would change before he knew it, because when you were a teenager your life really only stretches in your imagination about two weeks ahead, and they both knew that it wasn't going to get better by then. Or, probably, anytime soon after that.

"He all right?" said Liam, as she walked slowly back out to the car. The adrenaline had leached out of her, and Jess's shoulders slumped with exhaustion. She opened the rear door to fetch her jacket and bag, and his eyes, in the rearview mirror, took it all in.

"He'll live."

"Little bastards. I was just talking to your neighbor. Someone ought to do something." He adjusted his mirror. "I'd teach them a lesson myself if I didn't have to watch out for my license. Boredom, that's what it is. They don't know what else to do with themselves but pick on someone. Make sure you got all your stuff, Jess."

She had to half climb into the car to reach her coat. And as she did, she felt something under her feet. Semisolid, cylindrical. She moved her foot, reached down into the footwell, and came up with a fat roll of banknotes. She stared at it in the half dark, then at what had fallen down beside it. A laminated identity card, the kind you would use at an office. Both must have fallen out of Mr. Nicholls's pocket when he was slumped on the backseat. Before she could think about it she stuffed them into her bag.

"Here," she said, reaching into her purse, but Liam raised a hand.

"No. I've got it. You've enough on your plate." He gave her a wink. "Give one of us a ring when you want picking up. On the house. Dan's cleared it."

"But —"

"No buts. Out you get now, Jess. Make sure that boy of yours is okay. I'll see you at the pub."

She felt almost tearful with gratitude. She stood there, one hand raised, as he circled the car park and shouted out of the driver's window: "You should tell him, though, if he'd just try to look a bit more normal, he might not get his head bashed in so often."

CHAPTER SEVEN: JESS

She dozed through the small hours on the plastic hospital chair, waking occasionally from discomfort and the sound of distant tragedies in the ward beyond the curtain. She watched the newly stitched Nicky as he finally slept, wondering how she was supposed to protect him. She wondered what was going on in his head. She wondered, with a clench of her stomach that no longer seemed to go away, what was coming next. A nurse popped her head around the curtain at seven and said she'd made her some tea and toast. This small act of kindness caused her to fight back embarrassed tears. The consultant stopped by shortly after eight, and said Nicky would probably spend another night while they checked that there was no internal bleeding. There was a shadow they hadn't quite got to the bottom of on the X-ray and they wanted to be sure. The best thing Jess could do would be to go home and get some rest. Nathalie rang to say she'd taken Tanzie to school with her kids and that everything was fine.

Everything was fine.

She got off the bus two stops before her house, walked round to Leanne Fisher's, knocked on her door and told her, with as much politeness as she could muster, that if Jason came anywhere near Nicky again she would have the police on him. Whereupon Leanne Fisher spat at her and said if Jess didn't fuck right off she'd put a brick through her effing window. There was a burst of laughter from within the house as Jess walked away.

It was pretty much the response she'd expected.

She let herself into her empty home. She paid the water bill with what would have been the rent money. She paid the electric with her cleaning money. She showered and changed and did her lunchtime shift at the pub, so lost in thought that Stewart Pringle rested his hand on her arse for a full ten seconds before she noticed. She poured his half pint of Best Bitter slowly over his shoes.

"What did you do that for?" Des yelled when Stewart complained.

"If you're so okay with it, you stand there and let him rest his hand on your arse," she said, and went back to cleaning the glasses.

"She has a point," Des said.

She vacuumed the entire house before Tanzie came home. She was so tired she should have been comatose, but in fact she was so angry it was possible she did it all at double speed. She couldn't stop herself. She cleaned and folded and sorted because if she didn't she would take Marty's old sledgehammer down from the two hooks in the musty garage, walk round to the Fishers' house, and do something that would finish them all off completely. She cleaned because if she didn't she would stand in her over-grown little back garden, lift her face to the sky, and scream and scream and scream, and she wasn't sure she'd be able to stop.

By the time she heard the footsteps on the path, the house floated in a toxic fug of furniture polish and kitchen cleaner. She took two deep breaths, coughed a bit, then made herself take one more before she opened the door, a reassuring smile already plastered on her face. Nathalie stood on the path, her hands on Tanzie's shoulders. Tanzie walked up to her, put her arms around her waist, and held her tightly, her eyes shut.

"He's okay, sweetheart," Jess told her, stroking her hair. "It's all right. It's just a silly boys' fight."

Nathalie touched Jess's arm, gave a tiny shake of her head. "You take care," she said, and left.

Jess made Tanzie a sandwich and watched her wander away into the shady part of the garden to do algorithms and told herself she would let her know about St. Anne's tomorrow. She would definitely tell her tomorrow.

And then she disappeared into the bathroom and unrolled the money she had found in Mr. Nicholls's taxi. Four hundred and eighty pounds. She laid it out in neat piles on the floor with the door locked.

Jess knew what she should do. Of course she did. It wasn't her money. It was a lesson she had drummed into the kids: You don't steal. You don't take what is not yours. Do the right thing, and you will be rewarded for it in the end.

Do the right thing.

But a new, darker voice had begun a low internal hum in her ear. Why should you give it back? He won't miss it. He was passed out in the car park, in the taxi, in his house. It could have fallen out anywhere. It was only luck that you found it, after all. And what if someone else from round here had picked it up? You think they would have handed it back to him?

His security card said the name of his company was Mayfly. His first name was Ed.

She would take the money back to Mr. Nicholls. Her brain whirred round and round in time with the clothes dryer.

And still she didn't do it.

Jess never used to think about money. Marty worked five days a week for a local taxi firm, handled all the finances, and they generally had enough for him to go down to the pub a couple of nights a week and for her to have the odd night out with Nathalie. They took the occasional holiday. Some years they did better than others, but they got by.

And then Marty got fed up with making do. There was a camping holiday in Wales where it rained for eight days solid and Marty became more and more dissatisfied, as if the weather were something to be taken personally. "Why can't we go to Spain or somewhere hot?" he'd mutter, staring out through the flaps of the sodden tent. "This is crap. This isn't a bloody holiday."

He got fed up with his work; he found more and more to complain about. The other drivers were against him. The controller was cheating him. The passengers were tight.

And then he started with the schemes. The knockoff T-shirts for a band that fell out of the charts as quickly as it had arrived. The pyramid scheme they joined two weeks too late. Import-export was the thing, he told Jess confidently, arriving home from the pub one night. He had met a bloke who could get cheap electrical goods from India, and they could sell them on to someone he knew. And then — surprise, surprise — the someone who was going to sell them on turned out not to be the sure thing Marty had been promised. And the few people who did buy the appliances complained that they blew their electricity supply, and the rest of them rusted, even in the garage, so their meager savings turned into a pile of useless white goods that had to be loaded, fourteen a week, into Marty's car and taken to the dump.

And then came the Rolls-Royce. At least Jess could see the sense in that one: Marty would spray it metallic gray, then rent himself out as a chauffeur for weddings and funerals. He'd bought it off eBay from a man in the Midlands, and made it halfway down the M6 before it conked out. Something to do with the starter motor, the mechanic said, peering under the bonnet. But the more he looked at it, the more seemed wrong with it. The first winter it spent on the drive, mice got into the upholstery so they needed money to replace the backseats before he could rent it out. And then it turned out that replacement upholstered Rolls-Royce seats were about the only thing you couldn't get on eBay. So it sat there in the garage, a daily reminder of how they never quite managed to get ahead.

She'd taken over the money when Marty started to spend the better part of each day in bed. Depression was an illness, everyone said so. Although, from what his mates said, he didn't seem to suffer it on the two evenings he still managed to drag himself to the pub.

When Jess peeled all the bank statements from their envelopes and retrieved the savings book from its place in the hall desk, she had finally seen for herself the trouble they were in. She'd tried to talk to him a couple of times, but he'd just pulled the duvet over his head and said he couldn't cope. It was around then that he'd suggested he might go home to his mum's for a bit. If she was honest, Jess was relieved to see him go. It was hard enough coping with Nicky — who was still a silent, skinny wraith — Tanzie, and two jobs.

"Go," she'd said, stroking his hair. She

remembered thinking how long it had been since she'd touched him. "Go for a couple of weeks. You'll feel better for a bit of a break." He had looked at her silently, his eyes red rimmed, and squeezed her hand.

That had been two years ago. Neither of them had ever seriously raised the possibility of his coming back.

She tried to keep things normal until Tanzie went to bed, asking what she'd had to eat at Nathalie's, telling her what Norman had done while she was out. She combed Tanzie's hair, then sat on her bed and read her an old Harry Potter, as if she were a much younger child, and for once Tanzie didn't tell her that actually she'd rather do some maths.

When Jess was sure that Tanzie was asleep, she rang the hospital. The nurse said that Nicky was comfortable: X-rays had shown no evidence that his lung was punctured. The small facial fracture would have to heal by itself.

She rang Marty, who listened in silence, then asked, "Does he still wear all that stuff on his face?"

"He wears a bit of mascara, yes."

There was a long silence.

"Don't say it, Marty. Don't you dare say

it." She put the phone down before he could.

And then the police rang at a quarter to ten and said that Jason Fisher had denied all knowledge.

"There were fourteen witnesses," she said, her voice tight with the effort of not shouting. "Including the man who runs the fish-and-chip shop. They jumped my son. There were four of them."

"Yes, but witnesses are only any use to us if they can identify the perpetrators, madam. And Mr. Brent says it wasn't clear who was actually doing the fighting." He let out a sigh as if she should know what teenage boys were like. "I have to tell you, madam, the Fishers claim your son started it."

"He's about as likely to start a fight as the Dalai bloody Lama. We're talking about a boy who can't put a duvet in its cover without worrying it might hurt someone."

"We can only act on the evidence, madam."

The Fishers. With their reputation, she'd be lucky if a single person "remembered" what they'd seen.

For a moment Jess let her head fall into her hands. They would never let up. And it would be Tanzie next, once she started secondary school. She would be a prime

target with her love of maths and her odd-
ness and her total lack of guile. Jess went
cold. She thought about Marty's sledgehammer in the garage, and how it would feel to
walk down to the Fishers' house and —

The phone rang. She snatched it up.
"What now? Are you going to tell me he
beat himself up, too? Is that it?"

"Mrs. Thomas?"

She blinked.

"Mrs. Thomas? It's Mr. Tsvangarai."

"Oh. Mr. Tsvangarai, I'm sorry. It — it's
not a great time." She held out her hand in
front of her. It was shaking.

"I'm sorry to call you so late, but it's a
matter of some urgency. I have discovered
something of interest. It's called the Maths
Olympiad." He spoke the words carefully.

"The what?"

"It's a new thing, in Scotland, for gifted
students. A maths competition. And we still
have time to enter Tanzie."

"A maths competition?" Jess closed her
eyes. "You know, that's really nice, Mr. Tsvangarai, but we have quite a lot going on here
right now, and I don't think I —"

"Mrs. Thomas, the prizes are five hundred
pounds, a thousand pounds, and five thousand pounds. Five thousand pounds. If she
won, you'd have at least the first year of

your St. Anne's school fees sorted out."

"Say that again."

Jess sat down on the chair as he explained in greater depth.

"This is an actual thing?"

"It is an actual thing."

"And you really think she could do it?"

"There is a category especially for her age group. I cannot see how she could fail."

Five thousand pounds, a voice sang in her head. Enough to get her through the first two years.

"What's the catch?"

"No catch. Well, you have to do advanced maths, obviously. But I can't see that this would be a problem for Tanzie."

She stood up and sat down again.

"And of course you would have to travel to Scotland."

"Details, Mr. Tsvangarai. Details." Her head was spinning. "This is for real, right? This isn't a joke?"

"I am not a funny man, Mrs. Thomas."

"Fuck. *Fuck!* Mr. Tsvangarai, you are an absolute beauty."

She could hear his embarrassed laugh.

"So . . . what do we do now?"

"Well, they waived the qualifying test after I sent over some examples of Tanzie's work. I understand they are very keen to have children from less-advantaged schools. And between you and me, it is, of course, an enormous benefit that she's a girl. But we have to decide quickly. You see, this year's Olympiad is only five days away."

Five days. The deadline for registration at St. Anne's was tomorrow.

She stood in the middle of the room, thinking. Then she ran upstairs, pulled Mr. Nicholls's money from its nest among her tights, and before she could think she stuffed it into an envelope, scrawled a note, and wrote ADMISSIONS OFFICE, ST. ANNE'S in careful letters on the front. She would drop it in on the way to clean tomorrow.

She would pay it back. Every penny.

But right now she didn't have a choice.

That night, Jess sat at the kitchen table and worked out a rough plan. She looked up the schedule for trains to Edinburgh, laughed a bit hysterically, then looked up the cost of three coach tickets (£187, including the £13 it would cost to get to the station) and the cost of putting Norman in a kennel for a week (£94). She put the palms of her hands into her eye sockets and let them stay there for a bit. And then, when the children were asleep, she dug out the keys to the Rolls-Royce, went outside, brushed the mouse droppings off the driver's seat and tried the ignition.

It turned over on the third attempt.

Jess sat in the garage that always smelled of damp, surrounded by old garden furniture, bits of car, plastic buckets, and let the engine run. Then she leaned forward and peeled back the faded tax disc. It was almost two years out of date. And she didn't have insurance.

She turned off the ignition and sat in the dark as the smell of oil gradually faded from the air, and she thought, for the hundredth time: Do the right thing.

Chapter Eight:
Ed

Ed.Nicholls@mayfly.com: Don't forget what I told you. Can remind you of deets if you lose the card.
Deanna1@yahoo.com: I won't forget. Whole night engraved on my memory. ;-)

Ed.Nicholls@mayfly.com: Did you do what I told you?
Deanna1@yahoo.com: Just sorting now.
Ed.Nicholls@mayfly.com: Let me know if you get good results!
Deanna1@yahoo.com: Well, based on your past performance, I'd be amazed if it was anything but! ;-0

Deanna1@yahoo.com: Nobody's ever done for me what you did for me.
Ed.Nicholls@mayfly.com: Really. It was nothing.
Deanna1@yahoo.com: You want to hook up again, next weekend?

Ed.Nicholls@mayfly.com: Bit busy at the mo. I'll let you know.
Deanna1@yahoo.com: I think it worked out well for both of us. ;-)

The detective let him finish reading the two sheets of paper, then slid them toward Paul Wilkes, Ed's lawyer.

"Have you got any comment on those, Mr. Nicholls?"

There was something excruciating about seeing private e-mails laid out in an official document: the eagerness of his early replies, the barely veiled double entendres, the smiley faces (what was he, fourteen?).

"You don't have to say anything," Paul said.

"That whole exchange could be about anything." Ed pushed the documents away from him. " 'Let me know if you get good results.' I could have been telling her to do something sexual. It could be, like, e-mail sex."

"At eleven fourteen a.m.?"

"So?"

"In an open-plan office?"

"I'm uninhibited."

The detective removed his glasses and gave him a hard look. "E-mail sex? Really? That's what you were doing here?"

"Well, no. Not in that case. But that's not the point."

"I would suggest it is totally the point, Mr. Nicholls. There are reams of this stuff. You talk about keeping in touch" — he flicked through the papers — " 'to see if I can help you out some more.' "

"But it's not how it sounds. She was depressed. She was having a bad time getting rid of her ex. I just wanted to . . . make things a little easier for her. I keep telling you."

"Just a few more questions."

They had questions, all right. They wanted to know how often he had met Deanna. Where they had gone. What the exact nature of their relationship was. They didn't believe him when Ed said he didn't know much about her life, and nothing about her brother.

"Oh, come on!" Ed protested. "You've never had a relationship based on sex?"

"Ms. Lewis doesn't say it was based on sex. She says the two of you were involved in a 'close and intense' relationship, that you had known each other since your college days, and that you were determined to make her go ahead with this deal, that you pressed it on her. She says she had no idea that in taking your advice she was doing anything illegal."

"But she's . . . she's making it sound like we had much more of a relationship than we did. And I didn't force her to do anything."

"So you admit that you gave her the information."

"I'm not saying that! I'm just saying —"

"I think what my client is saying is that he cannot be held responsible for any misconceptions Ms. Lewis might have held about their relationship," Paul interjected. "Or what information she might have passed on to her brother."

"And we were not having a relationship. Not that kind of relationship."

The detective shrugged. "You know what? I don't really care what the nature of your relationship was. I don't care if you knobbed her halfway to next Wednesday. What is of interest to me, Mr. Nicholls, is that you gave this young woman information that on the twenty-eighth of February, she told a friend, was 'going to bring us some serious profit.' And her and her brother's bank accounts show that they were, in fact, brought some 'serious profit.' "

An hour later, bailed for a fortnight, Ed sat in Paul's office. Paul poured them both a whiskey. Ed was becoming oddly used to the taste of strong alcohol in daylight hours.

"I can't be held responsible for what she told her brother. I can't go around checking whether every potential partner has a brother who works in finance. I was just trying to help her."

"Well, you certainly did that. But the SFA and the SOCA won't care what your motives were, Ed. She and her brother made a barrow load of money, and they did it illegally on information you gave her."

"Can we stop talking in acronyms? I have no idea who you're talking about."

"Well, try to imagine every serious crime-fighting body that has anything to do with finance. Or crime. That's basically who is investigating you right now."

"You make it sound like I'm actually going to be charged." Ed put the whiskey on the table beside him.

"I think it's extremely likely, yes. And I think we may be in court pretty quickly. They're trying to speed up these cases."

Ed stared at him. Then his head sank into his hands. "This is a nightmare. I just . . . I just wanted her to go away, Paul. That's all."

"Well, the best we can hope for at the moment is that we can convince them that you're just a geek who was in over his head."

"Great."

"You got any better ideas?"

Ed shook his head.

"Then just sit tight."

"I need to do something, Paul. I need to get back to work. I don't know what to do if I'm not working. I'm going nuts down there in Nowheresville."

"Well, if I were you, I'd stay put for now. The SFA may well leak this and then the shit is really going to hit the fan. The media will be all over you. The best thing you can do is hide out down there in 'Nowheresville' for another week or so." Paul scribbled a note on his legal pad.

Ed gazed at the upside-down writing. "Do you really think this will get into the papers?"

"I don't know. Probably. It might be a good idea to talk to your family, anyway, just so they're prepared for any negative publicity."

Ed rested his hands on his knees. "I can't."

"You can't what?"

"Tell my dad about all this. He's sick. This would . . ." He shook his head. When he finally looked up, Paul was watching him steadily.

"Well, that's got to be your decision. But as I said, I think it would be wise for you to remain somewhere out of reach if and when it all blows up. Mayfly obviously doesn't want you anywhere near its offices until it's all sorted out. There's too much money riding on SFAX. So you need to steer clear of anyone associated with the company. No calls. No e-mails. And if anyone does happen to locate you, for God's sake, don't say anything. To anyone." He tapped his pen, signaling the end of the conversation.

"So I should hide in the middle of nowhere, keep schtum, and twiddle my thumbs until I get sent to prison."

Paul stood, closed the file on his desk. "Well, we're putting our best team on it. And we'll do everything we can to make sure it doesn't come to that."

Ed stood blinking on the steps of Paul's office, surrounded by the lead-stained buildings, the couriers tugging helmets from sweaty heads, bare-legged women laughing on their way to eat sandwiches in the park, and felt an acute pang for his old life. The one with his Nespresso machine in his office and his secretary nipping out for sushi and his apartment with the views over the city, and the worst thing being the prospect of having to lie on the couch in the creatives' room and listen to the Suits drone on about profit and loss. He had never really measured his life by that of anyone else, but now he felt cripplingly envious of the people around him with their everyday concerns, their ability to get on a Tube back to their own homes, their families. What did he have? Weeks of being stuck in an empty house with nobody to talk to, facing the prospect of imminent prosecution.

He missed work more than he had ever missed his wife. He missed it like a constant mistress; he missed having a routine. He thought back to the previous week, to waking up on his sofa at Beachfront with no idea how he had got there, his mouth as dry as if it had been packed with cotton wool, his glasses neatly folded on the coffee table. It was the third time in as many weeks that he'd been so drunk he couldn't remember how he'd got home, the first time he had woken with empty pockets.

He checked his phone (new, only three imported contacts). There were two voice-mail messages from Gemma. Nobody else had called. Ed sighed and pressed Delete, then set off along the sunbaked pavement toward the car park. He wasn't really a drinker. Lara had always insisted alcohol gave you belly fat and complained that he snored if he had more than two. But he wanted a drink right now like he had rarely wanted anything.

Ed sat for a while in his empty flat, got a bite to eat at a pizza restaurant, sat again in his flat, and then climbed back into his car and drove toward the coast. Deanna Lewis danced before him the whole way out of London. How could he have been so stupid? Why had he not thought about the possibility that she would tell someone else? Or was he actually missing something more sinister here? Had she and her brother planned this? Was it some sort of psychotic revenge strategy for dumping her?

With every mile, Ed grew angrier. He might as well have given her the keys to his flat, his bank-account details — like his ex-wife — and let Deanna wipe him out. That would actually have been better. At least he would have kept his job, his friend. Shortly before the Godalming exit, now overcome with rage, Ed pulled over on the motorway and dialed her mobile number. The police had taken his old mobile, with all his stored contacts as evidence. He thought he remembered her number, though. And he had his opening line: What the hell did you think you were doing?

But the number was dead.

Ed sat in a lay-by, his phone in his hand, slowly letting his anger dissipate. He hesitated, then rang Ronan's number. It was one of only a handful he knew by heart.

It rang several times before he answered.

"Ronan —"

"I'm not allowed to talk to you, Ed." He sounded weary.

"Yeah. I know. I just — I just wanted to say —"

"Say what? What do you want to say, Ed?"

Ed's voice stalled at the sudden fury in Ronan's voice.

"You know what? I don't actually care so much about the insider-trading thing. Although obviously it's a bloody disaster for the company. But you were my mate. My oldest friend. I would never have done that to you."

A click, and the phone went dead.

Ed sat there and allowed his head to drop onto the wheel for a few minutes. He waited until the humming in his mind leached away to nothing, and then he signaled, pulled out slowly, and drove toward Beachfront.

"What do you want, Lara?"

"Hey, baby. How are you?"

"Uh . . . not so good."

"Oh no! What is the matter?"

He never knew if it was an Italian thing, but she had a way, his ex-wife, of making you feel better. She would cradle your head, run her fingers through your hair, fuss around you, cluck maternally. By the end it had irritated him, but now, on the empty road in the dead of night, he felt nostalgic for it.

"It's . . . a work thing."

"Oh. A work thing." That instinctive bristle in her voice.

"How are you, Lara?"

"Mamma is driving me crazy. And there is a problem with the roof in the apartment."

"Any jobs?"

She made a sound with her teeth against her lips. "I got a callback for a West End show and then they say I look too old. Too old!"

"You don't look too old."

"I know! I can look sixteen! Baby, I need to talk to you about the roof in the apartment."

"Lara, it's your place. You got a settlement."

"But they say it's going to cost lots of money. Lots of money. I have nothing."

"What happened to the settlement?" He kept his voice steady.

"There is nothing. My brother needed

some money for his business, and you know Papi's health is not good. And then I had some credit cards . . ."

"All of it?"

"I don't have enough for the roof. It's going to leak this winter, they said. Eduardo . . ."

"Well, you could always sell the print you took from my apartment in December." His solicitor had implied it was his own fault for not changing the locks on the doors. Everyone else did, apparently.

"I was sad, Eduardo. I miss you. I just wanted a reminder of you."

"Right. Of the man you said you couldn't even stand to look at anymore."

"I was angry when I said that." She pronounced it "engry." By the end she was always engry. He rubbed at his eyes, flicked the indicator to signal his exit onto the coast road.

"I just wanted some reminders of when we were heppy."

"You know, maybe the next time you miss me, you could take away, like, a framed photo of us, not a fourteen-thousand-pound limited-edition screen print of Mao Tse-tung."

"Don't you care that I have no one to turn to?" Her voice dropped to a whisper, almost unbearably intimate. It made his balls tighten reflexively. And she knew it.

Ed glanced in his rearview mirror. "Well, why don't you ask Jim Leonards?"

"What?"

"His wife called me. She's not very happy, funnily enough."

"It was only once! Once I went out with him. And it is nobody's business who I date!" Ed could picture her, one perfectly manicured hand raised, fingers splayed in frustration at having to deal with "the most annoying man on earth." "You left me! Am I supposed to be a nun my whole life?"

"You left me, Lara. On the twenty-seventh of May, on the way back from Paris. Remember?"

"Details! You always twist my words with details! This is exactly why I had to leave you!"

"I thought it was because I only loved my work and didn't understand human emotions."

"I left you because you have a tiny dick! Tiny, *tiny* dick! Like a pawn!"

"You mean prawn."

"Prawn. Crayfish, whatever is smallest thing! *Tiny!"*

"Then I think you actually mean shrimp. You know, given you just walked off with a valuable limited-edition print, I think you could at least have granted me 'lobster.' But sure. Whatever."

He still wondered what those Italian curses actually meant. He drove for several miles that later he would not recall driving. And then he sighed, turned on the radio, and fixed his gaze on the seemingly endless black road ahead.

Gemma rang just as he was turning down the coast road. Ed answered before he'd had time to think about why he shouldn't.

"Don't tell me. You're really busy."

"I'm driving."

"And you have a hands-free thing. Mum wanted to know if you're going to be there for their anniversary lunch."

"What anniversary lunch?"

"Oh, come on, Ed. I told you about it months ago."

"I'm sorry. I haven't got access to my diary right now."

Gemma took a deep breath. "Mum's doing a special lunch at home for them. Dad's coming out of hospital just for that. She wanted us to be there. You said you'd be able to come."

"Oh. Yeah."

"Yeah what? You remember? Or yeah,

you're coming?"

He tapped his fingers on the steering wheel. "I don't know."

"Look, Dad was asking for you yesterday. I told him you're tied up with a work project, but he's so frail, Ed. This is really important to him. To both of them."

"Gemma, I've told you —"

Her voice exploded into the interior of the car. "Yeah, I know, you're too busy. You've told me you've got stuff going on."

"I have got stuff going on! You have no idea!"

"Oh no, I couldn't possibly hope to understand, could I? Just the stupid social worker who doesn't earn a six-figure fucking salary. This is our dad, Ed. This is the man who sacrificed everything to buy you a fucking education. He thinks the sun shines out of your backside. And he's not going to last much longer. You need to get down there and show your face and say the things that sons are meant to say to their dying fathers, okay?"

"He's not dying."

"How the fuck would you know? You haven't been to see him in two months!"

"Look, I will go. It's just I've got to —"

"Bullshit. You're a businessman. You make

stuff happen. Make this happen. Or I swear I —"

"I'm losing you, Gem. Sorry, the reception's really patchy here. I —" He began to make *shhh* noises.

"One lunch," she said, her social-work voice on, all calm and conciliatory. "One little lunch, Ed."

He spotted a police car up ahead and checked the speedometer. A filthy Rolls-Royce, one headlight dimmed, sat half up on the verge under the orange glow of a sodium light. A small girl stood beside it holding an enormous dog on a lead. Her head turned slowly as he passed.

"And yes, I do understand that you have a lot of commitments, and your job is really important. We all understand that, Mr. Big Swinging Technodick. But is just one awkward family lunch too much to ask?"

"Hang on, Gem. There's an accident up ahead."

Beside the girl stood a ghostly teenager — boy? girl? — with a shock of dark hair, shoulders slumped. And, turning briefly away from a policeman, who was writing something, was another child — no, a small woman, her hair tied back into a scrappy ponytail. She was lifting her hands in exasperation — a gesture that reminded him of

Lara. *You are so ennoying!*

He had driven a farther hundred yards before he realized that he knew that woman. He racked his brain: bar? Holiday park? He had a sudden image of her taking his car keys, a memory of her removing his glasses in his house. What was she doing out there with children at this time of night? He pulled over and glanced into the rearview mirror, watching. He could just make out the group. The little girl had sat down on the dark verge, the dog a mountainous black lump beside her.

"Ed? Are you okay?" Gemma's voice broke into the silence.

Afterward he wouldn't be entirely sure what had made him stop. Perhaps it was an attempt to delay his arrival back in that empty house. Perhaps in a life that had gone so far off the rails, making himself part of such a scene no longer seemed like an odd thing to do. Perhaps it was just that he wanted to convince himself, against all available evidence, that he was not entirely an arsehole.

"Gem, I'll have to call you back. It's someone I know."

He pulled over and did a three-point turn, driving back down the dimly lit road slowly until he reached the police car. He pulled up on the other side of the road.

"Hi," Ed said, lowering the window. "Can I help?"

CHAPTER NINE: TANZIE

Tanzie's happy mood disappeared when she first saw Nicky's swollen face. It didn't really look like him, and she'd had to make her eyes stay very firmly on his when they would have liked to go somewhere else, even to the stupid picture of galloping horses on the wall opposite, which didn't even look like horses. She wanted to tell him about the maths competition and how they'd registered at St. Anne's, but she couldn't — not with the smell of hospital in her nose and Nicky's eye all the wrong shape. Tanzie found herself thinking, the Fishers did this, the Fishers did this; and she felt a bit scared because she couldn't believe anyone they knew would do this for no reason.

When Nicky got up to go down the corridor, she put her hand gently into his, and even though normally he would have told her to "Scoot, small fry," he just squeezed her fingers a bit.

Mum had to have all the usual arguments with the hospital people about how, no, she wasn't his actual mum, but as good as. And, no, he didn't have a social worker. And it always made Tanzie feel a bit odd, like Nicky wasn't a proper part of their family, even though he was.

He walked out of the room really slowly, and he remembered to thank the nurse. "Nice lad, isn't he?" she said. "Polite."

Mum was gathering up his things. "That's the worst bit," she said. "He just wants to be left alone."

"Doesn't really work like that round here, though, does it?" The nurse smiled at Tanzie. "Take care of your brother, eh?"

As she walked toward the main entrance behind him, Tanzie wondered what it said about their family when every single conversation they had now seemed to end with a funny look and the words "Take care."

Mum cooked dinner and gave Nicky three different-colored pills to take, and they sat watching television on the sofa together. It was *Total Wipeout,* which normally made Nicky pretty much wee himself laughing, but he had barely spoken since they'd returned home, and Tanzie didn't think it was because his jaw hurt. Mum was busy upstairs. Tanzie could hear her dragging drawers out and going backward and forward across the landing. She was so busy she didn't even notice it was way past bedtime.

Tanzie nudged Nicky very gently with her finger. "Does it hurt?"

"Does what hurt?"

"Your face."

"What do you mean?"

"Well . . . it's a funny shape."

"So's yours. Does that hurt?"

"Ha ha."

"I'm fine, Titch. Drop it." And then, when she stared at him, "Really. Just . . . forget it. I'm fine."

Mum came in and put the lead on Norman. He was lying on the sofa and didn't want to get up, and it took her about four goes to drag him out of the door. Tanzie was going to ask her if she was taking him for a walk, but then the part came on where the wheel knocks the contestants off their little pedestals into the water and Tanzie forgot. Then Mum came back in.

"Okay, kids. Get your jackets."

"Jackets? Why?"

"Because we're leaving. For Scotland." She made it sound perfectly normal.

Nicky didn't look round from the television. "We're leaving for Scotland . . . ?"

"Yup. We're going to drive."

"But we haven't got a car."

"We're taking the Rolls."

Nicky glanced at Tanzie, then back at Mum. "But you haven't got insurance."

"I've been driving since I was twelve years old. And I've never had an accident. Look, we'll stick to the B roads and do most of it overnight. As long as nobody pulls us over, we'll be fine."

They both stared at her.

"But you said —"

"I know what I said. But sometimes the ends justify the means."

"What does that mean?"

Mum threw her hands up in the air. "Nicky, there's a maths competition that could change our lives and it's in Scotland. Right now, we haven't got the money for the fares. That's the truth of it. I know it's not ideal to drive, and I'm not saying it's right, but unless you two have a better idea, then let's just get into the car and get on with it."

"Um, don't we need to pack?"

"It's all in the car."

Tanzie knew Nicky was thinking what she was thinking — that Mum had finally gone mad. But she had read somewhere that mad people were like sleepwalkers — it was best not to disturb them. So she nodded really slowly, like this was all making good sense. She fetched her jacket and they walked through the back door and into the garage, where Norman was sitting in the backseat and giving them the look that said, "Yeah. Me, too." It smelled a bit musty in the car, and she didn't really want to put her hands down on the seats because she had also read somewhere that mice wee all the time, like nonstop, and mouse wee could give you about eight hundred diseases. "Can I just run and get my gloves?" she said. Mum looked at her like she was the crazy one, but she nodded, so Tanzie ran and put them on and thought she felt a bit better.

Nicky eased his way gingerly into the front seat, and wiped at the dust on the dashboard with his fingers.

Mum opened the garage door, started the engine, reversed the car carefully out onto the drive. Then she climbed out, closed and locked the garage securely. Then sat and thought for a minute. "Tanze. Have you got a pen and paper?"

She fished around in her bag and handed her one. Mum didn't want her to see what she was writing but Tanzie peeped through the seats.

FISHER YOU LITTLE WASTE OF SKIN I HAVE TOLD THE POLICE THAT IF ANYONE BREAKS IN IT WILL BE YOU AND THEY ARE WATCHING

She got out of the car and pinned it to the bottom part of the door, where it wouldn't be visible from the street. Then she climbed back into the half-eaten driver's seat and, with a low purr, the Rolls set off into the night.

It took them about ten minutes to work out that Mum had forgotten how to drive. The things that even Tanzie knew — mirror, signal, maneuver — she kept doing in the wrong order, and she drove leaning forward over the steering wheel, clutching it like the grannies who drove at fifteen m.p.h. around the town center and scraped their doors on the pillars in the municipal car park.

They passed the Rose and Crown, the industrial area with the five-man car wash and the carpet warehouse. Tanzie pressed her nose to the window. They were officially leaving town. The last time she had left town was on the school journey to Durdle Door when Melanie Abbott was sick all down herself in the coach and started a vomit chain reaction around the whole of 5C.

"Just keep calm," Mum muttered to herself. "Nice and calm."

"You don't look calm," said Nicky. He was playing Nintendo, his thumbs a blur on each side of the little glowing screen.

"Nicky, I need you to map read. Don't play Nintendo right now."

"Well, surely we just go north."

"But where is north? I haven't driven around here for years. I need you to tell me where I should be going."

He glanced up at the signpost. "Do we want the M3?"

"I don't know. I'm asking you!"

"Let me see." Tanzie reached through from the back and took the map from Nicky's hands. "What way up do I hold it?"

They drove through the roundabout twice, while she wrestled with the map, and then they were on the road out of town. Tanzie vaguely remembered this road: they had once come this way when Mum and Dad were trying to sell the air conditioners. "Can you turn the light on at the back, Mum?" she said. "I can't read anything."

Mum turned in her seat. "The button should be above your head."

Tanzie reached up and clicked it with her thumb. She could have taken her gloves off, she thought. Mice couldn't walk upside down. Not like spiders. "It's not working."

"Nicky, you'll have to map read." She looked over, exasperated. "Nicky."

"Yeah. I will. I just need to get these golden stars. They're five thousand points." Tanzie folded the map as best she could and pushed it back through the front seats. Nicky's head was bent low over his game, lost in concentration. To be fair, golden stars were really hard to get.

"Will you put that thing down!"

He sighed, snapped it shut. They were going past a pub she didn't recognize, and now a new hotel. Mum said they were looking for the M3, but Tanzie hadn't seen any signs for the M3 for ages. Beside her Norman started a low whine: she figured they had around thirty-eight seconds before Mum said it was shredding her nerves.

She made it to twenty-seven.

"Tanzie, please stop the dog. It's making it impossible to concentrate. Nicky. I really need you to read the map."

"He's drooling everywhere. I think he needs to get out." Tanzie shifted to the side.

Nicky squinted at the signs in front of them. "If you stay on this road I think we'll end up in Southampton."

"But that's the wrong way."

"That's what I said."

The smell of oil was really strong. Tanzie wondered whether something was leaking. She put her glove over her nose.

"I think we should just head back to where we were and start again," Nicky said.

With a grunt Mum swung the car off at the next exit. They all tried to ignore the grinding noise as she turned the wheel to the right and headed back down the other side of the dual motorway.

"Tanzie. Please do something with the dog. Please." One of the Rolls's pedals was so stiff she almost had to stand up on it just to change gear. She looked up and pointed toward the turnoff for the town. "What am I doing, Nicky? Coming off here?"

"Oh, God. He's farted. Mum, I'm suffocating."

"Nicky, please can you read the map."

Tanzie remembered now that Mum hated driving. She wasn't good at processing information quickly enough. She always said she didn't have the right synapses. Plus, to be fair, the smell now seeping through the car was so bad it made it hard to think straight.

Tanzie began to gag. "I'm dying!"

Norman turned his big old head to look at her, his eyes sad, like she was being really mean.

"But there are two turnings. Do I take this one or the next?"

"Definitely the next. Oh no, sorry — it's this one."

"What?" Mum wrenched the car off the motorway, narrowly avoiding the grass verge, and onto the exit. The car juddered as they hit the curb and Tanzie had to let go of her nose to grab Norman's collar.

"For Christ's sake, can you just —"

"I meant the next one. This one takes us miles out of the way."

"We've been on the road almost half an hour and we're farther away than when we started. Jesus, Nicky, I —"

It was then that Tanzie saw the flashing blue light. She willed the police car to go past. But instead it drew nearer and nearer until its blue lights filled the car.

Nicky turned painfully in his seat. "Um, Jess, I think they want you to pull over."

"Shit. Shit shit shit. Tanzie, you didn't hear that." Mum took a deep breath, adjusted her hands on the wheel as she started to slow.

Nicky slumped a little lower in his seat. "Um, Jess?"

"Not now, Nicky."

The police car was pulling over, too. Tanzie's palms had begun to sweat. *It will all be fine.*

"I guess this isn't the time to tell you I brought my stash with me."

CHAPTER TEN:
JESS

So there she was, standing on the grass verge of the motorway at eleven forty at night with two policemen who were both acting not like she was a major criminal, which was sort of what she'd expected, but worse — like she was just really, really stupid. Everything they said had a patronizing edge to it: So are you often in the habit of taking your family out for a late-night drive, madam? With only one headlight working? Were you not aware, madam, that your tax disc is two years out of date? They hadn't actually looked up the whole no-insurance thing yet. So there was that to look forward to.

Nicky was sweating, waiting for them to locate his stash. Tanzie was a pale, silent ghost a few feet away, her sequined jacket glittering under the lights as she hugged Norman's neck for reassurance.

Jess had only herself to blame. It could

hardly get any worse.

And then Mr. Nicholls turned up.

She felt the remaining color drain from her face as his window wound down. And a million thoughts flashed through her head — like who was going to mind the children when she went to prison, and if it was Marty, would he remember things like the fact that Tanzie's feet grew occasionally and then would he buy her new shoes instead of waiting until her toenails curled in on her toes? And who would look after Norman? And why the hell hadn't she done what she should have done in the first place and just given Ed Nicholls back his stupid roll of money? And was Ed about to tell the police that on top of everything else, she was a thief?

But he didn't. He asked if he could help.

Policeman Number One turned slowly to look Ed over. Number One was a barrel-chested man with an upright bearing, the kind who took himself seriously, and bristled if everyone else didn't. "And you are?"

"Edward Nicholls. I know this woman. What is it? Car trouble?" He looked at the Rolls as if he couldn't believe it was actually on the road.

"You could say that," said Policeman Number Two.

"Out-of-date tax disc," Jess muttered, trying to ignore the hammering in her chest. "I was trying to drive the kids somewhere. And now I guess I'm driving it home again."

"You're not driving anywhere," said Policeman Number One. "Your car is now impounded. The tow truck is on its way. It is an offense under Section Thirty-three of the Vehicle Excise and Registration Act to drive on a public road without a valid tax disc. Which also means your insurance will be invalidated."

"I don't have any."

They both turned toward her.

"The car isn't insured. I'm not insured."

She could see Mr. Nicholls staring. What the hell? The moment they entered the details they would see it anyway. "We've had a bit of trouble. It was the only way I could see to get the kids from A to B."

"You are aware that driving your car without tax and insurance is a crime. And carries a possible jail sentence."

"And it's not my car." Jess kicked at a stone on the grass. "That's the next thing you're going to see when you do your whole database thing."

"Did you steal the vehicle, madam?"

"No, I did not steal the vehicle. It's been sitting in my garage for two years."

"That's not an answer to my question."

"It's my ex-husband's car."

"Does he know you've taken it?"

"He wouldn't know if I had a sex change and called myself Sid. He's been in north Yorkshire for the past —"

"You know, you really might want to stop talking now." Mr. Nicholls ran a hand over the top of his head.

"Who are you, her lawyer?"

"Does she need one?"

"Driving without tax and insurance is an offense under Section Thirty-three —"

"Yeah. You said. Well, I think you might want to get some advice before you say any more —"

"Jess," she said.

"Jess." Ed looked at the policemen. "Officers, does this woman actually need to go to the station? Because she's obviously really, really sorry. And given the hour, I think the kids need to go home."

"She'll be charged with driving without tax and insurance. Your name and address, madam?"

Jess gave it to Policeman Number One.

"The car is registered to that address, yes. But it's registered under a SORN, which means —"

"That it shouldn't be driven on a public

road. I know."

"Shame you didn't think about that before you came out, then, isn't it?" He gave her the kind of look that teachers reserve for making eight-year-olds feel small. And something in that look pushed Jess over the edge.

"You know what?" she said. "You honestly think I would have driven my kids anywhere at eleven o'clock at night if it hadn't been absolutely necessary? You really think I just sat there this evening in my little house and thought, I know, I'll take my kids and my bloody dog and just go and get us all into a whole heap of trouble and —"

"It's not my business what you were thinking, madam. My issue is you bringing an uninsured, possibly unsafe vehicle onto a public road."

"I was desperate, okay? And you won't find me on your damned database because I've never done anything wrong —"

"Or you just never got caught."

The two policemen gazed at her steadily. On the verge, Norman flopped down with a great sigh. Tanzie watched it all in silence, her eyes great hollows. *Oh, God,* Jess thought. She mumbled an apology.

"You will be charged with driving without the appropriate documents, Mrs. Thomas,"

Policeman Number One said, handing her a slip of paper. "I have to warn you that you will receive a court summons, and that you face a possible fine of up to five thousand pounds."

"Five grand?" Jess started to laugh.

"And you'll need to pay to get this" — the officer couldn't bring himself to say "car" — "out of the police pound. I have to tell you there is a fifteen-pound charge for every day that it remains there."

"Perfect. And how am I supposed to get it out of the pound if I'm not allowed to drive it?"

"I'd advise you to remove all your belongings before the tow truck arrives. Once it leaves here we cannot be held responsible for the vehicle's contents."

"Of course. Because obviously it would be way too much to hope for a car to be safe in a police pound," she muttered.

"But, Mum, how are we going to get home?"

There was a brief silence. The policemen turned away.

"I'll give you a lift," Mr. Nicholls said.

Jess stepped away from him. "Oh. No. No, thank you. We're fine. We'll walk. It's not far."

Tanzie squinted at her, as if trying to assess whether she was serious, then clambered wearily to her feet. Jess remembered that under her coat Tanzie was in her pajamas. Mr. Nicholls glanced at the children. "I'm headed back that way." He nodded toward the town. "You know where I live."

Tanzie and Nicky didn't speak, but Jess watched Nicky limp toward the car and start to haul out the bags. She couldn't make him carry all that stuff home. It was at least two miles.

"Thank you," she said stiffly. "That's very kind of you." She couldn't look him in the eye.

"What happened to your boy?" Policeman Number Two said.

"Look it up on your database," she snapped, and walked over to the pile of bags.

They drove away from the police in silence. Jess sat in the passenger seat of Mr. Nicholls's immaculate car, staring straight ahead at the road. She wasn't sure she had ever felt more uncomfortable. She could feel, even if she couldn't see, the children's stunned silence at the evening's turn of events. She had let them down. She watched the hedgerows turn to fencing and brick walls, the black lanes turn to streetlights.

She couldn't believe they had only been gone an hour and a half. It felt like a lifetime. A five-thousand-pound fine. An almost-certain driving ban. And a court appearance. Marty would go mental. And she had just blown Tanzie's last chance of going to St. Anne's.

Jess felt a lump rise in her throat.

"You okay?"

"Fine." She kept her face turned away from Mr. Nicholls. He didn't know. Of course he didn't know. For a brief, terrifying moment after she had agreed to get into his car, she had wondered if this was a trick. He would wait until the police had gone, then do something dreadful to get her back.

But it was worse. He was just trying to be helpful.

"Um, can you turn left here? We're down there. Go to the end, turn left, then the second turning on the right."

The picturesque part of town had fallen away half a mile back. Here on Danehall, the trees were skeletal even in summer, and burned-out cars stood on piles of bricks like civic sculptures on little pedestals. The houses came in three vintages, depending on your street: terraced, pebble-dashed, or tiny and built-in maroon brick with UPVC windows. He swung the car round to the left and onto Seacole Avenue, slowing as she pointed to her house. She looked round at the backseat and saw that during the short drive Tanzie had nodded off, her mouth hanging slightly open, her head resting against Norman, who leaned half his bulk against Nicky's body. Nicky looked out of the window impassively.

"So where were you trying to get to?"

"Scotland." She rubbed her nose. "It's a long story."

He waited.

Her leg had started to jiggle involuntarily. "I need to get my daughter to a Maths Olympiad. The fares were expensive. Although not as expensive as getting pulled over by the Old Bill, it turns out."

"A Maths Olympiad."

"I know. I'd never heard of one either until a week ago. Like I said, it's a long story."

"So what are you going to do?"

Jess looked into the backseat, at Tanzie, who snored gently. She shrugged. She couldn't say the words.

Mr. Nicholls suddenly caught sight of Nicky's face. He stared, as if seeing it for the first time.

"Yeah. That's another story."

"You have a lot of stories."

Jess couldn't work out if he was deep in

thought or if he was just waiting for her to get out of the car. "Thanks. For the lift. It was kind of you."

"Well, I owe you one. I'm pretty sure it was you who got me home from the pub the other night. I woke up on my sofa with my car safely in the pub car park and the world's most malevolent hangover." He paused. "I also have a vague memory of being an arsehole. Possibly for the second time."

"It's fine," she said, as blood rushed to her ears. "Really."

Nicky had opened the car door, making Tanzie stir. She rubbed her eyes and blinked at Jess. Then she gazed slowly around her at the car, the night's events reregistering on her face. "Does this mean we're not going?"

Jess gathered up the bags at her feet. This was not a conversation to have in front of an audience. "Let's go inside, Tanze. It's late."

"Does this mean we're not going to Scotland?"

Jess smiled awkwardly at Mr. Nicholls. "Thanks again." She hauled her bags out onto the pavement. The air was surprisingly chill. Nicky stood outside the gate, waiting.

Tanzie's voice cracked. "Does this mean I don't get to go to St. Anne's?"

Jess tried to smile. "Let's not talk about it now, sweetie."

"But what are we going to do?" said Nicky.

"Not now, Nicky. Let's just get indoors."

"You now owe the police five grand. How are we going to get to Scotland?"

"Kids? Please? Can we just go indoors?"

With a groan, Norman heaved himself off the backseat and ambled out of the car.

"You didn't say we'll sort something out." Tanzie's voice was panicky. "You always say we'll sort something out."

"We'll sort something out," Jess said, dragging the duvets out of the boot.

"That's not the voice you use when we're really going to sort something out." Tanzie began to cry.

It was so unexpected that at first Jess could do nothing but stand there in shock. "Take these." She thrust the duvets at Nicky, and leaned her upper half into the car, trying to maneuver Tanzie out. "Tanzie . . . sweetheart. Come out. It's late. We'll talk about this."

"Talk about me not going to St. Anne's?"

Mr. Nicholls was staring at his steering wheel. Jess suspected this was now all too much for him, and began apologizing under her breath. "She's tired," she said, trying to put her arm around her daughter. Tanzie

154

shifted away. "I'm so sorry."

It was at that point Mr. Nicholls's phone rang.

"Gemma," he said wearily. Jess heard an angry buzzing, as if a wasp had been trapped in the receiver.

"I know," he said quietly.

"I just want to go to St. Anne's," Tanzie cried. Her glasses had fallen off — Jess hadn't had time to take her to the optician to tighten them — and she covered her eyes with her hands. "Please let me go. Please, Mum. I'll be really good. Just let me go there."

"Shhh." A lump rose in Jess's throat. Tanzie never begged for anything. "Tanzie . . ." On the pavement, Nicky turned away.

Mr. Nicholls said something into his phone that she couldn't make out. Tanzie had begun to sob. She was a deadweight.

"Come on, sweetheart," Jess said, tugging at her.

Tanzie had braced herself against the door. "Please, Mum. Please. Please."

"Tanzie, you cannot stay in the car."

"Please . . ."

"Out. C'mon, baby."

"I'll drive you," Mr. Nicholls said.

Jess's head bumped against the door frame. "What?"

"I'll drive you to Scotland." He had put down his phone and was still looking at his steering wheel. "Turns out I've got to go to Northumberland. Scotland's not that much farther. I'll drop you there."

Everyone fell silent. At the end of the street there was a burst of laughter and a car door slammed. Jess straightened her ponytail, which had gone askew. "Look, it's really nice of you to offer, but we can't accept a lift from you."

"Yeah," said Nicky, leaning forward. "Yeah, we can, Jess." He glanced at Tanzie. "Really. We can."

"But we don't even know you. I can't ask you to —"

Mr. Nicholls didn't look at her. "It's just a lift. It's really not a big deal."

Tanzie sniffed and rubbed at her nose. "Please? Mum?"

Jess looked at her, and at Nicky's bruised face, then back at Mr. Nicholls. She had never wanted to sprint from a car so badly. "I can't offer you anything," she said, and her voice broke slightly. "Anything at all."

He raised one eyebrow, swiveled his head toward the dog. "Not even to vacuum my backseats afterward?"

The breath that left her chest probably sounded slightly more relieved than was

156

diplomatic. "Well . . . okay, that I can do."

"Right," he said. "Then I suggest we all get a few hours' sleep and I'll pick you up first thing tomorrow."

CHAPTER ELEVEN:
ED

It took Edward Nicholls about fifteen minutes after he had left Danehall estate to question what the bloody hell he had just done. He had just agreed to transport his stroppy cleaner, her two weird kids, and an enormous reeking dog all the way to Scotland. What the hell had he been thinking? He could hear Gemma's voice, the skepticism with which she had repeated her statement: "You're taking a little girl you don't know and her family to the other end of the country, and it's an 'emergency.' Right." He could hear the quotation marks. A pause. "Pretty, is she?"

"What?"

"The mother. Big tits? Long eyelashes? Damsel in distress?"

"That's not it. Er . . ." He hadn't been able to say anything with them in the car.

"I'll take both those as a yes, then." She sighed deeply. "For Christ's sake, Ed."

Tomorrow morning he would pop by, apologize, and explain that something had come up. She'd understand. She probably felt weird about sharing a car with a near stranger, too. She hadn't exactly jumped at the offer.

He would donate something toward the kid's train fare. It wasn't his fault the woman — Jess? — had decided to drive an untaxed, uninsured car, after all. If you looked at it on paper — the cops, the weird kids, the nighttime joyriding — she was trouble. And Ed Nicholls did not need any more trouble in his life.

With these thoughts in his head, he washed, brushed his teeth, and fell into the first decent sleep he'd had in weeks.

He pulled up outside the gate shortly after nine. He had meant to be there earlier but couldn't remember where the house was, and given that the council estate was a sprawling mass of Identi-Kit streets, he had driven up and down blindly for almost thirty minutes until he recognized Seacole Avenue.

It was a damp, still morning, the air heavy with moisture. The street was empty, apart from a ginger cat, which stalked its way along the pavement, its tail a question mark.

Danehall seemed a little less unfriendly in daylight, but he still found himself double-checking that he'd locked the car once he'd stepped out of it.

He gazed up at the windows. Pink and white bunting hung in one of the upstairs rooms, and two hanging baskets swung listlessly from the front porch. A car sat under a tarpaulin in the next driveway. And then he saw that dog. Jesus. The size of it. Ed pictured it lolling over his backseat the previous evening. A faint echo of its scent had remained when he climbed back in this morning.

He opened the latch of the gate warily in case the dog went for him, but it simply turned its enormous head with mild indifference, walked to the shade of a weedy tree, and flopped down on its side, lifting a desultory front leg as if in the vague hope it might get its stomach scratched.

"I'll pass, thanks," Ed said.

He walked up the path and paused at the door. He had his little speech all prepared.

Hi, I'm really sorry, but something very important has come up with work and I'm afraid I'm not going to be able to take the next couple of days off. I'd be happy, however, to contribute something to your daughter's Olympiad fund. I think it's great that she's working so hard at her studies. So here's her train fare.

If it sounded a little less convincing this morning than it had done last night, well, it couldn't be helped. He was about to knock when he saw the ripped note, half attached to the door with a pin, flapping in the breeze:

FISHER YOU LITTLE WASTE OF SKIN I
HAVE TOLD THE POLICE

As he straightened up the door opened. The little girl stood there. "We're all packed," she said, squinting, her head tilted to one side. "Mum said you wouldn't come, but I knew you would so I said I wouldn't let her unpack the suitcases until ten. And you made it with fifty-three minutes to spare. Which is actually about thirty-three minutes better than I estimated."

He blinked.

"Mum!" She pushed the door open. Jess was standing in the hallway, as if she had stopped dead halfway down it. She was wearing a pair of cutoff jeans and a shirt with the sleeves rolled up. Her hair was clipped up. She did not look like someone preparing to travel the length of the country.

"Hi." Ed smiled awkwardly.

"Oh. Okay." Jess shook her head. And he knew the child had been telling the truth: she really hadn't expected him to turn up. "I'd offer you a coffee, but I got rid of the last of the milk before we set off last night."

The boy sloped past, rubbing his eyes. His face was still swollen, and now colored an impressionist palette of purples and yellows. He gazed at the pile of holdalls and bin bags in the hall and said, "Which of these are we taking?"

"All of them," said the little girl. "And I packed Norman's blanket."

Jess looked at Ed warily. He made to open his mouth, but nothing came out. The entire length of the hallway was lined with battered paperbacks.

"Can you pick up this bag, Mr. Nicholls?" The little girl tugged it toward him. "I did try and lift it earlier because Nicky can't pick stuff up right now, but it's too heavy for me."

"Sure." He found himself stooping, but stopped for a moment before he lifted it. How was he going to do this?

"Listen. Mr. Nicholls . . ." Jess was in front of him. She looked as uncomfortable as he did. "About this trip —"

And then the front door flew open. A woman stood in jogging bottoms and a

T-shirt, a baseball bat raised in her hand.

"Drop them!" she roared.

He froze.

"Put your hands up!"

"Nat!" Jess shouted. "Don't hit him!"

He lifted them slowly, turning to face her.

"What the —" The woman looked past Ed at her. "Jess? Oh, my God. I thought someone was in your house."

"Someone is in my house. Me."

The woman dropped the bat, then looked in horror at him. "Oh, my God. It's . . . oh, God, oh, God, I'm so sorry. I saw the front door and I honestly thought you were a burglar. I thought you were . . ." She laughed nervously, then pulled an agonized face at Jess, as if he couldn't see her. "You know who."

Ed let out a breath. The woman put the bat behind her and tried to smile. "You know how it is around here . . ."

He took a step backward and gave a small nod. "Okay, well . . . I just need to get my phone. Left it in the car."

He edged past her with his palms up and headed down the path. He opened and shut the car door, then locked it again, just to give himself something to do, trying to think clearly over the ringing in his ears. Just drive off, a little voice said. Just go. You never have to see her again. You do not need this right now.

Ed liked order. He liked to know what was coming. Everything about this woman suggested the kind of . . . *boundarylessness* that made him nervous.

He was halfway up the path when he heard them talking behind the half-closed door, their voices carrying across the little garden.

"I'm going to tell him no."

"You can't, Jess." The boy's voice. "Why?"

"Because it's too complicated. I work for him."

"You clean his house. That's not the same thing."

"We don't know him, then. How can I tell Tanzie not to get in cars with men she doesn't know, and then do exactly that?"

"He wears glasses. He's hardly going to be a serial killer."

"Tell that to Dennis Nilsen's victims. And Harold Shipman's."

"You know way too many serial killers. We'll set Norman on him if he does anything bad." The boy's voice again.

"Yes. Because Norman has been so useful, protecting this family in the past."

"Mr. Nicholls doesn't know that, does he?"

"Look. He's just some bloke. He probably got caught up in the drama last night. It's obvious he doesn't want to do it. We'll . . . we'll just let Tanzie down gently."

Tanzie. Ed watched her running around the back garden, her hair flying out behind her. He watched the dog shambling back toward the door, half dog, half yak, leaving an intermittent snail trail of drool behind him.

"I'm wearing him out so that he'll sleep most of the journey." She appeared in front of him, panting.

"Right."

"I'm really good at maths. We're going to an Olympiad so I can win money to go to a school where I can do A-level maths. Do you know what my name is, converted to binary code?"

He looked at her. "Is Tanzie your full name?"

"No. But it's the one I use."

He blew out his cheeks. "Um. Okay. 01010100 01100001 01101110 01111010 01101001 01100101."

"Did you say 1010 at the end? Or 0101?"

"1010. Duh." He used to play this game with Ronan.

"Wow. You actually spelled it right." She walked past him and pushed the door. "I've

165

never been to Scotland. Nicky keeps trying to tell me there are herds of wild haggis. But that's a lie, right?"

"To the best of my knowledge they're all farmed these days," he said.

Tanzie stared at him. Then she beamed, and sort of growled at the same time.

And Ed realized he was headed for Scotland.

The two women fell silent as he pushed the door open. Their eyes dropped to the bags that he picked up in each hand.

"I need to get some stuff before we go," he said, as he let the door swing behind him. "And you left out Gary Ridgway. The Green River Killer. But you're fine. They were all nearsighted, and I'm farsighted."

It took half an hour to leave town. The lights were out on the top of the hill and that, combined with Easter holiday traffic, slowed the queue of cars to a bad-tempered crawl. Jess sat in the car beside him, silent and awkward, her hands pressed together between her knees.

He had the air conditioner on, but it couldn't disguise the smell of the dog, so he turned it off and they sat with all four windows open instead. Tanzie kept up a constant stream of chatter.

"Have you been to Scotland before?"

"Where do you come from?"

"Do you have a house there?"

"Why are you staying here then?"

He had some work to sort out, he said. It was easier than "I'm awaiting possible prosecution and a jail term of up to seven years."

"Do you have a wife?"

"Not anymore."

"Were you unfaithful?"

"Tanzie," said Jess.

He blinked. Glanced into the rearview mirror. "Nope."

"On *Jeremy Kyle* one person is usually unfaithful. Sometimes they have another baby and they have to do a DNA test and usually when it's right, the woman looks like she wants to hit someone. But mostly they just start crying."

Tanzie squinted out of the window.

"They're a bit mad, these women, mostly. Because the men have all got another baby with someone else. Or lots of girlfriends. So statistically they're really likely to do it again. But none of the women ever seem to think about statistics."

"I don't really watch *Jeremy Kyle,*" he said, glancing at the GPS.

"Nor do I. Only when I go to Nathalie's

house when Mum's working. She records it while she's cleaning so she can watch it in the evenings. She has forty-seven episodes on her hard drive."

"Tanzie," Jess said. "I think Mr. Nicholls probably wants to concentrate."

"It's fine."

Jess was twisting a strand of her hair. She had her feet up on the seat. Ed really hated people putting their feet on seats. Even if they did take their shoes off.

"So why did your wife leave you?"

"Tanzie."

"I'm being polite. You said it was good to make polite conversation."

"I'm sorry," Jess said.

"Really. It's fine." He addressed Tanzie through the rearview mirror: "She thought I worked too much."

"They never say that on *Jeremy Kyle.*"

The traffic cleared, and they headed out onto the dual carriageway. It was a beautiful day, and he was tempted to take the coast road, but he didn't want to risk getting caught in traffic again. The dog whined, the boy played Nintendo, his head down in intense concentration, and Tanzie grew quieter. He turned the radio on — a hits channel — and for a moment or two he started to think this could be okay. It was just a day out of his life, if they didn't hit too much traffic. And it was better than being stuck in the house.

"The GPS reckons about eight hours if we don't hit any jams," he said.

"By motorway?"

"Well, yeah." He glanced left. "Even a top-of-the-range Audi doesn't have wings." He tried to smile, to show her he was joking, but Jess was still straight-faced.

"Uh . . . there's a bit of a problem."

"A problem."

"Tanzie gets sick if we go fast."

"What do you mean 'fast'? Eighty? Ninety?"

"Um . . . actually, fifty. Okay, maybe forty."

Ed glanced into the rearview mirror. Was it his imagination or had the child grown a little paler? She was gazing out of the window, her hand resting on the dog's head. "Forty?" He slowed. "You're joking, right? You're saying we have to drive to Scotland via B roads?"

"No. Well, maybe. Look, it's possible she's grown out of it. But she doesn't travel by car very much and we used to have big problems with it and . . . I just don't want to mess up your nice car."

Ed glanced into the rearview mirror again. "We can't take the minor roads — that's ridiculous. It would take days to get there. Anyway, she'll be fine. This car is brand new. It has award-winning suspension. Nobody gets sick in it."

She looked straight ahead. "You don't have kids, do you?"

"Why do you ask?"

"No reason."

It took twenty-five minutes to disinfect and shampoo the backseat, and even then every time he put his head inside the interior Ed got a faint whiff of vomit. Jess borrowed a bucket from a petrol station and used shampoo that she had packed in one of the kids' bags. Nicky sat on the verge beside the garage, hiding behind a pair of oversized shades, and Tanzie sat with the dog, holding a balled tissue to her mouth, like a consumptive.

"I'm so sorry," Jess kept saying, her sleeves rolled up, her face set in a grim line of concentration.

"It's fine. You're the one cleaning it."

"I'll pay for you to get your car valeted afterward."

He raised an eyebrow at her. He was laying a plastic bin bag over the seat so that the kids wouldn't get damp when they sat down again.

"Well, okay, I'll do it. It will smell better, whatever."

Sometime later they climbed back into the car. Nobody remarked on the smell. He ensured his window was as low as it could go, and began reprogramming the GPS.

"So," he said. "Scotland it is. Via B roads." He pressed the "destination" button. "Glasgow or Edinburgh?"

"Aberdeen."

He looked at Jess.

"Aberdeen. Of course." He looked behind him, trying not to let the despair seep into his voice. "Everyone happy? Water? Plastic bag on seat? Sick bags in place? Good. Let's go."

Ed heard his sister's voice as he pulled back onto the road. *Ha ha ha, Ed. Served.*

It began to rain shortly after Portsmouth. Ed drove along the back roads, keeping at a steady thirty-eight all the way, feeling the fine spit of raindrops from the half inch of window he had not felt able to close. He found he had to focus on not putting his foot too far down on the accelerator the whole time. It was a constant frustration, going at this sedate speed, like having an itch you couldn't quite scratch. In the end he switched on cruise control.

Given their pace, he had time to study Jess surreptitiously. She remained silent, her head mostly turned away from him, as if he had done something to annoy her. He remembered her in his hallway now, demanding money, her chin tilted up — she was quite short. She still seemed to think he was an arsehole. Come on, he told himself. Two, three days maximum. And then you never have to see them again. Let's play nice.

"So . . . do you clean many houses?"

She frowned a little. "Yes."

"You have a lot of regulars?"

"It's a holiday park."

"Did you . . . Was it something you wanted to do?"

"Did I grow up wanting to clean houses?" She raised an eyebrow, as if checking that he had seriously asked that question. "Um, no. I wanted to be a professional scuba diver. But I had Tanze and I couldn't work out how to get the pram to float."

"Okay, it was a dumb question."

She rubbed her nose. "It's not my dream job, no. But it's fine. I can work around the kids and I like most of the people I clean for."

Most of.

"Can you make a living out of it?"

Her head shot round. "What do you mean?"

"Just what I said. Can you make a living? Is it lucrative?"

She looked away from him. "We get by."

"No, we don't," said Tanzie, from the back.

"Tanze."

"You're always saying we haven't got enough money."

"It's just a figure of speech." Jess blushed.

"So what do you do, Mr. Nicholls?" said Tanzie.

"I work for a company that creates software. Do you know what that is?"

"Of course."

Nicky looked up. In the rearview mirror Ed watched him remove his earbuds. When the boy saw him looking, he glanced away.

"Do you design games?"

"Not games, no."

"What, then?"

"Well, for the last few years we've been working on a piece of software that we hope will move us closer to a cashless society."

"How would that work?"

"Well, when you buy something or pay a bill, you wave your phone, which has a thing a bit like a bar code, and for every transaction you pay a tiny, tiny amount, like nought point nought one of a pound."

"We would pay to pay?" said Jess. "No one will want that."

"That's where you're wrong. The banks love it. Retailers like it because it gives them one uniform system instead of cards, cash, checks . . . and you'll pay less per transaction than you do on a credit card. So it works for both sides."

"Some of us don't use credit cards unless we're desperate."

"Then it would just be linked to your bank account. You wouldn't, like, have to do anything."

"So if every bank and retailer picks this up, we won't get a choice."

"That's a long way off."

There was a brief silence. Jess pulled her knees up to her chin and wrapped her arms around them. "So basically the rich get richer — the banks and the retailers — and the poor get poorer."

"Well, in theory, perhaps. But that's the joy of it. It's such a tiny amount you won't notice it. And it will be very convenient."

Jess muttered something he didn't catch.

"How much is it again?" said Tanzie.

"Point nought one per transaction. So it works out as a little less than a penny."

"How many transactions a day?"

"Twenty? Fifty? Depends how much you do."

"So that's fifty pence a day."

"Exactly. Nothing."

"Three pounds fifty a week," said Jess.

"One hundred and eighty-two pounds a year," said Tanzie. "Depending on how close the fee actually is to a penny. And whether it's a leap year."

Ed lifted one hand from the wheel. "At the outside. Even you can't say that's very much."

Jess turned in her seat. "What does one hundred and eighty-two pounds buy us, Tanze?"

"Two supermarket pairs of school trousers, four school blouses, a pair of shoes. A gym kit and a five-pack of white socks. If you buy them from the supermarket. That comes to eighty-five pounds ninety-seven. The one hundred is exactly nine point two days of groceries, depending on whether anyone comes round and whether Mum buys a bottle of wine. That would be the supermarket's brand." Tanzie paused. "Or one month's council tax for a Band D property. We're Band D, right, Mum?"

"Yes, we are. Unless we get rebanded."

"Or an out-of-season three-day holiday at the holiday village in Kent. One hundred and seventy-five pounds, inclusive of VAT." She leaned forward. "That's where we went last year. We got an extra night free because Mum mended the man's curtains. And they had a waterslide."

There was another brief silence.

Ed was about to speak when Tanzie's head appeared between the two front seats. "Or a whole month's cleaning of a four-bedroom house from Mum, laundering of sheets and towels included, at her current rates. That would be three hours' cleaning, one point three hours laundering." She leaned back in her seat, apparently satisfied.

They drove three miles, turned right at a T-junction, left onto a narrow lane. Ed wanted to say something but his voice had temporarily disappeared. Behind him, Nicky put his earbuds back in and turned away. The sun hid briefly behind a cloud.

"Still," said Jess, putting her bare feet up on the dashboard, and leaning forward to turn up the music, "let's hope you do really well with it, eh?"

CHAPTER TWELVE:
JESS

Jess's grandmother had often said that the key to a happy life was a short memory. Admittedly, that was before she got dementia and used to forget where she lived, but Jess took her point. She had to forget about that money. She was never going to survive being stuck in a car with Mr. Nicholls if she let herself think too hard about what she had done. Marty used to tell her she had the world's worst poker face: her feelings floated across her features like reflections on a still pond. She would blurt out a confession within hours. Or she would go crazy with the tension and start plucking at bits of the upholstery with her fingernails.

She sat in the car and listened to Tanzie chatting, and she told herself she would find a way to pay it all back before he discovered what she had done. She would take it out of Tanzie's winnings. She would work it out somehow. She told herself he was just a man who had offered them a lift and with whom she had to make polite conversation for a few hours a day.

And periodically she glanced behind her at the two kids and thought, *What else could I have done?*

It shouldn't have been hard to sit back and enjoy the ride. The country lanes were banked with wildflowers, and when the rain cleared, the clouds revealed skies the azure blue of 1950s postcards. Tanzie wasn't sick again, and with every mile they traveled from home she found her shoulders starting to inch downward from her ears. She saw now that it had been months since she had felt even remotely at ease. Her life these days held a constant underlying drumbeat of worry: What were the Fishers going to do next? What was going on in Nicky's head? What was she to do about Tanzie? And the grim bass percussion underneath it all: Money. Money. Money.

"You okay?" said Mr. Nicholls.

Hauled from her thoughts, Jess muttered, "Fine. Thanks." They nodded awkwardly at each other. He hadn't relaxed. It was obvious in his intermittently tightened jaw, the way his knuckles showed white on the steering wheel. Jess wasn't sure what on earth had been behind his decision to offer to drive, but she was pretty sure he had regretted it ever since.

"Um, is there any chance you could stop with the tapping?"

"Tapping?"

"Your feet. On the dashboard."

She looked at her feet.

"It's really distracting."

"You want me to stop tapping my feet."

He looked straight ahead through the windscreen. "Yes. Please."

She let her feet slide down, but she was uncomfortable, so after a moment she lifted them and tucked them under her on the seat. She rested her head on the window.

"Your hand."

"What?"

"Your hand. You're hitting your knee now."

She had been tapping it absentmindedly. "You want me to stay completely still while you drive."

"I'm not saying that. But the tapping thing is making it hard for me to focus."

"You can't drive if I'm moving any part of my body?"

"That's not it."

"What is it, then?"

"It's tapping. I just find . . . tapping . . . irritating."

Jess took a deep breath. "Kids, nobody is

to move. Okay? We don't want to irritate Mr. Nicholls."

"The kids aren't doing it," he said mildly. "It's just you."

"You do fidget a lot, Mum."

"Thanks, Tanze." Jess clasped her hands in front of her. She sat and clenched her teeth and concentrated on staying still. She closed her eyes and cleared her mind of money, of Marty's stupid car, of her worries for the children, letting them float away with the miles. And as the breeze from the open window rippled over her face and the music filled her ears, just briefly she felt like a woman in a different sort of life altogether.

They stopped for lunch at a pub somewhere outside Oxford, unfurling themselves and letting out little sighs of relief as they cracked joints and stretched cramped limbs. Mr. Nicholls disappeared into the pub and she sat on a picnic table and unpacked the sandwiches she had made hastily that morning when it turned out they were going to get a lift after all.

"Marmite," said Nicky, arriving back and peeling apart two slices of bread.

"I was in a rush."

"Have we got anything else?"

"Jam."

He sighed, and reached into the bag. Tanzie sat on the end of the bench, already lost in maths papers. She couldn't read them in the car because it made her nauseated, so she wanted to take every opportunity to work. Jess watched her scribbling algebraic equations on her exercise book, lost in concentration, and wondered for the hundredth time where she had come from.

"Here," said Mr. Nicholls, arriving with a tray. "I thought we could all do with some drinks." He pushed two bottles of cola toward the kids. "I didn't know what you wanted, so I got a selection." He had bought a bottle of Italian beer, what looked like a half of cider, a glass of white wine, another cola, a lemonade and a bottle of orange juice. He had a mineral water. A small mountain of different-flavored crisps sat in the middle.

"You bought all that?"

"There was a queue. I couldn't be bothered to come back out to ask."

"I — I haven't got that much cash."

"It's a drink. I'm not buying you a house."

And then his phone rang. He grabbed it and strode off across the car park, a palm pressed to the back of his neck, already talking as he went.

"Shall I see if he wants one of our sandwiches?" Tanzie said.

Jess watched him, one hand thrust deep in a pocket, until he was out of sight. "Not just now," she said.

Nicky said nothing. When she asked him which bit hurt the most, he just muttered that he was fine.

"It'll get easier," Jess said, reaching out a hand. "Really. We'll have this break, get Tanze sorted, and work out what to do. Sometimes you need time away to figure things out in your head. It makes everything clearer."

"I don't think what's in my head is the problem."

She gave him his painkillers, and watched him wash them down with cola.

Nicky took the dog off for a walk, his shoulders hunched, and his feet dragging. She wondered if he had cigarettes. He was out of sorts because his Nintendo had run out of charge some twenty miles back. Jess wasn't sure he knew what to do with himself when he wasn't surgically attached to a gaming device.

They watched him go in silence.

Jess thought of the way his few smiles had steadily grown fewer, of his watchfulness, the way he seemed like a fish out of water, pale and vulnerable, in the rare hours he was out of his bedroom. She thought of his face, resigned, expressionless, in that hospital. Who was it who had said you were only as happy as your unhappiest child?

Tanzie bent over her papers. "I'm going to live somewhere else when I'm a teenager, I think."

Jess looked at her. "What?"

"I think I might live in a university. I don't really want to grow up near the Fishers." She scribbled a figure in her workbook, then rubbed out one digit, replacing it with a four. "They scare me a bit," she said quietly.

"The Fishers?"

"I had a nightmare about them."

Jess swallowed. "You don't need to be scared of them," she said. "They're just stupid boys. What they did is what cowards do. They're nothing."

"They don't feel like nothing."

"Tanze, I'm going to work out what to do about them, and we're going to fix it. Okay? You don't need to have nightmares. I'm going to fix it."

They sat in silence. The lane was silent, apart from the sound of a distant tractor. Birds wheeled overhead in the infinite blue. Mr. Nicholls was walking back slowly. He had straightened up, as if he had resolved something, and his phone was loose in his hand. Jess rubbed at her eyes.

"I think I've finished the complex equations. Do you want to see?"

Tanzie held up a page of numbers. Jess looked at her daughter's lovely open face. She reached forward and straightened the glasses on Tanzie's nose. "Yes," she said, her smile bright. "I would totally love to look at some complex equations."

It took two and a half hours to do the next leg of the journey. Mr. Nicholls took two calls during the journey, one from the woman called Gemma, which he cut off (his ex-wife?) and one that had obviously to do with his business. A woman with an Italian accent called just after they pulled into a petrol station, and at the words "Eduardo, baby," Mr. Nicholls ripped his phone from the hands-free holder and went and stood outside by the pump. "No, Lara," he said, turning away from them. "We've discussed this . . . Well, your solicitor is wrong . . . No, calling me a lobster really isn't going to make any difference."

Nicky slept for an hour, his blue-black hair flopping over his swollen cheekbone, his face untroubled in sleep. Tanzie sang under her breath and stroked the dog. Norman slept, farted audibly several times, and slowly infused the car with his odor. Nobody complained. It actually masked the lingering smell of vomit.

"Do the kids need to grab some food?" Mr. Nicholls said, as they finally drove into the suburbs of some large town. Huge, shining office blocks punctuated each half mile, their frontages bearing management- or technology-based names she'd never heard of: Accsys, Technologica, and Avanta. The roads were lined with endless stretches of car parks. Nobody walked.

"We could find a McDonald's. There's bound to be loads of them around here."

"We don't eat McDonald's," she said.

"You don't eat McDonald's."

"No. I can say it again, if you like. We don't eat McDonald's."

"Vegetarian?"

"No. Actually, could we just find a supermarket? I'll make sandwiches."

"McDonald's would probably be cheaper, if it's about money."

"It's not about the money."

Jess couldn't tell him: as a single parent, there were certain things she could not do. Which were basically the things that everyone expected a single parent to do: claim benefits, smoke, live in council housing, feed your kids McDonald's. Some things she couldn't help, but others she could.

He let out a little sigh, his gaze fixed ahead. "Okay, well, we could find somewhere to stay and then see whether they have a restaurant attached."

"I had kind of planned we'd just sleep in the car."

Mr. Nicholls pulled over to the side of the road and turned to face her. "Sleep in the car?"

Embarrassment made her spiky. "We have Norman. No hotel's going to take him. We'll be fine in here."

He pulled out his phone and began tapping into a screen. "I'll find a dog-friendly place. There's bound to be one somewhere, even if we have to drive a bit farther."

Jess could feel the color bleeding into her cheeks. "Actually, I'd rather you didn't."

He kept tapping on the screen.

"Really. We . . . we don't have the money for hotel rooms."

Mr. Nicholls's finger stilled on the phone. "That's crazy. You can't sleep in my car."

"It's only a couple of nights. We'll be fine. We would have slept in the Rolls. It's why I brought the duvets."

Tanzie watched from the rear seat.

"I have a daily budget. And I'd like to stick to it. If you don't mind." Twelve pounds a day for food. Maximum.

He looked at her as if she were mad.

"I'm not stopping you from getting a hotel," she added. She didn't want to tell him she'd actually prefer it if he did.

"This is nuts," he said finally.

They drove the next few miles in silence. Mr. Nicholls had the air of a man who was quietly pissed off. In a weird way, Jess preferred it. And if Tanzie did as well as everyone seemed to think she would at the Olympiad, they could blow a little of her winnings on train tickets. The thought of ditching Mr. Nicholls made her feel so much better that she didn't say anything when he pulled into the Travel Inn.

"I'll be back in a minute," he said, and walked off across the car park. He took the keys with him, jangling them impatiently in his hand.

"Are we staying here?" Tanzie said, rubbing at her eyes and looking around.

"Mr. Nicholls is. We're going to stay in the car. It will be an adventure!" Jess said.

There was a brief silence.

"Yay," said Nicky.

Jess knew he was uncomfortable. But what else could she do? "You can stretch out in the back. Tanze and I will sleep in the front.

It will be fine."

Mr. Nicholls walked back out, shielding his eyes against the early-evening sun. She realized he was wearing the exact same outfit she had seen him wear in the pub that night.

"They had one room left. A twin. You guys can take it. I'll see if there's somewhere else nearby."

"Oh no," she said. "I told you. I can't accept any more from you."

"I'm not doing it for you. I'm doing it for your kids."

"No," she said, trying to sound a little more diplomatic. "It's very kind of you, but we'll be fine out here."

He ran a hand through his hair. "You know what? I can't sleep in a hotel room knowing that there's a boy who just got out of a hospital sleeping in the backseat of a car twenty feet away. Nicky can have the other bed."

"No," she said reflexively.

"Why?"

She couldn't say.

His expression darkened. "I'm not a pervert."

"I didn't say you were."

"So why won't you let your son share a room with me? He's as tall as I am, for

188

Christ's sake."

Jess flushed. "He's had a tough time lately. I just need to keep an eye on him."

"What's a pervert?" said Tanzie.

"I could charge up my Nintendo," said Nicky from the backseat.

"You know what? This is a ridiculous discussion. I'm hungry. I need to get something to eat." Mr. Nicholls poked his head in through the door. "Nicky, do you want to sleep in the car or in the hotel room?"

Nicky looked sideways at Jess. "Hotel room. And I'm not a pervert, either."

"Am I a pervert?" said Tanzie.

"Okay," said Mr. Nicholls. "Here's the deal. Nicky and Tanzie sleep in the hotel room. You can sleep on the floor with them."

"But I can't let you pay for a hotel room for us, then make you sleep in the car. Besides, the dog will howl all night. He doesn't know you."

Mr. Nicholls rolled his eyes. He was clearly losing patience. "Okay, then. The kids sleep in the hotel room. You and I sleep in the car with the dog. Everyone's happy." He didn't look happy.

"I've never stayed in a hotel. Have I stayed in a hotel, Mum?"

There was a brief silence. Jess could feel the situation sliding away from her.

189

"I'll mind Tanze," said Nicky. He looked hopeful. His face, where it wasn't bruised, was the color of putty. "A bath would be good."

"Would you read me a story?"

"Only if it has zombies in it." Jess watched as Nicky half smiled at Tanzie.

"Okay," she said. And she tried to fight the wave of nausea at what she had just agreed to.

The mini-mart squatted in the shadow of a food distribution company, its windows bright with exclamation marks and offers of crispy fish bites and fizzy drinks. Jess bought rolls and cheese, crisps, and overpriced apples and made the kids a picnic supper, which they ate on the grassy slope around the car park. On the other side the traffic thundered past in a purple haze toward the south. She offered Mr. Nicholls some of their meal, but he peered at the contents of her bag and said thanks but he'd eat in the restaurant.

Once he was out of sight, Jess relaxed. She set the kids up in their room, feeling faintly wistful that she wasn't in with them. It was on the ground floor, facing the car park. She had asked Mr. Nicholls to park as close to their window as possible, and Tanzie made her go outside three times, just so she could wave at Jess through the curtains and squash her nose sideways against the glass.

Nicky disappeared into the bathroom for an hour, the taps running. He came out, switched on the television, and lay on the bed, looking simultaneously exhausted and relieved.

Jess laid out his pills, got Tanzie bathed and into her pajamas, and warned them not to stay up too late. "And no smoking," she warned him. "Seriously."

"How can I?" he said. "You've got my stash."

Tanzie lay on her side, working her way through her maths books. Jess fed and walked the dog, sat in the passenger seat with the door open, ate a cheese roll, and waited for Mr. Nicholls to finish his meal.

It was a quarter past nine, and she was struggling to read a newspaper in the fading light when he appeared. He was holding a phone in a way that suggested he had just come off another call, and he seemed about as pleased to see her as she was him. He opened the door, climbed in, and shut it.

"I've asked Reception to ring me if anyone cancels a booking." He stared ahead at the windscreen. "Obviously I didn't tell them I'd be waiting in their car park."

Norman was lying on the tarmac, looking as if he'd been dropped from a great height. She wondered whether she should bring him in. Without the children in the back, and with the encroaching darkness, it felt even odder to be in the car beside Mr. Nicholls.

"Are the kids okay?"

"They're very happy. Thank you."

"Your boy looks pretty bashed up."

"He'll be all right."

There was a long silence. He looked at her. Then he put both hands on the wheel and leaned backward in his seat. He rubbed his eyes with the heels of his hands and turned to face her. "Okay . . . so have I done something else to upset you?"

"What?"

"You've acted all day like I'm bugging you. I apologized for the thing in the pub the other night. I've done what I can to help you out here. And yet still I get the feeling I've done something wrong."

"You . . . you haven't done anything wrong," she stammered.

He studied her for a minute. "Is this, like, a woman's 'There's nothing wrong' when actually what you mean is that I've done something massive and I'm actually supposed to guess? And then you get really mad if I don't?"

"No."

"You see, now I don't know. Because that 'no' might be part of the woman's 'There's nothing wrong.' "

"I'm not speaking in code. There's nothing wrong."

"Then can we just ease up around each other a bit? You're making me really uncomfortable."

"I'm making you uncomfortable?"

His head swiveled slowly toward her.

"You've looked like you regretted offering us this lift since the moment we got into the car. In fact, since before we got in." *Shut up, Jess,* she warned herself. *Shut up. Shut up. Shut up.* "I'm not even sure why you did it."

"What?"

"Nothing," she said, turning away. "Forget it."

He stared ahead of him out of the windscreen. He looked suddenly really, really tired.

"In fact, you could just drop us at a station tomorrow morning. We won't bother you anymore."

"Is that what you want?" he said.

She drew her knees up to her chest. "It might be the best thing."

The skies darkened to pitch around them. Twice Jess opened her mouth to speak, but nothing came out. Mr. Nicholls stared through the windscreen at the closed curtains of the hotel room, apparently deep in thought.

She thought of Nicky and Tanzie, sleeping peacefully on the other side, and wished she were with them. She felt sick. Why couldn't she have just pretended? Why couldn't she have been nicer? She was an idiot. She had blown it all again.

It had grown chill. Finally, she pulled Nicky's duvet from the backseat and thrust it at him. "Here," she said.

"Oh." He looked at the huge picture of Super Mario. "Thanks."

She called the dog in, reclined her seat just far enough for it not to be touching him, and then she pulled Tanzie's duvet over herself. "Good night." She stared at the plush interior a matter of inches from her nose, breathing in the new-car smell, her mind a jumble. How far away was the station? How much would the fare cost? They would have to pay for an extra day's bed-and-breakfast somewhere, at least. And what was she going to do with the dog? She could hear Norman's faint snore and thought grimly that she was damned if she would vacuum that rear seat now.

"It's half past nine." Mr. Nicholls's voice broke into the silence.

Jess lay very still.

"Half. Past. Nine." He let out a deep sigh. "I never thought I'd say it, but this is actually worse than being married."

"What, am I breathing too loud?"

He opened his door abruptly. "Oh, for Christ's sake," he said, and set off across the car park.

Jess pushed herself upright and watched him jogging across the road to the mini-mart, disappearing into its fluorescent-lit interior. He reappeared a few minutes later with a bottle of wine and a packet of plastic cups.

"It's probably awful," he said, climbing back into the driver's seat. "But right now I couldn't give a toss."

She gazed at the bottle.

"Truce, Jessica Thomas? It's been a long day. And a shitty week. And, spacious as it is, this car isn't big enough for two people who aren't talking to each other."

He looked at her. His eyes were exhausted and stubble was starting to show through on his chin. It made him seem curiously vulnerable.

She took a cup from him. "Sorry. I'm not

used to people helping us out. It makes me . . ."

"Suspicious? Crabby?"

"I was going to say it makes me think I should get out more."

He let out a breath. "Right." He glanced down at the bottle. "Then let's — oh, for crying out loud."

"What?"

"I thought it was a screw top." He stared at it as if it were just one more thing designed to annoy him. "Great. I don't suppose you have a bottle opener?"

"No."

"You think they'll exchange it?"

"Did you take the receipt?"

He let out a deep sigh, which she interrupted. "No need," she said, taking it from him. She opened her door and climbed out. Norman's head shot up.

"You're not going to smash it into my windscreen?"

"Nope." She peeled off the foil. "Take off your shoe."

"What?"

"Take off your shoe. It won't work with flip-flops."

"Please don't use it as a glass. My ex did that once with a stiletto, and it was really, really hard pretending that champagne smelling of feet was an erotic experience."

She held out her hand. He finally took his shoe off and handed it to her. As he looked on, Jess placed the base of the wine bottle inside it and, holding the two together carefully, stood alongside the hotel and thumped them hard against the wall.

"I suppose there's no point me asking you what you're doing."

"Just give me a minute," she said through gritted teeth, and thumped again.

Mr. Nicholls shook his head slowly.

She straightened up and glared at him. "You're more than welcome to suck the cork out, if you'd rather."

He held up his hand. "No, no. You go ahead. Broken glass in my socks is exactly how I hoped to end tonight."

Jess checked the cork and thumped again. And there — a centimeter of it protruded from the neck of the bottle. Thump. Another centimeter. She held it carefully, gave it one more thump, and there it was: she pulled the rest of the cork gently from the neck and handed it to him.

He stared at it, and then at her. She handed him back his shoe.

"Wow. You're a useful woman to know."

"I can also put up shelves, replace rotting floorboards, and make a fan belt out of a

197

tied stocking."

"Really?"

"Not the fan belt." She climbed into the car and accepted the plastic cup of wine. "I tried it once. It shredded before we'd got thirty yards down the road. Total waste of Marks & Spencer opaques." She took a sip. "And the car stank of burned tights for weeks."

Behind them, Norman whimpered in his sleep.

"Truce," Mr. Nicholls said, and held up his cup.

"Truce. You're not going to drive afterward, are you?" she said, holding up her own.

"I won't if you won't."

"Oh, very funny."

And suddenly the evening became a little easier.

Chapter Thirteen: Ed

So these were the things Ed discovered about Jessica Thomas, once she'd had a drink or two (actually, four or five) and stopped being chippy:

One, the boy wasn't actually her kid. He was the son of her ex and her ex's ex, and given that both of them had effectively walked out on him, she was pretty much the only person he had left. "Kind of you," he said.

"Not really," she said. "Nicky is as good as mine. He's been with me since he was eight. He looks out for Tanzie. And besides, families are different shapes now, right?" The defensive way she said it made him think she had had this conversation many times before.

Two, the little girl was ten. He did some mental arithmetic, and Jess cut in before he said a word.

"Seventeen."

"That's . . . young."

"I was a wild kid. I knew everything. I actually knew nothing. Marty came along, I dropped out of school, and then I got pregnant. I wasn't always going to be a cleaner, you know. My mum was a teacher." Her gaze had slid toward him, as if she knew this fact would shock.

"Okay."

"Retired now. She lives in Cornwall. We don't really get on. She doesn't agree with what she calls my life choices. I never could explain that once you have a baby at seventeen, there are no choices."

"Not even now?"

"Nope." She twisted a lock of hair between her fingers. "Because you never quite catch up. Your friends are at college, you're at home with a tiny baby. You haven't even had time to think about what your ambitions might be. Your friends are starting their careers, you're down at the housing office trying to find somewhere to live. Your friends are buying their first cars and houses and you're trying to find a job that you can fit round child care. And all the jobs you can fit round school hours have really crappy wages. And that was before the economy went splat. Oh, don't get me wrong. I don't regret having Tanzie, not for a minute. And I don't regret taking Nicky on. But if I had my time again, sure, I'd have had them after I had done something with my life. It would be nice to be able to give them . . . something better."

She hadn't bothered to put the seat back up while she told him this. She lay propped on her elbow facing him under the duvet and her bare feet rested on the dashboard. Ed found he didn't mind them so much.

"You could still have a career," he said. "You're young. I mean . . . you could get an after-school nanny or something?"

She actually laughed. A great seal bark, "Ha!" Her laugh was big, abrupt, and awkward, at odds with her size and shape. She sat bolt upright and took a swig of her wine. "Yeah. Right, Mr. Nicholls. Sure I could."

Three, she liked fixing things. She sometimes wondered if she could have made that her career. She did odd jobs around the council estate, from rewiring plugs to tiling people's bathrooms. "I did everything around the house. I'm good at making stuff. I can even block-print wallpaper."

"You make your own wallpaper?"

"Don't look at me like that. It's in Tanzie's room. I made her clothes, too, until recently."

"Are you actually from the Second World War? Do you save jam jars and string, too?"

"So what did you want to be?"

"What I was," he said. And then he realized he didn't want to talk about it and changed the subject.

Four, she had seriously tiny feet. As in she bought child-sized shoes. (Apparently they were cheaper.) After she'd said this he had to stop himself from sneaking looks at her feet like some kind of weirdo.

Five, before she'd had children, she could drink four double vodkas in a row and still walk a straight line. "Yup, I could hold my drink. Obviously not enough to remember birth control."

She almost never drank at home. "When I'm working at the pub and someone offers me one, I just take the cash. And when I'm at home, I worry that something might happen to the kids and I'll need to be together." She stared out of the window. "Now I think about it, this is the closest thing I've had to a night out in . . . five months."

"A man who shut a door in your face, two bottles of rot-gut wine, and a car park."

"I'm not knocking it."

She didn't explain what made her worry so much about the kids. He thought back to Nicky's face and decided not to ask.

Six, she had a scar under her chin from when she'd fallen off a bike and a piece of gravel had been lodged in it for two whole weeks. She tried to show him, but the light in the car wasn't strong enough. She also had a tattoo on the base of her spine. "A proper tramp stamp, according to Marty. He wouldn't talk to me for two whole days after I got it." She paused. "I think that's probably why I got it."

Seven, her middle name was Rae. She had to spell it out every single time.

Eight, she didn't mind cleaning, but she really, really hated people treating her as if she were "just" a cleaner. (He had the grace to color a little here.)

Nine, she hadn't had a date in the two years since her ex had left.

"You haven't had sex for two and a half years?"

"I said he left two years ago."

"It's a reasonable calculation."

She pushed herself upright and gave him a sideways look. "Three and a half, actually. If we're counting. Apart from one, um, episode last year. And you don't have to look so shocked."

"I'm not shocked," he said, and tried to rearrange his face. He shrugged. "Three and a half years. I mean, it's only, what, a quarter of your adult life? No time at all."

"Yeah. Thanks for that." And then he wasn't sure what happened, but something in the atmosphere changed. She mumbled something that he couldn't make out, pulled her hair into another ponytail — she tied her hair back for no reason when she felt nervous, he noticed, as if she needed to be doing something — and said maybe it was really time for them to be getting some sleep.

Ed thought he would lie awake for ages. There was something oddly unsettling about being in a darkened car just an arm's length from an attractive woman you had just shared two bottles of wine with. Even if she was huddled under a SpongeBob SquarePants duvet. He looked out of the sunroof at the stars, listened to the lorries rumbling toward London, and thought that his real life — the one with his company and his office and the never-ending hang-over of Deanna Lewis — was now a million miles away.

"Still awake?"

He turned his head, wondering if she'd been watching him. "No."

"Okay," came the murmur from the passenger seat. "Truth game."

He raised his eyes to the roof. "Go on, then."

"You first."

He couldn't come up with anything.

"You must be able to think of something."

"Okay, why are you wearing flip-flops?"

"That's your question?"

"It's freezing out. It's been the coldest, wettest spring since records began. And you're wearing flip-flops."

"Does it bug you that much?"

"I just don't understand it. You're obviously cold."

She pointed a toe. "It's spring."

"So?"

"So. It's spring. Therefore the weather will get better."

"You're wearing flip-flops as an expression of faith."

"If you like."

He couldn't think of how to reply to this.

"Okay, my turn."

He waited.

"Did you think about driving off and leaving us this morning?"

"No."

"Liar."

"Okay. Maybe a bit. Your neighbor wanted to smash my head in with a baseball bat and your dog smells really bad."

"Pfft. Any excuse."

He heard her shift in the seat. Her feet disappeared under the duvet. Her hair smelled of coconut.

"So why didn't you?"

He thought for a minute before he responded. Perhaps it was because he couldn't see her face. Perhaps the drink and the late hour had lowered his defenses, because he wouldn't normally have answered like he did. "Because I've done some stupid stuff lately. And maybe some part of me just wanted to do something I could feel good about."

Ed thought she was going to say something. He sort of hoped she would. But she didn't.

He lay there for a few minutes, gazing out at the sodium lights and listening to Jessica Rae Thomas's breathing and thought how much he missed just sleeping near another person. Most days he felt like the loneliest man on the planet. He thought about those tiny feet and polished toenails and realized he had probably had too much to drink. *Don't be an idiot, Nicholls,* he told himself, and turned so that he had his back to her.

And then he must have fallen asleep, because suddenly it was cold and pale gray outside and his arm was numb and he was so groggy that it took two whole minutes to figure out that the banging he could hear was the security guard knocking on the driver's window to tell them they couldn't sleep there.

Chapter Fourteen:
Tanzie

There were four different types of Danish pastry at the breakfast buffet and three different types of fruit juice, and a whole rack of those little individual packets of cereal that Mum said were uneconomical and would never buy. She had knocked on the window at a quarter past eight to tell them they should wear their jackets to breakfast and stuff as many of each of them as they could into their pockets. Her hair had flattened on one side and she had no makeup on. Tanzie guessed the car hadn't been that much of an adventure after all.

"Not the butters or jams. Or anything that needs cutlery. Rolls, muffins, that kind of thing. Don't get caught." She looked behind her to where Mr. Nicholls seemed to be having an argument with a security guard. "And apples. Apples are healthy. And maybe some slices of ham for Norman."

"Where am I meant to put the ham?"

"Or a sausage. Wrap it in a napkin."

"Isn't that stealing?"

"No."

"But —"

"It's just taking a bit more than you're likely to eat at that exact moment. You're just . . . Imagine you're a guest with a hormone disorder and it makes you really, really hungry."

"But I haven't got a hormone disorder."

"But you could have. That's the point. You're that hungry, sick person, Tanze. You've paid for your breakfast, but you need to eat a lot. More than you would normally eat."

Tanzie folded her arms. "You said it was wrong to steal."

"It's not stealing. It's just getting your money's worth."

"But we didn't pay for it. Mr. Nicholls did."

"Tanzie, just do as I say, please. Look, Mr. Nicholls and I are going to have to leave the car park for half an hour. Just do it, then come back to the room and be ready to leave at nine. Okay?" Jess leaned through the window and kissed Tanzie, then trudged back toward the car, her jacket wrapped around her. She stopped, turned back, and shouted, "Don't forget to brush your teeth.

And don't leave any of your maths books."

Nicky came out of the bathroom. He was wearing his really tight black jeans and a T-shirt that said WHATEVS across the front.

"You're never going to get a sausage in those," Tanzie said, staring at his jeans.

"I bet I can hide more than you can," he said.

Her eyes met his. "You're on," Tanzie said, and ran to get dressed.

Mr. Nicholls leaned forward and squinted through his windscreen as Nicky and she walked across the car park. To be fair, Tanzie thought, she would probably have squinted at them, too. Nicky had stuffed two large oranges and an apple down the front of his jeans and waddled across the asphalt like he'd had an accident in his trousers. She was in her sequined jacket, despite feeling too hot, because she'd packed the front of her hoodie with little packets of cereal and if she didn't wear her jacket she looked like she might be pregnant. With baby robots.

They couldn't stop laughing.

"Just get in, get in," said Mum, throwing their overnight bags into the boot as she glanced behind her. "What did you get?"

Mr. Nicholls set off down the road. Tanzie could see him glancing in the mirror as they took turns unloading their haul and handing it forward to Mum.

Nicky pulled a white package from his pocket. "Three Danish pastries. Watch out — the icing got a bit stuck to the napkins. Four sausages and a few slices of bacon in a paper cup for Norman. Two slices of cheese, a yogurt, and —" He tugged his jacket over his crotch, reached down, grimacing, tensing, and pulled out the fruit. "I can't believe I managed to fit those in there."

"There is nothing I can say to that that's in any way appropriate mother-son conversation," Mum said.

Tanzie had six small packets of cereal, two bananas, and a jam sandwich. She sat eating from one of the packets while Norman stared at her and two stalactites of drool grew longer and longer from his lips until they were pooling on the seat of Mr. Nicholls's car.

"That woman behind the poached eggs definitely saw us."

"I told her you had a hormone disorder," Tanzie said. "I told her you had to eat twice your body weight three times a day or you would faint in their dining room and you might actually die."

"Nice," said Nicky.

"You win on numbers," she said, counting out his items. "But I win extra points for skill." She leaned forward and, as everyone watched, she carefully lifted the two polystyrene cups of coffee from each of her pockets, packed with paper napkins so that they would stay upright. She handed one to Mum and the other she placed in the cup holder next to Mr. Nicholls.

"You are a genius," Mum said, peeling off the lid. "Oh, Tanze, you have no idea how much I needed this." She took a sip, closing her eyes. Tanzie wasn't sure if it was that they'd done so well with the buffet, or just that Nicky was laughing for the first time in ages, but for a moment her mum looked happier than she had since Dad left.

Mr. Nicholls just stared like they were a bunch of aliens.

"Okay, so we can make sandwiches for lunch with the ham, cheese, and sausages. You guys can eat the pastries now. Fruit for dessert. Want one?" She held an orange toward Mr. Nicholls. "It's a bit warm still. But I can peel it."

"Uh, kind of you," he said, tearing his gaze away. "But I think I'll just stop at a Starbucks."

■ ■ ■ ■

The next part of the journey was actually quite nice. There were no traffic jams and Mum persuaded Mr. Nicholls to put on her favorite radio station and sang along to six songs, getting louder with each one. She made Tanzie and Nicky join in, too, and Mr. Nicholls looked fed up at first, but Tanzie noticed that after a few miles he was nodding his head like he was actually enjoying himself. The sun got really hot and Mr. Nicholls slid the roof back. Norman sat bolt upright so that he could smell the air as they were going along and it meant that he didn't squish them into each door, which was also nice.

It reminded Tanzie a bit of when Dad lived with them and they would sometimes go on outings in his car. Except Dad always drove too fast and they could never agree on where to stop and eat. And Dad would say he didn't understand why they couldn't just blow some money on a pub lunch and Mum would say that she'd made the sandwiches now and it would be silly to waste them. And Dad would tell Nicky to get his head out of whatever game he was playing and enjoy the damn scenery and Nicky would mutter that he hadn't actually asked to come, which would make Dad even madder.

And then Tanzie thought that while she did love Dad, she probably preferred this trip without him.

After two hours Mr. Nicholls said he needed to stretch, and Norman needed to wee, so they stopped at the edge of a country park. Mum put some of the buffet haul out and they sat in the shade at a proper wooden picnic table and ate. Tanzie did some revision (prime numbers and quadratic equations), then took Norman for a walk around the woods. He was really happy and stopped every two minutes to sniff at something, and the sun kept sending little moving spotlights through the trees and they saw a deer and two pheasants and it was like they were actually on holiday.

"You okay, lovey?" Mum said, walking up with her arms crossed. From where they stood they could just see Nicky talking to Mr. Nicholls at the table through the trees. "Feeling confident?"

"I think so," she said.

"Did you go through the old test papers last night?"

"Yes. I do find the prime-number sequences a bit difficult, but I wrote them all down and when I saw the sequencing laid out I found it easier."

"No more nightmares about the Fishers?"

"Last night," Tanzie said, "I dreamed about a cabbage that could roller-skate. It was called Kevin."

Mum gave her a long look. "Right."

It was cooler in the forest, and it smelled of good damp, mossy and green and alive, not like the damp in their back room, which just smelled moldy. Mum stopped on the path and turned back toward the car. "I told you good things happen, didn't I?" She waited for Tanzie to catch up. "Mr. Nicholls is going to get us there tomorrow. We'll have a quiet night, get you through this competition, and you'll start at your new school. Then, hopefully, all our lives will change a little for the better. And this is fun, isn't it? This is a nice trip?"

She kept her eyes on the car as she spoke and her voice did that thing where she was saying one thing and thinking about something else. Tanzie noticed she'd put her makeup on while they were in the car. "Mum," she said.

"Yes?"

"We did sort of steal the food from that buffet, didn't we? I mean, if you look at it

215

proportionally, we did take more than our share."

Mum stared at her feet for a minute, thinking. "If you're really worried, when we get your prize money we'll put five pounds in an envelope and send it to them. How does that sound?"

"I think, given the items we took, it would probably be nearer six pounds. Probably six pounds fifty," Tanzie said.

"Then that's what we'll send them. And now I think we should work really, really hard to get this fat old dog of yours to run around a bit, so that (a) he's tired enough to sleep the next leg of the journey, and (b) it might encourage him to go to the loo here and not fart his way through the next eighty miles."

They hit the road again. It rained. Mr. Nicholls had had One of His Phone Calls with a man called Sidney and talked about share prices and market movements and looked a bit serious, so Mum didn't sing for a bit. Tanzie tried not to sneak looks at her maths papers (Mum said it would make her sick). Her legs kept sticking to Mr. Nicholls's leather seats and she was sort of regretting wearing her shorts. Plus Norman had rolled in something in the woods and she kept getting this whiff of something really bad, but she didn't want to say anything in case Mr. Nicholls decided he'd had enough of them and their stinky dog. So she just held her nose with her fingers and tried to breathe through her mouth, only letting herself open her nostrils every thirty lampposts.

"What are you thinking about, Tanze?" Mum looked back through the seats.

"I was thinking about permutations and combinations."

Mum did that smile that she did when she didn't really get what Tanzie was saying.

"Well, I was thinking about that fruit salad at the breakfast bar. Like that's a combination — it doesn't matter whether the apples, pears, and bananas are in any order, right? But with permutations it does."

Mum still looked blank. Mr. Nicholls looked in the rearview mirror and then turned to Mum.

"Okay, so imagine pulling colored socks from a drawer. If you have six pairs of different-colored socks in the drawer — say twelve in total — there are six times five times four times three different combinations you could pull them out in, right?" he said.

"But if all twelve had different colors,

you'd have a really big number of different ways of pulling them out — nearly half a billion."

"That sounds pretty much like our sock drawers," said Mum.

Mr. Nicholls looked back at Tanze and grinned. "So, Tanze, if you have a drawer with twelve socks but you can't see them, how many do you have to pull out to decide if there are at least two pairs?"

Tanzie was thinking about this for ages, so she didn't hear when Mr. Nicholls started talking to Nicky.

"You bored? You want to borrow my phone?"

"Really?" Nicky pushed himself upright from his slumped position.

"Sure. It's in the pocket of my jacket."

With Nicky glued again to a screen, Mum and Mr. Nicholls started talking. It was possible they'd forgotten anyone else was in the car.

"Still thinking about socks?" she said.

"Oh no. Those problems can fry your brain. I'll leave that to your daughter."

There was a short silence.

"So, tell me about your wife."

"Ex-wife. And no thanks."

"Why not? You weren't unfaithful. I'm guessing she wasn't, or you would have made that face."

"What face?"

Another short silence. Maybe ten lamp-posts.

"I'm not sure I would ever have made *that* face. But no. She wasn't. And no, I don't really want to discuss it. It's —"

"Private?"

"I just don't like talking about personal stuff. Do you want to talk about your ex?"

"In front of his children? Yup, that's always a great idea."

Nobody spoke for a few miles. Mum started tapping on the window. Tanzie glanced over at Mr. Nicholls. Every time Mum tapped, a little muscle tweaked in his jaw.

"So what shall we talk about, then? I'm not very interested in software and I'm guessing you have zero interest in what I do. I don't understand sock-related maths. And there are only so many times I can point at a field and say: 'Oh, look, cows.' "

Mr. Nicholls sighed.

"Come on. It's a long way to Scotland."

There was a thirty-lamppost silence. Nicky was taking pictures out of the window with Mr. Nicholls's phone.

"Lara. Italian. Model."

"Model." Mum laughed this great big

laugh. "Of course."

"What's that supposed to mean?" Mr. Nicholls said grumpily.

"All men like you go out with models."

"What do you mean, men like me?"

Mum pressed her lips together.

"What do you mean, men like me? Come on."

"Rich men."

"I'm not rich."

Mum shook her head. "Noooo."

"I'm not."

"I think it depends on how you define rich."

"I've seen rich. I'm not rich. I'm well-off, yes. But I'm a long way from rich."

Mum turned to him. He really had no idea whom he was dealing with. "Do you have more than one house?"

He signaled and swung the wheel. "I might."

"Do you have more than one car?"

He glanced sideways. "Yes."

"Then you're rich."

"Nope. Rich is private jets and yachts. Rich is staff."

"So what am I?"

Mr. Nicholls shook his head. "Not staff. You're . . ."

"What?"

"I'm just trying to imagine your face if I'd referred to you as my staff."

Mum started to laugh. "My woman servant. My cleaning wench."

"Yeah. Or those. Okay, well, what would you say is rich?"

Mum pulled one of the buffet apples from her bag and bit into it. She chewed for a minute before speaking. "Rich is paying every single bill on time without thinking about it. Rich is being able to have a holiday or get through Christmas without having to borrow against January and February. Actually, rich would be just not thinking about money all the bloody time."

"Everyone thinks about money. Even rich people."

"Yes, but you're just thinking what to do with it to make more money. Whereas I'm thinking how the hell we can get enough of it to get through another week."

Mr. Nicholls made a *harrumph*ing sound. "I can't believe I'm driving you to Scotland and you're giving me a hard time because you've misguidedly decided I'm some kind of Donald Trump."

"I'm not giving you a hard time."

"Noooo."

"I'm just pointing out that there's a difference between what you consider to be

221

rich and what is actually rich."

There was a sort of awkward silence. Mum blushed like she'd said too much and started eating her apple with big, noisy bites, even though she would have told Tanzie off if she had eaten like that. Tanzie was distracted from sock permutations. She didn't want Mum and Mr. Nicholls to stop talking to each other because they were having quite a nice day, so she put her head through the front seats. "Actually, I read somewhere that to qualify for the top one percent in this country, you would need to earn more than a hundred and forty thousand pounds a year," she said helpfully. "So if Mr. Nicholls doesn't earn that much, then he probably *isn't* rich." She smiled and sat back in her seat.

Mum looked at Mr. Nicholls. She kept looking at him.

Mr. Nicholls rubbed his head. "I tell you what," he said after a while, "shall we stop off and get some tea?"

Moreton Marston looked like it had been invented for tourists. Everything was made of the same gray stone and was really old, and everyone's gardens were perfect, with tiny blue flowers creeping over the tops of walls, and immaculate little baskets of trailing leaves, like something out of a book. The shops were all the kind you get on Christmas cards. In the market square there was a woman dressed in Victorian clothing, selling buns from a tray, with groups of tourists wandering around taking pictures. Tanzie was so busy gazing out of the window that she didn't notice Nicky at first. It was only when they pulled into the parking space that she saw he had gone really white. She asked him whether his ribs were hurting, and he said no, and when she asked if he had an apple down his trousers that he couldn't get out, he said, "No, Tanze, just drop it," but the way he said it, there was definitely something. Tanzie looked at Mum, but she was busy not looking at Mr. Nicholls and Mr. Nicholls was busy making this big to-do about finding the best parking space. Norman just looked up at Tanzie, like "Don't even bother asking."

Everyone got out and stretched and Mr. Nicholls said they were all having tea and cake and it was his treat and please could we not make a big financial deal out of it as it was just tea, okay? Mum raised her eyebrows like she was going to say something and then just muttered, "Thank you," but not with good grace.

They sat down in a café whose name was

Ye Spotted Sowe Tea Shoppe, even though Tanzie would bet there were no tea shops in medieval times. Nobody else seemed to mind. Nicky got up to go to the loo. And Mr. Nicholls and Mum were at the counter choosing what to eat, so she clicked on Mr. Nicholls's phone and the first thing that came up was Nicky's Facebook page. She waited for a minute because Nicky got really annoyed if people looked at his stuff, and then when she was sure he really was in the loo, she made the screen go bigger so she could read it, and then she went cold. The Fishers had posted messages and pictures of men doing rude things to other men all over Nicky's timeline. They had called him "gimp" and "fagboy," and even though Tanzie didn't know what the words meant, she knew they were bad and she suddenly felt sick. She looked up and Mum was coming back holding a tray.

"Tanzie! Be careful with Mr. Nicholls's phone!"

The phone had clattered onto the edge of the table. She didn't want to touch it. She wondered if Nicky was crying in the loo. She would be.

When she looked up, Mum was staring at her. "What's wrong?"

"Nothing."

She sat down and pushed an orange cupcake on a plate across the table. Tanzie wasn't hungry anymore, even though it was covered with sprinkles.

"Tanze. What's wrong? Talk to me."

She pushed the phone slowly across the wooden table with the tip of her finger, like it was going to burn her or something. Mum frowned, and then looked down at it. She clicked on it and stared. "Jesus Christ," she said after a minute.

Mr. Nicholls sat down beside her. He had the biggest slice of chocolate cake Tanzie had ever seen. "Everyone happy?" he said. He looked happy.

"The little bastards," Mum said. And her eyes filled with tears.

"What?" Mr. Nicholls had a mouthful of cake.

"Is that like a pervert?"

Mum didn't seem to hear her. She pushed the chair back with a massive screech and began striding toward the toilets.

"That's the Gents, madam," a woman called, as Mum pushed the door open.

"I can read, thank you," Mum said, and she disappeared inside.

"What? What's going on now?" Mr. Nicholls struggled to swallow his mouthful. He glanced over at where Mum had gone.

Then, when Tanzie didn't say anything, he looked down at his phone and tapped it twice. He just kept staring. Then he moved the screen around like he was reading everything. Tanzie felt a bit weird. She wasn't sure he should be looking at that.

"Did . . . is this something to do with what happened to your brother?"

She wanted to cry. She felt like the Fishers had ruined the nice day. It was as if they had followed them here, like they would never get away from them. She couldn't speak.

"Hey," he said, as a great big tear plopped down on the table. "Hey." He held out a paper napkin toward her and Tanzie wiped her eyes, and when she couldn't hide the sob that burst upward, he moved around the table and put an arm around her and pulled her in for a hug. He felt big and solid and smelled of lemons and men. She hadn't smelled that man smell since Dad left and that made her even sadder.

"Hey. Don't cry."

"Sorry."

"Nothing to be sorry for. I'd cry if some-one did that to my sister. That's — that's . . ." He clicked the phone off. "Sheez." He shook his head and blew out his cheeks. "Do they do that to him a lot?"

"I don't know." She sniffed. "He doesn't say much anymore."

Mr. Nicholls waited until she had stopped crying and then he moved back around the table and ordered a hot chocolate with marshmallows, chocolate shavings, and extra cream. "Cures all known ills," he said, pushing it toward her. "Trust me. I know everything."

And the weird thing was it was actually true.

Tanzie had finished her chocolate and cupcake by the time Mum and Nicky came out of the loo. Mum put on this bright smile, like nothing was wrong, and had her arm around Nicky's shoulders, which actually looked a bit odd now that he was half a head taller than her. He slid into the seat beside her at the table and stared at his cake. Tanzie watched Mr. Nicholls looking at Nicky and wondered if he was going to say anything about what was on his phone, but he didn't. She thought maybe he didn't want Nicky to get embarrassed. Either way, the happy day, she thought sadly, was over.

Mum got up to check on Norman, who was tied up outside, and Mr. Nicholls ordered a second cup of coffee and started stirring it slowly, like he was thinking about something. He looked up at Nicky from under his eyebrows and said quietly, "So. Nicky. You know anything about hacking?"

She got the feeling she wasn't supposed to listen, so she just stared really hard at the quadratic equations.

"No," said Nicky.

Mr. Nicholls leaned forward over the table and lowered his voice. "Well, I think now might be a good time to start."

"Where are they?" Mum said when she came back, looking around the room.

"They've gone to Mr. Nicholls's car. Mr. Nicholls said they're not to be disturbed." Tanzie sucked the end of her pencil.

Mum's eyebrows shot somewhere into her hairline.

"Mr. Nicholls said you'd look like that. He said to tell you he's sorting it out. The Facebook thing."

"He's doing what? How?"

"He said you'd say that, too." She rubbed at a two, which looked a bit too much like a five and blew away the rubbings. "He said to tell you to please give them twenty minutes, and he's ordered you another cup of tea and you should have some cake while you're waiting. They'll come back and fetch us when they're finished. And also to tell you the chocolate cake is really good."

Mum didn't like it. Tanzie sat and finished her unit until she was happy with the answers while Mum fidgeted and looked out of the window and made as if to speak, then closed her mouth again. She didn't eat any chocolate cake. She left the five pounds that Mr. Nicholls had put on the table sitting there and Tanzie put her eraser on it because she was worried that when someone opened the door it would blow away.

Finally, just as the woman was sweeping up close enough to their table to send a silent message, the door opened, a little bell rang, and Mr. Nicholls walked in with Nicky. Nicky had his hands in his pockets and his hair over his eyes, but there was a little smirk on his face.

Mum stood up and looked from one to the other. You could tell she really, really wanted to say something, but she didn't know what.

"Did you try the chocolate cake?" Mr. Nicholls said. His face was all bland, like a game-show host's.

"No."

"Shame. It was really good. Thank you! Your cake is the best!" he called to the woman, who went all smiley and twinkly. Then Mr. Nicholls and Nicky went straight back out again, striding across the road like they'd been mates all their lives, leaving Tanzie and Mum to gather up their things and hurry out after them.

CHAPTER FIFTEEN: NICKY

There was this article in the newspaper once, about a hairless baboon. Her skin wasn't black all over, like you'd expect, but kind of mottled, pink and black. Her eyes were black rimmed, like she had this really cool eyeliner on, and she had one long pink nipple and one black one, like a simian, booby David Bowie.

But she was all on her own. It turns out baboons don't like difference. And literally not one baboon was prepared to hang out with her. So she was photographed in picture after picture, just out looking for food, all bare and vulnerable, without a single baboon mate. Because even though all the other baboons, like, knew she was still a baboon, their dislike of difference was stronger than any genetic urge they had to stick with her.

Nicky thought this one thing quite often: that there was nothing sadder than a lonely hairless baboon.

Obviously, Mr. Nicholls was about to give him a lecture on the dangers of social networking or say that he had to report it all to his teachers or the police or something. But he opened his car door, pulled out his laptop from the boot, plugged the power lead into a connector near his gearshift, and then plugged in a dongle so that they had broadband.

"Right," he said, as Nicky eased himself into the passenger seat. "Tell me everything you know about this little charmer. Brothers, sisters, dates of birth, pets, address — whatever you've got."

"What?"

"We need to work out his password. Come on — you must know something."

They were sitting in the car park. There was no graffiti here, no discarded shopping trolley. This was the kind of place where they walked actual miles to return a shopping trolley. Nicky would have bet money they had one of those Best Kept Village signs, too. A gray-haired woman loading her car beside them caught his eye and smiled. She actually smiled. Or maybe she smiled at Norman, whose big head was hanging over Nicky's shoulder.

"Nicky?"

"Yeah. I'm thinking." He reeled off everything he knew about Fisher. He went through his address, his sister's name, his mum's name. He actually knew his birthday, as it was only three weeks previously and his dad had bought him one of those quad bikes, which he'd smashed up within a week.

Mr. Nicholls kept tapping away. "Nope. Nope. Come on. There must be something else. What music does he like? What team does he support? Oh, look, he's got a Hotmail address. Great, we can put that in."

Nothing worked. And then Nicky had a sudden thought. "Tulisa. He's got a thing about Tulisa. The singer."

Mr. Nicholls tapped away at his keyboard, then shook his head.

"Try Tulisa's Arse," Nicky said.

Mr. Nicholls typed. "Nope."

"IShaggedTulisa. All one word."

"Nope."

"Tulisa Fisher."

"Mmm. Nope. Nice try, though."

They sat there, thinking.

"You could just try his name," said Nicky.

Mr. Nicholls shook his head. "Nobody's stupid enough to use his name as a password."

Nicky looked at him. Mr. Nicholls typed a few letters, then stared at the screen. "Well,

233

what do you know?" He leaned back in his seat. "You're a natural."

"So what are you doing?"

"We're just going to have a little play with Jason Fisher's Facebook page. Actually, I'm not going to do it. I'm . . . uh . . . I can't really risk anything on my IP address right now. But I know someone who can." He dialed a number.

"But won't he know it's down to me?"

"How? We're basically him right now. There'll be nothing tracing this to you. He probably won't even notice. Hang on. Jez? . . . Hey. It's Ed . . . Yeah. Yeah, I'm just under the radar for a bit. I need you to do me a favor. It'll take five minutes."

Nicky listened as he told Jez Jason Fisher's password and e-mail address. He said that Fisher had been "creating a few difficulties" for a friend. He looked at Nicky sideways as he said this. "Just have a bit of fun with it, yeah? Read through his stuff. You'll get the picture. I'd do it myself, but I've got to keep my hands super clean right now . . . Yeah, I'll explain when I see you. Appreciate it."

Nicky couldn't believe it was so easy. "Won't he hack me back, though?"

Mr. Nicholls put down his phone. "I'm going to take a punt here. But a boy who can't think further than his own name for a

234

password is not really overflowing with computer skills."

They sat there in the car and waited, refreshing Jason Fisher's Facebook page again and again. And like magic, things began to change. Man, Fisher was such a douche. His wall was full of how he was going to "do" this girl or that girl from school, or how so-and-so was a slag and how he'd battered pretty much everyone outside his crew. His messages were much the same. Nicky glimpsed one message that had his name in it, but Mr. Nicholls read it really fast, scrolled up, and said, "Yeah. You don't need to see that one." The only time Fisher didn't sound like a douche was when he messaged Chrissie Taylor and told her that he really liked her and did she want to come round his house? She didn't sound too keen, but he kept messaging her. He said he'd take her out somewhere "really dope" and that he could borrow his dad's car (he couldn't — he was underage). He told her she was the prettiest girl in school and that she was doing his head in and that if his mates knew she'd made him like this, they'd think he was "a mentalist."

"Who says romance is dead?" Mr. Nicholls murmured.

And so it began. Jez messaged two of

Fisher's friends and told them that he had decided he was antiviolence, and didn't want to hang out with them anymore. He messaged Chrissie and told her that he still liked her, but he had to get himself sorted out before he went out with her because he'd "picked up some stupid infection that the doctor says I need to get medicine for. I'll be nice and clean when we get together, though, eh?"

"Oh, man." Nicky was laughing so much that his ribs hurt. "Oh, man."

"Jason" told another girl named Stacy that he really liked her and that his mum had picked out some really nice clothes for him if she ever wanted to go out, and he sent the same thing to a girl called Angela in his year whom he had once called a scuzz. And Jez deleted a new message from Danny Kane, who had tickets for some big football match and said Jason could have one, but he'd have to let him know by the end of the day. Which was today.

He made Fisher's profile picture an image of a braying donkey. And then Mr. Nicholls stared at the screen, thinking, and picked up his mobile. "Actually, I think we should leave his photo there, mate, just for now," he told Jez.

"Why?" said Nicky, after he'd put down

the phone. The donkey thing was kind of excellent.

"Because it's better to be subtle. If we just stick to his private messages for now, it's entirely likely that he won't even spot them. We send them, then delete them at this end. We'll turn off his e-mail notifications. And so his friends, and this girl, will just think he's become even more of an idiot. And he won't have a clue why. Which is kind of the point."

He couldn't believe it. He couldn't believe someone could just mess with Fisher's life like that.

Jez rang back to say he'd logged out, and they shut down Facebook. "And that's it?" Nicky said.

"For now. It's only a bit of fun. But it made you feel better, right? And he's going to clean up your page so that none of the stuff Fisher put up is there anymore."

It was a bit embarrassing then because when Nicky breathed out, he did this kind of shudder. He did feel better. It wasn't like it really solved anything, but for once it was nice not to feel like the butt of the joke.

He messed with the hem of his T-shirt until his breathing went back to normal. It was possible Mr. Nicholls knew, because he looked out of the window like he was really interested even though there was nothing there apart from cars and old people.

"Why would you do all this? The hacking thing and driving us all the way to Scotland. I mean, you don't even know us."

Mr. Nicholls continued to stare out of the window and just for a moment it was like he wasn't really talking to Nicky anymore. "I sort of owe your mum one. And I don't like bullies. They didn't start with your generation, you know."

Mr. Nicholls sat there for a minute, and Nicky was suddenly afraid that he was going to try to make him talk about stuff. That he'd do that thing the counselor did at school, where he tried to act like he was your mate and said about fifty times that anything you said would be "just between us" until it sounded a little creepy.

"I'll tell you one thing."

Here it comes, Nicky thought. He wiped at his shoulder, where Norman had left a drool.

"Everyone I've ever met who was worth knowing was a bit different at school. You just need to find your people."

"Find my people."

"Your tribe."

Nicky pulled a face.

"You know, you spend your whole life feeling like you don't quite fit in anywhere. And then you walk into a room one day, whether it's at university or an office or some kind of club, and you just go, 'Ah. There they are.' And suddenly you feel at home."

"I don't feel at home anywhere."

"For now."

Nicky considered this. "So where was yours?"

"Computing room at the university. I was your basic geek. I met my best mate Ronan there. And then . . . my company." His face fell for a moment.

"But I'm stuck there until I finish school. And there's nothing like that where we live, no tribes." Nicky pulled his fringe down over his eyes. "You do things Fisher's way or you stay out of his way."

"So find your people online."

"How?"

"I don't know. Look up online groups for things you're . . . interested in? Lifestyle choices?"

Nicky registered his expression. "Oh. You think I'm gay, too, right?"

"No, I'm just saying that the Internet's a big place. There's always someone out there who shares your interests, whose life is like yours."

"Nobody's life is like mine."

Mr. Nicholls shut his laptop and slid it into a case. He unplugged everything and glanced over toward the café.

"We should head back. Your mum will be wondering what we're up to." He opened his door and then turned back. "You know, you could always write a blog."

"A blog?"

"Doesn't have to be under your real name. But it's a good way of talking about what's going on in your life. You put a few keywords in, and people will find you. People like you, I mean."

"People who wear mascara. And who don't like football or musical theater."

"And who have enormous stinking dogs and sisters who are maths prodigies. I bet you there's at least one person like that somewhere." He thought for a minute. "Maybe. Perhaps in Hoxton. Or Tupelo."

Nicky pulled at his fringe some more, trying to cover the bruise, which had gone this really grim yellow. "Thanks, but blogs are . . . not really my thing. Blogs are like for middle-aged women writing about their divorces and cats and stuff. Or nail varnish obsessives."

"Just putting it out there."

"Do you write one?"

"Nope." He climbed out of the car. "But

then I don't particularly want to talk to anyone." Nicky climbed out after him. Mr. Nicholls pointed his key chain and the car locked down with an expensive thunk. "In the meantime," he said, lowering his voice, "we didn't have this conversation, okay? It wouldn't go down too well if anyone knew I was teaching innocent kids how to hack into private information."

"Jess wouldn't mind."

"I'm not just talking about Jess."

Nicky held his gaze. "First rule of Geek Club. There is no Geek Club."

"The sock thing," said Tanzie, as they crossed the car park to meet them. She was holding up a napkin covered in scribbles. "I worked it out. If you had n number of socks, you'd have to sum a series of the fraction one over n to the power n." She adjusted her glasses.

"Got it in one. Exactly what I would have suggested," said Mr. Nicholls. And Mum looked at Nicky as though they were all basically people she had never met in her life.

Chapter Sixteen: Tanzie

Nobody really wanted to get back in the car. The novelty of spending hours in a car, even one as nice as Mr. Nicholls's, had worn off pretty quickly. This, Mum announced, like someone about to give an injection, would be the longest day. They were all to make themselves comfortable and make sure they'd been to the loo because Mr. Nicholls's aim was to drive almost to Newcastle, where he had found a B and B that took dogs. They would arrive at around ten p.m. After that, he had calculated that with one more day's driving they should arrive in Aberdeen. Mr. Nicholls would find them somewhere to stay close to the university, then Tanzie would be bright and fresh for the maths competition the next day. He looked at Tanzie. "Unless you think you've got used to this car enough for me to go above forty now?"

She shook her head.

"No." His face fell a bit. "Oh, well."

He caught sight of the backseat then and blinked. A couple of chocolate buttons had melted into the cream leather seats, and the footwell was crusty with mud from walking around the woods. Mr. Nicholls saw her looking at him and gave a half smile, like it really didn't matter, even though you could tell that it probably did, and turned back to the wheel.

"Okay, then," he said, and started the engine.

Everyone was silent for about an hour, while Mr. Nicholls listened to something on Radio 4 about technology. Mum read one of her books. Since the library had closed, she'd bought two paperbacks a week from the charity shop but only ever had time to read one.

The afternoon stretched and sagged, and the rain came down in thick, glassy sheets. Tanzie gazed out of the window and tried to do maths problems in her head, but it was hard to focus when she couldn't see her work. It was about six o'clock when Nicky began shifting around, like he couldn't get comfortable.

"When are we next stopping?"

Mum had nodded off briefly. She pushed herself upright abruptly, pretending she hadn't, and peered at the clock.

"Ten past six," Mr. Nicholls said.

"Could we stop for some food?" said Tanzie.

"I really need to walk around. My ribs are starting to hurt."

"Let's find somewhere to eat," Mr. Nicholls said. "We could divert into Leicester for a curry."

"I'd rather just get some sandwiches." Mum said. "We don't have time to sit down and eat."

Mr. Nicholls drove through a small town, then another, and followed the signs to a retail park. It had begun to get dark. The Audi crawled through it all, then finally stopped outside a supermarket and Mum climbed out with a loud sigh and ran in. They could see her through the rain-lashed window, standing in front of the chiller cabinets, picking things up and putting them down again.

"Why doesn't she just buy the ready-made ones?" muttered Mr. Nicholls, looking at his watch. "She'd be back out in two minutes."

"Too expensive," said Nicky, "and you don't know whose fingers have been in them. Jess did three weeks making sandwiches for a supermarket last year. She said that the woman next to her picked her nose in between shredding the chicken for the chicken Caesar wraps."

Mr. Nicholls went a bit quiet.

"Five to one it's supermarket-brand ham," said Nicky, watching.

"Supermarket-brand ham is two to one," Tanzie said.

"I'm going to go right out there and say sliced cheese," said Mr. Nicholls. "What odds will you give me on sliced cheese?"

"Not specific enough," said Nicky. "You have to go for Dairylea or cheaper supermarket-brand orange-colored slices. Probably with a made-up name."

"Pleasant Valley Cheese."

"Udderly Lovely Cheddar."

"That sounds disgusting."

"Grumpy Cow Slices."

"Oh, come on now, she's not that bad," Mr. Nicholls said.

Tanzie and Nicky started laughing.

Mum opened the door, and held up her carrier bag. "Right," she said brightly. "They had tuna paste on special. Who wants a sandwich?"

"You never want our sandwiches," Mum said as Mr. Nicholls drove through the town.

Mr. Nicholls turned on his directional

signal and pulled out onto the open road. "I don't like them. They remind me of being at school."

"So what do you eat?" Mum was tucking in. It had taken a matter of minutes for the whole car to smell of fish.

"In London? Toast for breakfast. Maybe some sushi or noodles for lunch. I have a takeaway place I order from in the evening."

"You have a takeaway? Every night?"

"If I'm not going out."

"How often do you go out?"

"Right now? Never."

Mum gave him a hard look.

"Well, okay, unless I'm getting drunk in your pub."

"You seriously eat the same thing every day?"

Mr. Nicholls seemed a bit embarrassed now. "You can get different curries."

"That must cost a fortune. So what do you eat when you're at Beachfront?"

"I get a takeaway."

"From the Raj?"

"Yeah. You know it?"

"Oh, I know it."

The car fell silent.

"What?" said Mr. Nicholls. "You don't go there? What is it? Too expensive? You're going to tell me it's easy to cook a baked potato, right? Well, I don't like baked potato. I don't like sandwiches. And I don't like cooking." It might have been because he was hungry, but he was suddenly quite grumpy.

Tanzie leaned forward through the seats. "Nathalie once found a hair in her Chicken Jalfrezi."

Mr. Nicholls opened his mouth to say something, just as she added, "And it wasn't from someone's head."

Twenty-three lampposts went by.

"You can worry too much about these things," Mr. Nicholls said.

Somewhere after Nuneaton, Tanzie started sneaking bits of her sandwich to Norman because the tuna paste didn't really taste like tuna, and the bread kept sticking to the roof of her mouth. Mr. Nicholls pulled into a petrol station.

"Their sandwiches will be awful," said Mum, gazing inside the kiosk. "They'll have been there for weeks."

"I'm not buying a sandwich."

"Do they do pasties?" said Nicky, peering inside. "I love pasties."

"They're even worse. They're probably full of dog."

Tanzie put her hands over Norman's ears.

"Are you going in?" Mum said to Mr. Nicholls, rummaging around in her purse. "Will you get these two some chocolate? Special treat."

"Crunchie, please," said Nicky, who had cheered up.

"Aero. Mint, please," Tanzie said. "Can I have a big one?"

Mum was holding out her hand. But Mr. Nicholls was staring off to his right. "Can you get them? I'm just going to pop across the road."

"Where are you going?"

He patted his stomach and he suddenly looked really cheerful. "There."

Keith's Kebabs had six plastic seats that were bolted to the floor, fourteen cans of Diet Coke arranged in its window, and a neon sign that was missing its first *b*. Tanzie peered through the window of the car, and watched Mr. Nicholls's walk become almost jaunty as he entered its strip-lit interior. He stared at the wall behind the counter, then pointed to a huge hunk of brown meat turning slowly on a spit. Tanzie considered what animal was shaped like that, and could only come up with buffalo. Maybe an amputee buffalo.

"Oh, man," said Nicky, as the man began

to carve, his voice a low moan of longing. "Can't we have one of those?"

"No," said Mum.

"I bet Mr. Nicholls would buy us one if we asked," he said.

Mum snapped, "Mr. Nicholls is doing quite enough for us. We're not going to mooch off him any more than we already have. Okay?"

Nicky rolled his eyes at Tanzie. "Fine," he said moodily.

And then nobody said anything.

"I'm sorry," said Mum after a minute. "I just . . . I just don't want him thinking we're taking advantage."

"But is it still taking advantage if someone offers you something?" Tanzie said.

"Eat an apple if you're still hungry. Or one of the breakfast muffins. I'm sure we've got a few left."

Nicky raised his eyes silently. Tanzie let out a sigh.

Mr. Nicholls opened the car door, bringing with him the smell of hot, fatty meat, and a kebab was swaddled in white, grease-stained paper. Two twin bungee ropes of drool dropped immediately from Norman's mouth. "You sure you don't want some?" he said cheerfully, turning toward Nicky and Tanzie. "I put only a bit of chili sauce on."

"No. That's very kind, but thank you," said Mum firmly, and gave Nicky a warning look.

"No, thanks," Tanzie said quietly. It smelled delicious.

"No. Thank you," said Nicky, and turned his face away.

Nuneaton, Market Bosworth, Coalville, Ashby de la Zouch, the signs passed by in a steady blur. They could have said Zanzibar and Tanzania for all Tanzie knew of where they actually were. She found herself repeating *Ashby de la Zouch, Ashby de la Zouch,* and thinking it would be a good name to have. *Hi — what's your name? I'm Ashby de la Zouch. Hey, Ashby! That's so cool!* Costanza Thomas was five syllables, too, but it didn't have the same rhythm. She considered *Constanza de la Zouch,* which was six, and then *Ashby Thomas,* which sounded flat by comparison.

Costanza de la Zouch.

Mum was reading again, with the passenger light on, and Mr. Nicholls kept shifting around in his seat, until finally he said, "That map — is there a restaurant or something up ahead?"

They had been back on the open road for 389 lampposts. Usually it was one of them

250

who asked to stop. Tanzie kept getting dehydrated and drinking too much, then needing a wee. Norman whined to go every twenty minutes, but they could never tell if he genuinely needed one or was as bored as they were and just wanted a little sniff around.

"You're still hungry?" Mum looked up.

"No. I — I need the loo."

Mum went back to her book. "Oh, don't mind us. Just go behind a tree."

"Not that kind of loo," he muttered.

"Well, it looks like Kegworth is the nearest town. I'm sure there'll be somewhere you could go. Or there might be a services if we can get past the bridge."

"How far?"

"Ten minutes?"

"Okay." He nodded, almost to himself. "Ten minutes is okay." His face was weirdly shiny. "Ten minutes is doable."

Nicky had his earbuds in and was listening to music. Tanzie was stroking Norman's big soft ears and thinking about string theory. And then suddenly Mr. Nicholls swerved the car abruptly into a lay-by. Everyone lurched forward. Norman nearly rolled off the seat. Mr. Nicholls threw open the driver's door, ran round the back, and as she turned in her seat, he crouched down

251

by a ditch, one hand braced on his knee, and began heaving. It was impossible not to hear him, even with the windows closed.

They all stared.

"Whoa," said Nicky. "That's a lot of stuff coming out of him. That's like . . . whoa, that's like the Alien."

"Oh, my God," said Mum.

"It's disgusting," Tanzie said, peering over the back shelf.

"Quick," said Mum. "Where's that kitchen roll, Nicky?"

They watched as she got out of the car and went to help him. He was doubled over. When she saw Tanzie and Nicky were staring out of the back window, she flicked her hand like they shouldn't look, even though she had been doing the exact same thing.

"Still want a kebab?" Tanzie said to Nicky.

"You're an evil sprite," he said, and shuddered.

Mr. Nicholls walked back to the car like someone who'd only just learned how to do it. His face had gone this weird pale yellow. His skin was dusted with tiny beads of sweat.

"You look awful," Tanzie told him.

He eased himself back into his seat. "I'll

be fine," he whispered. "Should be fine now."

Mum reached back through the seats and mouthed *plastic bag.* "Just in case," she said cheerfully, and opened her window a bit.

Mr. Nicholls drove slowly for the next few miles. So slowly that two cars kept flashing them from behind and one driver sat on his horn really angrily as he passed. Sometimes he veered a bit across the white line, like he wasn't really concentrating, but Tanzie registered Mum's determined silence and decided not to say anything.

"How long now?" Mr. Nicholls kept muttering.

"Not long," said Mum, even though she probably had no idea. She patted his arm, like he was a child. "You're doing really well."

When he looked at her, his eyes were anguished.

"Hang on in there," she said quietly, and it was like an instruction.

And then, about half a mile farther along, "Oh, God," he said, and slammed the brakes on again. "I need to —"

"Pub!" Mum yelled, and pointed toward a light just visible on the outskirts of the next village. "Look! You can make it!"

Mr. Nicholls's foot went down on the accelerator so that Tanzie's cheeks were pulled back. He skidded into the car park, threw the door open, staggered out, and hurled himself inside.

They sat there, waiting. The car was so quiet that they could hear the engine ticking.

After five minutes, Mum leaned across and pulled his door shut to keep the chill out. She looked back and smiled at them. "How was that Aero?"

"Nice."

"I like Aeros, too."

Nicky, his eyes closed, nodded to the music.

A man pulled into the car park with a woman wearing a high ponytail and looked hard at the car. Mum smiled. The woman did not smile back.

Ten minutes went by.

"Shall I go and get him?" Nicky said, pulling out his earbuds and peering at the clock.

"Best not," said Mum. Her foot had started tapping.

Another ten minutes passed. Finally, when Tanzie had taken Norman for a walk around the car park and Mum had done some stretches on the back of the car because she said she was bent out of shape, Mr. Nicholls emerged.

He looked whiter than anyone Tanzie had ever seen, like paper. He looked like someone had rubbed at his features with a cheap eraser.

"I think we might need to stop here for a bit," he said.

"In the pub?"

"Not the pub," he said, glancing behind him. "Definitely not the pub. Maybe . . . maybe somewhere a few miles away."

"Do you want me to drive?" Mum said.

"No," everyone said at once, and she smiled and tried to look like she wasn't offended.

The Bluebell Haven was the only place within ten miles that had a vacancy sign. It had eighteen stationary RVs, a playground with two swings and a sandpit, and a sign that said NO DOGS.

Mr. Nicholls let his face drop against the steering wheel. "We'll find somewhere else." He winced and doubled over. "Just give me a minute."

"No need."

"You said you can't leave the dog in the car."

"We won't leave him in the car. Tanzie," said Mum. "The sunglasses."

There was a mobile home by the front

255

gate marked RECEPTION. Mum went in first, and Tanzie put the sunglasses on and waited outside on the step, watching through the bubbled-glass door. The fat man who raised himself wearily from a chair said she was lucky as there was only one still available, and they could have it for a special price.

"How much is that?" said Mum.

"Eighty pounds."

"For one night? In a stationary RV?"

"It's Saturday."

"And it's seven o'clock at night and you had nobody in it."

"Someone might still come."

"Yeah. I heard Madonna was having a pint and a packet of chips down the road and looking for somewhere to park her entourage."

"No need to be snarky."

"No need to rip me off. Thirty pounds," Mum said, pulling the notes from her pocket.

"Forty."

"Thirty-five." Mum held out a hand. "It's all I've got. Oh, and we've got a dog."

He lifted a meaty hand. "Read the sign. No dogs."

"He's a guide dog. For my little girl. I'd remind you that it's illegal to bar a person on the grounds of disability."

Nicky opened the door and, holding her elbow, guided Tanzie in. She stood motion-less behind her dark glasses while Norman stood patiently in front of her. They had done this twice when they'd had to catch the coach to Portsmouth after Dad had left.

"He's well trained," Mum said. "He'll be no trouble."

"He's my eyes," Tanzie said. "My life would be nothing without him."

The man stared at Tanzie's hand, and then at her face. His jowls reminded Tanzie of Norman's. She had to remember not to glance up at the television.

"You're busting my balls, lady."

"Oh, I do hope not," Mum said cheerfully.

He shook his head, withdrew his huge hand, and moved heavily toward a key cabinet. "Golden Acres. Second lane, fourth on the right. Near the toilet block."

Mr. Nicholls was so ill by the time they reached the static that it was possible he didn't even notice where they were. He kept moaning softly and clutching his stomach and when he saw the word "Toilets" he let out a little cry and disappeared. They didn't see him for the best part of an hour.

Golden Acres wasn't gold and didn't look

anything like even half an acre, but Mum said any port in a storm. There were two tiny bedrooms, and the sofa in the living room converted into another bed. Mum said that Nicky and Tanzie could stay in the room with twin beds, Mr. Nicholls could go in the other, and she would have the sofa. It was actually okay in their bedroom, even if Nicky's feet did hang over the end of his bed and everywhere smelled of cigarettes. Mum opened some windows for a bit, then made up the beds with the duvets and ran the water until it came hot because she said Mr. Nicholls would probably want a shower when he came back in.

Tanzie inspected the chemical loo in the bathroom, then pressed her nose to the window and counted all the lights in the other stationary RVs. (Only two seemed to be occupied. "That lying git," said Mum.)

She had put her phone on to charge for precisely fifteen seconds when it rang. She started and picked it up, still plugged into the wall.

"Hello? Des?" Her hand flew to her mouth. "Oh, God. Des, I'm not going to make it back in time."

A series of muffled explosions at the other end.

"I'm really sorry. I know what I said. But

things have gone a bit crazy. I'm in . . ." She pulled a face at Tanzie. "Where are we?"

"Near Ashby de la Zouch," she said.

"Ashby de la Zouch," Mum said. And then, her hand in her hair, "Ashby de la Zouch. I know. I'm really sorry. The journey didn't quite go as I planned and our driver got sick and my phone ran out and with all the . . . What?" She glanced at Tanzie. "I don't know. Probably not before Tuesday. Maybe even Wednesday. It's taking longer than we thought."

Tanzie could definitely hear him shouting then.

"Can't Chelsea cover it? I've done enough of her shifts. I know it's the busy period. I know, Des, I'm really sorry. I've said I —." She paused. "No. I can't get back before then. No. I'm really . . . What do you mean? I've never missed a shift this past year. I — Des? . . . Des?" She broke off and stared at the phone.

"Was that Des from the pub?" Tanzie liked Des from the pub. Once she had sat outside with Norman on a Sunday afternoon, waiting for Mum, and he had given her a packet of scampi fries.

At that minute, the door to the RV opened, and Mr. Nicholls pretty much fell in. "Lie down," he muttered, and he pulled

259

himself briefly upright, before collapsing onto the floral sofa cushions. He looked up at Mum with a gray face and big hollow eyes. "Lying down. Sorry," he mumbled.

Mum just sat there, staring at her mobile.

He blinked at her. "Were you trying to reach me?"

"He's sacked me," Mum said. "I don't believe it. He's bloody sacked me."

Chapter Seventeen:
Jess

The night took on a weird, disjointed quality, the hours running into each other, fluid and endless. Jess had never seen a man be so ill without actually hacking up a kidney. She gave up trying to sleep. She stared at the caramel-colored, wipe-clean walls of the caravan, read a bit, nodded off. Mr. Nicholls groaned beside her, occasionally getting up to shuffle backward and forward to the toilet block. She closed the kids' door and sat waiting for him in the little caravan, sometimes dozing on the far end of the L-shaped sofa, handing him water and tissues when he staggered in.

Shortly after three, Mr. Nicholls said he wanted a shower. She made him promise to leave the bathroom door unlocked, took his clothes down to the launderette (a washer-dryer in a shed), and spent three pounds twenty on a sixty-minute cycle. She didn't have any change for the dryer.

He was still in the shower when she arrived back at the caravan. She draped his clothes from hangers over the heater, hoping they might dry a bit by morning, then knocked quietly on the door. There was no answer, just the sound of running water, and a belch of steam. She peeped around the door. The glass was clouded but she could make him out, slumped and exhausted on the floor. She waited a moment, staring at his broad back pressed against the glass panel, a pale inverted triangle, surprisingly muscular, then watched as he lifted his hand and ran it wearily over his face.

"Mr. Nicholls?" she whispered behind him, then again when he didn't say anything. "Mr. Nicholls?"

He turned then, and saw her. His eyes were red rimmed and his head had sunk deep into his shoulders.

"Fucksake. I can't even get up. And the water's starting to go cold," he said.

"Want me to help?"

"No. Yes. Ah, Jesus."

"Hold on."

She held up the towel, whether to shield him or herself, she wasn't sure, reached in, and turned off the shower, soaking her arm. Then she crouched down, so that he could cover himself, and leaned in. "Put your arm around my neck."

"You're tiny. I'll just pull you over."

"I'm stronger than I look."

He didn't move.

"You're going to have to help me here. I'm not up to a fireman's lift."

His wet arm slid around her, he hooked the towel around his waist. Jess braced herself against the wall of the shower, and finally, shakily, they stood. Usefully, the RV was so small that at every step there was a wall for him to lean on. They made their way unsteadily to the couch.

"This is what my life has come to." He groaned, eyeing the bucket, as she placed it beside the sofa.

"Yup." Jess viewed the peeling wallpaper, the nicotine-stained paintwork. "Well, I've had better Saturday nights myself."

It was a little after four. Her eyes were gritty and sore, and she closed them for a minute.

"Thanks," he said weakly.

"What for?"

He pushed himself upright. "For bringing a loo roll out to me in the middle of the night. For washing my disgusting clothes. For helping me out of the shower. And for not once acting like it was my own fault for buying a dodgy doner from a place called Keith's Kebabs."

"Even though it was your own fault."

"See? Now you're spoiling it."

He lay back on the pillow, his forearm over his eyes. She tried not to look at the broad expanse of chest above the strategically placed towel. She couldn't remember when she had last seen a man's naked torso other than at Des's ill-advised Pub Beach Volleyball Match the previous August.

"Go and lie down in the bedroom. You'll be more comfortable."

He opened one eye. "Do I get a Sponge-Bob duvet?"

"You get my pink stripy one. But I promise not to regard it as any reflection whatsoever on your masculinity."

"Where will you sleep?"

"Out here. It's fine," she said, as he started to protest. "I'm not sure I'll sleep much anyway."

He let her lead him into the tiny bedroom. He groaned as he fell onto the bed, as if even that caused him discomfort, and she pulled the duvet over him gently. The shadows under his eyes were ash colored and his voice had become drowsy. "I'll be ready to go in a couple of hours."

"Sure you will," she said, observing the

ghostly pallor of his skin. "Take your time."

"Where the hell are we, anyway?"

"Oh, somewhere on the Yellow Brick Road."

"Is that the one with the godlike lion that saves everyone?"

"You're thinking of Narnia. This one is cowardly and useless."

"Figures."

And finally he slept.

Jess left the room silently and lay down on the narrow sofa, trying not to look at the clock. She and Nicky had studied the map while Mr. Nicholls was in the toilet block the previous evening and had reconfigured the journey as best they could.

We still have plenty of time, she told herself. And then, finally, she, too, fell asleep.

All was silent within Mr. Nicholls's room well into the morning. Jess thought about waking him, but each time she made a move toward his door, she remembered the sight of him slumped against the shower cabinet and her fingers stilled on the handle. She opened the door only once, when Nicky pointed out that it was possible he had choked to death on his own vomit. He seemed the faintest bit disappointed when it turned out Mr. Nicholls was just in a really deep sleep. The children took Norman up the road — Tanzie in her dark glasses for authenticity — bought supplies from a convenience store, and breakfasted in whispers. Jess converted the remaining bread into sandwiches ("Oh, good," said Nicky), cleaned the caravan — for something to do — and left a voice mail for Des, apologizing again. He didn't pick up.

Then the door of the little room opened with a squeak and Mr. Nicholls emerged, blinking, in his T-shirt and boxers. He raised a palm in greeting. A long crease bisected his cheek from the pillow. "We are in . . . ?"

"Ashby de la Zouch. Or somewhere nearby. It's not quite Beachfront."

"Is it late?"

"Quarter to eleven."

"Quarter to eleven. Okay." His jaw was thick with stubble, and his hair stuck up on one side. Jess pretended to read her book. He smelled of warm, sleepy male. She had forgotten what a weirdly potent scent that was.

"Quarter to eleven." He rubbed at the stubble on his chin, then walked unsteadily to the window and peered out. "I feel like I've been asleep for a million years." He sat down heavily on the sofa cushion opposite her, running his hand over his jaw.

"Dude," said Nicky from beside Jess. "Jailbreak alert."

"What?"

Nicky waved a ballpoint. "You need to put the prisoners back in the pen."

Mr. Nicholls stared at him, then turned to Jess, as if to say, *Your son has gone mad.*

Following Nicky's gaze, Jess looked down and swiftly away. "Oh, God."

Mr. Nicholls frowned. " 'Oh, God' what?"

"You could at least have taken me out to dinner first," she said, standing to clear the breakfast things. She felt her ears go pink.

"Oh." Mr. Nicholls looked down and adjusted himself. "Sorry. Right. Okay." He stood, and made for the bathroom. "I'll, uh, I . . . am I okay to have another shower?"

"We saved you some hot water," said Tanzie, who was head down over her exam sheet in the corner. "You smelled really bad yesterday."

He emerged twenty minutes later, his hair damp and smelling of shampoo, his face clean shaven. Jess was busy whisking salt and sugar into a glass of water and trying not to think about naked bits of Mr. Nicholls. She handed it to him.

"What's that?" He pulled a face.

"Rehydrating solution. To replace some of

what you lost last night."

"You want me to drink a glass of salty water? After I've spent all night being sick?"

"Just drink it." While he was grimacing and gagging, she fixed him some plain toast and black coffee. He sat across the little Formica table, took a sip of coffee and a few tentative bites of toast, and ten minutes later, in a voice that held some surprise, acknowledged that he did actually feel a bit better.

"Better, as in able-to-drive-without-having-an-accident better?"

"By having an accident, you mean —"

"Not crashing into a lay-by."

"Thank you for clarifying that." He took another, more confident, bite of toast. "Yeah. Give me another twenty minutes, though. I want to make sure I'm —"

"Safe in cars."

"Ha." He grinned, and it was pleasing to see him smile. "Yes. Quite. Oh, man, I do feel better." He ran a hand across the plastic-covered table and took a swig of coffee, sighing with apparent satisfaction. He finished the first round of toast, asked if there was any more going, then looked around the table. "Although, you know, I might feel even better if you weren't all staring at me while I eat. I'm worried some other part of me is poking out."

"You'll know," said Nicky, "because we'll all run screaming."

"Mum said you nearly brought up an organ," said Tanzie. "I was wondering what it felt like."

He glanced up at Jess and stirred his coffee. He didn't shift his gaze until she had blushed. "Truthfully? Not so different from most of my Saturday nights, these days."

Tanzie studied her exam sheet before folding it up carefully. "The thing about numbers," she said, as if they had been having a different conversation altogether, "is they're not always numbers. I mean, i is imaginary. Pi is transcendent. And so is e. But if you stick them together, e to the power of i times pi is minus one. So they make a number that isn't there. Because minus one isn't a number; it's a place where a number should be."

"Well, that makes perfect sense," said Nicky.

"Does to me," said Mr. Nicholls. "I feel pretty much like a space where a body should be." He drank the rest of his coffee and put down his cup. "Okay. I'm good. Let's hit the road."

The landscape altered by the mile as they

269

drove through the afternoon, the hills growing steeper and less bucolic, the walls that banked them morphing from hedgerows into flinty gray stone. The skies opened, the light around them grew brighter, and they passed the distant symbols of an industrial landscape: redbrick factories, huge power stations that belched mustard-colored clouds. Jess watched surreptitiously as Mr. Nicholls drove, at first wary that he would suddenly clutch his stomach, and then later with a vague satisfaction at the sight of normal color returning to his face.

"I don't think we're going to make Aberdeen today," he said, and there was a hint of apology in his voice.

"Let's just get as far as we can and do the last stretch early tomorrow morning."

"That's exactly what I was going to suggest."

"Still loads of time."

"Loads."

She let the miles roll by, dozed intermittently, and tried not to worry about all the things she needed to worry about. She positioned her mirror surreptitiously so that she could watch Nicky in the backseat. His bruises had faded, even in the short time they had been away. He seemed to be talking more than he had been. But he was still closed to her. Sometimes Jess worried he would be like that for the rest of his life. It didn't seem to make any difference how often she told him she loved him, or that they were his family. "You're too late," her mother had said when Jess told her he was coming to live with them. "With a child that age, the damage has been done. I should know."

As a schoolteacher, her mother could keep a class of thirty eight-year-olds in a narcoleptic silence, could steer them through tests like a shepherd streaming sheep through a pen. But Jess couldn't remember her ever smiling at her with pleasure, the kind of pleasure you're meant to get just from looking at someone you gave birth to.

She had been right about many things. She had told Jess on the day she started secondary school: "The choices you make now will determine the rest of your life." All Jess heard was someone telling her she should pin down her whole self, like a butterfly. That was the thing: when you put someone down all the time, eventually they stopped listening to the sensible stuff.

When Jess had Tanzie, young and daft as she had been, she'd had enough wisdom to know she was going to tell her how much she loved her every day. She would hug her

271

and wipe her tears and flop with her on the sofa with their legs entwined like spaghetti. She would cocoon her in love. When Tanzie was tiny, Jess slept with her in their bed, her arms wrapped around her — Marty would haul himself grumpily into the spare room, moaning that there wasn't any room for him. She barely even heard him.

And when Nicky had turned up two years later, and everyone had told her she was mad to take on someone else's child, a child who was already eight years old and from a troubled background — *you know how boys like that turn out* — she'd ignored them. Because she could see instantly in the wary little shadow who had stood a minimum twelve inches away from anyone, a little of what she had felt. Because she knew that something happened to you when your mother didn't hold you close, or tell you all the time that you were the best thing ever, or even notice when you were home: a little part of you sealed over. You didn't need her. You didn't need anyone. And without even knowing you were doing it, you waited. You waited for anyone who got close to you to see something they didn't like in you, something they hadn't seen initially, and to grow cold and disappear, too, like so much sea mist. Because there had to be something wrong, didn't there, if even your own mother didn't really love you?

It was why she hadn't been devastated when Marty left. Why would she be? He couldn't hurt her. The only things Jess really cared about were those two children and letting them know they were okay. Because even if the whole world was throwing rocks at you, if you had your mother at your back, you'd be okay. Some deep-rooted part of you would know you were loved. That you deserved to be loved. Jess hadn't done much to be proud of in her life, but the thing she was most proud of was that Tanzie knew it. Strange little bean that she was, Jess knew she knew it.

She was still working on Nicky.

"Are you hungry?" Mr. Nicholls's voice woke her from a half doze.

She pushed herself upright. Her neck had calcified, as bent and stiff as a wire coat hanger. "Starving," she said, turning awkwardly toward him. "You want to stop somewhere for lunch?"

The sun had emerged. It shone in actual rays off to their left, strobing a vast, open field of green. God's fingers, Tanzie used to call them. Jess reached for the map in the glove compartment, ready to look up the location of the next services.

Mr. Nicholls glanced at her. He seemed almost embarrassed. "Actually, you know what? I could really go for one of your sandwiches."

CHAPTER EIGHTEEN: ED

The Stag and Hounds B and B wasn't listed in any accommodations guides. It had no Web site, no brochures. It wasn't hard to work out why. The pub sat alone on the side of a bleak, windswept moor, and the mossy plastic garden furniture that stood outside its gray frontage suggested an absence of casual visitors or, perhaps, the triumph of hope over experience. The bedrooms, apparently, were last decorated several decades previously — they bore shiny pink wallpaper, lace curtains, and a smattering of china figurines in place of anything useful, like, say, shampoo or tissues. There was a communal bathroom at the end of the upstairs corridor, where the fixtures were an ancient green and ringed with lime scale. A small box-shaped television in the twin room deigned to pick up three channels, each of those with a faint static buzz. When Nicky discovered the plastic doll in a crocheted wool ball dress that squatted over the loo roll, he was awestruck. "I actually love this," he said, holding her up to the light to inspect her glittery synthetic hem. "It's so bad it's actually cool."

Ed couldn't believe places like this still existed. But he had been driving for a little more than eight hours at forty m.p.h., the Stag and Hounds was twenty-five pounds per night per room — a rate even Jess was pleased with — and they were happy to let Norman in.

"Oh, we love dogs." Mrs. Deakins waded through a small flock of excitable Pomeranians. She patted her head, on which a carefully pinned structure sat. "We love dogs more than humans, don't we, Jack?" There was a grunt from somewhere downstairs. "They're certainly easier to please. You can bring your lovely big fella into the snug tonight, if you like. My girls love to meet a new man." She gave Ed a faintly saucy nod as she said this.

She opened the two doors and waved a hand inside.

"So, Mr. and Mrs. Nicholls, you'll be right next door to your children. You're the only guests tonight, so it should be nice and quiet. We have a selection of cereals for breakfast or Jack will do you egg on toast.

He does a lovely egg on toast."

"Thank you."

She handed him the keys, held his gaze a millisecond longer than was strictly necessary. "I'm going to guess you like yours . . . gently poached. Am I right?"

Ed glanced behind him, checking that she was addressing him.

"I am, aren't I?"

"Um . . . however they come."

"However . . . they . . . come," she repeated slowly, her eyes not leaving his. She raised one eyebrow, smiled at him again, then headed downstairs, her pack of small dogs a moving hairy sea around her feet. From the corner of his eye he could see Jess smirking.

"Don't." He dropped their bags onto the bed.

"I bags first bath." Nicky rubbed at the small of his back.

"I need to study," said Tanzie. "I have exactly seventeen and a half hours until the Olympiad." She gathered her books under her arm and disappeared into the next room.

"Come and give Norman a walk first, sweetheart," Jess said. "Get some fresh air. It'll help you sleep later."

Jess unzipped a holdall, and pulled a

hoodie over her head. When she lifted her arms, a crescent of bare stomach was briefly visible, pale and oddly startling. Her face emerged through the neck opening. "We'll be gone for at least half an hour. Or we . . . could make it longer." As she adjusted her ponytail, she glanced toward the stairs and lifted an eyebrow at him. "Just . . . saying."

"Funny."

He could hear her laughing as they disappeared. Ed lay down on the nylon bedspread, feeling his hair lift slightly with static electricity, and pulled his phone from his pocket.

"So here's the good news," said Paul Wilkes. "The police have completed their initial investigations. The preliminary results show no obvious motive on your side. There is no evidence that you extracted a profit from Deanna Lewis or her brother's trading activities. More pertinent, there is no sign that you made any money at all from the launch of SFAX other than the same share gains that would be made by any employee. Obviously, there would be a higher proportion of profit, given your overall shareholding, but they can find no links to offshore accounts or any attempt to conceal on your side."

"That's because there were none."

"Also, the investigating team says that they have uncovered a number of accounts in Michael Lewis's family's names, which suggests a clear attempt to conceal his actions. They have obtained trading records that show he was trading a large volume immediately prior to the announcement — another red flag for them."

Paul was still talking but the signal was patchy, and Ed struggled to hear him. He stood and walked over to the window. Tanzie was running round and round the pub garden, shrieking happily. The small yappy dogs were following her. Jess was standing, her arms folded, laughing. Norman was in the middle of the space, gazing at them all, a bemused, immovable object in a sea of madness. He put his hand over his other ear. "Does that mean I can come back now? Is it sorted out?" He had a sudden vision of his office: a mirage in a desert.

"Hold your horses. Here's the less-good news. Michael Lewis wasn't just trading stocks; he was trading options on the stock."

"Trading what?" He blinked. "Okay. You're now speaking Polish."

"Seriously?" There was a short silence. Ed pictured Paul in his wood-paneled office, rolling his eyes. "Options allow a trader to leverage his or, in this case, her investment, and generate substantially more in profits."

"But what does that have to do with me?"

"Well, the level of profits he generated from the options is significant, so the whole case moves up a gear. Which brings me to the bad news."

"That wasn't the bad news?"

Paul sighed. "Ed, why didn't you tell me you'd written Deanna Lewis a damn check?"

Ed blinked. The check.

"She cashed a check written by you for five thousand pounds to her bank account."

"So?"

"So," and here, from the elaborately slow and careful tenor of his voice, it was possible to picture the eyes roll again, "it links you financially to what Deanna Lewis was doing. You enabled some of that trade."

"But it was just a few grand to help her out! She had no money!"

"Whether or not you extracted a profit from it, you had a clear financial interest in Lewis, and it came just before SFAX went live. The e-mails we could argue were inconclusive, but this means it's not just her word against yours, Ed."

He stared out at the moorland. Tanzie was jumping up and down and waving a stick at the slobbering dog. Her glasses had gone askew on her nose and she was laughing. Jess scooped her up from behind and hugged her.

"Meaning?"

"Meaning, Ed, defending you just got a whole lot tougher."

Ed had only utterly disappointed his father once in his whole life. That's not to say he wasn't a general disappointment — he knew his father would have preferred a son who was more obviously in his own mold: upright, determined, driven. A sort of filial marine. But he managed to override whatever private dismay he felt at this quiet, geeky boy, and decided instead that as he so clearly couldn't sort him out, an expensive education would.

The fact that the meager funds their parents saved over their working years sent Ed to private school and not his sister was the great Unacknowledged Resentment of their family. He often wondered whether, if they had known then what a huge emotional hurdle they were planting in front of Gemma, they still would have done it. Ed never could convince her that it was purely because she was so good at everything that they never felt the need to send her. He was the one who spent every waking hour in his room or glued to a screen. He was the one who was hopeless at sports.

But no, against all available evidence, Bob Nicholls, former military policeman and later head of security for a small northern building society, was convinced that an expensive minor private school, with the motto "Sports maketh the man," would maketh his son. "This is a great opportunity we're giving you, Edward. Better than your mother or I ever had," he said repeatedly. "Don't waste it." So at the end of Ed's first year, when he opened the report, which used the words *disengaged* and *lackluster performance* and, worst of all, *not really a team player,* he stared at the letter as Ed watched uncomfortably while the color drained from his face.

Ed couldn't tell him he didn't really like the school, with its braying packs of mocking, overentitled posh boys. He couldn't tell him that no matter how many times they made him run round the rugby field he was never going to like rugby. He couldn't explain that it was the possibilities of the pixelated screen, and what you could create from it, that really interested him. And that he felt he could make a life out of it. His father's face actually sagged with disappointment, with the sheer bloody waste of it all, and Ed realized he had no choice.

"I'll do better next year, Dad," he said.

Now Ed Nicholls was due to report to the City of London police in a matter of days.

He tried to imagine the expression his father would wear when he heard that his son — the son he now boasted about to his ex-army colleagues ("Of course I don't understand what it is he actually does, but apparently all this software stuff is the future") — was quite possibly about to be prosecuted for insider trading. He tried to picture his father's head turning on that frail neck, the shock pulling his weary features down even as he tried to disguise it, and his gently pursed lips as he grasped there was nothing he could say or do.

So Ed made a decision. He would ask his lawyer to prolong the proceedings as long as possible. He would throw every penny of his own money at the case to delay the announcement of his supposed crime. But he could not go to that family lunch, no matter how ill his father was. He would be doing his father a favor. By staying away he would actually be protecting him.

Ed Nicholls stood in the little pink hotel bedroom that smelled of air freshener and disappointment and stared out at the bleak moors, at the little girl who had flopped onto the damp grass and was pulling the ears of the dog as he sat, tongue lolling, an expression of idiotic ecstasy on his great features, and he wondered why — given that he was so evidently doing the right thing — he felt like a complete shit.

CHAPTER NINETEEN: JESS

Tanzie was nervous. She refused supper and declined to come downstairs even for a break, preferring to curl up on the pink nylon coverlet and plow through her maths papers while nibbling on what remained of the breakfast picnic. Jess was surprised: her daughter rarely suffered from nerves when it came to anything maths related. She did her best to reassure her, but it was hard when she had no idea what she was talking about.

"We're nearly there! It's all good, Tanze. Nothing to worry about."

"Do you think I'll sleep tonight?"

"Of course you'll sleep tonight."

"But if I don't, I might do really badly."

"Even if you don't sleep, you'll do fine. And I've never known you to not sleep."

"I'm worried that I'll worry too much to sleep."

"I'm not worried that you'll worry. Just

relax. You'll be fine. It will all be fine."

When Jess kissed her, she saw that Tanzie had chewed her nails right down to the quick.

Mr. Nicholls was in the garden. He walked up and down where she and Tanzie had been half an hour earlier, talking avidly into his phone. He stopped and stared at it a couple of times, then stepped up onto a white plastic garden chair, presumably to get better reception. He stood there, wobbling, utterly oblivious to the curious glances of those inside as he gesticulated and swore.

Jess gazed through the window of the bar, unsure whether to go and interrupt him. There were a few old men gathered around the landlady as she chatted from the other side of the counter. They looked at Jess incuriously over their pints.

"Work, is it?" The landlady followed her gaze through the window.

"Oh. Yes. Never stops." Jess raised a smile. "I'll take him a drink."

Mr. Nicholls was seated on a low stone wall when she finally walked out. His elbows were on his knees and he was staring at the grass.

Jess held out the pint and he stared at it for a moment, then took it from her.

"Thanks." He looked exhausted.

"Everything okay?"

"No." He took a long gulp of his beer. "Nothing's okay."

She sat down a few feet away. "Anything I can help with?"

"No."

They sat in silence. It was so peaceful there, with nothing around them except the breeze rippling across the moors, and the gentle hum of conversation from inside. She was going to say something about the landscape when his voice broke into the still air.

"Fuck it," Mr. Nicholls said vehemently. "Just fuck it."

Jess flinched.

"I just can't believe my fucking life has turned into this . . . mess." His voice cracked. "I can't believe that I can work and work for years and the whole thing can fall apart like this. For what? For fucking what?"

"It's only food poisoning. You'll —"

"I'm not talking about the fucking kebab." He dropped his head into his hands. "But I don't want to talk about it." He shot her a warning look.

"Okay."

"That's the thing. Legally, I'm not meant to talk to anyone about any of this."

287

She didn't look at him.

"I can't tell a soul."

She stretched out a leg and gazed at the sunset. "Well, I don't count, do I? I'm a cleaning wench."

He let out a breath. "Fuck it," he said again.

And then he told her, his head down, his hands raking his short dark hair. He told her about a girlfriend with whom he couldn't think how to break up nicely, and how his whole life had come crashing down. He told her about his company and how he should have been there now, celebrating the launch of his last six years' obsessive work. And how instead he had to stay away from everything and everyone he knew all the while facing the prospect of prosecution. He told her about his dad and about the lawyer who had just rung to inform him that shortly after he returned from this trip his presence would be required at a police station in London where he would be charged with insider trading, a charge that could win him up to twenty years in prison. By the time he'd finished, she felt winded.

"Everything I've ever worked for. Everything I cared about. I'm not allowed to go into my own office. I can't even go back to my flat in case the press hear of it and I let slip what's happened. I can't go and see my own dad because then he'll die knowing what a bloody idiot his son is. And the stupid thing is, I miss him. I really miss him."

Jess digested this for a few minutes. He smiled bleakly at the sky. "And you know the best bit? It's my birthday."

"What?"

"Today. It's my birthday."

"Today? Why didn't you say anything?"

"Because I'm thirty-four years old, and a thirty-four-year-old man sounds like a dick talking about birthdays." He took a swig of his beer. "And what with the whole food-poisoning thing, I didn't feel I had much to celebrate." He looked sideways at Jess. "Plus you might have started singing 'Happy Birthday' in the car."

"I'll sing it out here."

"Please don't. Things are bad enough."

Jess's head was reeling. She couldn't believe all the stuff Mr. Nicholls was carrying around. If he had been anyone else, she might have put her arm around him, attempted to say something comforting. But Mr. Nicholls was prickly.

"Things will get better, you know," she said, when she couldn't think of anything else to say. "Karma will get that girl who messed you up."

He pulled a face. "Karma?"

"It's like I tell the kids. Good things happen to good people. You just have to keep faith —"

"Well, I must have been a complete shit in a past life."

"Come on. You still have property. You have cars. You have your brain. You have expensive lawyers. You can work this out."

"How come you're such an optimist?"

"Because things do come right."

"And that's from a woman who doesn't have enough money to catch a train."

Jess kept her gaze on the craggy hillside. "Because it's your birthday, I'm going to let that one go."

Mr. Nicholls sighed. "Sorry. I know you're trying to help. But right now I find your positivity exhausting."

"No, you find driving hundreds of miles in a car with three people you don't know and a large dog exhausting. Go upstairs and have a long bath and you'll feel better. Go on."

He trudged inside, the condemned man, and she sat and stared out at the slab of green moorland in front of her. She tried to imagine what it would be like to be facing prison, not to be allowed near the things or the people you loved. She tried to imagine someone like Mr. Nicholls doing time.

After a while, she walked inside with the empty glasses. She leaned over the bar, where the landlady was watching an episode of *Homes Under the Hammer.* The men sat in silence behind her, watching it, too, or gazing rheumily into their pints.

"Mrs. Deakins? It's actually my husband's birthday today. Would you mind doing me a favor?"

Mr. Nicholls finally came downstairs at eight thirty, wearing the same clothes he'd worn that afternoon. And the previous afternoon. Jess knew he had bathed, though, as his hair was damp and he was clean shaven.

"So what's in your bag, then? A body?"

"What?" He walked over to the bar. He gave off a faint scent of Wilkinson Sword soap.

"You've worn the same clothes since we left."

He looked down, as if to check. "Oh. No. These are clean."

"You have the same T-shirt and jeans? For every day?"

"Saves thinking about it."

She looked at him for a minute, then

291

decided to bite back what she had been about to say. It was his birthday after all.

"Oh. You look nice," he said suddenly, as if he'd only just noticed.

She had changed into a blue sundress and a cardigan. She had planned to save it for the Olympiad, but figured that this was important. "Well, thank you. One has to make the effort to fit one's surroundings, doesn't one?"

"What — you left your flat cap and dog-haired jeans behind?"

"You're about to be sorry for your sarcasm. Because I have a surprise in store."

"A surprise?" He looked instantly wary.

"It's a good one. Here." Jess handed him one of two glasses she had prepared earlier, to Mrs. Deakins's amusement. They hadn't made a cocktail here since 1997, Mrs. Deakins had observed, as Jess checked the dusty bottles behind the optics. "I figure you're well enough."

"What is this?" He stared at it suspiciously.

"Scotch, triple sec, and orange juice."

He took a sip. And then a larger one. "This is all right."

"I knew you'd like it. I made it especially for you. It's called a Mithering Bastard."

The white plastic table sat in the middle of

the threadbare lawn, with two place settings of stainless-steel cutlery and a candle in a wine bottle in the middle. Jess had wiped the chairs with a bar cloth so that there was no moss left on them and now pulled one out for him.

"We're eating alfresco. Birthday treat." She ignored the look he gave her. "If you would like to take your seat, I'll go and inform the kitchen that you're here."

"It's not breakfast muffins, is it?"

"Of course it's not breakfast muffins." She pretended to be offended. As she walked toward the kitchen, she muttered, "Tanzie and Nicky had the rest of those."

When she arrived back at the table, Norman had flopped down on Mr. Nicholls's foot. Jess suspected that Mr. Nicholls would quite like to have moved it, but she had been sat on by Norman before and he was a deadweight. You just had to pray that he shifted before your foot went black and fell off.

"How was your aperitif?"

Mr. Nicholls gazed at his empty cocktail glass. "Delicious."

"Well, the main course is on its way. I'm afraid it's just the two of us this evening, as the other guests had prior arrangements."

"Teenager-heavy soap opera and some

completely insane algebraic equations?"

"You know us too well." Jess sat down in her chair, and, as she did, Mrs. Deakins picked her way across the lawn, the Pomeranians yapping at her feet. She held aloft two plates.

"There you go," she said, placing them on the table. "Steak and kidney. From Ian up the road. He does a lovely meat pie."

Jess was so hungry by then she thought she could probably have eaten Ian. "Fantastic. Thank you," she said, laying a paper napkin on her lap.

Mrs. Deakins stood and gazed around, as if seeing the setting for the first time. "We never eat out here. Lovely idea. I might offer it to my other customers. And those cocktails. I could make a package of it."

Jess thought about the old men in the bar. "Shame not to," she said, passing the vinegar across to Mr. Nicholls. He seemed temporarily stunned.

Mrs. Deakins rubbed her hands on her apron. "Well, Mr. Nicholls, your wife is certainly determined to show you a good time on your birthday," she said with a wink.

He glanced up at her. "Oh. There's never a quiet moment with Jess," he said, letting his gaze slide back to hers.

"So how long have you two been married?"

"Ten years."

"Three years."

"The children are from my previous marriages," Jess said, slicing into the pie.

"Oh! That's —"

"I rescued her," said Mr. Nicholls. "From the side of the road."

"He did."

"That's very romantic." Mrs. Deakins's smile wavered a little.

"Not really. She was being arrested at the time."

"I've explained all that. Wow, these chips are delicious."

"You have. And those policemen were very understanding. Considering."

Mrs. Deakins had started to back away. "Well, that's lovely. It's nice that you're still together."

"We get by."

"We have no choice right now."

"That's true, too."

"Could you bring out some red sauce?"

"Oh, good idea. Darling."

As she disappeared, Mr. Nicholls nodded toward the candle and the plates. And then he looked up at Jess and he was no longer scowling. "This is actually the best pie and

chips I've ever eaten in a weird bed-and-
breakfast somewhere I've never heard of on
the north Yorkshire moors."

"I'm so glad. Happy birthday."

They ate in companionable silence. It was
astonishing how much better a hot meal and
a strong cocktail could make you feel.
Norman groaned and flopped over onto his
side, releasing Mr. Nicholls's foot. Ed
stretched his leg speculatively, perhaps trying to see whether he still could.

He looked up at her, and raised his re-
freshed cocktail glass. "Seriously. Thank
you." Without his glasses on, she noticed
now that he had ridiculously long eyelashes.
It made her feel weirdly conscious of the
candle in the middle of the table. It had
been a bit of a joke when she'd asked for it.

"Well . . . it was the least I could do. You
did rescue us. From the side of the road. I
don't know what we would have done."

He speared another chip and held it aloft.
"Well, I like to look after my staff."

"I think I preferred it when we were married."

"Cheers." He grinned at her, his eyes
wrinkling. And it was so genuine and unexpected that she found herself grinning back.

"Here's to tomorrow. And Tanzie's future."

"And a general absence of more crap."

"I'll drink to that."

The evening crept into night, eased by alcohol, and the happy knowledge that nobody had to sleep in a car, or needed frequent, urgent access to a bathroom. Nicky came down, gazed suspiciously from under his fringe at the men in the snug, who gazed equally suspiciously back at him, and retreated to his bedroom to watch television. Jess drank three glasses of acidic Liebfraumilch, went inside to check on Tanzie and take her some food. She made her promise she would not study later than ten o'clock. "Can I keep working in your room? Nicky has the telly on."

"That's fine," Jess said.

"You smell of wine," Tanzie said pointedly.

"That's because we're sort of on holiday. Mums are allowed to smell of wine when they're sort of on holiday."

"Hm." She gave Jess a severe look and turned back to her books.

Nicky was sprawled on one of the single beds watching television. She shut the door behind her and sniffed the air.

"You haven't been smoking, have you?"

"You've still got my stash."

"Oh yes." She had completely forgotten. "But you slept without it. Last night and the night before."

"Mm."

"Well, that's good, right?"

He shrugged.

"I think the words you were looking for are: 'Yes, it's great that I no longer need illegal substances simply to fall asleep.' Right, up you get for a minute. I need you to help me lift a mattress." When he didn't move, she said, "I can't sleep in there with Mr. Nicholls. We'll make another bed on the floor of your room, okay?"

He sighed, but he got up and helped. He didn't wince anymore when he moved, she noticed. On the carpet beside Tanzie's bed, the mattress left just enough room for them to slide in and out of the door, which now only opened six inches.

"This is going to be fun if I need the loo in the night."

"Go last thing. You're a big boy." She told Nicky to turn off the television at ten so as not to disturb Tanzie, and left them both upstairs.

The candle had long since expired in the stiff evening breeze, and when they could no longer see each other, they moved indoors. The conversation had meandered from parents and first jobs on to relationships. Jess told him about Marty and how he had once bought her an extension cord for her birthday, protesting, "But you said you needed one!" In turn, he told her about Lara the Ex and how on her birthday he had once arranged for a chauffeur to pick her up for a surprise breakfast at a smart hotel with her friends, then spend the morning in Harvey Nichols with a personal shopper and an unlimited budget. And how when he'd met her for lunch, she had complained bitterly because he hadn't taken the whole day off work. Jess thought she'd quite like to slap Lara the Ex's overly made-up face. (She had invented this face: it was probably more drag queen than was strictly necessary.)

"Did you have to pay her alimony?"

"Didn't have to, but I did. Until she let herself into the apartment and helped herself to my stuff for the third time."

"Did you get it back?"

"It wasn't worth the hassle. If a silk screen of Mao Tse-tung is that important to her, she can have it."

"What was it worth?"

"What?"

"The painting."

He shrugged. "A few grand."

"You and I speak different languages, Mr. Nicholls."

"You think? Okay, then, how much maintenance does your ex pay you?"

"Nothing."

"Nothing?" His eyebrows had lifted to somewhere round his hairline. "Nothing at all?"

"He's a mess. You can't punish someone for being a mess."

"Even if it means you and the kids have to struggle?"

How could she explain? It had taken her two years to work it out herself. She knew the kids missed him, but she was secretly relieved Marty had gone. She was relieved that she didn't have to worry about whether he was going to hijack their futures with his next ill-thought-out scheme. She was weary of his black moods and that he was permanently exhausted by the children. Mostly she was tired of never doing anything right. Marty had liked the sixteen-year-old Jess: the wild, impulsive, responsibility-free Jess. Then he had weighed her down with responsibility and hadn't liked who had emerged from under it.

"When he's sorted himself out, I'll make sure he contributes his share again. But we're okay." Jess glanced upstairs to where Nicky and Tanzie were sleeping. "I think this will be our turning point. And besides, you probably won't understand this, and I know everyone thinks they're a bit odd, but I'm the lucky one having them. They're kind and funny." She poured herself another glass of wine and took a gulp. It was definitely getting easier to drink.

"They're nice kids."

"Thank you," she said. "Actually, I realized something today. The last few days have been the first time I can remember where I just got to be with them. Not working, not running around doing housework or shopping or trying to catch up on all the stuff. It's been nice just hanging out with them, if that doesn't sound daft."

"It doesn't."

"And Nicky's sleeping. He never sleeps. I'm not sure what you did for him, but he seems —"

"Oh, we just redressed the balance a little."

Jess raised her glass. "Then one good thing happened on your birthday: you cheered up my boy."

"That was yesterday."

She thought for a moment. "You didn't vomit once."

"Okay. Stop now."

Mr. Nicholls's whole body had finally relaxed. He leaned back, his long legs stretched out under the table. For some time now one of them had been resting against hers. She had thought fleetingly that she should move it, and hadn't, and now she couldn't without looking as if she were making a point. She felt it, an electric presence, against her bare leg.

She quite liked it.

Because something had happened somewhere between the pie and chips and the last round, and it wasn't just drink. She wanted Mr. Nicholls not to feel angry and hopeless. She wanted to see that big, sleepy grin of his, the one that seemed to defuse all the suppressed anger spread across his face.

"You know, I've never met anyone like you," he said, gazing at the table.

Jess had been about to make a joke about cleaners and baristas and staff, but instead she just felt this great lurch in the pit of her belly and found herself picturing the taut *V* of his bare torso in the shower. And then she wondered what it would be like to have sex with Mr. Nicholls.

The shock of this thought was so great that she nearly said it out loud — *I think it*

would be nice to have sex with Mr. Nicholls.
She looked away, blushing, and gulped the remaining quarter glass of wine.

Mr. Nicholls was looking at her. "Don't take offense. I meant it in a good way."

"I'm not taking offense." Even her ears had gone pink.

"You're just the most positive person I've ever met. You never seem to feel sorry for yourself. Every obstacle that comes your way, you just scramble over it."

"Ripping my trousers and falling over in the process."

"But you keep going."

"When someone helps me."

"Okay. This simile is becoming confusing." He took a swig of his beer. "I just . . . wanted to tell you. I know it's nearly over. But I've enjoyed this trip. More than I expected to."

It was out before she knew what she was saying. "Yeah. Me, too."

They sat. He was looking at her leg. She wondered if he was thinking what she was thinking.

"Do you know something, Jess?"

"What?"

"You've stopped fidgeting."

They looked up at each other. She wanted to look away, but she couldn't. Mr. Nicholls had just been a means of moving forward out of an impossible mess. Now all Jess could see were his big dark eyes, the backs of his strong hands, the way his torso shifted under his T-shirt.

You need to get back on the horse.

He looked away first.

"Whoa! Look at the time. We should really get some sleep. You said we had to get up early." His voice was just a bit too loud.

"Yup. Nearly eleven already. I think I calculated that we need to leave here by seven to make it there for midday. Does that sound right to you?"

"Uh . . . sure."

She swayed a little when she stood up, and reached for his arm, but he'd already moved away.

They arranged an early breakfast, bade Mrs. Deakins a slightly-too-hearty good night, and made their way slowly up the stairs at the back of the pub. Jess was barely aware of what was said, for she was acutely conscious of him behind her. Of the way her hips moved when she walked. *Is he watching me?* Her mind swirled and dipped in unexpected directions. She wondered, briefly, what it would feel like if he were to lean forward and kiss her bare shoulder. She thought she might have made a small, involuntary sound at the thought of it.

They stopped on the landing, and she turned to face him. It felt as if, three days in, she'd only just seen him.

"Good night, then, Jessica Rae Thomas. With an *a* and an *e*."

Her hand came to rest on the door handle, and her breath caught in her throat. It had been so long. Would it really be such a bad idea? She pushed down on the handle and leaned in. "I'll . . . see you in the morning."

"I'd offer to make you coffee. But you're always up first."

She didn't know what to say. It was possible she was just gazing at him.

"Um . . . Jess?"

"What?"

"Thanks. For everything. The sickness stuff, the birthday surprise . . . In case I don't get a chance to say this tomorrow" — he gave her a lopsided smile — "as ex-wives go, you were definitely my favorite."

She pushed at the door. She was going to say something, but she was distracted by the fact that the door didn't move. She turned and pushed down on the handle again. It gave, opened an inch, and no more.

"What?"

"I can't open the door," she said, putting both her hands on it. Nothing.

Mr. Nicholls walked over and pushed. It gave the tiniest amount. "It's not locked," he said, working the handle. "There's something blocking it."

She squatted down, trying to see, and Mr. Nicholls turned on the landing light. Through the two inches of door space, she could just make out Norman's bulk on the other side of the door. He was lying on the mattress, his huge back to Jess.

"Norman," she hissed. "Move."

Nothing.

"Norman."

"If I push, he'll have to wake up, right?" Mr. Nicholls began leaning on the door. He rested his full weight on it. Then he pushed. "Jesus Christ," he said.

Jess shook her head. "You don't know my dog."

He let go of the handle and the door shut with a gentle click. They stared at each other.

"Well . . . ," he said finally. "There are two beds in here. It'll be fine."

She grimaced. "Um. Norman is sleeping on the other single. I moved the mattress in there earlier."

He looked at her wearily then. "Knock on the door?"

"Tanzie is stressed. I can't run the risk of

waking her. It's fine. I'll . . . I'll . . . just sleep on the chair."

Jess headed down to the bathroom before he could contradict her. She washed and brushed her teeth, gazing at her alcohol-flushed skin in the plastic-framed mirror and trying to stop her thoughts chasing themselves in circles.

When she arrived back at the room, Mr. Nicholls was holding up one of his dark gray T-shirts. "Here," he said, and threw it at her as he walked past to the bathroom. Jess changed into it, trying to ignore the vague eroticism of its scent, pulled the spare blanket and a pillow out of the wardrobe, and curled up in the chair, struggling to bring her knees up to a position that made it comfortable. It was going to be a long night.

Some minutes later, Mr. Nicholls opened the door and turned off the overhead light. He was wearing a white T-shirt and a pair of dark blue boxers. She saw that his legs bore the long, visible muscles of someone who does no-excuses exercise. She knew immediately how they would feel against her own. The thought made her swallow.

The little bed sagged audibly as he climbed in.

"Are you comfortable like that?"

"Totally fine!" she said too loudly. "You?"

"If one of these springs impales me while I sleep, you have my permission to take the car the rest of the way."

He gazed at her across the room for a moment longer, then turned out the bedside light.

The darkness was total. Outside, a faint breeze moaned through unseen gaps in the stone, trees rustled, and a car door slammed, its engine roaring a protest. In the next room, Norman whined in his sleep, the sound only partially muffled by the thin plasterboard wall. Jess could hear Mr. Nicholls breathing, and although she had spent the previous night only inches from him, she was acutely conscious of his presence in a way she hadn't been twenty-four hours earlier. She thought of the way he had made Nicky smile, of the way his fingers rested on a steering wheel.

She thought about an expression she had heard Nicky use a few weeks ago: YOLO — You only live once, and remembered how she had told him she thought it was just an excuse idiots used for doing pretty much anything they felt like doing, no matter what the consequences.

She thought about Liam, and how she

knew in her gut that he was probably having sex with someone right this minute — that ginger barmaid from the Blue Parrot, maybe, or the Dutch girl who drove the flower van. She thought about a conversation she'd had with Chelsea when Chelsea had told her she should lie about her kids because no man would ever fall in love with a single mother of two, and how Jess had gotten angry with her because deep down she knew she was probably right.

She thought about the fact that even if Mr. Nicholls didn't go to prison, she would probably never see him again after this trip.

And then, before she could think too hard about anything else, Jess eased herself silently out of the chair, letting the blanket fall to the floor. It took only four steps to reach the bed, and she hesitated, her bare toes curled in the acrylic carpet, even then not quite sure what she was doing. You only live once. And then in the inky dark there was a faint movement and she saw Mr. Nicholls turn to face her as she lifted the cover and climbed in.

Jess was chest to chest against him, her cool legs against his warm ones. There was nowhere else to go in this tiny bed, with the sag of the mattress pushing them closer together and its edge like a cliff drop just inches behind her. They were so close that she could breathe in the remnants of his aftershave, his toothpaste. She could feel the rise and fall of his chest, as her heart thumped erratically against his. She tilted her head a little, trying to read him. He put his right arm across the duvet, a surprisingly heavy weight, gathering her in closer to him. With his other, he took her hand and enclosed it slowly in his. It was dry and soft, and inches from her mouth. She wanted to lower her face to his knuckles and trace her lips along them. She wanted to reach her mouth up to his . . .

You only live once.

She lay there in the dark, paralyzed by her own longing.

"Do you want to have sex with me?" she said into the darkness.

There was a long silence.

"Did you hear what —"

"Yes," he said. "And . . . no." He spoke again before she could turn completely to stone. "I just think it would make things too complicated."

"It's not complicated. We're both young, lonely, a bit pissed. And after tonight we're never going to see each other again."

"How so?"

"You'll go back to London and lead your

city life, and I'll be down on the coast lead-
ing mine. It doesn't have to be a big deal."

He was silent for a minute. "Jess . . . I
don't think so."

"You don't fancy me." She prickled with
embarrassment, remembering suddenly
what he'd said about his ex. Lara was a
model, for crissakes. She shifted away from
him, and his hand tightened around hers.

"You're beautiful." His voice was a murmur in her ear.

She waited. His thumb brushed over her
palm. "So . . . why won't you sleep with
me?"

He didn't say anything.

"Look. Here's the thing. I haven't had sex
in three years. I sort of need to get back on
the horse, and I think it — you — would be
great."

"You want me to be a horse."

"Not like that. I need a metaphorical
horse."

"And now we're back to the weird meta-
phors."

"Look, a woman you say you find beautiful is offering you no-strings sex. I don't
understand the problem."

"There's no such thing as no-strings sex."

"What?"

"Someone always wants something."

"I don't want anything from you."

She felt him shrug. "Not now, maybe."

"Wow." She turned onto her side. "She really got to you, didn't she?"

"I just . . ."

Jess slid her foot along his leg. "You think I'm trying to lure you in? You think this is me trying to entrap you with my womanly wiles? My womanly wiles, a nylon bedspread, and pie and chips?" She interlinked her fingers with his, let her voice drop to a whisper. She felt unleashed, reckless. She thought she might actually faint with how much she wanted him then. "I don't want a relationship, Ed. With you or anyone. There's no room in my life for the whole one-plus-one thing." She tilted her face so that her mouth was inches from his. "I'd have thought that would be obvious."

He moved his hips an awkward fraction away from hers. "You are . . . incredibly persuasive."

"And you are . . ." She hooked her leg around him, pulling him closer. His hardness made her briefly giddy.

He swallowed.

Her lips were millimeters from his now. All the nerves of her body had somehow concentrated themselves in her skin. Or maybe his skin — she could no longer tell.

"It's the last night. At worst we can exchange a glance over the vacuum cleaner and I'll just remember this as a nice night with a nice guy who actually was a nice guy." She let her lips graze his chin. It carried the faint trace of stubble. She wanted to bite it. "You, of course, will remember it as the greatest sex you ever had."

"And that's it." His voice was thick, distracted.

Jess moved closer. "That's it," she murmured.

"You'd have made a great negotiator."

"Do you ever stop talking?" She moved forward until her lips met his. She almost jolted. She felt the pressure of his mouth on hers as he ceded to her, the sweetness of him. And she no longer cared about anything. She wanted him. She burned with it.

And then he pulled back. She felt, rather than saw, Ed Nicholls gazing at her. His eyes were black in the darkness, unfathomable. He moved his hand and as it brushed lightly against her stomach she gave a faint, involuntary shiver.

"Fuck," he said quietly. "Fucking fuck." And then, with a groan, he said, "You will actually thank me for this tomorrow."

And he gently disentangled himself from her, climbed out of bed, walked over to the chair, sat down, and, with a great sigh, hauled the blanket over himself and turned away.

CHAPTER TWENTY:
ED

Ed Nicholls had thought that spending eight hours in a damp car park was the worst possible way to spend a night. Then he'd concluded that the worst way to spend a night was hoicking your guts up in a stationary RV somewhere near Derby. He was wrong on both counts. The worst way to spend a night, it turned out, was in a tiny room a few feet from a slightly drunk, good-looking woman who wanted to have sex with you and whom you had, like an idiot, rebuffed.

Jess fell asleep, or pretended to: it was impossible to tell. Ed sat in the world's most uncomfortable chair, staring out of the narrow gap in the curtains at the black moonlit sky, his right leg going to sleep, and his left foot freezing cold where it wouldn't fit under the blanket. He tried not to think about the fact that if he hadn't leaped out of that bed, he could be there, curled around her right now, his lips pressed against her skin, those lithe legs tangled with his . . .

No.

Either (a) the sex would have been terrible, they would have been mortified afterward, and the five hours spent traveling to the Olympiad would have been excruciating. Or (b) the sex would have been fine, they would have woken up embarrassed, and the journey would still have been excruciating. Worse, they could have ended up with (c): the sex would have been off the scale (he slightly suspected this one was correct — he kept getting a hard-on just thinking about her mouth), they would develop feelings for each other based purely on sexual chemistry, and (d) would then have to adjust to the fact that they had nothing in common and were just completely unsuited in every other way, or (e) they would find they were not entirely unsuited, but then he would be sent to prison. And none of these considered that Jess had actual kids, kids who needed stability in their lives and not someone such as he: he liked children as a concept, in the same way that he liked the Indian subcontinent — that is, it was nice to know it existed, but he had no knowledge about it and had never felt any real desire to spend time there.

And all this was without the added factor that he was obviously crap at relationships, had only just come out of the two most disastrous examples anyone could imagine, and the odds of his getting it right with someone else on the basis of a lengthy car journey that had begun because he couldn't think of how to get out of it were lower than a very low thing indeed.

And the whole horse conversation had been, frankly, weird.

And these points could be supplemented by the wilder possibilities that he had completely failed to consider. What if Jess was a psycho, and all that stuff about not wanting a relationship was just a way to reel him in? She didn't seem that sort of girl, sure.

But neither had Deanna.

Ed sat pondering this and other tangled things, and wishing he could talk a single one of them through with Ronan, until the sky turned orange then neon blue and his leg became completely dead and his hangover, which had formerly manifested itself as a vague tightness at his temples, turned into an emphatic, skull-crushing headache. Ed tried not to look at Jess as the outline of her face and body under the duvet became clear in the encroaching light.

And he tried not to feel wistful for a time when having sex with a woman you liked had just been about having sex with a woman you liked and hadn't involved a series of equations so complex and unlikely that probably only Tanzie could have got anywhere near understanding them.

"Come on. We're running late." Jess shepherded Nicky — a pale, T-shirt-clad zombie — toward the car.

"I didn't get any breakfast."

"That's because you wouldn't get up when I told you. We'll get you something on the way. Tanze. Tanzie? Has the dog been to the loo?"

The morning sky was the color of lead and seemed to have descended to a point around their ears. A faint drizzle promised heavier rain. Ed sat in the driver's seat as Jess ran around, organizing, scolding, promising, in a fury of activity. She had been like this since he'd woken, groggily, from what seemed like twenty minutes' sleep. He didn't think she had met his eye once. Tanzie climbed silently into the backseat.

"You okay?" He yawned and looked at the little girl in the rearview mirror.

She nodded silently.

"Nerves?"

She didn't say anything.

"Been sick?"

She nodded.

"It's all the rage on this trip. You'll be great. Really."

She gave him the look he would have given any adult if they had said the same, then turned to stare out of the window, her face round and pale. Ed wondered how late she had stayed up studying.

"Right." Jess shoved Norman into the backseat. He brought with him an almost overwhelming scent of wet dog. She checked that Tanzie had done up her belt, climbed into the passenger seat, and finally turned to Ed. Her expression was unreadable. "Let's go."

Ed's car no longer looked like his car. In just three days its immaculate cream interior had acquired new scents and stains, a fine sprinkling of dog hair, jumpers and shoes that now lived on seats or wedged underneath them. The floor crunched underfoot with dropped sweet wrappers and crisps. The radio stations were no longer on settings he understood.

But something had happened while he was driving along at forty m.p.h. The faint sense

that he should actually have been somewhere else had begun to fade, almost without his being aware of it. He found himself
glancing at the people they passed, buying
food, driving their cars, walking their children to and from school in worlds completely different from his own, knowing
nothing of his own little drama several
hundred miles south. It made it all seem
reduced in size, a model village of problems
rather than something that loomed over
him.

Despite the pointed silence from the
woman beside him, Nicky's sleeping face in
the rearview mirror ("Teenagers don't really
do Before Eleven O'clock," Tanzie explained), and the occasional foul eruptions
of the dog, it slowly dawned on him as they
crept closer to their destination that he was
feeling a complete lack of the relief he had
expected to feel at the prospect of having
his car, his life, back to himself. What he
felt was more complex. Ed fiddled with the
speakers, so that the music was loudest in
the rear seats and temporarily silent in the
front.

"You okay?"

Jess didn't look round. "I'm fine."

Ed glanced behind him, making sure

nobody was listening. "About last night," he began.

"Forget it."

He wanted to tell her that he regretted it. He wanted to tell her that his body had actually hurt with the effort of not climbing back into that sagging single bed. But what would have been the point? Like she'd said the previous evening, they were two people who had no reason to see each other ever again.

"I can't forget it. I wanted to explain —"

"Nothing to explain. You were right. It was a stupid idea." She tucked her legs under her and stared away from him out of the window.

"It's just my life is too —"

"Really. It's not an issue. I just" — she let out a deep breath — "I just want to make sure we get to the Olympiad on time."

"But I don't want us to end it all like this."

"There's nothing to end." She put her feet on the dashboard. It felt like a statement. "Let's go."

"How many miles is it to Aberdeen?" Tanzie's face appeared between the front seats.

"What, left?"

"No. From Southampton."

Ed pulled his phone from his jacket and

handed it to her. "Look it up on the Maps app."

She tapped the screen, her brow furrowed. "About five hundred and eighty?"

"Sounds about right."

"So if we're doing forty miles an hour, we'd have had to do at least six hours' driving a day. And if I didn't get sick, we could have done it —"

"In a day. At a push."

"One day." Tanzie digested this, her eyes trained on the Scottish hillsides in the distance ahead. "But we wouldn't have had such a nice time then, would we?"

Ed glanced sideways at Jess. "No, we wouldn't."

It took a moment before Jess's gaze slid back toward him. "No, sweetheart," she said after a beat. And her smile was oddly rueful. "No, we wouldn't."

The car ate the miles sleekly and efficiently. They crossed the Scottish border, and Ed tried — and failed — to raise a cheer. They stopped once for Tanzie to go to the loo, once twenty minutes later for Nicky to go ("I can't help it. I didn't have to go when Tanze did"), and three times for Norman (two were false alarms). Jess sat silently beside him, checking her watch and chewing at her nails. Nicky watched groggily out the window at the empty landscape, at the few flinty houses set into rolling hills. Ed wondered what would happen to Nicky after this was over. He wanted to suggest fifty other things to help him, but he tried to imagine someone suggesting things to him at the same age, and guessed he would have taken no notice at all. He wondered how Jess would keep him safe when they returned home.

The phone rang and he glanced over, his heart sinking. "Lara."

"Eduardo. Baby. I need to talk to you about this apartment."

He was aware of Jess's sudden rigidity, the flicker of her gaze. He wished, suddenly, that he hadn't chosen to answer the call.

"Lara, I'm not going to discuss this now."

"It's not a lot of money. Not for you. I spoke to my solicitor and he says it would be nothing for you to pay for it."

"I told you before, Lara, we made a final settlement."

He was suddenly conscious of the acute stillness of three people in the car.

"Eduardo. Baby. I need to sort this out with you."

"Lara —"

Before he could say anything more, Jess

reached over and grabbed the phone. "Hello, Lara," she said. "Jess here. I'm awfully sorry but he can't pay for any more of your stuff, so there's really no point in ringing him anymore."

A short silence. Then an explosive: "Who is this?"

"I'm his new wife. Oh, and he'd like his Chairman Mao picture back. Perhaps just leave it with his lawyer. Okay? In your own time. Thanks so much."

The resulting silence had the same quality as the few seconds before an atomic explosion. But before any of them could hear what happened next, Jess flipped the Off button, and handed it back to him. He took it gingerly, and turned it off.

"Thank you," he said. "I think."

"You're welcome." She didn't look at him when she spoke.

Ed glanced into his rearview mirror. He couldn't be sure, but he thought Nicky was trying very hard not to laugh.

Somewhere between Edinburgh and Dundee, on a narrow, wooded lane, they had to slow down and then stop for a herd of cows in the road. The animals moved around the car, gazing in at its inhabitants with vague curiosity, a moving black sea, eyes rolling in woolly black heads. Norman stared back.

"Aberdeen Angus," said Nicky.

Suddenly, without warning, Norman hurled his whole body, snarling and growling at the window. The car jolted to one side, the backseat a chaotic mass of arms and noise and writhing dog. Nicky and Jess fought to reach him.

"Mum!"

"Norman! Stop!" The dog was on top of Tanzie, his face hard against the window. Ed could just make out her glittery pink jacket, flailing underneath him.

Jess lunged over the seat at the dog, grabbing for his collar. They dragged Norman back down from the window. He whined, shrill and hysterical, straining at their grasp, great gobs of drool spraying across the interior.

"Norman, you big idiot! What the hell —"

"He's never seen a cow before," Tanzie said, struggling upright.

"Jesus, Norman." Nicky grimaced.

"You okay, Tanze?"

"I'm fine."

The cows continued to part around the car, unmoved by the dog's outburst. Through the now steamed windows they could just make out the farmer at the rear, walking slowly and impassively, with the same lumbering gait as his bovine charges. He gave the barest of nods as he passed, as if he had all the time in the world. Norman whined and pulled against his collar.

"I've never seen him like that before." Jess straightened her hair and blew out through her cheeks. "Perhaps he could smell beef."

"I didn't know he had it in him," Ed said.

"My glasses." Tanzie held up the twisted piece of metal. "Mum. Norman broke my glasses."

It was a quarter past ten.

"I can't see anything without my glasses." Jess looked at Ed. *Shit.*

"Okay," he said. "Grab a plastic bag. I'm going to have to put my foot down."

The Scottish roads were wide and empty, and Ed drove so fast that the GPS had to repeatedly reassess its timing to their destination. Every minute they gained was an imaginary air punch in his head. Tanzie was sick twice. He refused to stop to allow her to vomit into the road.

"She's really ill," Jess said.

"I'm fine," Tanzie kept saying, her face wedged into a plastic bag. "Really."

"You don't want to stop, sweetheart? Just for a minute?"

"No. Keep going. Bleurgh —"

There wasn't time to stop. Not that this made the car journey any easier to bear. Nicky had turned away from his sister, his hand over his nose. Even Norman's head was thrust as far out the window, into the fresh air, as he could get it.

He would get them there. He felt filled with purpose in a way that he hadn't in months. And finally, Aberdeen loomed before them, its buildings vast and silver gray, the oddly modern high-rises thrusting into the distant sky. He headed for the center, watched as the roads narrowed and became cobbled streets. They came through the docks, the enormous tankers on their right, and that was where the traffic slowed, and his confidence began to unravel. They sat in an increasingly anxious silence, Ed punching in alternative routes across Aberdeen that offered no time gain. The GPS started to work against him, adding back the time it had subtracted. It was fifteen, nineteen, twenty-two minutes until they reached the university building. Twenty-five minutes. Too many.

"What's the delay?" said Jess, to nobody in particular. She fiddled with the radio buttons, trying to find the traffic reports. "What's the holdup?"

"It's just sheer weight of traffic."

"That's such a lame expression," said Nicky. "Of course a traffic jam is sheer weight of traffic. What else would it be down to?"

"There could have been an accident," said Tanzie.

"But the jam itself would still comprise the traffic," Ed mused. "So technically, the problem is still the sheer weight of traffic."

"No, the volume of traffic slowing itself down is something completely different."

"But it's the same result."

"But then it's an inaccurate description."

Jess peered at the GPS. "Can we just focus here, people? Are we in the right place? I wouldn't have thought the docks would be near the university."

"We have to get through the docks to get to the university."

"You're sure?"

"I'm sure, Jess." Ed tried to suppress the tension in his voice. "Look at the GPS."

There was a brief silence. In front of them the traffic lights changed through two cycles without anybody moving. Jess, on the other hand, moved incessantly, fidgeting in her seat, peering around her to see if there was some clear route they might have missed. He couldn't blame her. He felt the same.

"I don't think we've got time to get new glasses," he murmured to her, when they'd sat through the fourth cycle.

"But she can't see without them."

"If we look for a chemist, we're not going to make it there for midday."

She bit her lip, then turned round in her seat. "Tanze? Is there any way you can see through the unbroken lens? Any way at all?"

A pale green face emerged from the plastic bag. "I'll try," it said.

Traffic stopped and stalled. They grew silent, the tension within the car ratcheting up. When Norman whined, they growled, "Shut up, Norman!" as one. Ed felt his blood pressure rising. Why hadn't they left half an hour earlier? Why hadn't he worked this out better? What would happen if they missed it? He glanced sideways to where Jess was tapping her knee nervously and guessed that she was thinking the same thing. And then finally, inexplicably, as if the gods had been toying with them, the traffic cleared.

He flung the car through the cobbled streets, Jess yelling, *"Go! Go!"* and leaning forward on the dashboard as if she were a coachman driving a horse. He skidded the car around the bends, almost too fast for the GPS, which hiccupped its instructions, and entered the university campus, then followed the small printed signs that had been placed haphazardly on random poles until they found the Downes Building, an unlovely 1970s office block in the same gray granite as everything else.

The car screeched into a parking space in front of it, and as Ed cut the ignition, everything stopped. He let out a long breath and glanced at the clock. It was six minutes to twelve.

"This is it?" Jess said peering out.

"This is it."

Jess appeared suddenly paralyzed, as if she couldn't believe they were actually there. She undid her seat belt and stared at the car park, at the boys strolling in as if they had all the time in the world, reading off electronic devices, accompanied by tense-looking parents. The kids were all wearing private school uniforms. "I thought it would be . . . bigger," she said.

Nicky gazed out through the dank gray drizzle. "Yeah. Because advanced maths is such a crowd-pleaser."

"I can't see anything," said Tanzie.

"Look, you guys go in and register. I'll get her some glasses."

Jess turned to him. "But they won't be the right prescription."

"It'll be better than nothing. Just go. *Go.*"

He could see her staring after him as he skidded out of the car park and headed back toward the city center.

It took seven minutes and three attempts to find a chemist large enough to sell reading glasses. Ed screeched to a halt so dramatic that Norman shot forward and his great head collided with his shoulder. The dog resettled himself on the backseat, grumbling.

"Stay here," Ed told him, and bolted inside.

The shop was empty aside from an old woman with a basket and two assistants talking in lowered voices. He skidded around the shelves, past tampons and toothbrushes, corn plasters and reduced Christmas gift sets until he finally found the stand by the till. Dammit. He couldn't remember if she was far- or nearsighted. He reached for his phone to ask, then remembered he didn't have Jess's number.

"Fuck. Fuck. Fuck." Ed stood there, trying to guess. Tanzie's glasses looked as if they might be pretty strong. He had never seen her without them. Would that mean she was more likely to be nearsighted? Didn't all children tend to be nearsighted?

It was adults who held things away from them to see, surely. He hesitated for about ten seconds and then, after a moment's indecision, pulled them all from their rack, far- and nearsighted, mild and super strength, and dumped them on the counter in a clear plastic-wrapped pile.

The girl broke off her conversation with the old woman. She looked down at the glasses, then up at him. Ed saw her clock the drool on his collar and tried to wipe it surreptitiously with his sleeve. This succeeded in smearing it across his lapel.

"All of them. I'll take all of them," he said. "But only if you can ring them up in less than thirty seconds."

She looked over at her supervisor, who gave Ed a penetrating stare, then an imperceptible nod. Without a word, the girl began to ring them up, carefully positioning each pair in a bag. "No. No time. Just chuck them in," he said, reaching past her to thrust them into the plastic carrier.

"Do you have a loyalty card?"

"No. No loyalty card."

"We're doing a special three for two offer on diet bars today. Would you like —"

Ed scrambled to pick up the glasses that had fallen from the counter. "No diet bars," he said. "No offers. Thank you. I just need to pay."

"That'll be a hundred and seventy-four pounds," she said finally. "Sir."

She peered over her shoulder then, as if half expecting the arrival of a prank television crew. But Ed scribbled his signature, grabbed the carrier bag, and ran for the car. He heard "No manners" in a strong Scottish accent as he left.

There was nobody in the car park when he returned. He pulled up right outside the door, leaving Norman clambering wearily onto the backseat, and ran inside, down the echoing corridor. "Maths competition? Maths competition?" he yelled at anyone he passed. A man pointed wordlessly to a laminated sign. Ed bolted up a flight of steps two at a time, along another corridor, and into an anteroom. Two men sat behind a desk. On the other side of the room stood Jess and Nicky. She took a step toward him. "Got them." He held up the carrier bag, triumphantly. He was so out of breath he could barely speak.

"She's gone in," she said. "They've started."

He looked up at the clock, breathing hard. It was seven minutes past twelve.

"Excuse me?" he said to the man at the

desk. "I need to give a girl in there her glasses."

The man looked up slowly. He eyed the plastic bag Ed held in front of him.

Ed leaned right over the desk, thrusting the bag toward him. "She broke her glasses on the way here. She can't see without them."

"I'm sorry, sir. I can't let anyone in now."

Ed nodded. "Yes. Yes, you can. Look, I'm not trying to cheat or sneak anything in. I just didn't know her glasses type so I had to buy every pair. You can check them. All of them. Look. No secret codes. Just glasses." He held the bag open in front of him. "You have to take them in to her so she can find a pair that fits."

The man gave a slow shake of his head. "Sir, we can't allow anything to disrupt the other —"

"Yes. Yes, you can. It's an emergency."

"It's the rules."

Ed stared at him hard for a full ten seconds. Then he straightened up, put a hand to his head, and started to walk away from him. He could feel a new pressure building inside him, like a kettle juddering on a hot plate. "You know something?" he said, turning around. "It has taken us three solid days and nights to get here. Three days in which

I have had my very nice car filled with vomit, and unmentionable things done to my upholstery by a dog. I don't even like dogs. I have slept in a car with a virtual stranger. Not in a good way. I have stayed places no reasonable human being should have to stay. I have eaten an apple that had been down the too-tight trousers of a teenage boy and a kebab that for all I know contained human flesh. I have left a huge, huge personal crisis in London and driven five hundred and eighty miles with people I don't know — very nice people — because even I could see that this competition was really, really important to them. Vitally important. Because all the little girl in there cares about is maths. And if she doesn't get a pair of glasses she can actually see through, she can't compete fairly in your competition. And if she can't compete fairly, she blows her only chance to go to the school that she really, really needs to go to. And if that happens, you know what I'll do?"

The man stared.

"I will go into that room of yours, and I will walk around to every single maths paper and I will rip them into teeny-tiny pieces. And I will do it very, very quickly, before you have a chance to call your security guards. And you know why I will do this?"

The man swallowed. "No."

"Because all this has to have been worth something." Ed went back to him and leaned close to him. "It has to."

Something had happened to Ed's face. He could feel it, the way it seemed to have twisted itself into shapes he had never felt before. And in the way Jess stepped forward and gently put her hand on his arm.

She passed the man the bag of glasses. "We'd be really, really grateful if you took her the glasses," she said quietly.

The man stood up and walked around the desk toward the door. He kept his eyes on Ed at all times. "I'll see what I can do," he said. And the door closed gently behind him.

They walked out to the car in silence, oblivious to the rain. Jess unloaded the bags. Nicky stood off to the side, his hands thrust as far into his jeans pockets as he could manage. Which, given the tightness of his jeans, wasn't very far.

"Well, we made it." She allowed herself a small smile.

"I said we would." Ed nodded toward the car. "Shall I wait here until she's finished?"

She wrinkled her nose. "No. You're fine. We've held you up long enough."

Ed felt his smile sag a little. "Where will you sleep tonight?"

"If she does well, I might treat us to a fancy hotel. If she doesn't . . ." She shrugged. "Bus shelter." The way she said this suggested she didn't believe it.

She walked around to the rear door of the car. Norman, who had glanced at the rain and decided not to get out, looked up at her.

Jess stuck her head through the door. "Norman, time to go."

A small pile of bags sat on the wet ground behind the Audi. She hauled a jacket out of a bag and handed it to Nicky. "Come on, it's cold."

The air held the salt tang of the sea. It made him think suddenly of Beachfront. "So . . . is this . . . it?"

"This is it. Thank you for the lift. I . . . we . . . all appreciate it. The glasses. Everything."

They looked at each other properly for the first time that day, and there were about a billion things he wanted to say.

Nicky lifted an awkward hand. "Yeah. Mr. Nicholls. Thanks."

"Oh. Here." Ed reached into his pocket for the phone he had pulled from the glove compartment and tossed it to him. "It's a backup. I, um, don't need it anymore."

"Really?" Nicky caught it with one hand and gazed at it, disbelieving.

Jess frowned. "We can't take that. You've done enough for us."

"It's not a big deal. Really. If Nicky doesn't take it, I'll only have to send it off to one of those recycling places. You're just saving me a job."

Jess glanced down at her feet as if she were going to say something else. And then she looked up and hauled her hair briskly into an unnecessary ponytail.

"Well. Thanks again." She thrust a hand toward him. Ed hesitated, then shook it, trying to ignore the sudden flash of memory from the previous evening.

"Good luck with your dad. And the lunch. And the whole work thing. I'm sure it will come out good. Remember, good things happen." When she pulled her hand away, he felt weirdly as if he'd lost something. She turned and looked over her shoulder, already distracted. "Right. Let's find somewhere dry to stick our stuff."

"Hold on." Ed hauled a business card from his jacket, scribbled a number, and walked over to her. "Call me."

One of the numbers was smudged. He saw her staring at it.

"That's a three." He altered it, then shoved his hands into his pockets, feeling like an awkward teenager. "I'd like to know how Tanzie gets on. Please."

She nodded. And then she was gone, propelling the boy in front of her like a particularly vigilant shepherd. He stood and watched them, lugging their oversized hold-alls and the huffing, recalcitrant dog, until they rounded the corner of the gray concrete building and were gone.

The car was silent. Even in the hours when nobody spoke, Ed had become used to the faintly steamed windows, the vague sense of constant movement that came from being in close confinement with other people. The muffled ping of Nicky's games console. Jess's constant fidgeting. Now he gazed around the car's interior and felt as if he was standing in a deserted house. He saw the crumbs and the apple core that had been stuffed into the rear ashtray, the melted chocolate, the newspaper folded into the pocket of the seat. His damp clothes on wire hangers across the rear windows. He saw the maths book, half wedged down the side of the seat, which Tanzie had evidently missed in her hurry to get out, and won-dered whether to take it to her. But what was the point? It was too late.

It was too late.

He sat in the car park, watching the last of the parents walking to their cars, killing time as they waited for their charges. He leaned forward and rested his head on the steering wheel for some time. And then, when his was the only car left there, he put his key into the ignition and drove away.

Ed had gone about twenty miles before he became aware of quite how tired he was. The combination of three nights of broken sleep, a hangover, and hundreds of miles of driving hit him like a demolition ball, and he felt his eyes drooping. He turned up the radio, opened his windows, and when that failed, he pulled into a roadside café to get some coffee.

Although it was lunchtime, the cafe was half empty. A couple of suited men sat at opposite ends of the room, lost in mobile phones and paperwork, the wall behind them offering sixteen different permutations of sausage, egg, bacon, chips, and beans. Ed grabbed a newspaper from the stand and made his way to a table. He ordered coffee from the waitress.

"I'm sorry, sir, but at this time of day we reserve tables for those eating." Her accent was strong enough that he had to think quite hard to work out what she had said.

"Oh. Right. Well, I —"

MAJOR UK TECHNOLOGY COMPANY IN INSIDER TRADING PROBE

He stared at the newspaper headline.

"Sir?"

"Mm?" His skin began to prickle.

"You have to order some food. If you want to sit down."

"Oh."

The Financial Services Authority confirmed last night that it is investigating a traded UK technology company for insider trading worth millions of pounds. The investigation is understood to be taking place on both sides of the Atlantic, and involves the London and New York stock exchanges and the SEC, the US equivalent to the FSA.

Nobody has yet been arrested, but a source within the City of London police said that this was "simply a matter of time."

"Sir?"

She'd said it twice before he heard her. He looked up. A young woman, her nose freckled, her natural hair teased and fluffed into a kind of matted arrangement. "What would you like to eat?"

"Whatever." His mouth was the consistency of powder.

A pause.

"Um. Do you want me to tell you today's specials? Or some of our more popular dishes?"

Simply a matter of time.

"We do an all-day Burns breakfast —"

"Fine."

"And we . . . You want the Burns breakfast?"

"Yes."

"Do you want white or brown bread with that?"

"Whatever."

He felt her staring at him. Then she scribbled a note, tucked her pad carefully into her waistband, and walked away. And he sat and stared at the newspaper on the Formica table. Over the past seventy-two hours he might have felt like the whole world had gone topsy-turvy, but that had been a mere taste of what was about to come.

"I'm with a client."

"This won't take a minute." He took a

breath. "I'm not going to be at Dad's lunch."

A short, ominous silence.

"Please tell me I'm hallucinating through my ears."

"I can't. Something's come up."

"Something."

"I'll explain later."

"No. You wait. Hold on."

He heard the muffled sound of a hand over a phone. Possibly a clenched fist. "Sandra, I need to take this outside. Back in a . . ." Footsteps. And then, as if someone had turned up the volume to full blast: "Really? Are you fucking kidding me? Really?"

"I'm sorry."

"I can't believe I'm hearing this. Do you have any idea how hard Mum's worked to pull it together? Do you have any idea how much they're looking forward to seeing you? Dad sat down last week and worked out how long it had been since they last saw you. December, Ed. That's four months. Four months in which he's got more and more sick and you have fucking well failed to do anything useful other than send him some stupid fucking magazines."

"He said he liked *The New Yorker.* I thought it gave him something to do."

343

"He can barely fucking see, Ed. As you'd know if you'd bothered to come up. And Mum gets so bored reading those long pieces that her brain actually starts to seep through her ears."

On and on she went. It was like having a hair dryer turned on full blast in his ear.

"She's actually cooked your favorite food rather than Dad's for Dad's birthday lunch. That's how much she wants to see you. And now, twenty-four hours before the actual thing, you just announce that you can't come? No explanation? What the hell is this?"

His ears actually grew warm. He sat there, closed his eyes. When he opened them, it was twenty to two. The Olympiad would now be more than three quarters through. He thought of Tanzie in that university hall, her head bent over her papers, the floor around her littered with redundant spectacles. He hoped for her sake that, faced with a pageful of figures, she would relax and do the thing she was so plainly made to do. He thought of Nicky, sloping around outside, perhaps trying to find somewhere for a sneaky smoke.

He thought of Jess, seated on a holdall, the dog at her side, her hands clasped together on her knees as if in prayer, convinced that if she wished hard enough, good things would finally happen.

"You are a bloody disgrace for a human being, Ed. Really." His sister's voice was choked by tears.

"I know."

"Oh, and don't think I'm going to tell them. I'm not doing your damned dirty work for you."

"Gem. Please, there is a reason —"

"Don't even think about it. You want to break their hearts, then you do it. I'm done here, Ed. I can't believe you're my brother."

Ed swallowed hard as she put down the phone. And then he let out a long slow, shuddering breath. What was the difference? It was only half of what they would all say if they knew the truth.

It was there, in the half-empty restaurant, seated on a red leatherette banquette and facing a slowly congealing breakfast he didn't want, that Ed finally understood how much he missed his father. He would have given anything just to see that reassuring nod, to watch that somehow reluctant smile break over his face. He hadn't missed his home for the fifteen years since he had left it, yet suddenly he felt so homesick that it overwhelmed him. He sat in the restaurant staring out of the faintly greasy window at the cars whizzing past on the motorway and something he couldn't quite identify broke over him like the rolling of a vast wave. For the first time in his adult life, even through the divorce, the investigation, the thing with Deanna Lewis, Ed Nicholls found he was fighting back tears.

He sat and pressed his hands into his eyes and tightened his jaw until he could think about nothing other than the feeling of his back teeth pressing against each other.

"Is everything okay?"

The young waitress's eyes were vaguely wary, as if she were trying to assess whether this man was going to be trouble.

"Fine," he said. He had meant to sound reassuring, but his voice cracked on the word. And then, when she didn't seem convinced: "Migraine."

Her face relaxed immediately. "Oh. Migraine. Sympathies. They're buggers. You got something for it?"

Ed shook his head, not trusting himself to speak.

"I knew there was something wrong." She stood in front of him for a moment. "Hold on." She walked over to the counter, one hand reaching up to the back of her head, where her hair was pinned into an elaborate twist. She leaned over, fumbling toward something he couldn't see, then walked back slowly. She glanced behind her, then dropped two pills in a foil casing on his table.

"I'm not meant to give customers pills, obviously, but these are great. Only thing that works for mine. Don't drink any more coffee, though — it'll make it worse. I'll get you some water."

He blinked at her, then down at the pills.

"It's okay. They're nothing dodgy. Just Migra-gone."

"That's very kind of you."

"They take about twenty minutes. But then — oh! Relief!" Her smile wrinkled her nose. Kind eyes under all the mascara, he saw now.

She took away his coffee mug, as if to protect him from himself. Ed found himself thinking about Jess. Good things happen. Sometimes when you least expect them.

"Thank you," he said quietly.

"You're welcome."

And then his phone rang. The sound echoed in the roadside café and he gazed down at the screen as he stemmed the sound. Not a number he recognized.

"Mr. Nicholls?"

"Yes?"

"It's Nicky. Nicky Thomas. Um. I'm really

sorry to bother you. But we need your help."

CHAPTER TWENTY-ONE: NICKY

It had been obvious to Nicky that this was a bad idea from the moment they had pulled into the car park. Every other kid at that place — apart from maybe one or two at the most — was a boy. Every single one was at least two years older than Tanze. Most looked like they were not unfamiliar with the Asperger's scale. They wore wool blazers, bad haircuts, braces, the well-worn shirts of the properly middle class. Their parents drove Volvos. Tanzie, in her pink trousers and denim jacket with the felt flowers that Jess had sewn on, was as out of place as if she had been dropped there from outer space.

Nicky knew Tanzie was uncomfortable, even before Norman had broken her glasses. She had grown quieter and quieter in the car, locked in her own little world of nerves and car sickness. He had tried to nudge her out of it — this was actually an act of epic

selflessness, as she smelled pretty bad —
but by the time they had hit Aberdeen, she
had retreated so far inside herself that she
was unreachable. Jess was so focused on getting there that she couldn't see it. She was
all tied up with Mr. Nicholls, the glasses,
and the sick bags. She hadn't considered
for a minute that kids from private schools
could be just as mean as kids from
McArthur's.

Jess had been at the desk registering Tanzie and collecting her name tag and paperwork. Nicky had been checking out Mr.
Nicholls's phone and had stood off to the
side with Norman to keep him out of
everyone's way, so he hadn't really paid any
attention to the two boys who had gone to
stand next to Tanzie as she peered up at the
desk plan at the entrance to the hall. He
couldn't hear them because he had his earbuds in, and he was listening to Depeche
Mode without really noticing anything at
all. Until he caught sight of Tanzie's crest-
fallen face. And he pulled an earbud from
one ear.

The boy with the braces was staring at
her, a slow up and down. "You are at the
right place? You know that the Justin Bieber
fan convention is down the road?"

The skinnier boy laughed.

Tanzie looked at them with round eyes.

"Have you been to an Olympiad before?"

"No," she said.

"*Quel* surprise. I can't say many Olympians bring furry pencil cases. Have you got your furry pencil case, James?"

"I think I forgot mine. Oh, dear."

"My mum made it for me," Tanzie said stiffly.

"Your mum made it for you." They looked at each other. "Is it your lucky pencil case?"

"Do you know anything about string theory?"

"I think she's more likely to know about stink theory. Or . . . hey, James, can you smell something unpleasant? Like vomit? Do you think someone's a bit nervous?"

Tanzie ducked her head and bolted past them into the loos.

"That's the Gents!" they cried, and fell about laughing.

Nicky had been struggling to tie Norman's lead to a radiator. Now as the boys made to walk into the main hall he stepped forward and put his hand on the back of Braces' neck. "Hey, kid. *Hey!*"

The boy spun round. His eyes widened. Nicky moved in, so that his voice was a low whisper. He was suddenly glad that he had a weird yellow tinge to his skin and a scar on the side of his face. "Dude. A word. You ever speak to my sister like that again — anyone's sister — and I will personally come back here and tie your legs into a complex equation. You got that?"

He nodded, his mouth open.

Nicky gave him his best Fisher Psycho Stare. Long enough for the boy to do one of those massive Adam's-apple-bobbing gulps. "Not nice being nervous, is it?"

The boy shook his head.

Nicky patted him on the shoulder. "Good. Glad we're straight. Go do your sums." He turned and began to walk toward the loos.

One of the teachers stepped in front of him then, one hand raised, his face questioning. "Excuse me? Did I just see you —"

"Wishing him luck? Yes. Great kid. Great kid." Nicky shook his head, as if in admiration, then headed for the Gents to fetch Tanzie.

When Jess and Tanzie emerged from the ladies', Tanzie's top was damp where Jess had scrubbed at it with soap and water, her face blotchy and pale.

"You don't want to pay any attention to a little squirt like that, Tanze," Nicky said, climbing to his feet. "He was just trying to put you off."

"Which one was it?" Jess's expression was flinty. "Tell me, Nicky."

Yeah. Because Jess going in all guns blazing was going to be exactly the start to the competition that Tanzie needed. "I, um, don't think I could recognize him. Anyway, I sorted it."

He kind of liked the words. *I sorted it.*

"But I can't see, Mum. What am I going to do if I can't see?"

"Mr. Nicholls is getting you some glasses. Don't worry."

"But what if he doesn't? What if he doesn't even come back?"

I wouldn't, Nicky thought, if I were him. They had wrecked his nice car. And he looked about ten years older than when they had set off.

"He'll come back," Jess said.

"Mrs. Thomas. We need to start. Your daughter has thirty seconds to take her seat."

"Look, is there any way we can delay the start by a few minutes? We really, really need to get her some glasses. She can't see without them."

"No, madam. If she's not in her place in thirty seconds, I'm afraid we'll have to start without her."

"Then can I go in? I could read her the

353

questions?"

"But I can't write without my glasses."

"Then I'll write for you."

"Mum . . ."

Jess knew she was beaten. She looked over at Nicky and gave a vague shake of her head that said, *I don't know what to do.*

Nicky crouched beside her. "You can do this, Tanze. You can. You can do this stuff standing on your head. Just hold the paper really, really close to your eyes and take your time."

She was staring blindly into the hall. Beyond the door the students were shuffling into place, dragging chairs under desks, arranging pencils in front of them.

"And as soon as Mr. Nicholls gets here, we'll bring the glasses in to you."

"Really. Just go in and do your best and we'll be waiting here. Norman will just be on the other side of the wall. We all will. And then we'll go and get some lunch. Nothing to stress about."

The woman with the clipboard walked over. "Are you going to take part in the competition, Costanza?"

"Her name's Tanzie," Nicky said. The woman didn't seem to hear. Tanze nodded mutely and allowed herself to be led to a desk. She looked so damned little.

"You can do it, Tanze!" His voice burst out of him suddenly, bouncing off the walls of the hall, so that the man at the back tutted. "Back of the net, Titch!"

"Oh, for goodness' sake," someone muttered.

"Back of the net!" Nicky yelled again, so that Jess looked at him in shock.

And then a bell rang, the door closed in front of them with a solid *thunk,* and it was just Nicky, Jess, and Norman on the other side, with a couple of hours to kill.

"Right," said Jess, when she finally tore her gaze away from the door. She put her hands into her pockets, took them out again, straightened her hair, and sighed. "Right."

"He will come," said Nicky, who was suddenly not entirely sure he would.

"I know that."

The silence that followed was long enough that they were forced to smile awkwardly at each other. The corridor emptied slowly, apart from one organizer who murmured to himself as he ran his pencil down a list of names.

"Probably stuck in traffic."

"It was pretty bad."

Nicky could picture Tanzie on the other side of the door, squinting at her papers, looking around for help that wouldn't come. Jess stared up at the ceiling, swore softly, then tied and retied her ponytail. He guessed she was picturing the same.

And then there was the sound of a distant commotion and Mr. Nicholls appeared, running down the corridor like a crazy man and holding aloft a plastic bag that looked as if it might be entirely full of pairs of glasses. And as he launched himself at the desk and started arguing with the organizers — the kind of argument that comes from someone who knows there is no way in the world he is going to lose — the relief Nicky felt was so overwhelming that he had to go outside, slump against the wall, and drop his head to his knees until his breathing no longer threatened to turn into a huge, gulping sob.

It was weird saying good-bye to Mr. Nicholls. They stood by his car in the drizzle and Jess was acting all *oh, I don't care,* even though she obviously did. And Nicky really wanted to thank him for the whole hacking thing, driving them all that way and just being, you know, weirdly decent, but then Mr. Nicholls went and gave him his spare phone and all that came out was this strangulated "Thanks." And then that was it. And he and

Jess were walking across the campus car park with Norman, pretending they couldn't hear Mr. Nicholls's car driving away.

They stopped by the corridor, and Jess stashed their bags in the cloakroom. Then she turned to Nicky and brushed non-existent fluff from his shoulder. "Well," she said, "let's go and walk this dog, shall we?"

It was true that Nicky didn't talk much. It wasn't that he didn't have stuff to say. It was just that there was nobody he really wanted to say it to. Ever since he had gone to live with Dad and Jess, when he was eight, people had been trying to get him to talk about his "feelings," like they were a big rucksack he could just drag around with him and open up for everyone to examine the contents. But half the time he didn't even know what he thought. He didn't have opinions about politics or the economy or what happened to him. He didn't even have an opinion about his real mum. She was an addict. She liked drugs more than she liked him. What else was there to say?

Nicky went to counseling for a bit, like the social workers said he should. The woman seemed to want him to get mad about what had happened to him. Nicky had told her he wasn't angry because he understood that his mum couldn't look after him. It wasn't as if it was personal. If he had been any other kid, she would have dumped him just the same. She was just . . . sad. He had seen so little of her when he was small that he didn't even really feel like she had anything to do with him.

But the counselor kept saying: "You must let it out, Nicholas. It's not good for you to internalize what happened to you." She gave him two little stuffed figures and wanted him to act out "how your mother's abandonment made you feel."

Nicky didn't like to tell her that it was the thought of having to sit in her office playing with dolls and being called Nicholas that made him feel destructive. He just wasn't a particularly angry person. Not with his real mum, not even with Jason Fisher, although he didn't expect anyone to understand. Fisher was just an idiot who didn't have the brainpower to do anything but hit out. Fisher knew on some deep level that he had nothing, that he was never going to be anything. He was a phony, and nobody liked him, not really. So he turned it all outward, transferred his bad feelings to the nearest available person (see? The therapy had done something useful).

So when Jess said they should go for a

walk, a little bit of Nicky was wary. He
didn't want to get into some big conversation about his feelings. He didn't want to
discuss any of it. He was all braced to
deflect, and then she scratched her head a
bit, and said, "Is it just me, or does it feel a
bit weird without Mr. Nicholls?"

This was what they talked about:

The unexpected beauty of some of Aberdeen's buildings.

The dog.

Whether either of them had brought
plastic bags for the dog.

Which of them was going to kick that
thing under the parked car so that nobody
trod in it.

The best way to clean the toes of your
shoes on grass.

Whether it was actually possible to clean
the toes of your shoes on grass.

Nicky's face, as in did it hurt? (Answer:
no, not anymore.)

Other bits of him, as in did they? (No, no,
and a bit, but it was improving.)

His jeans, as in why didn't he pull them
up so that his underwear wasn't always
showing?

Why his underwear was actually his own
business.

Whether they should tell Dad about the Rolls. Nicky told her she should pretend it had been nicked. What would he know? And it would serve him right. But Jess said she couldn't lie to him because that wouldn't be fair. And then she went quiet for a while.

Was he okay? Did he feel better being away from home? Was he worried about going home? This was where Nicky stopped talking and started shrugging. What was there to say?

This was what they didn't talk about:

What it would be like if they actually went home with five thousand pounds.

If Tanzie went to that school and he left school before sixth form, whether Jess would want him to pick her up from St. Anne's every day.

The takeaway that they would definitely get tonight in celebration. Possibly not a kebab.

That Jess was plainly freezing, even if she insisted she was fine. All the little hairs on her arms were standing bolt upright.

Mr. Nicholls. Most notably, where Jess had actually slept the previous night. And why they had kept stealing looks at each other like a pair of teenagers all morning, even while they were grumping at each other. Nicky honestly thought she thought they were all stupid sometimes.

But it was kind of okay, the talking thing. He thought he might even do it more often.

They were waiting outside the doors when they finally opened at two o'clock. Tanzie walked out in the first batch, her furry pencil case clutched in front of her, and Jess held out her arms wide, all braced for celebration.

"So? How was it?"

She looked at them steadily.

"Did you ace it, Titch?" said Nicky, grinning.

And then, abruptly, Tanzie's face crumpled. Everyone froze, then Jess stooped and pulled her close, maybe to hide the shock on her face, and Nicky put his arm around Tanzie's on the other side, and Norman sat on her feet. As the other kids filed past, she told them what had happened, through muffled sobs.

"I lost the whole first half hour. And I didn't understand some of their accents. And I couldn't see properly. And I got really nervous, and I kept staring at my paper and then by the time I got the glasses, it took me ages to find a pair that fit me and then I couldn't even understand the first question."

Jess scanned the corridor for the organizers. "I'll talk to them. I'll explain what happened. I mean, you couldn't see. That's got to count for something. Maybe we could get them to adjust the score to take it into account."

"No. I don't want you talking to them. I didn't understand the first question, even when I got the right glasses. I couldn't make it work the way they said it should work."

"But maybe —"

"I messed it up," Tanzie wailed. "I don't want to go over it. I just want to go."

"You didn't mess anything up, sweetheart. Really. You did your best. That's all that matters."

"But it's not, is it? Because I can't go to St. Anne's without the money."

"Well, there must be . . . Don't worry, Tanze. I'll work something out."

It was her least convincing smile ever. And Tanzie wasn't stupid. She cried like someone heartbroken. Nicky had honestly never seen her like that. It actually made him want to cry a bit, too.

"Let's go home," he said when it became unbearable.

But that made Tanzie cry harder.

Jess looked up at him, her face completely lost, and it was like she was asking him, *Nicky, what shall I do?* And the fact that right now even Jess didn't know made him feel like something had gone really wrong with the world. And then he thought: I really, really wish Jess hadn't confiscated my stash. He didn't think he had ever needed a smoke more in his life.

They waited in the hallway as the other competitors retreated into cars with their parents, and suddenly, unexpectedly, Nicky realized he did feel angry. He was angry with the stupid boys who had put his little sister off her stroke. He was angry with the stupid maths competition and its rules that wouldn't bend a tiny bit for a little girl who couldn't see. He was angry that they had come all this way across an entire country just to fail again. Like there was nothing this family could do that turned out right. Nothing at all.

When the hallway had emptied finally, Jess reached into her back pocket and wrenched out a small rectangular card. She thrust it at him. "Call Mr. Nicholls."

"But he's halfway home by now. And what can he do?"

Jess bit her lip. She half turned away from

him, then back again. "He can take us to Marty."

Nicky stared at her.

"Please. I know it's awkward, but I can't think what else to do. Tanzie needs something to help her up again, Nicky. She needs to see her dad."

He was back within half an hour. He had just been down the road, he said, having a bite to eat. Nicky thought afterward that if he had been thinking more clearly, he might have wondered why Ed hadn't gone very far, and why it had taken him so long to have a snack. But he was too busy arguing with Jess, a few feet from the car.

"I know you don't want to see your dad, but —"

"I'm not going."

"Tanzie needs this." Her face had that determined set, where you knew she was making out that she was taking your feelings into account, but actually she was just going to make you do what she wanted you to do.

"This is really not going to make anything better."

"For you, maybe. Look, Nicky, I know you have very mixed feelings about your dad right now, and I don't blame you. I know it's been a very confusing time —"

"I'm not confused."

"Tanzie is at rock bottom. She needs something to give her a lift. And Marty is not that far away." She put out a hand and touched his arm. "Look, if you really don't want to see him when you get there, you can just stay in the car, okay? I'm sorry," she said when he didn't say anything. "I'm not exactly desperate to see him, either. But we do have to do this."

What could he tell her? What could he tell her that she would believe? And he supposed there was 5 percent of him that still wondered whether he was the one who was wrong.

Jess walked back to Mr. Nicholls, who had been leaning against his car watching. Tanzie sat silently inside. "Please. Will you give us a lift to Marty's? His mum's, I mean. I'm sorry. I know you've probably had enough of us and we've been a complete pain, but . . . but I haven't got anyone else to ask. Tanzie . . . she needs her dad. Whatever I — we — think of him, she needs to see her dad. It's only a couple of hours from here."

He looked at her.

"Okay, maybe more if we have to go slowly. But please — I need to turn this round. I really need to turn this round."

Mr. Nicholls stepped to one side and opened the passenger door. He bent down a little so that he could smile at Tanzie. "Let's go."

They all looked relieved. But it was a bad idea. A really bad idea. If only they'd asked him about the wallpaper, Nicky could have told them why.

CHAPTER TWENTY-TWO:
JESS

The last time Jess had seen Maria Costanza was the day she had delivered Marty to her in Liam's brother's van. Marty had spent the last hundred miles to Glasgow asleep under a duvet, and as Jess stood in her immaculate front room and tried to explain her son's breakdown, she had looked at her as if Jess had personally tried to kill him.

Maria Costanza had never liked her. She'd thought her son deserved better than a sixteen-year-old schoolgirl with home-dyed hair and glittery nails, and nothing Jess had ever done since had changed Maria's fundamentally low opinion of her. She thought what Jess did with the house was peculiar. She thought the fact that Jess made most of the children's clothes herself was willfully eccentric. It never occurred to her to ask why she made their clothes, or why they couldn't afford to pay someone else to decorate. Or why when the kitchen sink overflowed, it was Jess who ended up under the sink wrestling with the U-bend.

She had tried. She really had. She was polite, she didn't swear. She was faithful to Marty. She produced the world's most amazing baby, and kept her clean, fed, and cheerful. It took Jess about five years to grasp that she wasn't the problem. Maria Costanza was just one of life's lemon suckers. Jess wasn't sure she had ever seen her smile spontaneously unless it was to report some piece of news about one of her friends or neighbors — a slashed tire or a terminal illness, maybe.

She had tried to ring her twice, on Mr. Nicholls's phone, but got no answer.

"Granny's probably still at work," she told Tanzie, ringing off. "Or perhaps they've gone to see the new baby."

"You still want me to head over there?" Mr. Nicholls glanced at her.

"Please. I'm sure they'll be home by the time we get there. She never goes out in the evening."

Nicky's eyes met hers in the mirror and slid away. Jess didn't blame him for being negative. If Maria Costanza's reaction to Tanzie had been lukewarm, her discovery that she had a grandson she hadn't even known about was met with the same enthusiasm she would have expressed had they announced a family case of scabies. Jess couldn't tell whether she was offended because he had existed for so long without her knowledge or whether her inability to explain him without referring to illegitimacy and her son's involvement with an addict meant that she just found it easier to ignore him altogether

"You looking forward to seeing Daddy, Tanze?" Jess turned in her seat. Tanzie was leaning against Norman, her face solemn and exhausted. Her eyes slid to Jess's and she gave the smallest of nods.

"It will be great to see him. And Granny," Jess said brightly. "I'm not sure why we didn't think of it sooner."

They drove in silence. Tanzie dozed, resting against the dog. Nicky sat and watched the darkening sky. She didn't feel like putting music on. She didn't dare let the children see how she felt about what had happened in Aberdeen. She couldn't let herself think about it. *One thing at a time,* she told herself. *Just get Tanzie back on track. And then I'll work out what to do next.*

"You okay?" Mr. Nicholls asked.

"Fine." She could see he didn't believe her. "She'll feel better once she sees her dad. I know it."

"She could always do another Olympiad, next year. She'll know what to expect then."

Jess tried to smile. "Mr. Nicholls. That sounds suspiciously like optimism."

He turned to her, and his eyes were full of sympathy.

She was relieved to be back in his car. She had begun to feel oddly safe there, like nothing really bad could happen while they were all inside it. Jess pictured being in the front room of Costanza's little house, trying to explain the events that had led them there. She pictured Marty's face when she told him about the Rolls-Royce. She saw them all waiting at a bus stop tomorrow, the first stage in an interminable journey home. She wondered briefly whether she could ask Mr. Nicholls to mind Norman till they got back. Thinking about this made her remember how much this whole escapade had cost, and she pushed the thought away. One thing at a time.

And then she must have nodded off, because someone had hold of her arm.

"Jess?"

"Nngh?"

"Jess? I think we're here. That GPS says this is her address. Does this look right to you?"

She pushed herself upright, uncricking her

neck. The windows of the neat, white terraced house gazed unblinkingly back at her.
Her stomach lurched reflexively.

"What's the time?"

"Just before seven." He waited while she
rubbed her eyes. "Well, the lights are on,"
he said. "I'm guessing they're home."

He turned in his seat as she pushed herself
upright. "Hey, kids, we're here. Time to see
your dad."

Tanzie's hand gripped Jess's tightly as they
walked up the path. Nicky had refused to
get out of the car, saying he'd wait with Mr.
Nicholls. Jess decided she'd let Tanzie go in
before she went back and tried to reason
with him.

"Are you excited?"

Tanzie nodded, her little face suddenly
hopeful and, just briefly, Jess sensed that
she had done the right thing. They would
salvage something out of this trip, even if it
killed her. Whatever issues she and Marty
had could be sorted out later.

Two new small barrels sat by the front
steps, filled with a purple flower she didn't
recognize. She straightened her jacket,
smoothed the hair from Tanzie's face,
leaned forward, and wiped a bit of something from the corner of her mouth, and

then she rang the doorbell.

Maria Costanza saw Tanzie first. She gazed at her, and then up at Jess, and several expressions, none quite identifiable, flickered rapidly across her face.

Jess answered them with her cheeriest smile. "Hi, Maria. We, um, were in the area, and I just thought we couldn't pass without seeing Marty. And you."

Maria Costanza stared at her.

"We did try to call," Jess continued, her voice a singsong, and odd to her ears. "Quite a few times. I would have left a message, but —"

"Hi, Granny." Tanzie ran forward and threw herself at her grandmother's waist. Maria Costanza's hand went down and she let it rest limply against Tanzie's back. She had dyed her hair a shade too dark, Jess noted absently. Maria Costanza stayed like that for a moment, then glanced at the car, where Nicky stared out impassively from the rear window.

God, would it kill you to express some enthusiasm, just once? Jess thought. "Nicky will be over in a minute," she said, keeping the smile firmly on her face. "He's just woken up. I'm . . . giving him a moment."

They stood and faced each other, waiting. "So . . . ," Jess said.

"He — he's not here," Maria Costanza said.

"Is he at work?" She had sounded more eager than she had intended. "I mean, it's lovely if he's feeling . . . well enough to work."

"He's not here, Jessica."

"Is he ill?" Oh, Christ, she thought. Something's happened. And then she saw it. An emotion she was not sure she'd ever seen on Maria Costanza's features. Embarrassment.

Jess watched her attempt to cover it. "So where is he?"

"You . . . I think you should talk to him." Maria Costanza brought a hand to her mouth, as if to prevent herself saying more, then extricated herself gently from her grandchild. "Hold on. I'll get you his address."

"His address?"

She left Tanzie and Jess standing on the doorstep, and disappeared down the little hallway, half closing the door behind her. Tanzie looked up quizzically. Jess smiled reassuringly. It wasn't quite as easy as it had been.

The door opened again. She handed over a piece of paper. "It will take you maybe one hour, maybe an hour and a half, depending on the traffic." Jess registered her stiff features, then looked past her to the little hallway, where nothing had changed in the fifteen years she had known her. Nothing at all. And somewhere in the back of Jess's head a little bell began to chime.

"Right," she said, and she wasn't smiling anymore.

Maria Costanza couldn't hold her gaze. She stooped then, and put her palm against Tanzie's cheek. "You come back and stay with your *nonna* soon, yes?" She looked up at Jess. "You bring her back? It's been a long time."

That look of mute appeal, of acknowledgment in her duplicity, was more unnerving than almost anything Maria Constanza had ever done in the years of their relationship.

Jess swept Tanzie toward the car.

Mr. Nicholls looked up. He didn't say anything.

"Here." Jess handed him the paper. "We need to go here." Wordlessly he began to program the postcode into the GPS. Her heart was thumping.

She looked in the rearview mirror. "You knew," she said when Tanzie finally put her earphones in.

Nicky pulled at his fringe, gazing out at

his grandmother's house. "It was the last few times we've spoken to him on Skype. Granny would never have had that wallpaper."

She didn't ask him where Marty was. She thought she probably had an idea even then.

They drove the hour in silence. Jess couldn't speak. A million possibilities ran through her head. Occasionally she looked into the mirror, watching Nicky. His face was closed, turned resolutely toward the roadside. She began slowly to reconsider his reluctance to come here, even to speak to his father these last few months, casting it in a new light.

They drove through the dusky countryside to the outskirts of a new town and a housing development where the houses were box fresh, laid out in careful, sweeping curves, and new cars gleamed outside like statements of intent. Mr. Nicholls pulled up to Castle Court, where four cherry trees stood like sentinels along the narrow pavement upon which she suspected nobody ever walked. The house looked newly built; its Regency-style windows gleamed, its slate roof shone in the drizzle.

She stared at it out of the window.

"You okay?" They were the only two words Mr. Nicholls had spoken the entire journey.

"You wait here a minute, kids," Jess said, and climbed out.

She walked up to the front door, double-checked the address on the piece of paper, then rapped with the brass knocker. Inside she could hear the sound of a television, and see the vague shadow of someone moving under bright light.

She knocked again. She barely felt the rain.

Footsteps in the hallway. The door opened and a blond woman stood in front of her. She wore a dark red wool dress and matching pumps, and her hair was cut in one of those styles that women wear when they work in retail or banking but don't want to look like they've entirely given up on the idea of being a rock chick.

"Is Marty here?" Jess said. The woman made as if to speak, then looked Jess up and down, at her flip-flops, at her crumpled white trousers, and in the several seconds that followed, from the faint hardening of her expression, Jess could see she knew. She knew about her.

"Wait there," she said.

The door half closed, and Jess heard her shout down the narrow corridor. "Mart? Mart?"

Mart.

She heard his voice, muffled, laughing, saying something about television, and then the woman's voice dropped. Jess saw their shadows behind the frosted-glass panels. And then the door opened and he stood there.

Marty had grown his hair. He had a long, floppy fringe, swept carefully to one side like a teenager. He wore jeans she didn't recognize, in deep indigo, and he had lost weight. He looked like someone she didn't know. And he had gone quite, quite pale. "Jess."

She couldn't speak.

They stared at each other. He swallowed. "I was going to tell you."

Right up to that point a part of her had refused to believe it could be true. Right up to that point she had thought there must be some huge mistake, that Marty was staying with a friend or he was ill again and Maria Costanza, with her misplaced pride, just couldn't face admitting it. But there was no mistaking what was right in front of her.

It took her a moment to find her voice. "This? This is . . . where you've been living?"

Jess stumbled backward, now taking in the immaculate front garden, the living room, just visible through the window. Her hip bumped against a car on the drive and she put out her hand to support herself. "All this time? We've been scratching around for the last two years just to stay warm and fed and you're here with an executive home and a — a brand-new Toyota?"

Marty glanced awkwardly behind him. "We need to talk, Jess."

And then she saw the wallpaper in his dining room. The thick stripe. And it all fell into place. His insistence that they only speak at set times. The lack of a landline phone number. Maria Costanza's assurance that he was sleeping whenever she rang outside the usual time. Her determination to get Jess off the telephone as quickly as possible.

"We need to talk?" Jess was half laughing now. "Yes, let's talk, Marty. How about I talk? For two years I've not made a single demand on you — not for money or time or child care or help of any kind. Because I thought you were ill. I thought you were depressed. I thought you were living with your *mother.*"

"I *was* living with Mum."

"Till when?"

He compressed his lips.

"Till when, Marty?" Her voice was shrill.

"Fifteen months."

"You were with your mum fifteen months?"

He looked at his feet.

"You've been here fifteen months? You've been here more than a year?"

"I wanted to tell you. But I knew that you'd —"

"What — kick up a fuss? Because you're here living a life of luxury while your wife and kids are back at home scrabbling around in the crap you left behind?"

"Jess . . ."

She was briefly silenced as the door opened abruptly. A little girl appeared behind him, her hair a virgin sheet of blond, wearing a Hollister sweatshirt and Converse trainers. She tugged at his sleeve. "It's your program, Marty," she began, and then she saw Jess and stopped.

"Go to your mum, babe," he said quietly, his gaze flicking sideways. He put his hand gently on her shoulder. "I'll be through in a minute."

She looked at Jess warily. She was the same age as Tanzie. "Go on." He pulled the door behind him.

And that was when Jess's heart actually broke.

"She . . . she has *kids*?"

He swallowed. "Two."

Her hands went to her face, and then her hair. She turned and walked blindly back down the path. "Oh, God. Oh, God."

"Jess, I never set out to —"

She spun round and flew at him. She wanted to smash his stupid face and his expensive haircut. She wanted him to know the pain he had put his children through. She wanted him to pay. He ducked behind the car, and almost without knowing what she was doing, she found she was kicking at it, at its oversized wheels, its gleaming panels, the stupid bright white shiny stupid immaculate stupid car.

"You lied! You lied to all of us! And I was trying to protect you! I can't believe . . . I can't —" She kicked and felt the faint satisfaction as the metal gave, even as the pain shot up her foot. She kicked again and again, not caring, her fists raining blows on the window.

"Jess! The car! Are you fucking mad?"

She rained blows down on that car because she could not rain the blows on him. She hit with her hands and her feet, not caring, sobbing with fury, her rasping breath loud in her ears. And when he wrenched her off it, wedging himself between her and the car, his grip tight on her arms, she felt a momentary flicker of fear that her life had spun utterly out of control. And then she looked into his eyes, his coward's eyes, and there was a loud buzzing in her head. She wanted to smash —

"Jess."

Mr. Nicholls's arm was around her waist, easing her backward.

"Get off me!"

"The kids are watching. Come on now." A hand on her arm.

She couldn't breathe. A moan rose up through her whole body. She allowed herself to be pulled a few steps back. Marty was shouting something she couldn't hear through the din in her head.

"Come . . . come away."

The kids. She looked at the car, and saw Tanzie's face, wide-eyed with shock, Nicky a motionless silhouette behind her. She looked to the other side, at the house where two small, pale faces watched from the living room, their mother behind them. When she saw Jess looking, she lowered the blind.

"You're mad," yelled Marty, staring at the dented panels of the car. "Completely effing mad."

She had begun to shake. Mr. Nicholls put his arms around her, and steered her into his car. "Get in. Sit down," he said, closing the door once she was inside. Marty was walking slowly down the pathway toward them, his old swagger suddenly visible now that she was the one in the wrong. She thought he was about to pick a fight, but when he was about fifteen feet away he peered into the car, stooping slightly as if to check, and then she heard the rear door open behind her and Tanzie was out and running toward him.

"Daddy!" she cried, and he swept her up in his arms and then Jess had to look away because she no longer knew what she felt about anything.

She wasn't sure how long she sat there, staring at the footwell. She couldn't think. She couldn't feel. She heard murmuring voices on the pathway, and at one point, Nicky reached forward and touched her shoulder lightly. "I'm sorry," he said, his voice cracking.

She reached behind and gripped his hand fiercely. "Not. Your. Fault," she whispered.

The door opened finally and Mr. Nicholls put his head in. His face was wet, and rain dripped from his collar. "Okay. Tanzie's going to stay here for a couple of hours."

She stared at him, suddenly alert. "Oh no," she began. "He doesn't get to have her. Not after what he's —"

"This isn't about you and him, Jess."

Jess turned toward the house. The front door was slightly ajar. Tanzie was already inside. "But she can't stay there. Not with them . . ."

He climbed into the driver's seat, then he reached across and took her hand. His was ice cold and damp.

"She's had a bad day and she asked if she could spend some time with him. And, Jess, if this really is his life now, then surely she has to be part of it."

"But it's not —"

"Fair. I know."

They sat there, the three of them, staring at the brightly lit house. Her daughter was in there. With Marty's new family. It was as if someone had reached in, gripped her heart, and ripped it out through her ribs.

She couldn't take her eyes from the window. "What if she changes her mind? She'll be all alone. And we don't know them. I don't know this woman. She could be —"

"She's with her dad. She'll be okay."

She stared at Mr. Nicholls. His face was sympathetic, but his voice was oddly firm. "Why are you on his side?"

"I'm not on his side." His fingers closed around hers. "Look, we'll all go find somewhere to eat. We'll be back in a couple of hours. We stay close by and we can come back for her anytime if she needs us."

"No. I'll stay," said a voice from behind. "I'll stay with her. So that she's not by herself."

Jess turned. Nicky was gazing out of the window. "Are you sure?"

"I'll be fine." His face was a blank. "Anyway, I sort of want to hear what he says."

Mr. Nicholls saw Nicky to the front door. She watched her stepson, his long, lanky legs in his skinny black jeans, his diffident, awkward way of standing as the door opened to let him in. The blond woman tried to smile at him. She peered surreptitiously past him at the car. It was possible, Jess observed distantly, that the woman was actually frightened of her. The door closed behind them. Jess shut her eyes, not wanting to imagine what was going on behind that door.

And then Mr. Nicholls was in the car, bringing with him a blast of cold air. "Come on," he said. "It's okay. We'll be back before you know it."

They sat in a roadside café. She couldn't eat. She drank coffee and Mr. Nicholls bought a sandwich and just sat there, opposite her. She wasn't sure he knew what to say. Two hours, she kept telling herself. Two hours and then I can have them back. She wanted to be back in the car with her children, away from here. Away from Marty and his lies and his new girlfriend and pretend family. She watched the clock hands edge round and let her coffee cool. Every minute felt like infinity.

And then, ten minutes before they were due to leave, the phone rang. Jess snatched it up. A number she didn't recognize. Marty's voice. "Can you leave them with me tonight?"

It knocked the breath clean out of her.

"Oh no," she said when she could find her voice. "You don't get to keep them, just like that."

"I'm just . . . trying to explain it all to them."

"Well, good luck with that. Because I'm damned if I understand it." Her voice lifted in the little café. She saw the people at the nearby tables turn their heads.

"I couldn't tell you, Jess, okay? Because I knew you'd react like you did."

"Oh, so it's my fault. Of course it is!"

"We were over. You knew it as well as I did."

She was standing. She wasn't aware of

having got to her feet. Mr. Nicholls, for some reason, stood, too. "I couldn't give a flying fuck about you and me, okay? But we've been living on the breadline since you left, and now I find out you're living with someone else, supporting her kids. Even as you said you couldn't lift a finger for ours. Yes, it's just possible I'm going to react badly to that one, Marty."

"It's not my money I'm living on. It's Linzie's money. I can't use her money to pay for your kids."

"My kids? *My* kids?" She was out from behind the table now, walking blindly toward the door. She was dimly aware of Mr. Nicholls summoning the waitress.

"Look," said Marty, "Tanzie really wants to stay over. She's obviously upset about this maths thing. She asked me to ask you. Please."

Jess couldn't speak. She just stood in the cold car park, her eyes closed, her knuckles white around the phone.

"And I really want to sort things out with Nicky."

"You are . . . unbelievable."

"Just . . . just let me sort things out with the kids, please? You and I, we can talk afterward. But just tonight, while they're here. I've missed them, Jess. I know it's all my fault. I know I've been rubbish. But I'm actually glad it's all out there. I'm glad you know what's going on. And I just . . . I want to move forward now."

She stared ahead of her. In the distance a police car's blue lights flashed. Her foot had begun to throb. Finally she said, "Put Tanzie on."

There was a short silence, the sound of a door. Jess took a deep breath.

"Mum?"

"Tanze? Sweetheart? Are you okay?"

"I'm fine, Mum. They've got terrapins. One has a gammy leg. It's called Mike. Can we get a terrapin?"

"We'll talk about it." She could hear a saucepan clash in the background, the sound of a tap running. "Um, you really want to spend the night? You don't have to, you know. You just . . . you do whatever makes you feel happy."

"I would quite like to stay. Suze's nice. She's going to lend me her *High School Musical* pajamas."

"Suze?"

"Linzie's daughter. It's going to be like a sleepover. And she has those beads where you make a picture and stick it together with an iron."

"Right."

There was a brief silence. Jess could hear muffled talking in the background.

"So what time are you picking me up tomorrow?"

She swallowed, and tried to keep her voice level. "After breakfast. Nine o'clock. And if you change your mind, you just call me, okay? Anytime. And I'll pick you up straightaway. Even if it's the very middle of the night. It doesn't matter."

"I know."

"I'll come anytime. I love you, sweetie. Anytime you want to call."

"Okay."

"Will you . . . will you put Nicky on?"

"Love you. Bye."

Nicky's voice was unreadable. "I've told him I'll stay," he said. "But only to keep an eye on Tanze."

"Okay. I'll make sure we're somewhere close by. Is she . . . the woman . . . is she okay? I mean, will you all be okay?"

"Linzie. She's fine."

"And you . . . you're all right with this? He's not —"

"I'm fine."

There was a long silence.

"Jess?"

"Yes?"

"Are you okay?"

She screwed her eyes shut. She took a silent breath, put her hand up, and wiped at the tears that were running down her cheeks. She hadn't known there were that many tears in her. She didn't answer Nicky until she could be sure they hadn't soaked her voice, too. "I'm fine, lovey. You have a good time and don't worry about me. I'll see you both in the morning."

Mr. Nicholls was behind her. He took his phone from her in silence, his eyes not leaving her face. "I've found us somewhere to sleep where they'll let us take the dog."

"Is there a bar?" Jess asked, wiping at her eyes with the back of her hand.

"What?"

"I need to get drunk, Ed. Really, really drunk." He held out an arm and she took it. "And I think I may have broken my toe."

Chapter Twenty-Three:
Ed

So once upon a time Ed met a girl who was the most optimistic person he had ever known. A girl who wore flip-flops in the hope of spring. She seemed to bounce through life like Tigger; the things that would have felled most people didn't seem to touch her. Or if she did fall, she bounced right back. She fell again, plastered on a smile, dusted herself off, and kept going. He never could work out whether it was the single most heroic or the most idiotic thing he'd ever seen.

And then he stood on the curb outside a four-bedroom executive home somewhere near Carlisle and watched as that same girl saw everything she'd believed in stripped away until nothing was left but a ghost who sat in his passenger seat gazing unseeing through the windscreen. The sound of her optimism draining away was audible. And something cracked open in his heart.

He booked a holiday cabin on the side of a lake, twenty minutes from Marty's — or rather his girlfriend's — house. He couldn't find a hotel within a hundred miles that would take the dog, but the last receptionist he had spoken to, a jovial woman who called him "duck" eight times, told him of a new place she knew, run by her friend's daughter-in-law. He had to pay for three days, their minimum stay, but he didn't care. Jess didn't ask. He wasn't sure she even noticed where they were.

They picked up the keys from Reception, he followed the path through the trees, they pulled up in front of the cabin. He unloaded Jess and the dog and saw them inside. She was limping badly by then. He remembered suddenly the ferocity with which she had kicked the car. In flip-flops.

"Have a long bath," he said, flicking on all the lights and closing the curtains. It was too dark outside by now to see anything. "Go on. Try to relax. I'll go get us some food. And maybe an ice pack."

She turned and nodded. The smile she raised in thanks was barely a smile at all.

The closest supermarket was a super-market in name only — sitting under flickering strip lights were two baskets of tired vegetables and shelves of canned food with brand names he hadn't heard of. He bought a couple of ready meals, bread, coffee, milk, frozen peas, and painkillers for her foot. And a couple of bottles of wine. He needed a drink, too.

He was standing at the checkout when his phone beeped. He wrestled it out of his pocket, wondering if it was Jess. And then he remembered that her phone had run out of credit two days previously.

Hello darling. So sorry you can't make tomorrow. We do hope to see you before too long. Love Mum. PS Dad sends his love. Bit poorly today.

"Twenty-two pounds eighty."

The girl had said it twice before he registered.

"Oh. Sorry." He fished around for his card, and held it out to her.

"Card machine's not working. There's a sign."

Ed followed her eyes. "Cash or check only," it said in laboriously outlined ballpoint letters. "You're kidding me, right?"

"Why would I be kidding you?" She chewed, meditatively, at whatever was in her mouth.

"I'm not sure I've got enough cash on me," Ed said.

She gazed at him impassively.

"You don't take cards?"

"It's what the sign says."

"Well . . . do you not have a manual card machine?"

"Most people round here pay cash," she said. Her expression said it was obvious that he was not from around here.

"Okay. Where's the nearest cash machine?"

"Carlisle." She blinked at him slowly. "If you haven't got the money, you'll have to put the food back."

"I've got the money. Just give me a minute."

He dug around in his pockets, ignoring the barely suppressed sighs and rolled eyes from those behind him. By some miracle he was able to scrape up cash for everything but the onion bhajis. He counted it all out and she raised her eyebrows ostentatiously as she rang it up, and shoved the bhajis to one side. Ed, in turn, shoved it all into a carrier bag that would give way even before he reached the car, and tried not to think about his mother.

He was cooking when Jess limped downstairs. Or rather, he had two plastic trays rotating noisily in the microwave, which was about as far as he had ever immersed himself in the culinary arts. She was wearing a bathrobe and had her hair wrapped in a white bath-towel turban. He had never understood how women did that. His ex had done it, too. He used to wonder if it was something women got taught, like periods and hand washing. Her bare face was beautiful.

"Here." Ed held out a glass of wine.

She took it from him. He had started a fire, and she sat down in front of the flames, apparently still lost in her thoughts. He handed her the frozen peas for her foot, then busied himself with the rest of the microwave meals, following the instructions on the packaging.

"I texted Nicky," he told her as he stabbed the plastic film with a fork. "Just to tell him where we were staying."

She took another sip of her wine. "Was he okay?"

"He was fine. They were just about to eat." She flinched slightly as he said this, and Ed immediately regretted planting that little domestic tableau in her imagination. "How's your foot?"

"Hurts."

She took a huge swig of her wine and he saw she'd downed the glass already. She got up, wincing, so that the peas fell onto the floor and poured herself another. Then, as if she'd just remembered something, she reached into the pocket of the robe, and held up a clear plastic bag.

"Nicky's stash," she said. "I decided this qualified as an appropriate moment for appropriating his drugs."

She said it almost defiantly, waiting for him to contradict her. When he didn't, she dragged a tourist guide from the glass coffee table onto her lap, on which she proceeded to roll a haphazard joint. She lit it, and inhaled deeply. She tried to smother a cough, then inhaled again. Her towel turban had started to slide and, irritated, she tugged it off, so that her wet hair fell around her shoulders. She inhaled again, closed her eyes, and held it out toward him.

"Is that what I could smell when I came in?"

She opened one eye. "You think I'm a disgrace."

"No. I think one of us should be in a state to drive, just in case Tanzie wants picking up. It's fine. Really. You go ahead. I think . . . you need —"

"A new life? To pull myself together? A good seeing to?" She laughed mirthlessly. "Oh no. I forgot. I can't even do that right."

"Jess —"

She raised a hand. "Sorry. Okay. Let's eat."

They ate at the little laminated table beside the kitchen area. The curries were serviceable, but Jess barely touched hers.

As he put the plates on the side and prepared to wash up, she faced him. "I've been a total idiot, haven't I?"

Ed leaned back against the kitchen units, a plate in his hand. "I don't see how —"

"I worked it all out in the bath. I've been blathering to the kids all these years about how if you look out for people and do the right thing, it will all be okay. Don't steal. Don't lie. Do the right thing. Somehow the universe will see you right. Well, it's all bullshit, isn't it? Nobody else thinks that way."

Her voice was slightly slurred, its edges frayed with pain.

"It's not —"

"No? Two years I've been flat broke. Two years I've been protecting him, not adding to his stress, not bothering him about his own children. And all the while he's been living like that, with his new girlfriend." She shook her head in wonder. "I didn't suspect a thing. Not for one minute. And I worked it out, while I was in the bath . . . that whole 'do as you would be done by' thing? Well, it only works if everyone else does it. And nobody does. The world is basically full of people who couldn't give a shit. They'll tread all over you if it means they get what they want. Even if it's their own kids they're treading on."

"Jess . . ."

He walked through the kitchen until he was inches from her. He couldn't think what to say. He wanted to put his arms around her, but something about her held him back. She poured herself another glass of wine and lifted it in a salute.

"I don't care about that woman, you know. That's not it. He was right — the two of us were over a long time ago. But all that crap about not being able to help his own kids? Refusing even to think about helping Tanze with school fees?" She took a long gulp of her drink and blinked slowly. "Did you see that girl's top? You know how much a Hollister top costs? Sixty-seven pounds. Sixty-seven pounds for a child's sweatshirt. I saw the price tag when Druggie Aileen brought one round." She wiped angrily at her eyes. "You know what he sent Nicky for his birthday in February? A ten-pound gift certificate. A ten-pound gift certificate for the computer games shop. You can't even buy a computer game for ten pounds. Only secondhand. And the stupid thing is we were all really pleased. We thought it meant that Marty was getting better. I told the kids that ten pounds, when you're not working, is actually quite a lot of money."

She started to laugh. An awful, desolate sound. "And all the time . . . all the time he was in that executive home with his immaculate new sofa and his matchy-matchy curtains and his bloody boy-band haircut. And he didn't even have the balls to tell me."

"He's a coward," he said.

"Yup. But I'm the idiot. I've dragged the kids halfway around the country on some wild-goose chase because I thought I could somehow better their chances. I've put us thousands of pounds into debt. I've lost my job at the pub. I've pretty much destroyed Tanzie's self-confidence by putting her through something I should never have made her do. And for what? Because I refused to see the truth."

"The truth?"

"That people like us never get on. We never move upward. We just rattle around at the bottom."

"That's not how it is."

"What do you know?" There was no anger in her voice, just confusion. "How could you possibly understand? You're being done for one of the most serious crimes in the City. Strictly speaking, you did do it. You told your girlfriend what shares to buy so that she would make herself a heap of money. But you'll get off."

He stopped lifting his glass somewhere near his mouth.

"You will. You'll get a couple of weeks inside, maybe a suspended sentence even, and a big fine. You've got expensive lawyers who will keep you out of any real trouble. You've got people who will argue for you, fight for you. You have houses, cars, resources. You don't really need to worry. How could you possibly understand what it's like for us?"

"That's not fair," he said gently.

She turned away, and inhaled, closing her eyes and exhaling upward, the sweet smoke drifting toward the ceiling.

Ed sat down beside her and took it from between her fingers. "I think maybe that isn't such a good idea."

She snatched it back. "Don't tell me what's a good idea."

"I don't think this is going to help."

"I don't care what you —"

"I'm not the enemy here, Jess."

She shot him a look, then turned and

stared at the fire. He couldn't tell whether she was waiting for him to get up and leave.

"I'm sorry," she said eventually, and her voice was stiff, like cardboard.

"It's fine."

"It's not fine." She sighed. "I shouldn't . . . I shouldn't take it out on you."

"It's okay. It's been a crappy day. Look, I'm going to have a bath, and then I think we should just get some sleep."

"I'll be up when I've finished this." She inhaled again.

Ed waited for a moment, then left her staring at the fire. It was a mark of how tired he was that he didn't think any further than the bath.

He must have nodded off in the water. He had run it deep, pouring in whatever unguents and potions he could find, and sinking in gratefully, letting the hot water ease out some of the tensions of the day.

He tried not to think. Not about Jess, downstairs, staring bleakly into the flames, not about his mother, a couple of hours away, awaiting a son who wouldn't come. He just needed a few minutes of not having to think about anything. He lowered his head into the water as far as he could and still breathe.

He dozed. But some strange tension seemed to have crept into Ed's bones: he couldn't quite relax, even as he closed his eyes. And then he became aware of the sound; a distant revving noise, uneven and dissonant — a whining chain saw, or a driver learning how to accelerate. He opened an eye, wishing it would just go away. He had assumed that this place, of all places, might offer the tiniest bit of peace. Just one night with no noise or drama. Was it really so much to ask?

"Jess?" he called when it became too irritating. He wondered if there was a music system downstairs. Something she could turn on to drown it out.

And then he realized the source of his vague discomfort: it was his own car he could hear.

He sat there, bolt upright, for a split second, then leaped from the bath, wrapping a towel around his waist. He ran down the stairs two at a time, past the empty sofa, past Norman, who lifted his head quizzically from his spot in front of the fire, and wrestled with the front door until he had it open. A blast of cold air hit him. He was just in time to see his car bunny-hopping its way forward from its place in front of the cabin, along the curved gravel drive. He leaped off the steps and as he ran he could just make out Jess at the wheel, craning forward to see through the windscreen. She didn't have any headlights on.

"Jesus Christ. *Jess!*" He sprinted across the grass, still dripping, one hand clutching at the towel around his waist, trying to cross the lawn to block her before she could get round the drive to the road. Her face turned briefly toward him, her eyes widening as she saw him. There was an audible crunch as she wrestled with the gears.

"Jess!"

He was at the car. He threw himself at the bonnet, thumping it, then at the side, wrenching at the driver's door. It opened before she could fumble for the lock, sending him swinging sideways.

"What the hell are you doing?"

But she didn't stop. He was running now, unnaturally long strides, braced against the swinging door, one hand on the wheel, the gravel sharp under his feet. The towel had long since disappeared.

"Get off!"

"Stop the car! *Jess, stop the car!*"

"Get off, Ed! You'll get hurt!" She batted at his hand, and the car swerved dangerously to the left.

"What the —" With a leap he managed to

wrestle the keys from the ignition. The car juddered and stalled abruptly. His right shoulder collided hard with the door. Jess's nose hit the steering wheel with a crack.

"Fuck." Ed landed heavily on his side, his head hitting something hard. *"Fuck it."* He lay on the ground winded, his head spinning. It took a second for his thoughts to clear, and then he scrambled unsteadily to his feet, hauling himself up by the still-open door. He could see, through blurred vision, that they were feet from the lake, its shoreline an inky black near his wheels. Jess's arms rested against the wheel, her face buried in the gap between them. He reached across her and pulled on the hand brake, before she could somehow set the thing in motion again.

"What the hell were you doing? What were you *doing*?" Adrenaline and pain coursed through him. The woman was a nightmare. "Jesus, my head. Oh no. Where's my towel? Where's the damn towel?"

Lights were flicking on in the other cabins. He glanced up, and there were silhouettes in windows that he hadn't known were there, figures looking out at him. He cupped himself as best he could with one hand and half walked, half ran for the towel, which was lying muddied on the path. As he walked, he lifted his other hand toward them as if to say, *Nothing to see here* (given the cold night air, this had swiftly become true), and a couple of them shut their curtains hurriedly.

She was sitting where he had left her. "Do you know how much you've drunk tonight?" he yelled, through the open door. "How much dope you've smoked? You could have killed yourself. You could have killed us both."

He wanted to shake her. "Are you really so determined to dig yourself deeper and deeper into more crap? What the hell is wrong with you?"

And then he heard it. She had her head in her hands and she was crying into them, a soft, desolate sound. "I'm sorry."

Ed deflated a little, hitched the towel around his waist. "What the hell were you doing, Jess?"

"I wanted to get them. I couldn't leave them there. With him."

He took a breath, made a fist and released it. "But we've discussed this. They're absolutely fine. Nicky said he'd call if there were any problems. And we're going to get them first thing tomorrow. You know that. So what the hell —"

"I'm scared, Ed."

"Scared? Of what?"

Her nose was bleeding, a dark scarlet trickle winding its way down to her lip, her eyes smudged black with mascara. "I'm scared that . . . I'm scared that they'll like it at Marty's." Her face crumpled. "I'm scared they won't want to come back."

And Jess Thomas came to rest, gently, against him, her face buried in his bare chest. And finally Ed put his arms around her and held her close and let her cry.

He had heard religious people talk about having revelatory experiences. Like there was one moment where everything became clear to them and all the crap and ephemera just floated away. It had always seemed pretty unlikely to him. But then Ed Nicholls had one such moment in a log cabin beside a stretch of water that might have been a lake, or might well have been a canal for all he could tell, somewhere near Carlisle.

And he realized in that moment that he had to make things right. He felt Jess's injustices more fiercely than he had ever felt anything for himself. He realized, as he held her to him and kissed the top of her head and felt her cling to him, that he would do anything he could to make her and her kids happy, to keep them safe and give them a fair chance.

He didn't ask himself how he could know this after four days. It just seemed clearer to him than anything he had worked out in entire decades before.

"It's going to be okay," he said softly into her hair. "It's going to be okay because I'm going to make it okay."

Then he told her, in the quiet tones of someone offloading a confession, that she was the most amazing woman he had ever met. And when she lifted her swollen eyes to his, Ed mopped her bleeding nose, and he dropped his lips gently onto hers, and he did what he had wanted to do for the past forty-eight hours, even if he had been initially too dumb to know it. He kissed her. And when she kissed him back — tentatively at first, and then with a fierce, gratifying passion, her hand stealing up to his neck, her eyes closing — he picked her up and carried her back to the house. And in the only way he could offer that he was sure wouldn't be misunderstood, he tried to show her.

Because in that one moment, Ed Nicholls saw that he had been more like Marty than he was like Jess. He had been that coward who spent his life running from things rather than facing up to them. And that had to change.

"Jess?" he said softly into her skin, sometime later as he lay awake, marveling at the 180-degree swings of life in general. "Will you do something for me?"

"Again?" she said sleepily. Her hand rested lightly on his chest. "Good God."

"No. Tomorrow." He leaned his head into hers.

She shifted, so that her leg slid across his. He felt her lips on his skin. "Sure. What do you want?"

He gazed up at the ceiling. "Will you come with me to my dad's?"

CHAPTER TWENTY-FOUR: NICKY

So Jess's favorite saying (next to "It's all going to be fine" and "We'll work something out" and "Oh, Christ, *Norman!*") is that families come in all different shapes and sizes. "It's not all two point three now," she says, like if she says it enough times we'll all have to actually believe it.

Well, if our family was a weird shape before, it's pretty much insane now.

I don't really have a full-time mum, not like you probably have a mum, but it looks like I've acquired another part-time version. Linzie. Linzie Fogarty. I'm not sure what she makes of me: I can see her watching me out of the corner of her eye, trying to work out if I'm going to do something dark and Gothic or chew up a terrapin or something. Dad said she's somebody high up in the local council. He said it like he was really proud, like he's gone up in the world. I'm not sure he ever looked at Jess the way he looks at her.

For about the first hour after we got here I just felt really awkward, like I basically just acquired one more place to feel like I didn't fit. The house is really tidy and they don't have any books, unlike ours, where Jess has stuffed them into pretty much every room except the bathroom and there's usually one by the loo anyway. And I kept staring at Dad because I couldn't believe he'd been living here like a totally normal person while lying to us all the time. It made me hate her, like I hate him.

But then Tanzie said something at supper, and Linzie burst out laughing, and it was this really goofy, honking laugh — *Foghorn Fogarty,* I thought — and she clamped her hand over her mouth and she and Dad exchanged a look like it was a sound she should have tried really, really hard not to make. And something about the way her eyes wrinkled up made me think maybe she was okay.

I mean, her family has just taken on a weird shape, too. She had two kids, Suze and Josh, and Dad. And suddenly there's me — Gothboy, as Dad calls me, like that's funny — and Tanze, who has taken to wearing two pairs of glasses on top of each other because she says the one pair isn't quite right; and Jess going nutso on her driveway, kicking holes in her car; and Mr. Nicholls, who definitely has a thing about Mum, hanging around and calmly trying to sort everyone out like the only grownup in the place. And no doubt Dad has had to tell her about my biological mum, who might also end up on her driveway one day, shouting like that first Christmas after I moved in with Jess when she threw bottles at our windows and screamed herself hoarse until the neighbors called the police. So all things considered, Foghorn Fogarty might honestly be feeling like her family isn't in quite the shape she expected, either.

I don't really know why I'm telling you this. It's just that it's three thirty a.m. and everyone else in this house is asleep and I'm in Josh's room with Tanzie and he has his own computer — both of them have their own computers (Macs, no less) — and I can't remember his codes to do any gaming. But I've been thinking about what Mr. Nicholls said about blogging and how somehow if you write it and put it out there, like that baseball audience in *Field of Dreams,* your people might just come.

You probably aren't my people. You're probably people who made a typo while doing a search on discount tires or porn or something. But I'm putting it out here anyway. Just in case you happen to be anything like me.

Because this last twenty-four hours has made me see something. I might not fit in the way that you fit with your family, neatly, a little row of round pegs in perfectly round holes. In our family all our pegs and holes belonged somewhere else first, and they're all sort of jammed in and a bit lopsided. But here's the thing. I don't know if it's being away from everything, or how intense these last few days have been, but I realized something when Dad sat down and told me it was good to see me and his eyes got all moist: my dad might be an arse, but he's my arse, and he's the only arse I've got. And feeling the weight of Jess's hand as she sat by my hospital bed, or hearing her try not to cry on the phone at the thought of leaving me here, and watching my little sister, who is trying to be really, really brave about the whole school thing, even though I can tell that her world has basically ended — it all made me see that I do sort of belong somewhere.

I think I sort of belong to them.

CHAPTER TWENTY-FIVE: JESS

Ed lay propped against the pillows, watching her do her makeup, painting over the bruises on her face with a little tube of concealer. She had just about covered the blue one on her temple where her head had bounced off the air bag. But her nose was purple, the skin stretched tight over a bump that hadn't been there before, and her upper lip bore the swollen, oversized look of a woman who had ill-advisedly indulged in backstreet plastic surgery. "You look like someone punched you in the nose."

Jess rubbed her finger gently over her mouth. "So do you."

"*It* did. My own car, thanks to you."

She tilted her head, gazing at his reflection behind her. He had this slow, lopsided grin, and his chin was a giant bristly shadow. She couldn't not smile back.

"Jess, I'm not sure there's really any point trying to cover it. You're going to look bashed up whatever you do."

"I thought I'd tell your parents, sorrow-fully, that I walked into a door. Maybe with a bit of a furtive sideways look at you."

He let out a sigh and stretched, closing his eyes. "If that's the worst they think of me by the end of today, I suspect I'll be doing quite well."

She gave up on her face, and shut her makeup bag. He was right: short of spending the day pressed against an ice pack, there was little she could do to make it look less battered. She ran a speculative tongue over her sore upper lip. "I can't believe I didn't feel this when we were . . . well, last night."

Last night.

She turned and crawled up the bed until she was lying full length alongside him, luxuriating in the feel of him against her. She couldn't believe that they had not even properly met each other a week previously. He opened his eyes, sleepily, reached out, and toyed lazily with a lock of her hair.

"That'll be the sheer power of my animal magnetism."

"Or the two joints and a bottle and a half of Merlot."

He hooked his arm around her neck and pulled her into him. She closed her eyes briefly, breathing in the scent of his skin. He smelled pleasingly of sex. "Be nice," he growled softly. "I'm a bit broken today."

"I'll run you a bath." She traced the mark on his head where it had hit the car door. They kissed, long and slow and sweet, and it raised a possibility.

"Are you okay?"

"Never felt better." He opened one eye.

"No. About lunch."

He looked briefly serious, and let his head fall back on the pillow. She regretted mentioning it. "No. But I guess I'll feel better when it's done."

She sat in the loo, agonizing in private, then rang Marty at a quarter to nine and told him she had something to sort out and that she would now pick the children up between three and four. She didn't ask. From now on, she had decided, she was just going to tell him how it was going to be. He put Tanzie on the phone, and she wanted to know how Norman had coped without her. The dog was stretched out in front of the fire, like a three-dimensional rug. She wasn't entirely sure he'd moved in twelve hours, besides to eat breakfast.

"He survived. Just."

"Dad said he's going to make bacon

sandwiches. And then we might go to the park. Just him and me and Nicky. Linzie's taking Suze to ballet. She has ballet lessons twice a week."

"That sounds great," Jess said. She wondered whether being able to sound cheerful about things that made her want to kick something was her superpower.

"I'll be back some time after three," she said to Marty, when he came back on the phone. "Please make sure Tanzie wears her coat."

"Jess," he said, as she was about to ring off.

"What?"

"They're great. The pair of them. I just —"

Jess swallowed. "After three. I'll ring if I'm going to be any later."

She walked the dog and when she returned, Ed was up and breakfasted. They drove the hour to his parents' house in silence. He had shaved and changed his T-shirt twice, even though they were both exactly the same. She sat beside him and said nothing, and felt, with the morning and the miles, the intimacy of the previous evening slowly seep away. Several times she opened her mouth to speak and then found she didn't know what to say. She felt as if someone had peeled a layer of skin off her, leaving all her nerve endings exposed. Her laugh was too loud, her movements unnatural and self-conscious. She felt as if she had been asleep for a million years and someone had just blasted her awake.

What she really wanted to do was touch him, to rest a hand on his thigh. And yet she wasn't sure whether, now that they were out of the bedroom and in the unforgiving light of day, that was appropriate. She wasn't entirely sure what he thought had taken place.

Jess lifted her bruised foot and placed the bag of refrozen peas back onto it. Taking it off and putting it back on again.

"You okay?"

"Fine." She had mostly done it for something to do. She smiled fleetingly at him and he smiled back.

She thought about leaning across and kissing him. She thought about running her finger lightly along the back of his neck so that he would look over at her like he had the previous night. About undoing her seat belt and edging across the front seat and forcing him to pull over, just so she could take his mind off things for another twenty minutes. And then she remembered Nathalie, who, three years previously, in an effort to be impulsive, had given Dean a surprise blow job while he was driving his truck. He had yelled, "What the hell do you think you're doing?" and plowed straight into the back of a Mini Metro, and before he'd had a chance to do himself up, Nathalie's aunt Doreen had come running out of the supermarket to see what had happened. She had never looked at Nathalie in quite the same way again.

So maybe not. As they drove she kept stealing looks at him. She found she couldn't see his hands without picturing them on her skin, and then that soft mop of hair traveling slowly down her bare stomach. Oh, God. She crossed her legs and stared out of the window.

But Ed's mind was elsewhere. He had grown quieter, the muscle in his jaw tightening, his hands a fraction too fixed on the wheel.

She turned to the front, adjusted the frozen peas, and thought about trains. And lampposts. And Maths Olympiads. They drove on in silence, their thoughts humming like twin wheels.

Ed's parents lived in a gray stone Victorian house at the end of a terrace, the kind of street where neighbors try to outdo each other with the neatness of their window boxes. Ed pulled up, let the engine tick down. He didn't move.

Almost without thinking, she reached out and touched his hand. He turned to her as if he'd forgotten she was there. "You sure you don't mind coming in with me?"

"Of course not," she stuttered.

"I'm really grateful. I know you wanted to get the kids."

She rested her hand on his briefly. "It's fine."

They walked up the path, and Ed paused, then knocked sharply on the front door. They glanced at each other, smiled awkwardly, and waited. And waited some more.

After about thirty seconds, he knocked again, louder this time. And then he crouched to peer through the letter box.

He straightened up and reached for his phone. "Odd. I'm sure Gem said the lunch was today. Let me check." He flicked through some messages, nodded, then knocked again.

"I'm pretty sure if anyone was there they would have heard," Jess said. The thought occurred, in passing, that it would be quite nice just for once to walk up to a house and have a clue what was happening on the other side of the door.

They startled at the stuttering sound of a sash window being raised above their heads. Ed took a step back and peered up at next door.

"Is that you, Ed?"

"Hi, Mrs. Harris. I'm after my parents. Any idea where they are?"

The woman grimaced. "Oh, Ed dear, they've gone to the hospital. I'm afraid your father took ill again early this morning."

Ed put his hand up to his eyes. "Which hospital?"

She hesitated. "The Royal, dear. It's about four miles away if you head for the dual motorway. You want to go left at the end of the road —"

"It's okay, Mrs. Harris. I know where it is. Thank you."

"Give him our best," she called, and Jess heard the window being pulled down. Ed was already opening the car door.

They reached the hospital in a matter of minutes. Jess didn't speak. She had no idea what to say. At one point she ventured, "Well, at least they'll be glad to see you." But it was a stupid thing to say and he was so deep in thought that he didn't seem to hear. He gave his father's name at the information desk and the receptionist ran a finger down her screen. "You know where Oncology is, yes?" she added, looking up from her screen.

They entered a steel lift and traveled up two floors. Ed gave his name on the intercom, cleaned his hands with the antibacterial lotion by the ward's door, and, when the doors finally clicked open, she followed him through.

A woman walked down the hospital corridor toward them. She was wearing a felt skirt and colored tights. Her hair was cut in a short, feathery style.

"Hey, Gem," he said, slowing as she drew near.

The woman looked at him, disbelieving. Her jaw dropped, and for a moment Jess thought she was going to say something.

"It's good to s—" he began. From nowhere, the woman's hand shot out, smacking Ed across the face. The sound actually echoed down the corridor.

Ed staggered backward, clutching his cheek. "What the —"

"You fucking wanker," she said. "You fucking, fucking wanker."

The two of them stared at each other, Ed lowering his hand as if to check for blood.

She shook her hand, looking quite surprised at herself, and then after a moment, held it gingerly toward Jess. "Hello, I'm Gemma."

Jess hesitated, then shook it carefully. "Um . . . Jess."

Gemma frowned. "The one with a child in need of urgent help."

When Jess nodded, Gemma looked her up and down slowly. Her smile was weary, rather than unfriendly. "Yes, I rather thought you might be. Right. Mum's down the end, Ed. You'd better come and say hello."

"Is he here? Is it Ed?" The woman's hair was gunmetal gray, pinned up in a neat twist. "Oh, Ed! It is you. Oh, darling. How lovely. But what have you done to yourself?"

He hugged her, then pulled back, ducking his face when she tried to touch his nose, and giving Jess the swiftest sideways look. "I . . . I walked into a door."

She pulled him close again, patting his back. "Oh, it is so good to see you."

He let her hold him for a minute, then gently disentangled himself. "Mum, this is Jess."

"I'm . . . Ed's friend."

"Well, how lovely to meet you. I'm Anne." Her gaze traveled briefly over Jess's face, taking in her bruised nose, the faint swelling on her lip. She hesitated just a moment, then perhaps decided not to ask. "I'm afraid I can't say Ed's told me an awful lot about you, but he never does tell me an awful lot about anything, so I'm very much looking forward to hearing it from you." She put her hand on Ed's arm and her smile wavered a little. "We did have a rather nice lunch planned but . . ."

Gemma took a step closer to her mother and began rummaging around in her handbag. "But Dad was taken ill again."

"He was so looking forward to this lunch. We had to put Simon and Deirdre off. They were just setting out from the Peak District."

"I'm sorry," Jess said.

"Yes. Well. Nothing to be done." She seemed to pull herself together. "You know, it really is the most revolting disease. I have to work quite hard not to take it all personally." She leaned into Jess with a rueful smile. "Sometimes I go into our bedroom and I call it the most dreadful names. Bob would be horrified."

Jess smiled back at her. "I'll give it a few from me, if you like."

"Oh, please do! That would be wonderful. The filthier, the better. And loud. It has to be loud."

"Jess can do loud," Ed said, dabbing at his lip.

There was a short silence.

"I bought a whole salmon," Anne said to nobody in particular.

Jess could feel Gemma studying her. Unconsciously she pulled at her T-shirt, not wanting her tattoo to show above her jeans. The words "social worker" always made her feel scrutinized.

And then Anne moved past her and was holding out her arms. The hungry way she pulled Ed to her again made Jess wince a little. "Oh, darling. Darling boy. I know I'm being a terribly clingy mum but do indulge me. It really is so lovely to see you." He hugged her back, his eyes raising to Jess's briefly, guiltily.

"My mother last hugged me in 1997," murmured Gemma. Jess wasn't sure she was aware that she had said it out loud.

"I'm not sure mine ever did," Jess said.

Gemma looked at her. "Um . . . about the whole whacking-my-brother thing. He's probably told you what I do for a living. I just feel obliged to stress that I don't usually hit people."

"I don't think brothers count."

There was a sudden flicker of warmth behind Gemma's eyes. "That's a very sensible rule."

"No problem," Jess said. "Anyway, I've wanted to do it quite often myself over the past few days."

Bob Nicholls lay in a hospital bed, a blanket up to his chin and his hands resting gently on its surface. His skin held a waxy, yellow pallor and the bones of his skull were almost visible beneath it. His head turned slowly toward the door as they entered. An oxygen mask sat on a bedside table, and two faint indents on his cheek told of its recent use. He was painful to look at.

"Hey, Dad."

Jess watched Ed struggle to hide his shock. He stooped toward his father and hesitated before touching him lightly on the shoulder.

"Edward." His voice was a croak

"Doesn't he look well, Bob?" said his mother.

His father studied him from under shadowed lids. When he spoke, it was slowly, and with deliberation.

"No. He looks like someone beat the living daylights out of him."

Jess could see the new color on Ed's cheekbone where his sister had hit him. She found herself reaching unconsciously toward her injured lip.

"Where's he been, anyway?"

"Dad, this is Jess."

His father's eyes slid toward her, his eyebrow lifting a quarter of an inch. "And what the hell happened to your face?" he whispered to her.

"I had an argument with a car. My fault."

"Is that what happened to him?"

"Yes."

He regarded her for a moment longer. "You look like trouble," he said. "Are you trouble?"

Gemma leaned forward. "Dad! Jess is Ed's friend."

He dismissed her. "If there's one small advantage to having very little time left, then surely it's that I can say whatever I like. She doesn't look offended. Are you offended? I'm sorry, I've forgotten your name. I don't seem to have any brain cells anymore."

"Jess. And no, I'm not offended."

He kept staring.

"And, yes, I probably am trouble," she said, holding his gaze.

His smile was slow to arrive, but when it came, she could imagine, fleetingly, how he must have looked before he got ill. "Glad to hear it. I always liked girls who were trouble. And this one has been head down in front of a computer for far too long."

"How are you, Dad?"

Bob Nicholls blinked. "I'm dying."

"We're all dying, Dad," Gemma said.

"Don't give me your social-worker sophistry. I am dying uncomfortably and rapidly. I have few faculties left, and very little dignity. I will probably not make the end of the cricket season. Does that answer your question?"

"I'm sorry," Ed said quietly. "I'm sorry I haven't been by."

"You've been busy."

"About that . . . ," Ed began. His hands were thrust deep in his pockets. "Dad. I need to tell you something. I need to tell you all something."

Jess stood up hurriedly. "Why don't I go and get us some sandwiches? Leave you to talk."

Jess could feel Gemma studying her. "I'll get drinks, too. Tea? Coffee?"

Bob Nicholls's head turned toward her. "You've only just got here. Stay."

Her eyes met Ed's. He gave a tiny shrug.

"What is it, dear?" His mother put a hand out to him. "Are you all right?"

"I'm fine. Well. I'm sort of fine. I mean I'm healthy. But . . ." He swallowed. "No, I'm not fine. There's something I have to tell you."

"What?" Gemma said.

"Okay." He took a deep breath. "Well, here it is."

"What?" said Gemma. "Jesus, Ed. What?"

"I'm being investigated for insider trading. I've been suspended from my company. Next week I have to go to a police station where I will in all likelihood be charged and I may go to prison."

To say the room fell silent was an understatement. It was as if someone had come in and sucked out all the available air. Jess thought she might pass out.

"Is this a joke?" said his mother.

"No."

"I really could go and get some tea," Jess said.

Nobody paid her any attention. Ed's mother sat down slowly on a plastic chair.

"Insider trading?" Gemma was the first to speak. "This — that's serious, Ed."

"Yeah. I do get that, Gem."

"Actual insider trading, like you see on the news?"

"That's the one."

"He's got good lawyers," Jess said.

Nobody seemed to hear.

"Expensive ones."

His mother's hand had risen halfway to her mouth. She lowered it slowly. "I don't understand. When did this happen?"

"A month or so ago. The insider-trading bit, anyway."

"A month ago? But why didn't you tell us? We could have helped you."

"You couldn't, Mum. Nobody can help."

"But prison? Like a criminal?" Anne Nicholls had gone quite pale.

"I think if you're sent to prison, you pretty much are a criminal, Mum."

"Well, they'll have to sort it out. They'll see that there's been some kind of mistake, but they'll sort it out."

"No, Mum. I'm not sure it's going to work out like that."

There was another long silence.

"Are you going to be all right?"

"I'll be fine. As Jess said, I have good lawyers. I have resources. They have already established that there was no financial gain for me."

"You didn't even make money out of it?"

"It was a mistake."

"A mistake?" said Gemma. "I don't get it. How do you do insider trading by mistake?"

Ed straightened his shoulders and looked at her. He took a breath, and his gaze flickered toward Jess. And then he looked up at the ceiling. "Well, I had sex with a woman. I thought I liked her. And then I realized she wasn't who I thought she was and I sort of wanted her to go away without it all getting messy. And what she wanted to do was travel. So I made a snap decision and told her a way I thought she could make a little extra money to pay off her debts and go traveling."

"You gave her inside information."

"Yup. On SFAX. Our big product launch."

"Jesus Christ." Gemma shook her head. "I can't believe I'm hearing this."

"And my name hasn't come out in the press yet. But it will." He put his hands into his pockets and looked steadily at his family. Jess wondered if only she could detect that his hand was shaking. "So . . . um . . . that's why I haven't been home. I was hoping I could keep it from you, maybe even sort it out so that you didn't have to know anything about it. But it turns out that's going to be impossible. And I wanted to say I'm sorry. I should have told you right away, and I should have spent more time here. But I . . . I didn't want you to know the truth. I didn't want you to see what a mess I'd made of everything."

Jess's right leg had begun to jiggle involuntarily. She concentrated on a really interesting floor tile and tried to make her leg stop. When she finally looked up, Ed was staring at his father. "Well?"

"Well what?"

"You're not going to say anything?"

Bob Nicholls lifted his head slowly from his pillow. "What do you want me to say?"

Ed and his dad stared at each other.

"You want me to say you've been an idiot? I'll say you've been an idiot. You want me to say you've ballsed up a brilliant career? I'll say that, too."

"Bob . . ."

"Well, what do you —" Abruptly, he started to cough, a hollow, rasping sound. Anne and Gemma lurched forward to help him, handing over tissues, glasses of water, fussing and clucking like a pair of hens.

Ed was standing at the foot of his father's bed.

"Prison?" his mother said again. "Actual *prison* prison?"

"Sit down, Mum. Deep breaths." Gemma steered her mother into a chair.

Nobody moved toward Ed. Why didn't somebody hug him? Why could they not see how alone he felt right at that minute?

"I'm sorry," he said quietly.

Jess could bear it no longer. "Can I say something?" She heard her voice, clear and slightly too loud. "I just want to tell you that Ed helped my two children when I couldn't. He drove us the length of the country, because we were desperate. As far as I'm concerned, your son is . . . wonderful."

They all looked up. Jess turned to his father. "He's kind, smart, and clever, even if I don't agree with all the things he does. He's nice to people he barely knows. Insider trading or no, if my son turns out as half the man your son is, then I'll be very happy. More than happy. I'll be ecstatic."

They were all staring at her.

She added: "And I thought that even before I had sex with him."

Nobody spoke. Ed stared fixedly at his feet.

"Well," Anne gave a faint nod, "that's, er, that's —"

"Enlightening," said Gemma.

Anne's voice trailed away. "Oh, Edward."

Bob sighed and closed his eyes. "Let's not get all Hollywood about this." He opened them again and signaled for the head of the bed to be raised a little. "Come here, Ed. Where I can see you. Wretched eyesight." He motioned for the glass again and his wife held it to his lips.

He swallowed painfully, then tapped the side of his bed, so that Ed sat down on it. He reached out a hand and rested it lightly on his son's. He was unbearably frail. "You're my son, Ed. You might be idiotic and irresponsible, but it doesn't make the slightest difference to what I feel about you." He frowned. "I'm pissed off that you could have thought it would."

"I'm sorry, Dad."

His father gave a slow shake of his head. "I'm afraid I can't be much help. Stupid, breathless . . ." He pulled a face, then swallowed painfully. His hand tightened around Ed's. "We all make mistakes. Go and take your punishment, then come back and start again."

Ed looked up at him.

"Do even better next time. I know you can."

It was at that point that Anne started to cry, helpless tears that she buried in her sleeve. Bob turned his head slowly toward her. "Oh, darling," he said softly. And that was when Jess opened the door silently and slid out.

She put some credit on her phone in the hospital shop, texted Ed to say where she was, and waited in A and E to get her foot looked at. Badly bruised, said a young Polish doctor, who didn't bat an eyelid when she told him how she had done it. He strapped it up, wrote a prescription for painkillers, handed her back her flip-flop, and advised her to rest. "Try not to kick any more cars," he said without looking up from his clipboard.

Jess hobbled back upstairs to Victoria Ward, sat on one of the plastic chairs in the corridor, and waited. It was warm and the people around her spoke in whispers. She may have nodded off briefly. She woke abruptly when Ed emerged from his father's room. She held out his jacket and he took it without a word. A moment later Gemma appeared in the corridor. His sister put her hand gently to the side of his face. "You bloody idiot."

His head dipped, hands shoved deep in his pockets, like Nicky.

"You stupid bloody stupid idiot. Call me."

He pulled back. His eyes were red rimmed.

"I mean it. I'll come with you to court. I might know some people in probation who could help get you into an open prison. I mean, you're not going to be category A, as long as you haven't done anything else." Her eyes flickered toward Jess and back to him. "You haven't done anything else, right?"

He leaned forward and hugged her, and maybe it was only Jess who noticed the way his eyes closed really tightly when he pulled away.

They emerged from the hospital into the luminous white of a spring day. Real life, inexplicably, seemed to have continued regardless. Cars reversed into spaces too small, strollers were disgorged from buses, a workman's radio blared as he painted a nearby railing. Jess found herself taking deep breaths, grateful to be away from the stale, medical air of the ward, the almost tangible specter of death that hung over Ed's father. Ed walked and looked straight ahead. He paused when they reached his car and unlocked it with an audible clunk. Then he stopped. It was as if he couldn't move. He stood there, one arm slightly outstretched, staring blankly at his car.

Jess waited for a minute, and then she walked slowly around it. She took the key from his hand. And finally, when his gaze slid toward her, she slid her arms tight around his waist and held him until his head came slowly down to rest, a soft deadweight upon her shoulder.

Chapter Twenty-Six: Tanzie

Nicky actually started a conversation at breakfast. They had been eating around the table like a television family — Tanzie had multigrain hoops, and Suze and Josh had chocolate croissants, which Suze said they had every day because it was their favorite — and it was a bit weird sitting there with Dad and his other family but not actually as bad as she'd thought. Dad was eating a bowl of bran flakes because he said he had to stay trim now, as he patted his stomach, although she wasn't sure why because it wasn't like he had a job. "Things in the pipeline, Tanze," he said whenever she asked what he was actually doing. She wondered if Linzie had a garage full of air-conditioning units that didn't work, too. Linzie didn't seem to eat anything. Nicky was toying with some toast — he rarely ate breakfast; until this trip Tanzie wasn't sure he had ever been up for breakfast — when he just looked at

Dad and said, "Jess works all the time. All the time. And I don't think it's fair."

Dad's spoon stopped halfway to his mouth, and Tanzie wondered whether he was going to get really angry, like he used to if Nicky said anything he felt was disrespectful. Nobody said anything for a minute. Then Linzie put her hand on Dad's and smiled. "He's right, love."

And Dad went a bit pink and said, yes, well, things were going to change a bit from now on and we all made mistakes, and because she felt a bit braver then, Tanzie said, no, strictly speaking, not all of us did make mistakes. She had made a mistake with her algorithms and Norman had made a mistake because of the cows and breaking her glasses, and Mum had made a mistake with the Rolls-Royce and getting arrested, but Nicky was the one person in their family who hadn't made any mistakes. But halfway through her saying it, Nicky kicked her hard under the table and gave her that look.

What? her eyes said to him.

Shut it, his said to her.

Grrr, don't tell me to shut it, hers said to him.

And then he wouldn't look at her.

"Would you like a chocolate croissant,

love?" Linzie said, and put one on her plate before Tanzie had even answered.

Linzie had washed and dried Tanzie's clothes overnight, and they smelled of orchid and vanilla fabric conditioner. Everything in that house smelled of something. It was as if nothing were allowed to just smell of itself. She had little plug-in things dotted around her baseboards that released "a luxurious scent of rare blossoms and rain forests" and bowls of potpourri and about a billion candles in the bathroom ("I do love my scented candles"). Tanzie's nose itched the whole time they were indoors.

After breakfast Linzie took Suze to ballet. Dad and Tanzie went to the park even though she hadn't been to the park in about two years because she had sort of grown out of it. But she didn't want to hurt Dad's feelings so she sat on the swing and let him push her a few times. Nicky stood and watched, with his hands stuffed into his pockets. He had left his Nintendo in Mr. Nicholls's car and she knew he really, really wanted a cigarette, but she didn't think he felt brave enough to smoke one in front of Dad.

There were chip-shop chips for lunch ("Don't tell Linzie," Dad said, patting his stomach again), and Dad asked questions about Mr. Nicholls, trying to sound all casual: "Who is he then, that bloke? Your mum's boyfriend?"

"No," said Nicky, in a way that made it hard for Dad to ask another question. Tanzie thought Dad was a bit shocked at how Nicky spoke to him. Not that he was rude, exactly, it's just that he didn't seem to care what Dad thought. And Nicky was now taller than him, but when Tanzie pointed it out, Dad didn't seem to think that was amazing at all.

And then Tanzie got cold because she hadn't brought her coat, so they went back and Suze was already home from ballet so they played some games and Nicky went upstairs to the computer. Then Tanzie and Suze went to her room and Suze said they could watch a DVD because she had her own DVD player and she watched a whole one by herself every night before she went to sleep.

"Doesn't your mum read to you?" Tanzie said.

"She doesn't have time. That's why she got me the DVD player," Suze said. She had a whole shelf of films, all her favorites, that she could watch up there when they were watching something she didn't like downstairs.

"Marty likes gangster films so they watch those," she said, her nose wrinkling, and it took Tanzie a few minutes to realize she was actually talking about her dad. And she didn't know what to say.

"I like your jacket," Suze said, peering into Tanzie's bag.

"My mum made it for me for Christmas."

"Your mum actually made it?" She held it up, so that the sequins Mum had sewn into the sleeves glinted in the light. "Oh, my God, is she like a fashion designer or something?"

"No," Tanzie said. "She's a cleaner."

Suze laughed as if Tanzie'd been joking.

"What are all those?" she said when she saw the maths papers in her bag.

This time Tanzie kept her mouth closed.

"Is that maths? Oh, my God, it's like . . . squiggles. It's like . . . Greek." She giggled, flicking through them, then holding them from two fingers, like they were something horrible. "Are they your brother's? Is he, like, a maths freak?"

"I don't know." Tanzie blushed because she was not very good at lying.

"Ugh. What a brainiac. Freaky. Geeky." She tossed them to one side, while she pulled out Tanzie's other clothes. "Does everything you own have sequins on it?"

Tanzie didn't say anything. She left the papers there on the floor because she didn't want to have to explain. And she didn't want to think about the Olympiad. And she just thought maybe it would be easier if she tried to be like Suze from now on because she seemed really happy and Dad seemed really happy here. And then, because she really didn't want to think about anything anymore, Tanzie said that maybe they should watch television downstairs.

They were three quarters of the way through *Fantasia* when Tanzie heard Dad calling, "Tanze, your mum's here." Mum stood on the doorstep with her chin up like she was ready for an argument. When Tanzie stopped and stared at her face, Mum put a hand to her lip as if she had only just remembered it was split, then said, "I fell over." Tanzie looked behind her to Mr. Nicholls who was sitting in the car, and Mum said, quick as anything, "He fell over, too." Even though she hadn't actually been able to see his face and she had just wanted to see whether they were getting in the car or if they were going to have to get a bus after all.

And Dad said, "Does everything you come into contact with these days suffer some kind of injury?" Mum gave him a look and he muttered something about repairs, then said he'd go and get her bag, and Tanzie let out a big breath and ran into Mum's arms because although she'd had a nice time at Linzie's house, she'd missed Norman and she wanted to be with Mum and she was suddenly really, really tired.

The cabin that Mr. Nicholls had rented was like something out of an advertisement for what old people want to do when they retire, or maybe pills for urine problems. It was on a lake and there were a few other houses, but they were mostly set back behind trees or at angles so that no single window looked directly at any other house. There were fifty-six ducks and twenty geese on the water, and all but three were still there by the time they'd had tea. Tanzie thought Norman might chase them, but he just flopped down on the grass and watched.

"Awesome," said Nicky, even though he didn't really like the outdoors at all. He inhaled deeply, then took two pictures on Mr. Nicholls's phone. She realized he hadn't smoked a cigarette for four days.

"Isn't it?" said Mum. She gazed out at the lake. She started to say something about paying their share, and Mr. Nicholls held up his hands and made this *"no no no no"* noise like he didn't even want to hear it, and Mum went a bit pink and stopped.

They had dinner on a barbecue outside — even though it was not really barbecue weather — because Mum said it would be a fun end to the trip, and when did she ever get time to do a barbecue, anyway? She seemed determined to make everyone happy and just chatted away about twice as much as anyone else, and she said she'd blown the budget because sometimes you had to count your blessings and live a little. It seemed like it was her way of saying thank you to Mr. Nicholls. So they had sausages and chicken thighs in spicy sauce and fresh rolls and salad, and Mum had bought two tubs of the good ice cream, not the cheap stuff that came in the white plastic cartons. She didn't ask anything about Dad's new house, but she did hug Tanzie a lot and said that she'd missed her and wasn't that silly because it was only one night after all.

They each told jokes, and even though Tanzie could only remember the one that went "What's brown and sticky?" (answer: a stick), everyone laughed, and they played the game where you put a broomstick to your forehead and the other end on the ground and run around it in circles until you fall over. Mum did it once, even though she could barely walk with her foot all strapped up and kept saying, *Ow, ow, ow,* as she went round in a circle. And that made Tanzie laugh because it was just nice to see Mum being silly for a change. And Mr. Nicholls kept saying, No, no, not for him, thanks, he would just watch. And then Mum limped over to him and said something really quiet in his ear and he raised his eyebrows and said, "Really?" And she nodded. And he said, "Well, all right, then." And when he crashed over, he actually made the ground vibrate a little. And even Nicky, who never did anything, did it, his legs sticking out like a daddy longlegs, and when he laughed, his laugh was really strange, like this *huh huh huh* sound, and then Tanzie decided she hadn't heard him laugh like that for ages. Maybe ever.

And she did it about six times until the world bucked and rolled beneath her and she collapsed on her back on the grass and watched the sky spin slowly around her and thought that was a bit like life for their family. Never quite the way it was meant to be.

They ate the food, and Mum and Mr. Nicholls had some wine, and Tanzie took all the scraps off the bones and gave them to Norman because dogs die if you give them chicken bones. And then they put their coats on and just sat out on the nice wicker chairs that went with the cabin, all lined up in a row in front of the lake, and watched the birds on the water until it got dark. "I love this place," said Mum into the silence. Tanzie wasn't sure anyone was meant to see it, but Mr. Nicholls reached over and gave Mum's hand a squeeze.

Mr. Nicholls seemed a little sad most of the evening. Tanzie wasn't sure why. She wondered if it was because they'd reached the end of the little trip. But the sound of the water lapping against the shore was really calm and peaceful and she must have fallen asleep because she vaguely remembered Mr. Nicholls carrying her upstairs and Mum tucking her in and telling her she loved her. But what she mostly remembered about that whole evening was that nobody talked about the Olympiad, and she was just really, really glad.

Because here's the thing. While Mum was getting the barbecue set up, Tanzie asked to borrow Mr. Nicholls's computer and looked up the statistics for children of low-income families at private schools. And she saw within a few minutes that the probability of her actually going to St. Anne's had always been in single-figure percentages. And she understood that it didn't matter how well she had done in that entrance test; she should have checked this figure before they had even left home because you only ever went wrong in life when you didn't pay attention to the numbers. Nicky came upstairs, and when he saw what she was doing, he stood there without saying anything for a minute, then patted her arm and said he would speak to a couple of people he knew at McArthur's to make sure they looked out for her.

When they were at Linzie's, Dad had told her that private school was no guarantee of success. He'd said it three times. *Success is all about what's inside you,* he said. *Determination.* And then he said Tanzie should get Suze to show her how she did her hair because maybe hers would look nice like that, too.

Mum said she would sleep on the couch that night so that Tanzie and Nicky could have the second bedroom, but Tanzie didn't think she did because when she woke up really thirsty in the middle of the night and went downstairs, Mum wasn't there. And in the morning Mum was wearing Mr. Nicholls's gray T-shirt that he wore every single day and Tanzie waited twenty minutes watching his door because she was curious to know what he was going to come down in.

A faint mist hung across the lake in the morning. It rose off the water like a magician's trick as everyone packed up the car. Norman sniffed around the grass, his tail wagging slowly. "Rabbits," said Mr. Nicholls (he was wearing another gray T-shirt). The morning was chill and the wood pigeons cooed softly in the trees and Tanzie had that sad feeling like you've been somewhere really nice and it's all come to an end.

"I don't want to go home," she said quietly, as Mum shut the boot.

She flinched. "What, love?"

"I don't want to go back home," Tanzie said.

Mum glanced at Mr. Nicholls and then she tried to smile, walked over slowly, and said, "Do you mean you want to be with your dad, Tanze? Because if that's what you really want, I'll —"

"No. I just like this house and it's nice here." She wanted to say, *And there's nothing to look forward to when we get back because everything is spoiled, and besides, here there are no Fishers,* but she could see from Mum's face that that was what she was thinking, too, because she immediately

446

looked at Nicky and he shrugged.

"You know, there's no shame in having tried to do something, right?" Mum gazed at them both. "We all did our best to make something happen, and it didn't happen, but some good things have come out of it. We got to see some parts of the country we would never have seen. We learned a few things. We sorted it out with your dad. We made some friends." It's possible she meant Linzie and her children, but her eyes were on Mr. Nicholls when she said it. "So all in all I think it was a good thing that we tried, even if it didn't go quite the way we'd planned. And, you know, maybe things won't be so bad once we get home."

Nicky's face didn't show anything. Tanzie knew he was thinking about money.

And then Mr. Nicholls, who had said barely anything all morning, walked around the car, opened the door, and said, "Yes. Well, I've been thinking about that. And we're going to make a little detour."

Chapter Twenty-Seven: Jess

They were a muted little group in the car on the way home. Even Norman no longer whined, as if he had accepted that this car was now his home. The whole time Jess had planned the trip, through the strange, frenetic few days of traveling, she hadn't really imagined any further than getting Tanzie to the Olympiad. She would get her there, Tanzie would sit the test, and everything would be okay. She hadn't given a thought to the possibility that the entire trip might take three days longer than she had planned. Or that she would be left with precisely £13.81 in cash to her name and a bank card that she was too frightened to feed into a cashpoint machine in case it didn't come back.

Jess mentioned none of this to Ed, who was silent, his gaze trained on the road ahead.

Ed. Jess repeated his name silently in her

head until it ceased to have any real meaning. When he smiled, Jess couldn't help smiling. When his face turned sad, something inside her broke a little. She watched him with her children, the easy way in which he admired some photograph Nicky had taken on his phone, the serious manner in which he considered a passing comment of Tanzie's — the kind of comment that would have caused Marty to roll his eyes to heaven — and she wished he had been in their lives long ago. When they were alone and he held her close to him, his palm resting with a hint of possession on Jess's thigh, his breath soft in her ear, she felt with a quiet certainty that it would all be okay. It wasn't that Ed would make it okay — he had his own problems to deal with — but somehow the sum of them added up to something better. *They* would make it okay.

Because she wanted Ed Nicholls. She wanted to wrap her legs around him in the dark and feel him inside her, to buck against him as he held her. She wanted the sweat and the pull and the solidity of him, his mouth on hers, his eyes on hers. They drove and she recalled the previous two nights in hot, dreamy fragments, his hands, his mouth, the way he had to stifle her when she came so that they wouldn't wake the children, and it was all she could do not to reach across and bury her face in his neck, to slide her hands up the back of his T-shirt for the sheer pleasure of it.

She had spent so long thinking only about the children, about work and bills and money. Now her head was full of him. When he turned to her, she blushed. When he said her name, she heard it as a murmur, spoken in the dark. When he handed her coffee, the brief touch of his fingers sent an electric pulse fizzing through her. She liked it when she felt his eyes settle on her, and she wondered what he was thinking.

Jess had no idea how to communicate any of this to him. She had been so young when she met Marty, and apart from one night in the Feathers with Liam Stubbs's hands up her shirt, she had never had even the beginnings of a relationship with anyone else.

Jess Thomas had not been on an actual date since school. It made her sound ridiculous, even to herself. She had to make him understand that he had changed everything.

"We'll keep going to Nottingham, if you guys are all okay," he said, turning to look at her. He still had the faintest bruise on the side of his nose. "We'll pitch up somewhere late. That way we'll make it home in one run on Thursday."

And then what? Jess wanted to ask. But she put her feet up on the dashboard, and said, "Sounds good."

They stopped for lunch at a service station. The children had given up asking if there was any chance they could eat anything but sandwiches, and now eyed the fast-food joints and upmarket coffee shops with something close to indifference. They unfolded themselves and paused to stretch.

"How about sausage rolls?" said Ed, pointing toward a concession. "Coffee and hot sausage rolls. Or Cornish pasties. My treat. Come on."

Jess looked at him.

"Come on, you food Nazi. We'll eat some fruit afterward."

"You're not afraid? After that kebab?"

His hand was above his brow, shielding his eyes from the sun so that he could see her better. "I've decided I like living dangerously."

He had come to her the previous night, after Nicky, who had been tapping silently away at Ed's laptop in the corner of the room, had finally gone to bed. She had felt like a teenager sitting there on the sofa opposite him, pretending to watch the television, waiting. But when Nicky sloped off,

Ed had opened up the laptop rather than moving straight to her.

"What's he doing?" she had said, as Ed peered at the screen.

"Creative writing," he said.

"Not gaming? No guns? No explosions?"

"Nothing."

"He sleeps," she had whispered. "He has slept every night we've been away. Without a spliff."

"Good for him. I feel like I haven't slept for several years."

He seemed to have aged a decade in the short time they had been away. And then he had reached out a hand to her and pulled her into him. "So," he had said softly, "Jessica Rae Thomas. Are you going to let me get some sleep tonight?"

She studied his lower lip, absorbing the feel of his hand on her hip. Feeling suddenly joyous. "No," she said.

"Excellent answer."

Now they changed direction, walking away from the mini-mart, weaving their way through clumps of disgruntled travelers looking for cashpoint machines or over-crowded toilets. Jess tried not to look as delighted as she felt at the thought of not making another round of sandwiches. She could smell the buttery pastry of the hot pies from yards away.

The children, clutching a handful of notes and Ed's instructions, disappeared into the long queue inside the shop. He walked back toward her, so that they were shielded from them by the crowds of people. .

"What are you doing?"

"Just looking." Every time he stood close to her Jess felt like she was a few degrees warmer than she should have been.

"Looking?"

"I find it impossible being close to you." His lips were inches from her ear, his voice a low rumble through her skin.

Jess felt her skin prickle. "What?"

"I just imagine myself doing filthy things to you. Pretty much the whole time. Completely inappropriate things."

He took hold of the front of her jeans and pulled her to him. Jess drew back a little, craning her neck to make sure they were out of sight. "That's what you were thinking about? While you were driving? All that time while you weren't speaking?"

"Yup." He glanced behind her toward the shop. "Well, that and food."

"My two favorite things, right there."

His fingers traced the bare skin underneath her top. Her stomach tensed pleasurably. Her legs had become oddly weak. She had never wanted Marty like she wanted Ed.

"Apart from sandwiches."

"Let's not talk about sandwiches. Ever again."

And then he placed the flat of his hand on the small of her back, so that they were as close as they could decently be. "I know I shouldn't be," he murmured, "but I woke up really happy." His face scanned hers. "I mean, like, really, stupidly happy. Like even though my whole life is a disaster, I just . . . I feel okay. I look at you, and I feel okay."

A great fat lump had risen in her throat. "Me, too," she whispered.

He squinted against the sun, trying to gauge her expression. "So I'm not . . . just a horse?"

"You are so not a horse. Well, in the nicest way I could say that you were —"

He dropped his head and kissed her. He kissed her and it was a kiss of utter certainty, the kind of kiss during which monarchs die and whole continents fall without your even noticing. When Jess extricated herself, it was only because she didn't want the children to see her lose the ability to stand.

"They're coming," he said.

Jess found herself staring at him goofily.

"Trouble." He glanced back at her as they approached, bearing their paper bags aloft. "That's what my dad said."

"Like you hadn't worked that one out by yourself." She held back, watching Ed chat to Nicky, the opening of paper bags as Nicky revealed what they'd chosen, waiting for the color on her cheeks to fade. She felt the sun on her skin, heard birdsong over people talking, revving cars, smelled petrol fumes and hot pastry, and the words echoed through her head, unbidden: this is what happiness feels like.

They set off slowly back to the car, faces already buried in paper bags. Tanzie walked a few paces ahead, her skinny legs kicking the ground listlessly as she walked, and it was then that Jess noticed something was missing.

"Tanze? Where are your maths books?"

She didn't turn around. "I left them at Dad's."

"Oh. Do you want me to call him?" She fumbled in her bag for her mobile phone. "I'll get him to pop them straight in the post. They'll probably arrive back before we do."

"No," she said. She inclined her head slightly toward her, but not quite meeting Jess's eye. "Thank you."

Nicky's eyes slid to Jess and back to his sister. And something heavy settled in her stomach.

By the time they reached their final overnight stop, it was almost nine o'clock and they were drooping. The children, who had been snacking on biscuits and sweets for most of the last leg of the journey, were exhausted and cranky, and headed straight upstairs to examine the sleeping arrangements. Norman followed behind them, and then Ed with the bags.

The hotel was vast and white and expensive looking, the kind of place Mrs. Ritter might have shown Jess on her camera phone and she and Nathalie would have sighed about afterward. Ed had booked it over the phone and when Jess had started to protest about the cost, there was a slight edge to his voice: "We're all tired, Jess. And my next bed may be at Her Majesty's Pleasure. Let's just stay somewhere nice tonight, okay?"

Three interlocking rooms in a corridor seemed to double as an annex to the main hotel. "My own room." Nicky sighed with relief as he unlocked number twenty-three. He lowered his voice as Jess pushed open the door. "I love her and everything, but you have no idea how much the Titch snores."

"Norman will like this," said Tanzie, as Jess opened the door to room twenty-four. The dog, as if in agreement, immediately flopped down at the side of the bed. "I don't mind sharing with Nicky, Mum, but he really does snore badly."

Neither of them seemed to question where Jess would be sleeping. She couldn't work out whether they knew and didn't mind, or whether they just assumed either she or Ed was still sleeping in the car.

Nicky borrowed Ed's laptop. Tanzie worked out how to operate the remote control for her television, and said she would watch one program, then go to sleep. She wouldn't talk about the missing maths books. She actually said, "I don't want to talk about it." Jess didn't think Tanzie had ever said those words to her.

"Just because something doesn't work out once, sweetheart, doesn't mean you can't try again," she said, laying out Tanzie's pajamas on her bed.

Tanzie's expression seemed to contain a knowledge that hadn't been there before. And her next words broke Jess's heart. "I think it's best if I just work with what we've got, Mum."

■ ■ ■ ■

"What do I do?"

"Nothing. She's just had enough for now. You can't blame her." Ed dropped the bags in the corner of the room. Jess sat on the side of the huge bed, trying to ignore her throbbing foot.

"But this isn't like her. She loves maths. Always has. And now she's acting like she doesn't want anything to do with it."

"It's been two days, Jess. Just . . . let her be. She'll work it out."

"You're so sure."

"They're smart kids." He walked over to the switch and turned the lights down, looking up at them until he'd got it dark enough. "Like their mother. But just because you bounce back like a rubber ball, it doesn't mean they always will."

She looked at him.

"That's not a criticism. I just think if you give her some time to decompress, she'll be okay. She is who she is. I can't see that changing."

He pulled his T-shirt over his head in a fluid motion and dropped it onto a chair. Her thoughts muddled immediately. Jess couldn't see his bare torso without wanting to touch it.

"How did you get so wise?" she said.

"Dunno. I guess it rubbed off." He took two steps toward her, and then he knelt down and pulled off her flip-flops, removing the one on her injured foot with extra care. "How's it feeling?"

"Sore. But okay."

He reached for her top. He unzipped it slowly and without asking, his eyes fixed on the skin it exposed. He seemed almost distant then, as if his thoughts were on her, yet miles away. The zip caught near the end, and she took it from him gently, her hands over his, unhitching the two sides so that he could peel it from her shoulders. He stood there for a moment, just looking at her.

He unhooked her belt, then unzipped her jeans, his fingers measured and precise. She watched them and her heart began to pulse in her ears.

"It's time, Jessica Rae Thomas, that someone looked after you."

Edward Nicholls washed her hair, his legs around her waist, as she lay back against him in the oversized bath. He rinsed it gently, smoothing it and wiping her eyes with a facecloth to stop shampoo from getting into them. She went to do it herself, but he stopped her. Nobody had ever washed her hair, outside a hairdresser's. It made her feel vulnerable and oddly emotional. When he was done, he lay in the steaming, scented water with his arms wrapped around her and kissed the tips of her ears. And then they agreed jointly that this had been quite enough romantic stuff, thank you; she felt him rise under her, and she swiveled, lowered herself onto him. And they fucked until the water sluiced out of the bath, and she couldn't work out whether the pain of her foot was greater than her need to feel him inside her.

Sometime later, they lay half submerged, legs entwined. And they started to laugh. Because it was a cliché to fuck in a shower but it was ridiculous to do it in a bath, and it was even more ridiculous to be in this much trouble and yet this happy. Jess twisted so that she lay along the length of him, and draped her arms around his neck and pressed her wet chest to his, and she felt with utter certainty that she would never be as close to another human being again. She held his face in her hands and she kissed his jaw and his poor bruised temple, and his lips, and told herself that whatever happened, she would always remember how this felt.

He brought his hand down over his face, wiping the moisture from it. He looked suddenly serious. "Do you think this is a bubble?"

"Um, there're lots of bubbles. It's a —"

"No. This. A bubble. We're on this weird journey, where the normal rules don't apply. Real life doesn't apply. This whole trip has been . . . like time out of real life."

Water was pooling on the bathroom floor.

"Don't look at that. Talk to me."

She dropped her lips to his collarbone, thinking. "Well," she said, lifting her head again, "in a little more than five days, we've dealt with illness, distraught children, sick relatives, unexpected acts of violence, busted feet, police, and car accidents. I'd say that was quite enough real life for anyone."

"I like your thinking."

"I like your everything."

"We seem to spend a lot of time talking rubbish to each other."

"Well, I like that, too."

The water had started to cool. She wriggled out of his arms and stood, reaching for the heated towel rail. She handed him a towel, wrapping one around herself, noting the casual luxury of a warm, fluffy hotel towel.

Ed rubbed at his hair vigorously with one hand. She wondered, briefly, whether Ed was so used to fluffy hotel towels that he didn't even notice. She felt suddenly bone weary.

She brushed her teeth, switched off the bathroom light, and when she turned back, he was already in the enormous hotel bed, holding back the covers to let her in. He flicked off the bedside lamp and she lay there beside him in the dark, feeling his damp skin against her own, wondering what it would be like to have this every night. She wondered if she would ever be able to lie quietly beside him without wanting to slide a leg over his.

"I don't know what's going to happen to me, Jess," he said into the dark, as if he could hear her thoughts. His voice was a warning.

"You'll be okay."

"Seriously. You can't do your optimism tricks on this one. Whatever happens, I'm probably going to lose everything."

"So? That's my default position."

"But I might have to go away."

"You won't."

"I might, Jess." His voice was uncomfortably firm.

And she spoke before she knew what she

was saying. "Then I'll wait," she said.

She felt his head tilt toward her, a question. "I'll wait for you. If you want me to."

He took three calls on the final leg home, all hands free. His lawyer — a man with an accent so grand he should have been announcing the arrival of the royal family at dinner — told him he was due at the police station the following Thursday. No, nothing had changed. Yes, said Ed, he understood what was happening. And yes, he had spoken to his family. The way he said it made her stomach tense. She couldn't help herself afterward. She reached over and took his hand. When he squeezed it back, he didn't look at her.

His sister rang to say his dad had had a better night. They had a long conversation about some insurance bonds that his father had been concerned about, some keys that were missing from a filing cabinet, and what Gemma had had for lunch. Nobody talked about dying. She said to say hello and Jess shouted hello back and felt a bit self-conscious and a bit pleased at the same time.

After lunch he took a call from a man called Lewis, and they discussed market values and percentages and the state of the mortgage market. It took Jess a while to realize he was talking about Beachfront.

"Time to sell," he said when he rang off. "Still. Like you said, at least I have assets to dispose of."

"What's it all going to cost you? The prosecution?"

"Oh. Nobody's saying. But reading between the lines, I think the answer is 'most of it.' "

She couldn't work out if he was more upset than he was letting on.

He tried to call someone else, but the voice mail kicked in. "It's Ronan here. Leave a message." He hung up without saying anything.

With every mile, real life moved steadily toward them like an encroaching tide: cold, unstoppable.

They finally arrived shortly after four. The rain had eased to a fine drizzle, the road looked oily with dampness, the sprawling streets of Danehall struggled to show spring promise. There was her house, looking somehow smaller and scruffier than Jess remembered it and, oddly, like something that had nothing to do with her. Ed pulled up outside, and she peered out of the window at the peeling paintwork on the upstairs windows that Marty had never got round to painting because, he said, really, you had to do a proper job, sanding it first and taking off the old paint and using filler to plug the gaps, and he had always been either too busy or too tired to do any of it. For a moment, she felt a wave of depression wash over her at the thought of all the problems that had been sitting there waiting for their return. And all the greater ones that she had created in her absence. And then she looked at Ed, who was helping Tanzie with her bag, and laughing at something Nicky said, leaning over to hear him better, and it passed.

He had stopped at a DIY superstore about an hour out of town — his detour — emerging with a great box of stuff that he had to wrestle into the back alongside their bags. It was possible he needed to tidy his house before he sold it. Jess couldn't think what you would do to that house to make it any nicer.

He dropped the last of the bags by the front door and stood there, holding the cardboard box. The children had disappeared immediately to their rooms, like creatures in some sort of homing experiment. Jess felt a bit embarrassed then by the cluttered little house, the wood-chip wallpaper, the rows of battered paperbacks.

"I'm going back to my dad's tomorrow."

A reflexive twinge at the thought of his going. "Good. That's good."

"Just for a few days. Until the police thing. But I thought I'd put these up first."

Jess looked down at the boxes.

"Security camera and motion-activated light. It shouldn't take more than a couple of hours."

"You bought that for us?"

"Nicky got beaten up. Tanzie plainly doesn't feel safe. I thought it would make you all feel better. You know . . . if I'm not here."

She stared at the box, at what it meant. She spoke before she knew what she wanted to say. "You — you don't have to do that," she stammered. "I'm good at DIY. I'll do it."

"On a ladder. With a busted foot." He raised an eyebrow. "You know, Jessica Rae Thomas, at some point you're going to have to let someone help you."

"Well, what shall I do, then?"

"Sit down. Stay still. Put your injured foot up. And then afterward I'll walk into town with Nicky and we'll buy a disgustingly unhealthy waste-of-money takeaway because it might be the last one I get for a while. And then we'll sit here and eat it, and afterward you and I will lie around gazing in awe at the size of each other's stomachs."

"Oh, my God, I love it when you talk dirty."

So she sat. Doing nothing. On her own sofa. And Tanzie came and sat with her for a while and Ed went up a ladder outside and waved the drill at her through the window and pretended that he was going to fall off until it made her anxious. "I've been in two different hospitals in eight days," she yelled at him through the window, crossly. "I do not want to make it a third." And then, because she was not very good at sitting still, she sorted some dirty washing and put a load in, but after that she sat down again and just let everyone else move because she had to admit that resting her foot was a lot less painful than trying to do things on it.

"Is that okay?" Ed asked.

She limped outside to see him. He stood back on the garden path, gazing up at the front of the house. "I figured if I put it there it'll catch anyone who comes not just in your front garden but who hangs around outside. It's got a convex lens, see?" She tried to look interested. She was wondering whether once the children had gone to bed, she could persuade him to stay over.

"And often, with these sorts of things, you find that just by having a camera there is a deterrent."

Would it really be that bad? He could always sneak out before they woke up. But then, who were they kidding? Nicky and Tanzie must have guessed something was going on, surely.

"Jess?"

He was standing in front of her.

"Mm?"

"All I have to do is drill a hole there, and feed the wires in through that wall. Hopefully I can put a little junction just inside and it should be fairly simple to connect it all up. I'm pretty good at wiring. DIY is the one thing Dad taught me that I was actually okay at."

He wore the satisfied look that men assume when in possession of power tools. He patted his pocket, checking for screws, then looked at her carefully. "Were you listening to a single thing I've said?"

Jess grinned at him guiltily.

"Oh, you're incorrigible," he said after a minute. "Honestly."

Glancing around to make sure nobody was looking, he hooked his arm gently

468

around her neck, pulled her close, and kissed her. His chin was thick with stubble. "Now let me get on. Undistracted. Go and dig out that takeaway menu."

Jess limped, smiling, into the kitchen and began rooting through the drawers. She couldn't remember the last time she had ordered a takeaway. She was pretty sure none of the menus were up to date. Ed went upstairs to connect the wiring. He shouted down that he was going to need to move some furniture to get at the baseboards.

"Fine by me," she yelled back. She heard the rumbling, thunderous sound of large things being dragged around the floor above her head as he tried to find the connection box, and marveled again that somebody other than her was going to do it.

And then she lay back on the sofa and started going through the fistful of old menus that she had uncovered in the tea-towel drawer, unpicking the pages of those splashed with sauce, or yellowed with age. She was pretty sure the Chinese place didn't exist anymore. Some business with environmental health. The pizza place was unreliable. The curry-house menu looked pretty standard, but she couldn't shake the thought of that curly little hair in Nathalie's Jalfrezi. Still, *Chicken Balti. Pilau Rice. Poppadums.*

She was so distracted that she didn't hear his footsteps as he came slowly down the stairs. "Jess?"

"I think this one will do it." She held up the menu. "I've decided a hair of unknown provenance is a small price to pay for a decent Jal—"

It was then that she saw his expression. And what he held, disbelieving, in his hand.

"Jess?" he said, and his voice sounded as if it belonged to someone else. "Why would my security pass be in your sock drawer?"

CHAPTER TWENTY-EIGHT: NICKY

When Nicky came downstairs, she was just sitting on the sofa staring straight ahead of her, like she was in a trance. The Black & Decker drill sat on the windowsill and the ladder was still propped against the front of the house.

"Has Mr. Nicholls gone to get the take-away?" Nicky was a little annoyed that he hadn't got to choose.

She didn't seem to hear him.

"Jess?"

Her face was sort of frozen. She gave a little shake of her head and said quietly, "No."

"He is coming back, though, right?" he said after a minute. He opened the fridge door. He didn't know what he expected to find. There was a pack of shriveled lemons and a half-empty jar of Branston pickles.

A long pause. "I don't know," she said. And then, "I don't know."

"So . . . we're not getting a takeaway?"

"No."

Nicky let out a groan of disappointment. "Well, I guess he'll have to come back at some point. I've got his laptop upstairs."

They'd obviously had some kind of row, but she wasn't behaving like she did when she and Dad had had a row. Then she would slam a door and you'd hear her muttering *Dick* under her breath, or wearing that really tight expression that said, *Why do I have to live with this idiot?* Now she looked like someone who'd just been given six months to live.

"Are you okay?"

She blinked and put a hand to her forehead, like she was taking her temperature. "Um. Nicky. I need . . . I need to lie down. Can you . . . can you sort yourself out? There's stuff. Food. In the freezer."

In all the years Nicky had lived with her, Jess had never asked him to sort himself out. Even that time she'd had the flu for two weeks. Before he could say anything, she turned and limped upstairs, really slowly.

At first Nicky thought Jess was just being melodramatic. But twenty-four hours later, Jess was still in her room. He and Tanzie hovered outside her door, talking in whispers. Then they took her in some tea and toast, but she was just staring at the wall. The window was still open, and it was getting cold outside. Nicky shut it and left to put the ladder and the drill back in the garage, which seemed really enormous without the Rolls in it. And when he came back a couple of hours later to collect her plate, the tea and toast were still there, lying cold on the bedside table.

"She's probably exhausted from all the traveling," said Tanzie, like an old lady.

But the next day Jess stayed in bed. When Nicky went in, the covers were barely rumpled and she was still wearing the same clothes she'd gone to bed in.

"Are you ill?" he said, opening the curtains. "Do you want me to call the doctor?"

"I just need a day in bed, Nicky," she said quietly.

"Nathalie came round. I said you'd call her. Something about cleaning."

"Tell her I'm ill."

"But you're not ill. And the police pound rang up to ask when you're picking up the car. And Mr. Tsvangarai rang up, but I didn't know what to say to him so I just let him leave a message on the answering machine."

"Nicky. Please?" Her face was so sad that he felt bad for even saying anything. She waited a moment, then pulled the duvet up to her chin and turned away.

Nicky got breakfast for Tanzie. He felt oddly useful in the mornings now. He wasn't even missing his stash. He let Norman into the garden and cleaned up after him. Mr. Nicholls had left the security light out by the window. It was still in its box, which had become damp because of the rain, but nobody had nicked it. Nicky picked it up, brought it inside, and sat there looking at it.

He thought about ringing Mr. Nicholls, but he didn't know what he would say if he did. And he felt a bit weird asking Mr. Nicholls to come back a second time. If someone wanted to be with you, after all, they just made it happen. Nicky knew that better than anyone. Whatever had gone on between him and Mum was serious enough that he hadn't come back for his laptop. Serious enough that Nicky wasn't sure he should interfere.

He cleaned his room. He walked along the seafront and took a few pictures on Mr. Nicholls's phone. He went online for a while, but he was bored by gaming. He stared out of the window at the roofs of the high street and the distant orange brick of the leisure center and he knew he didn't want to be an armor-clad droid shooting aliens out of the sky anymore. He didn't want to be stuck in this room. Nicky thought back to the open road, and the feeling of Mr. Nicholls's car taking them vast distances, that endless time when they didn't even know where they were headed next, and he realized that, more than anything, he wanted to be out of this little town.

He wanted to find his tribe.

Nicky had given it some considerable thought and concluded that by the afternoon of day two he was entitled to feel a little freaked out. School was due to start again soon, and he wasn't sure how he was meant to look after Jess as well as Titch and the dog and everything else. He vacuumed the house and rewashed the load of damp laundry that he found sitting in the washing machine, which had started to smell musty. He walked with Tanzie to the shop and they bought some bread and milk and dog food. He tried not to show it, but he was quite relieved that there was nobody hanging around outside to call him a fagboy or freak or whatever. And Nicky thought maybe, just maybe, Jess had been right and that things did change. And that maybe a new stage of his life was finally beginning.

A short time later, as he was going through the post, Tanzie arrived in the kitchen. "Can we go back to the shop?"

He didn't look up. He was wondering whether to open the official letter addressed to Mrs. J. Thomas. "We've just been to the shop."

"Then can I go by myself?"

He looked up then and started a little. She had done something weird to her hair, putting it up on one side with a load of glittery barrettes. She didn't look like Tanzie.

"I want to get Mum a card," she said. "To cheer her up a bit."

Nicky was pretty sure a card wasn't going to do it. "Why don't you make her one, Titch? Save your money."

"I always make her one. Sometimes it's nice to get a shop card."

He studied her face. "Have you got makeup on?"

"Only lipstick."

"Jess wouldn't let you wear lipstick. Take it off."

"Suze wears it."

"I don't think that's going to make Jess any happier about it, Titch. Look, take it off and I'll give you a proper makeup lesson

476

when you get back."

She pulled her jacket from the hook. "I'll rub it off on the way," she called over her shoulder.

"Take Norman with you," he yelled, because it was what Jess would have said. Then he made a cup of coffee and carried it upstairs. It was time to sort out Jess.

The room was dark. It was a quarter to three in the afternoon. "Leave it on the side," she murmured. The room held the fug of unwashed bodies and undisturbed air.

"It's stopped raining."

"Good."

"Jess, you need to get up."

She didn't say anything.

"Really. You need to get up. It's starting to honk in here."

"I'm tired, Nicky. I just need . . . a rest."

"You don't need rest. You're . . . you're like our household Tigger."

"Please, love."

"I don't get it, Jess. What's going on?"

She turned over, really slowly, then propped herself up on one elbow. Downstairs the dog had begun to bark at something, insistent, erratic. Jess rubbed at her eyes. "Where's Tanzie?"

"Gone to the shop."

"Has she eaten?"

"Yes. But mostly cereal. I can't really cook anything more than fish fingers, and she's sick of those."

She looked at Nicky, then out toward the window, as if weighing something up. And then she said, "He's not coming back." And her face sort of crumpled.

The dog was really barking outside now, the idiot. Nicky tried to stay focused on what Jess was saying. "Really? Never?"

A great fat tear rolled down her cheek. She wiped it away with the flat of her hand and shook her head. "You know the really stupid bit, Nicky? I actually forgot. I forgot I did it. I was so happy while we were away, it was like all the time before had happened to someone else. Oh, that bloody dog."

She wasn't really making sense. He wondered if she actually was ill.

"You could call him."

"I tried. He's not picking up."

"Do you want me to go over there?"

Even as he asked he slightly regretted it. Because even though he really liked Mr. Nicholls, he knew better than anyone that you couldn't make someone stay with you. There was no point trying to hang on to someone who didn't want you.

It's possible she'd told him because she

478

didn't have anyone else to tell. "I loved him, Nicky. I know it sounds stupid after such a short time, but I loved him." It was a shock to hear her say it. All that emotion, just blurted out there. But it didn't make him want to run. Nicky sat on the bed, leaned over, and although he still felt a bit weird about actual physical contact, he hugged her. And she felt quite small, even though he'd always thought of her as sort of bigger than he was. And she rested her head against him and he felt sad because for once he did want to say something, but he didn't know what.

It was at that point that Norman's barking got hysterical. Like when he saw the cows in Scotland. Nicky pulled back, distracted. "He sounds like he's going insane."

"Bloody dog. It'll be that Chihuahua from fifty-six." Jess sniffed and wiped at her eyes. "I swear it torments him on purpose."

Nicky climbed up off the bed and walked over to the window. Norman was in the garden, barking hysterically, his head thrust through the gap in the fence where the wood was rotten and two of the panels had half broken away. It took him a few seconds to register that he didn't look like Norman. This dog was rigidly upright, his hair bristling. Nicky pulled the curtain back farther, and it was then that he saw Tanzie across the road. There were two Fishers and a boy he didn't recognize and they had backed her up against the wall. As Nicky watched, one of them grabbed at her jacket and she tried to bat his hand away. "Hey! Hey!" he yelled, but they didn't hear him. His heart thumping, Nicky wrestled with the sash window but it refused to budge. He banged on the glass, trying to make them stop. "HEY! Shit. HEY!"

"What?" said Jess, swiveling in the bed.

"Fishers."

They heard Tanzie's high-pitched scream. As Jess dived out of bed, Norman stilled for a split second, then hurled himself against the weakest section of the fence. He went through it like a canine battering ram, sending pieces of wood splintering into the air around him. Straight toward the sound of Tanzie's voice. Nicky saw the Fishers spin round to see this enormous black missile coming for them and their mouths opened. And then he heard the screech of brakes, a surprisingly loud *whumph,* Jess's *Oh, God, oh, God,* and then a silence that seemed to go on and on forever.

CHAPTER TWENTY-NINE: TANZIE

Tanzie had sat in her room for almost an hour trying to draw Mum a card. She couldn't work out what to put on it. Mum seemed like she was sick, but Nicky said she wasn't really sick, not like Mr. Nicholls had been sick, so it didn't seem right to write a Get Well Soon card. She thought about writing "Be Happy!" but it sounded like an instruction. Or even an accusation. And then she thought about just writing "I love you," but she'd wanted to do it in red and all her red felt-tips had dried out. So then she thought she'd buy a card because Mum always said that Dad had never bought her a single one, apart from a really cheesy padded Valentine's Day card once when they were courting. And she would burst out laughing at the word "courting."

Mostly Tanzie just wanted her to cheer up. A mum should be in charge, taking care of things and bustling around downstairs, not lying up there in the dark, like she was really a million miles away. It made Tanzie scared. Ever since Mr. Nicholls had gone, the house had felt too quiet, and a massive lump had lodged itself in her stomach, like something bad was about to happen. She had crept into Mum's room that morning when she woke up and crawled into bed with her for a cuddle, and Mum had put her arms around her and kissed the top of her head.

"Are you ill, Mum?" she'd said.

"I'm just tired, Tanze." Mum's voice did sound like the saddest, tiredest thing in the world. "I'll get up soon. I promise."

"Is it . . . because of me?"

"What?"

"Not wanting to do maths anymore. Is that what's making you sad?"

And then Mum's eyes filled with tears, and Tanzie felt like she'd somehow made things even worse. "No, Tanze," she said, and pulled her close. "No, darling. It has absolutely nothing to do with you and maths. That is the last thing you should think."

But she didn't get up.

So Tanzie was walking along the road with two pounds fifteen in her pocket that Nicky had given her, even though she could tell he thought a card was a stupid idea, and wondering if it was better to get a cheaper card and some chocolate or if a cheap card spoiled the whole point of a card when a car pulled up alongside. She thought it was someone looking for directions to Beachfront (people were always asking for directions to Beachfront), but it was Jason Fisher.

"Oi. Freak," he said, and she kept walking. His hair was gelled up in spikes and his eyes were narrowed, like he spent his whole life squinting at things he didn't like.

"I said, Freak."

Tanzie tried not to look at him. Her heart had begun to thump. She walked a little bit faster.

He pulled forward and she thought maybe he was going to go away. But he stopped the car and got out and swaggered over so that he was in front of her and she couldn't actually go any farther without pushing past him. He leaned to one side, like he was explaining something to someone stupid. "It's rude not to answer someone when they're talking to you. Did your mum never tell you that?"

Tanzie was so frightened that she couldn't talk.

"Where's your brother?"

"I don't know." Her voice came out as a

whisper.

"Yes, you do, you little four-eyed freak. Your brother thinks he's been a bit clever messing around with my Facebook."

"He didn't," she said. But she was a really bad liar, and she knew as soon as she'd said it that he knew she was lying.

He took two steps toward her. "You tell him that I'm going to have him, the cocky little shit. He thinks he's so clever. Tell him I'm going to mess with his profile for real."

The other Fisher, the cousin whose name she never remembered, muttered something to him that Tanzie didn't hear. They were all out of the car now, walking slowly toward her.

"Yeah," Jason said. "Your brother needs to understand something. He messes with something of mine, we mess around with something of his." He lifted his chin and spat noisily on the pavement. It sat there in front of her, a great green slug.

She wondered if they could see how hard she was breathing.

"Get in the car."

"What?"

"Get in the fucking car."

"No." She began to back away from them. She glanced around her, trying to work out if anyone was coming down the road. Her heart hammered against her ribs like a bird in a cage.

"Get in the fucking car, Costanza." He said it like her name was something disgusting. She wanted to run then, but she was really bad at running — and she knew they would catch her. She wanted to cross the road and turn toward home, but it was too far. And then a hand landed on her shoulder.

"Look at her hair."

"You know about boys, Four Eyes?"

"Course she doesn't know about boys. Look at the state of her."

"She's got lipstick on, the little tart. Still fugly, though."

"Yeah, but you don't have to look at its face, do you?" They started laughing.

Her voice came out sounding like someone else's: "Just leave me alone. Nicky didn't do anything. We just want to be left alone."

"We just want to be left alone." Their voices were mocking. Fisher took a step closer. His voice lowered. "Just get into the fucking car, Costanza."

"Leave me alone!"

He started grabbing at her then, his hands snatching at her clothes. Panic washed over her in an icy wave, tightening her throat.

She tried to push him away. She might have been shouting, but nobody came. The two of them grabbed her arms and were pulling her toward the car. She could hear their grunts of effort, smell their deodorant, as her feet scrabbled for purchase on the pavement. And she knew like she knew anything that she should not get inside. Because as that door opened in front of her, like the jaws of some great animal, she suddenly remembered an American statistic for girls who got into strange men's cars. Your odds of survival dropped by 72 percent as soon as you put your foot in that footwell. That statistic became a solid thing in front of her. Tanzie took hold of it and she hit and she kicked and she bit and she heard someone swear as her foot made contact with soft flesh and then something hit the side of her head and she reeled and spun and there was a crack as she hit the ground. Everything went sideways. There was scuffling, a distant shout. And she lifted her head and her sight was all blurry, but she thought she saw Norman coming toward her across the road at a speed she'd never seen, his teeth bared and his eyes black, looking not like Norman at all but some kind of demon, and then there was a flash of red and the squeal of brakes and all Tanzie saw was something black flying into the air like a ball of washing. And all she heard was the scream, the screaming that went on and on, the sound of the end of the world, the worst sound you ever heard, and she realized it was her it was her it was the sound of her own voice.

CHAPTER THIRTY: JESS

He was on the ground. Jess ran, breathless, barefoot, into the street and the man was standing there, both hands on his head, rocking on his feet, saying, "I never even saw it. I never saw it. It just ran straight out into the road."

Nicky was beside Norman, cradling his head, white as a sheet and murmuring, "Come on, fella. Come on." Tanzie was wide-eyed with shock, her arms rigid at her sides.

Jess knelt. Norman's eyes were glass marbles. Blood seeped from his mouth and ear. "Oh no, you daft old thing. Oh, Norman. Oh no." She put her ear to his chest. Nothing. A great sob rose into her throat.

She felt Tanzie's hand on her shoulder, her fist grabbing a handful of her T-shirt and pulling at it again and again. "Mum, make it all right. Mum, make him all right." Tanzie dropped to her knees and buried her face in his coat. "Norman. Norman." And then she started to howl.

Beneath her shrieking, Nicky's words emerged garbled and confused. "They were trying to get Tanzie into the car. I was trying to get you, but I couldn't open the window. I just couldn't open it, and I was shouting and he went through the fence. He knew. He was trying to help her."

Nathalie came running down the road, her shirt fastened with the wrong buttons, hair half done in rollers. She wrapped her arms around Tanzie and held her close, rocking her, trying to stop the noise.

Norman's eyes had stilled. Jess lowered her head to his and felt her heart break.

"I've called the emergency vet," someone said.

She stroked his big soft ear. "Thank you," she whispered.

"We've got to do something, Jess." Nicky said it again, more urgently. "Now."

She put a trembling hand on Nicky's shoulder. "I think he's gone, sweetheart."

"No. You don't say that. You're the one who said we don't say that. We don't give in. You're the one who says it's all going to be okay. You don't say that."

And as Tanzie began to wail again, Nicky's face crumpled. And then he sobbed, one elbow bent across his face, huge, gasping sobs, as if a dam had finally broken.

Jess sat in the middle of the road, as the cars crawled around her, and the curious neighbors hovered on the front steps of their houses, and she held her old dog's enormous bloodied head on her lap and she lifted her face to the heavens and said silently, *What now? What the hell now?*

CHAPTER THIRTY-ONE: TANZIE

Mum brought her indoors. Tanzie didn't want to leave him. She didn't want him to die out there on the tarmac, alone, strangers staring at him with open mouths and murmured whispers, but Mum wouldn't listen. Nigel from next door came running out and said he would take over, and the next thing Mum had her arms tight around Tanzie. And as she kicked and screamed for him, Mum's voice was close in Tanzie's ear: "Sweetheart, it's all right, sweetheart, come on inside, don't look, it's all going to be okay." But as Mum closed the front door, head against hers, pulling Tanzie to her, and her eyes were blind with tears, Tanzie could hear Nicky sobbing behind them in the hallway, weird jagged sobs like it wasn't even something he knew how to do. And Mum was finally lying to her because it wasn't going to be okay, it never could be because it was actually the end of everything

Chapter Thirty-Two: Ed

"Sometimes," Gemma said, glancing behind her at the puce screaming child, arching its back at the next table, "I think the worst sort of parenting is not actually witnessed by social workers but by baristas." She stirred her coffee briskly, as if biting back a natural urge to say something.

The mother, her blond corkscrew curls cascading stylishly over her back, continued to ask the child in soothing tones to stop and drink its babycino. It ignored her.

"I don't see why we couldn't go to the pub," Ed said.

"At eleven fifteen in the morning? Jesus, why doesn't she just tell him to stop? Or take him out? Does nobody know how to distract a child anymore?"

The child screamed louder. Ed's head had begun to hurt. "We could go."

"Go where?"

"The pub. It would be quieter."

She stared at him, and then she ran a speculative finger across his chin. "Ed, how much did you drink last night?"

He had emerged from the police station spent. They had met his barrister afterward — Ed had already forgotten his name — with Paul Wilkes and two other solicitors, one of whom specialized in insider-trading cases. They sat around the mahogany table and spoke as if choreographed, laying out the prosecution case baldly so that Ed was in no doubt about what lay ahead. Against him: the e-mail trail, Deanna Lewis's testimony, her brother's phone calls, the FSA's new determination to clamp down on perpetrators of insider trading. His own check, complete with signature.

Deanna had sworn that she had not known what she was doing was wrong. She said Ed had pressed the money on her. She said that had she known what he was suggesting was illegal, she would never have done it. Nor would she have told her brother.

The evidence for him: that he had plainly not gained a cent from the transaction. His legal team said — in his opinion, a little too cheerfully — that they would stress his ignorance, his ineptitude, that he was new to money, the ramifications and responsibilities of directorship. They would claim that

Deanna Lewis knew very well what she was doing; that his and Deanna's short relationship was actually evidence of her and her brother's entrapment. The investigating team had been all over Ed's accounts and found them gratifyingly unrewarding. He paid the full whack of tax every year. He had no investments. He had always liked things simple.

And the check was not addressed to her. It was in her possession, but her name was in her own writing. They would assert that she had taken a blank check from his home at some point during the relationship, they said.

"But she didn't," he said.

Nobody seemed to hear.

It could go either way with the prison sentence, they told him, but whatever happened, Ed was undoubtedly looking at a hefty fine. And obviously the end of his time with Mayfly. He would be banned from holding a directorship, possibly for some considerable time. Ed needed to be prepared for all these things. They began to confer among themselves.

And then he had said it: "I want to plead guilty."

"What?"

The room fell silent.

"I did tell her to do it. I didn't think about it being illegal. I just wanted her to go away, so I told her how she could make some money."

They stared at each other.

"Ed —" his sister began.

"I want to tell the truth."

One of the solicitors leaned forward. "We actually have quite a strong defense, Mr. Nicholls. I think that given the lack of your handwriting on the check — their only substantive piece of evidence — we can successfully claim that Ms. Lewis used your account for her own ends."

"But I did give her the check."

Paul Wilkes leaned forward. "Ed, you need to be clear about this. If you plead guilty, you substantially increase your chance of a custodial sentence."

"I don't care."

"You will care for your own safety when you're doing twenty-three hours in solitary in Winchester," Gemma said.

He barely heard her. "I just want to tell the truth. That's how it was."

"Ed," his sister grabbed at his arm, "the truth has no place in a courtroom. You're going to make things worse."

But he shook his head and sat back in his chair. And then he didn't say anything more.

He knew they thought he was insane, but he didn't care. He couldn't bring himself to look exercised by any of it. He sat there, numb, his sister asking most of the questions. He heard *Financial Services and Markets Act 2000 blah blah blah.* He heard *open prison and punitive fines and Criminal Justice Act 1993 blah blah blah.* He honestly couldn't make himself care about any of it. So he was going to prison for a bit? So what? He had lost everything anyway, twice over.

"Ed? Did you hear what I said?"

"Sorry."

Sorry. It's all he seemed to say these days. Sorry, I didn't hear you. Sorry, I wasn't listening. Sorry, I fucked it all up. Sorry, I was stupid enough to fall in love with someone who actually believed I was an idiot.

And there it was: the now familiar clench at the thought of her. How could she have lied to him? How could they have sat side by side in that car for the best part of a week, and she hadn't even begun to let on what she had done?

How could she have talked to him of her financial fears? How could she have talked to him of trust, have collapsed into his arms, all the while knowing that she had stolen money right out of his pocket?

She hadn't even needed to say anything in the end. It was her silence that told him. The fractional delay between her registering the sight of the security card that he held, disbelieving in his hand, and her stuttering attempt to explain it.

I was going to tell you.

It's not what you're thinking. The hand to the mouth.

I wasn't thinking.

Oh, God. It's not —

She was worse than Lara. At least Lara had been honest, in her way, about his attractions. She liked the money. She liked how he looked, once she had shaped him according to what she wanted. He thought they had both understood, deep down, that their marriage was a kind of deal. He had told himself that everybody's marriages were, one way or another.

But Jess? Jess had behaved as if he were the only man she had ever truly wanted. Jess had let him think it was the real him she liked, even when he was puking, even with his bashed-up face, afraid to meet his own parents. She had let him think it was him.

"Ed?"

"Sorry?" He lifted his head from his hands.

"I know it's tough. But you will survive this." His sister reached across and squeezed his hand. Somewhere behind her the child screamed. His head pulsed.

"Sure," he said.

The moment she left he went to the pub.

They had fast-tracked the hearing, following his revised plea, and Ed spent the last few days before it took place with his father. It was partly down to choice, partly because he no longer had a flat in London that contained any furniture, everything having been packed for storage, ready for the completion of the sale.

It had sold for the asking price without a single viewing. The estate agent didn't seem to find this surprising. "We have a waiting list for this block," he said, as Ed handed him the spare keys. "Investors, wanting a safe place for their money. To be honest, it will probably just sit there empty for a few years until they feel like selling it."

For three nights Ed stayed at his parents' house, sleeping in his childhood room, waking in the small hours and running his fingers across the surface of the textured wallpaper behind his headboard, recalling the sound of his teenage sister's feet thundering up the stairs, the slam of her bedroom door as she digested whatever insult their father had directed her way this time. In the mornings he sat and had breakfast with his mother and slowly grasped that his father was never coming home. That they would never see him there again, flicking his paper irritably into straight corners, reaching without looking for his mug of strong black coffee (no sugar). Occasionally she would burst into tears, apologizing and waving Ed away as she pressed a napkin to her eyes. *I'm fine, I'm fine. Really, love. Just ignore me.*

In the overheated confines of room three, Victoria Ward, Bob Nicholls spoke less, ate less, did less. Ed didn't need to speak to a doctor to see what was happening. The flesh seemed to be disappearing from him, melting away, leaving his skull pulled into a translucent veil, his eyes great bruised sockets.

They played chess. His father often fell asleep midgame, drifting off during a move, and Ed would sit patiently at his bedside and wait for him to wake. And when his eyes opened, and he took a moment or two to register where he was, his mouth closing, and his eyebrows lowering, Ed would move a piece and act as if it had been a minute, not an hour, that he had been missing from the game.

They talked. Not about the important stuff. Ed wasn't sure either of them was built that way. They talked about cricket and the weather. Ed's father talked about the nurse with the dimples who always thought up something funny to tell him. He asked Ed to look after his mother. He worried she was doing too much. He worried that the man who cleared the gutters would overcharge her if he wasn't there. He was annoyed that he had spent lots of money in in the autumn having the moss removed from the lawn and he wouldn't get to see the results. Ed didn't try to argue. It would have seemed patronizing.

"So, where's the firecracker?" he said one evening. He was two moves from checkmate. Ed was trying to work out how to block him.

"The what?"

"Your girl."

"Lara? Dad, you know we got —"

"Not her. The other one."

Ed took a breath. "Jess? She's . . . uh . . . she's at home, I think."

"I liked her. She had a way of looking at you." He pushed his castle forward slowly onto a black square. "I'm glad you have her." He gave a slight nod. "Trouble," he murmured, almost to himself, and smiled.

Ed's strategy went to pieces. His father beat him in three moves.

Chapter Thirty-Three: Jess

The bearded man emerged from the swing doors wiping his hands on his white coat. "Norman Thomas?"

Jess had never considered that their dog might have a surname.

"Norman Thomas? Large, indeterminate breed?" he said, lowering his chin and looking straight at her.

She scrambled to standing in front of the plastic chairs. "He has suffered massive internal injuries," he said, with no preamble. "He has a broken hip and several broken ribs and a fractured front leg and we won't know what's going on inside until the swelling's gone down. And I'm afraid he's definitely lost the left eye." She noticed there were bright smears of blood on his blue plastic shoes.

She felt Tanzie's hand tighten in hers. "But he's still alive?"

"I don't want to give you false hope. The

next forty-eight hours will be critical."

Beside her Tanzie gave a low moan of something that might have been joy or anguish; it was hard to tell.

"Walk with me." He took Jess's elbow, turning his back on the children, and lowered his voice. "I have to say that I'm not sure, given the extent of his injuries, if the kindest thing wouldn't be to let him go."

"But if he does survive forty-eight hours?"

"Then he may stand some chance of recovery. But as I said, Mrs. Thomas, I don't want to give you false hope. He really isn't a well lad."

Around them the waiting clients were watching silently, their cats in pet carriers cradled on their laps, their small dogs panting gently under chairs. Nicky was staring at the vet, his jaw set in a tense line. His mascara was smudged around his eyes.

"And if we do proceed, it's not going to be cheap. He may need more than one operation. Possibly even several. Is he insured?"

Jess shook her head.

Now the vet became awkward. "I need to warn you that going forward, his treatment is likely to cost a significant sum. And there are no guarantees of recovery. It's very important that you understand that before we go any further."

It was her neighbor Nigel who had saved him, she heard later. He had run from his house carrying two blankets, one to wrap around the shivering Tanzie, the other to cover the body of the dog. Go indoors, he had instructed Jess. Take the kids indoors. But as he drew the tartan rug gently over Norman's head, he had paused, and said to Nathalie, "Did you see that?"

Jess hadn't heard him at first, over the sound of the crowd and Tanzie's muffled wailing and the children crying nearby because even though they didn't know him, they understood the utter sadness of a dog lying motionless in the road.

"Nathalie? His tongue. Look. I think he's panting. Here, let's pick him up. Get him in the car. Quick!" It had taken three of Jess's neighbors to lift him. They had laid him carefully on the rear seat, and had driven in a blur to the big veterinary practice on the outskirts of town. Jess loved Nigel for not once mentioning the blood that must have gotten all over his upholstery. They had rung her from the vet's and told her to get down there as fast as she could. Under her jacket, she was still in her pajamas.

"So what do you want to do?"

Lisa Ritter had once told Jess about a

huge deal her husband had done that had gone wrong. "Borrow five thousand and you can't pay it back, and it's your problem," she said, quoting him. "Borrow five million and it's the bank's problem."

Jess looked at her daughter's pleading face. She looked at Nicky's raw expression: the grief and love and fear that he finally felt able to express. She was the only person who could make this right. She was the only person who would ever be able to make it right.

"Do whatever it takes," she said. "I'll find the money. Just do it."

The short pause told her he thought she was a fool. But of a kind he was well used to dealing with. "Come this way, then," he said. "I need you to sign some paperwork."

Nigel drove them home. She tried to give him some money, but he waved her away gruffly and said, "What are neighbors for?" Belinda cried as she came out to greet them.

"We're fine," she muttered dully, her arm around Tanzie, who still shook intermittently. "We're fine. Thank you."

They would call, the vet said, if there was any news.

Jess didn't tell the kids to go to bed. She wasn't sure she wanted them to be alone in

505

their rooms. She locked the door, bolted it twice, and put an old film on. Then she made three mugs of cocoa, brought her duvet down, and sat under it, one child on each side of her, watching television that they didn't see, each alone with individual thoughts. Praying, praying that the telephone wouldn't ring.

CHAPTER THIRTY-FOUR: NICKY

This is the story of a family who didn't fit in. A little girl who was a bit geeky and liked maths more than makeup. And a boy who liked makeup and didn't fit into any tribes. And this is what happens to families who don't fit in — they end up broken and skint and sad. No happy ending here, folks.

Mum doesn't stay in bed anymore, but I catch her wiping her eyes as she washes up or gazes down at Norman's basket. She's busy all the time: working, cleaning, sorting out the house. She does it with her head down and her jaw set. She packed up three whole boxes of her paperback books and took them back to the charity shop because she said she'd never have time to read them and, besides, it's pointless believing in fiction.

I miss Norman. It's weird how you can miss something you only ever complained about. Our house is quiet without him. But since the first forty-eight hours passed, and the vet said he was in with a chance, and we all cheered on the phone, I've started to worry about other stuff. We sat on the sofa last night after Tanzie went to bed and the phone still didn't ring and then I said to Mum, "So what are we going to do?"

She looked up from the television.

"I mean, if he lives."

She let out a long breath, like this was something that had already occurred to her. And then she said, "You know what, Nicky? We didn't have a choice. He's Tanzie's dog, and he saved her. If you don't have a choice, then it's actually quite simple."

I could see that even though she really did believe this, and it might actually be quite simple, the extra debt is like a new weight settling on her. That with each new problem she just looks a bit older, and flatter, and wearier.

She doesn't talk about Mr. Nicholls.

I couldn't believe after how they'd been together that it could just end like that. Like one minute you can seem really happy and then nothing. I thought you got all that stuff sorted out when you get older, but clearly you don't. So that's something else to look forward to.

I walked up to her then, and I gave her a hug. And that might not be a big deal in your family, but I can tell you in mine it is. It's about the only stupid difference I can make.

So this is the thing I don't understand. I don't understand how our family can basically do the right thing and yet always end up in the crap. I don't understand how my little sister can be brilliant and kind and some sort of damn genius, and yet now wakes up crying and having nightmares, and I have to lie awake listening to Mum pottering across the landing at four a.m. trying to calm her down. And how my sister stays inside during the day, even though it's finally warm and sunny, because she's too afraid to go outside anymore in case the Fishers come back to get her. And how in six months' time she'll be at a school whose main message is that she should be like everyone else or she'll get her head kicked in, like her freak of a brother did. I think about Tanzie without maths, and it just feels like the whole universe has gone mad. It's like . . . cheeseburgers without the cheese, or a Jennifer Aniston headline without the word "heartbreak." I just can't imagine who Tanze will be if she doesn't do maths anymore.

I don't understand why I had just got used to sleeping and now I lie awake listening for nonexistent sounds downstairs, and how now when I want to go to the shop to buy a paper or some sweets, I feel sick again and have to fight the urge to look over my shoulder.

I don't understand how a big, useless, soppy dog, who has basically never done anything worse than dribble on everyone, had to lose an eye and get his insides rearranged just because he tried to protect the person he loves.

Mostly, I don't understand how the bullies and the thieves and the people who just destroy everything — the arseholes — get away with it. The boys who punch you in your kidneys for your dinner money, and the police who think it's funny to treat you like you're an idiot, and the kids who take the piss out of anyone who isn't just like them. Or the dads who walk right out and just start afresh somewhere new that smells of Febreze with a woman who drives her own Toyota and owns a couch with no marks on it and laughs at all his stupid jokes like he's God's gift and not actually a slimeball who lied to all the people who loved him for two years. Two whole years.

I'm sorry if this blog has just got really depressing, but that's how our life is right now. My family, the eternal losers. It's not much of a story, really, is it?

Mum always told us that good things happen to good people. Guess what? She doesn't say that anymore.

CHAPTER THIRTY-FIVE: JESS

The police came on the fourth day after Norman's accident. Jess watched the officer coming up the garden path through the living-room window and for one stupid minute she thought she had come to tell her Norman had died. A young woman, red hair pulled back in a neat ponytail. One Jess hadn't seen before.

She was coming in response to reports about a road traffic accident, she said, as Jess opened the door.

"Don't tell me," Jess said, walking back down the hall to the kitchen. "The driver's going to sue us for damaging his car." It was Nigel who had warned her this might happen. She had actually started to laugh when he said it.

The officer looked at her notebook. "Well, not at the moment, at least. The damage to his car seems to be minimal. And there have been conflicting statements as to whether he was exceeding the speed limit. But we've had various reports about what happened in the lead-up to the accident, and I was wondering if you could clarify a few things?"

"What's the point?" Jess said, turning back to the washing up. "Your lot never take any notice."

She knew how she sounded: like half the residents of the neighborhood — antagonistic, braced for confrontation, hard done by. She no longer cared. But the officer was too new, too keen, to play that game.

"Well, do you think you could tell me what happened, anyway? I'll only take five minutes of your time."

So Jess told her, in the flat tones of someone who didn't expect to be believed. She told her about the Fishers, and their history with them, and the fact that she now had a daughter who was afraid to play in her own garden. She told her about her daft cow-sized dog who was racking up bills at the vet's roughly equivalent to her buying him a suite in a luxury hotel. She told her how her son's sole aim now was to get as far from this town as possible, and how, thanks to the Fishers having made a misery of his exam year at school, this was unlikely to happen.

PC Kenworthy didn't look bored. She

stood, leaning against the kitchen cabinets, taking notes. Then she asked Jess to show her the fence. "There," Jess said, pointing through the window. "You can see where I've mended it, by the lighter wood. And the accident, if that's what we're calling it, happened about fifty yards up on the right." She watched the officer walk outside. Aileen Trent, pulling her shopping trolley, gave Jess a cheery wave over the hedge. Then, when she registered who was in the garden, she ducked her head and walked swiftly the other way.

The officer was out there for almost ten minutes. Jess was unloading the washing machine when she let herself back in.

"Can I ask you a question, Mrs. Thomas?" she said, closing the back door behind her.

"That's your job," Jess said.

"You've probably been through this a dozen times already. But your CCTV camera. Does it have any film in it?"

Jess watched the footage three times after PC Kenworthy called her into the station, sitting beside her on a plastic chair in interview suite three. It chilled her every time: the tiny figure, her sequined sleeves glinting in the sun, walking slowly along the edge of the screen, pausing to push her spectacles up her nose. The car that slows, the door that opens. One, two, three of them. Tanzie's slight step backward, the nervous glance behind, back down the road. The raised hands. And then they're on her and Jess cannot watch.

"I'd say that was pretty conclusive evidence, Mrs. Thomas. And on good-quality footage. The Crown Prosecution Service will be delighted," she said cheerfully, and it took Jess several seconds to grasp that she meant this. That somebody was actually taking them seriously.

At first Fisher had denied it, of course. He said they were "having a joke" with Tanzie. "But we have her testimony. And two witnesses who have come forward. And we have screenshots of Jason Fisher's Facebook account discussing how he was going to do it."

"Do what?"

Her smile faded for a minute. "Something not very nice to your daughter."

Jess didn't ask anything else.

They had received an anonymous tip that he used his name as his password. The eejit, PC Kenworthy said. She actually said "eejit." "Between us," she said, as she let Jess out, "that hacked evidence may not be strictly admissible in court. But let's just say it gave us a leg up."

The case was reported in vague terms at first. Several local youths, the local papers said. Arrested for assault of a minor and attempted kidnap. But they were in the newspapers again the following week, and named. Apparently, the Fisher family had been instructed to move out of their council house. The Thomases were not the only people they had been harassing. The housing association was quoted as saying the family had long been on a last warning.

Nicky held up the local newspaper over tea, and he read the story aloud. They were all silent for a moment, unable to believe what they had heard.

"It actually says the Fishers have to move somewhere else?" Jess said, her fork still halfway to her mouth.

"That's what it says," Nicky said.

"But what will happen to them?"

"Well, it says here, they're going to move to Surrey, to live with some relatives."

"Surrey? But —"

"They're not the housing association's responsibility anymore. None of them. Jason Fisher. And his cousin and his family." He scanned the page. "They're moving in with some uncle. And even better, there's a restraining order preventing them from returning to the neighborhood. Look, there're two pictures of his mum crying and saying they've been misunderstood and Jason wouldn't hurt a fly." He pushed the newspaper across the table toward her.

Jess read the story twice, just to check he'd understood it correctly. That she'd understood it correctly. "They actually get arrested if they come back?"

"See, Mum?" he said, chewing on a piece of bread. "You were right. Things can change."

Jess sat very still. She looked at the newspaper, then back at him, until he realized what he had called her, and she could see him coloring, hoping she wouldn't make a big deal out of it. So she swallowed and then she wiped both her eyes with the heels of her palms and stared at her plate for a minute before she began eating again. "Right," she said, her voice strangled. "Well. That's good news. Very good news."

"Do you really think things can change?" Tanzie's eyes were big and dark and wary.

Jess put down her knife and fork. "I think I do, love. I mean, we all have our down moments. But yes, I do."

And Tanzie looked at Nicky and back at Jess, and then she carried on eating.

■ ■ ■ ■

Life went on. Jess walked to the Feathers on a Saturday lunchtime, hiding her limp for the last twenty yards, and pleaded for her job back. Des told her he'd taken on a girl from the City of Paris. "Not the actual City of Paris. That would be uneconomical."

"Can she take apart the pumps when they go wrong?" Jess said. "Will she fix the cistern in the men's loo?"

Des leaned on the bar. "Probably not, Jess." He ran a chubby hand through his mullet. "But I need someone reliable. You're not reliable."

"Give me a break, Des. One missed week in two years. Please. I need this. I really need this."

He said he'd think about it.

The children went back to school. Tanzie wanted Jess there to pick her up every afternoon. Nicky got up without her having to go in six times to wake him. He was actually eating breakfast when she got out of the shower. He didn't ask to renew his prescription of antianxiety medication. The flick on his eyeliner was point perfect.

"I was thinking. I might not leave school.

I might want to stay on and do sixth form after all. And then, you know, I'll be around when Tanzie starts big school."

Jess blinked. "That's a great idea."

She cleaned alongside Nathalie, listening to her gossip about the final days of the Fishers — how they had pulled every plug socket off the walls, and kicked holes in the plaster in the kitchen before they'd left the house on Pleasant View. Someone — she pulled a face — had set fire to a mattress outside the housing association office on Sunday night.

"You must feel relieved, though, eh?" she said.

"Sure," Jess said.

"So are you going to tell me about this trip?" Nathalie straightened and rubbed her back. "I meant to ask, what was it like going all the way to Scotland with Mr. Nicholls? It must have been weird."

Jess leaned over the sink and paused, looking out the window at the infinite crescent of the sea. "It was fine."

"Didn't you run out of things to say to him, stuck in that car? I know I would."

Jess's eyes prickled with tears so that she had to pretend to be scrubbing at an invisible mark on the stainless steel. "No," she said. "Funnily enough. I didn't."

■ ■ ■ ■

Here was the truth of it: Jess felt the absence of Ed like a thick blanket, smothering everything. She missed his smile, his lips, his skin, the bit where a trace of soft dark hair snaked up toward his belly button. She missed feeling like she had when he was there, that she was somehow more attractive, more sexy, more everything. She missed feeling as if anything was possible. She couldn't believe losing someone you had known such a short time could feel like losing part of yourself, that it could make food taste wrong and colors seem dull.

Jess saw now that when Marty had left, everything she had felt had been related to practical matters. She had worried about how the children would feel with him gone. She had worried about money, about who would mind them if she had to do an evening shift at the pub, about who would take the bins out on a Thursday. But what she mostly felt was a vague relief.

Ed was different. Ed's absence was a kick in the guts first thing in the morning, a black hole in the dead of night. Ed was a constant running conversation in the back of her mind: *I'm sorry, I didn't mean, I love you.*

More than anything she hated the fact that a man who had seen only the best in her now thought the worst. To Ed she was now no better than any of the other people who had let him down or messed him up. In fact, she was probably worse. And it was all her fault. That was the thing she could never escape from. It was entirely her own fault.

She thought about it for three nights, then she wrote him a letter. These were the last lines.

> So in one ill-thought-out minute, I became the person I have always taught my children not to be. We are all tested eventually, and I failed.
>
> I'm sorry.
>
> I miss you.
>
> PS I know you'll never believe me. But I was always going to pay it back.

She put her phone number on it and twenty pounds in an envelope, marked FIRST IN-STALLMENT. And she gave it to Nathalie and asked her to put it with his post at Beachfront Reception. The next day, Nathalie said a for-sale sign had gone up outside number two. And she looked at Jess sideways and then stopped asking questions about Mr. Nicholls.

When five days had gone by and Jess realized he wasn't going to respond, she spent an entire night awake, and then she told herself firmly that she could lie around feeling miserable no longer. It was time to move on. Heartbreak was a luxury too costly for the single parent.

On Monday she made herself a cup of tea, sat down at the kitchen table, and called the credit-card company; she was told that she needed to up her minimum monthly payment. She opened a letter from the police that said that she would be fined a thousand pounds for driving without tax and insurance and that if she wanted to appeal the penalty, she should apply for a court hearing in the following ways. She opened the letter from the auto pound, which said she owed a hundred and twenty pounds up to the previous Thursday for the safekeeping of the Rolls. She opened the first bill from the vet and shoved it back in the envelope. There was only so much news you could digest in one day. She got a text from Marty, who wanted to know if he could come and see the kids at half term.

"What do you think?" she said to them,

over breakfast.

They shrugged.

After her cleaning shift on Tuesday she walked into town to the low-cost solicitors and paid them twenty-five pounds to draft a letter to Marty asking for a divorce and for back payments in child support.

"How long?" the woman asked.

"Two years."

The woman didn't even look up. Jess wondered what kinds of stories she heard every day. She tapped in some figures, then turned the screen to Jess's side of the desk. "That's what it comes to. Quite a sum. He'll ask to pay in installments. They usually do."

"Fine." Jess reached for her bag. "Do what you have to do."

She worked her way methodically through the list of things she needed to sort out, and she tried to see a bigger picture beyond that small town. Beyond a little family with financial problems, and a brief love story that had snapped in two before it had really begun. Sometimes, she told herself, life was a series of obstacles that just had to be negotiated, possibly through sheer act of will. She stared out at the muddy blue of the endless sea, gulped in the air, lifted her chin, and decided that she could survive this. She could survive most things. It was nobody's right to be happy, after all.

Jess walked along the pebbly beach, her feet sinking, stepping over the breakwaters, and counted her blessings on three fingers, as if she were playing a piano in her pocket: Tanzie was safe. Nicky was safe. Norman was getting better. That was what it all boiled down to, in the end, wasn't it? The rest was just detail.

Two evenings later, they sat in the garden on the old plastic furniture. Tanzie had washed her hair and was on Jess's lap while Jess tugged the comb through her wet tangles. Jess told them why Mr. Nicholls wouldn't be coming back.

Nicky stared at her. "From his pocket?"

"No. It had fallen out of his pocket. It was in a taxi. But I knew whose it was."

There was a shocked silence. Jess couldn't see Tanzie's face. She wasn't sure she wanted to look at Nicky's. Jess kept combing gently, smoothing her daughter's hair, her voice calm and reasonable, as if that might bring reason to what she had done.

"What did you do with the money?" Tanzie's head had become unusually still.

Jess swallowed. "I can't remember now."

"Did you use it for my registration?"

She kept combing. Smooth and comb.

Tug, tug, release. "I honestly can't remember, Tanzie. Anyway, what I did with it is irrelevant."

Jess could feel Nicky's eyes on her the whole time she spoke.

"So why are you telling us now?"

Tug, smooth, release.

"Because . . . because I want you to know that I made a terrible mistake and I'm sorry. Even if I planned to pay it back, I should never have taken that money. There was no excuse for it. And Ed — Mr. Nicholls — was well within his rights to leave when he found out because, well, the most important thing you have with another human being is trust." She tried to keep her voice measured and unemotional. It was becoming harder. "So I want you to know that I'm sorry I let you both down. I know that I've always told you how to behave, and then I did the complete opposite. I'm telling you because not telling you would make me a hypocrite. But I'm also telling you because I want you to see that doing the wrong thing has a consequence. In my case I lost someone I cared about. Very much."

They were both silent.

After a minute, Tanzie reached a hand round. Her fingers sought Jess's, and closed briefly around them. "It's okay, Mum," she said. "We all make mistakes."

Jess closed her eyes.

When she opened them again, Nicky lifted his head. He looked genuinely bemused. "He would have given it to you," he said, and there was a faint, but unmistakable, trace of anger in his voice.

Jess stared at him.

"He would have given it to you. If you'd asked."

"Yes," she said, and her hands stilled on Tanzie's hair. "Yes, that's the worst bit. I think he probably would have."

Chapter Thirty-Six: Nicky

A week went by. They caught the bus to see Norman every day. The vet had sewn up his eye socket so there wasn't an actual hole, but it still looked pretty grim. The first time Tanzie saw his face she burst into tears. They said he might bump into things for a while once he was up and about. They said he would spend a lot of time sleeping. Nicky didn't tell them he wasn't sure anyone would be able to tell the difference. Jess stroked Norman's head and told him he was a wonderful brave boy, and when his tail thumped gently on the tiled floor of his pen, she blinked a lot and turned away.

On Friday, Jess asked Nicky to wait in Reception with Tanzie, and she walked over to the front desk to speak to the woman about the bill. He guessed it was about the bill. They printed out a sheet of paper, then a second sheet, then, incredibly, a third, and she ran her finger the whole way down each page and made a little choking sound when it reached the bottom. They walked home that day, even though Jess was still limping.

The town started to get busier as the sea turned from mucky gray to glinting blue. It felt weird at first, the Fishers being gone. It was as if no one could actually believe it. Nobody's tires got slashed. Mrs. Worboys started to walk to bingo in the evenings again. Nicky got used to being able to walk to the shop and back and realized that the butterflies he still felt in his stomach didn't have to be there. He told them this repeatedly, but they refused to get the message. Tanzie didn't go outside at all unless Jess was with her.

Nicky didn't look at his blog for almost ten days. He had written his "my family of losers" post when Norman was hurt and he was so full of anger that he had had to get it out somewhere. He had never felt rage, real rage, where he had wanted to break stuff and hit people before, but for days after the Fishers had done what they did, Nicky felt it. It boiled in his blood like poison. It made him want to scream. For those awful few days, at least, writing it down and putting it out there had actually helped. It had felt like he was telling someone, even if that someone didn't really know who he was and probably didn't care. He just hoped that someone would hear what had happened, would see the injustice of it.

And then, after his blood had cooled, and they heard that the Fishers were going to have to pay, Nicky felt kind of like an idiot. It felt like that thing when you tell someone a bit too much and you feel exposed and spend the following weeks praying they'll forget what you told them, afraid they might use it against you. And what was the point of putting it out there, anyway? The only people who'd want to look at all that emotional crap were the kind of people who slowed down to look at car crashes.

He opened the post up at first because he was going to delete it. And then he thought, *No, people will have seen it. I'll look even more stupid if I take it down.* So he decided to write a short thing about the Fishers being evicted and that would be the end of it. He wasn't going to name them, but he wanted to post something good so that if anyone ever did come across what he had written, they wouldn't think his whole family was completely tragic. He read through what he'd written the previous week — the emotion and the rawness of it — and his toes actually curled with shame. He wondered who out there in cyberspace had read it. He wondered how many people in the world now thought he was a total fool as well as a freak.

And then he reached the bottom. And he saw the comments.

Hang on in there, Gothboy. People like that make me sick.

Your blog got sent to me by a friend and it made me cry. I hope your dog is okay. Please post and let us know when you get a chance.

Hey Nicky. I'm Viktor from Portugal. I don't know you but my friend linked to your blog on Facebook and I just wanted to say that I felt like you a year back and things did get better. Don't worry. Peace!

He scrolled down some more. There was message after message. He typed his name into Google: it had been copied and linked hundreds, then thousands of times. Nicky looked at the statistics, then sat back in his chair and stared in disbelief: 2,876 people had read it. In a single week. Almost 3,000 people had read his words. More than 400 of them had taken the trouble to send him a note about it. And only 2 had called him a wanker.

But that wasn't all. People had sent money. Actual money. Someone had opened an online donation account to help with the vet's fees and left a message telling him how he could access it using a PayPal account.

Hey Gothboy (is that your real name??) have you thought of a rescue dog? That way something good might come out of it. I enclose a contribution! Rescue centers always need donations ;-)

A little something to help with the vet's bills. Give your sister a hug from me. I'm so mad at what happened to you all.

My dog got hit by a car and was saved by the PDSA. I'm guessing you don't have one near you. I thought it would be nice, as someone helped me, to help you a little. Please accept my £10 toward his recuperation.

From a fellow girl maths geek. Please tell your little sister to keep on. Don't let them win.

There were 459 shares. Nicky counted 130 names on the donations page, £2 being the smallest donation, and £250 the highest. A total stranger had sent £250. The final tally sat at £932.50, the last having come in an hour previously. He kept refreshing the page and staring at the figure, wondering if they had put a period in the wrong place.

His heart was doing something strange. He placed his palm against his chest, wondering if this was what it felt like to have a heart attack. He wondered if he was going to die. What he wanted to do, though, he discovered, was laugh. He wanted to laugh at the magnificence of total strangers. At their kindness and their goodness and the fact that there were actual people out there being good and nice and giving money to people they had never met and never would. And because, most crazy of all, all that kindness, all that magnificence, was sitting there just because of his words.

Jess was standing by the cupboard holding a parcel of pink paper when he scooted into the living room. "Here," he said. "Look." He pulled at her arm, dragging her over to the sofa.

"What?"

"Put that down."

Nicky opened the laptop and placed it on her lap. She almost flinched, as if it were actually painful for her to be so close to something that belonged to Mr. Nicholls.

"Look." He pointed at the donations page. "Look at this. People have sent money. For Norman."

"What do you mean?"

"Just look, Jess."

She squinted at the screen, moving the page up and down as she read, then reread it. "But . . . we can't take that."

"It's not for us. It's for Tanzie. And Norman."

"I don't understand. Why would people we don't know send us money?"

"Because they're upset about what happened. Because they can see it wasn't fair. Because they want to help. I don't know."

"But how did they know?"

"I wrote a blog about it."

"You did what?"

"Something Mr. Nicholls told me. I just . . . put it out there. What was happening to us."

"Show me."

Nicky switched pages then and showed her the blog. She read it slowly, her brow furrowed in concentration, and he felt suddenly awkward, like he was showing her part of himself that he didn't show anyone. Somehow it was harder to show all that emotional stuff to someone you knew.

"So, how much is the vet?" he said when he could see that she'd finished.

She spoke like someone in a daze. "Eight hundred and seventy-eight pounds. And forty-two pence. So far."

Nicky lifted his hands in the air. "So we're okay, yes? Look at the total. We're okay!"

She looked at him and he could see on her face the exact expression he must have worn half an hour previously.

"It's good news, Jess! Be pleased!" And for a minute her eyes brimmed with tears. And then she looked so confused that he leaned forward and hugged her. This was his third voluntary hug in three years.

"Mascara," she said when she pulled back.

"Oh." He wiped under his eyes. She wiped hers.

"Good?"

"Fine. Me?"

She leaned forward and ran a thumb under the outer edge of his eye.

Then she let out a breath and suddenly she was a bit like the old Jess again. She stood up and brushed down her jeans. "We'll have to pay them all back, of course."

"Most of them are, like, three pounds. Good luck with working that out."

"Tanzie will sort it out." Jess picked up

the pink tissue parcel, and then, almost as an afterthought, she shoved it into a cupboard. She pushed her hair from her face. "And you have to show her the messages about maths. It's really important she sees those."

Nicky looked upstairs toward Tanzie's bedroom. "I will," he said, and just for a minute his mood dipped. "But I'm not sure it's going to make any difference."

Chapter Thirty-Seven: Jess

Norman came home. "It's time for us to say good-bye to our old hero, isn't it, old chap?" the vet said, patting Norman's side. The way he spoke to him, and the way that Norman immediately flopped to the ground for a tummy scratch, made Jess think this was not the first time he'd done it. As the vet dropped right down onto the floor, she caught a glimpse of the man beyond the careful professional manner. His broad smile, the way his eyes crinkled when he looked at the dog. And she heard Nicky's phrase running through her head, as it had done for days: the kindness of strangers.

"I'm glad you made the decision you did, Mrs. Thomas," he said, pushing himself back onto his feet while they diplomatically ignored the pistol crack of his knees. Norman stayed on his back, his tongue lolling, ever hopeful. Or perhaps just too fat to get up. "He deserved his chance. If I'd known how his injuries had come about, I would have been a bit less reticent about proceeding."

Tanzie stayed pressed close to Norman's enormous black body as they lumbered home, his lead wrapped twice around her fist. The walk from the vet's was the first time she had been outside in three weeks that she hadn't insisted on holding Jess's hand.

Jess had hoped that having him back would lift her daughter's spirits. But Tanzie was still a little shadow, tailing her silently around the house, peering around corners, waiting anxiously beside her form teacher at the end of the day for Jess's arrival at the school gates. At home she read in her room or lay silently on the sofa watching cartoons, one hand resting on the dog beside her. Mr. Tsvangarai had been off since term restarted — a family emergency — and Jess felt a reflexive sadness when she pictured him discovering Tanzie's determination to push mathematics from her life, the disappearance of the singular, quirky little girl she'd been. Sometimes she felt as if she had simply traded one unhappy, silent child for another.

St. Anne's rang to discuss Tanzie's orientation day at the school, and Jess had to tell them that she wasn't coming. The words were a squat dry frog in her throat.

"Well, we do recommend it, Mrs. Thomas. We find the children settle a lot better if they've familiarized themselves a little. It's good for her to meet a few fellow pupils as well. Is it a problem with getting time off from her current school?"

"No. I mean she — she's not coming."

"At all?"

"No."

A short silence.

"Oh," said the registrar. Jess heard her flicking through papers. "But this is the little girl with the ninety percent scholarship, yes? Costanza?"

She felt herself color. "Yes."

"Is she going to Petersfield Academy instead? Did they offer her a scholarship, too?"

"No. That's not it," Jess replied. She closed her eyes as she spoke. "Look, I don't suppose . . . Is there any way you could . . . increase the scholarship any further?"

"Further?" She sounded taken aback. "Mrs. Thomas, it was already the most generous scholarship we've ever offered. I'm sorry, but there's no question."

Jess pressed on, glad that nobody could see her shame. "If I could get the money together by next year, would you consider deferring her place?"

"I'm not sure whether that would be possible. Or even if it would be fair to the other candidates." She hesitated, perhaps suddenly conscious of Jess's silence. "But of course we'd certainly look at her favorably if ever she did want to reapply."

Jess stared at the spot on the carpet where Marty had brought a motorbike into the front room and it had leaked oil. A huge lump had risen into her throat. "Well, thank you for letting me know."

"Look, Mrs. Thomas," the woman said, her voice suddenly conciliatory, "there's still another week to go before we have to close the place. We'll hold it for you until the last possible minute."

"Thank you. That's very kind of you. But, really, there's no point."

Jess knew it and the woman knew it. It wasn't going to happen for them. Some leaps were just too big to make.

She asked Jess to pass on her best wishes to Tanzie for her new school. As she put the phone down, Jess imagined her already scanning her lists for the next suitable candidate.

She didn't tell Tanzie. Two nights previously

Jess discovered that Tanzie had removed all her maths books from her shelf and stacked them with Jess's remaining books on the upstairs landing, inserting them between thrillers and a historical romance so that she wouldn't notice. Jess put them in a neat pile in her wardrobe, where they couldn't be seen. She wasn't sure if this was saving Tanzie's feelings or her own.

Marty received the solicitor's letter and rang, protesting and blustering about why he couldn't pay. She told him it was out of her hands. She said she hoped they could be civil about it. She told him his children needed shoes. He didn't mention coming down at half term.

She got her job back at the pub. The girl from the City of Paris had apparently disappeared to the Texas Rib Shack three shifts after she'd started. Tips were better and there was no Stewart Pringle making random grabs at your backside.

"No loss. She didn't know not to talk during the guitar solo of 'Layla,' " Des mused. "What kind of barmaid doesn't know to keep quiet during the guitar solo of 'Layla'?"

She cleaned four days a week with Nathalie, and avoided number two Beachfront. She preferred jobs like scrubbing ovens, where she was unlikely to accidentally look through the window and catch sight of it, with its jaunty blue-and-white for-sale placard. If Nathalie thought she was behaving a little oddly, she didn't say anything.

She put an advert in the local newsagent's offering her services as a handyperson. No Job Too Small. Her first job came in less than twenty-four hours later: putting up a bathroom cabinet for a pensioner in Aden Crescent. The old woman was so happy with the result that she gave Jess a five-pound tip. She said she didn't like having men in her house and that in the forty-two years she had been married to her husband he had only ever seen her with her good wool vest on. She recommended Jess to a friend who managed a nursing home and needed a washer replaced and carpet gripper installed. Two other jobs followed, also pensioners. Jess sent a second installment of cash to number two Beachfront. Nathalie dropped it in. The for-sale sign was still up.

Nicky was the only one in the family who seemed genuinely cheerful. It was as if the blog had given him a new sense of purpose. He wrote it most evenings, posting about Norman's progress, pictures from his life, chatting with new friends. He met up with one of them IRL, he said, translating that for Jess: "In Real Life." He was all right, he said. And no, not like that. He wanted to go to open days at two different colleges. He was speaking to his form tutor about how to apply for a hardship grant. He'd looked it up. He smiled, often several times a day and without being asked, dropped to his knees with pleasure when he saw Norman wagging his tail in the kitchen, waved unself-consciously at Lila, the girl from number forty-seven (who, Jess noticed, had dyed her hair the same shade as his), and played an air guitar solo in the front room. He walked into town frequently, his skinny legs seeming to gain a longer stride, his shoulders not exactly back, but not slumped, defeated, as they had been in the past. Once he even wore a yellow T-shirt.

"Where's the laptop gone?" Jess said when she went into his room one afternoon and found him working away on their old computer.

"I took it back." He shrugged. "Nathalie let me in."

"Did you see him?" she said, before she could stop herself.

Nicky's eyes slid away. "Sorry. His stuff's there, but it's all boxed up. I'm not sure he stays there anymore."

It shouldn't have been a surprise, but as Jess made her way downstairs she found herself holding her stomach with both hands, as if she had been punched.

CHAPTER THIRTY-EIGHT: ED

His sister accompanied him to court several weeks later, on a day that woke still and hot. Ed had told his mother not to come. By then they were never sure whether it was a good idea to leave Dad for any length of time. As they crawled across London, his sister leaned forward in her taxi seat, her fingers tapping impatiently on her knee, her jaw set in a tight line. Ed felt perversely relaxed.

The courtroom was nearly empty. Thanks to the unholy combination of a particularly grisly murder at the Old Bailey, a political love scandal, and the public meltdown of a young British actress, the two-day trial had not registered as a big news story, just enough for an agency court reporter and a trainee from the *Financial Times.* And Ed had already pleaded guilty, against the advice of his legal team.

Deanna Lewis's claims of innocence had

been somewhat undermined by the evidence of a friend, a banker, who had apparently informed her in no uncertain terms that what she was about to do was indeed insider trading. The friend was able to produce an e-mail she had sent informing Deanna as much, and one in return from Deanna accusing the friend of being "picky," "annoying," and "frankly a little too involved in my business. Don't you want me to have a chance to move forward?"

Ed stood and watched the court reporter scribbling away, and the solicitors leaning in to each other, pointing to bits of paper, and it all felt rather anticlimactic.

"I am minded that you confessed your guilt and that, as far as Ms. Lewis and yourself are concerned, this appears to be isolated criminal behavior, motivated by factors other than money. This cannot be said of Michael Lewis."

The FSA, it turned out, had tracked other "suspicious" trades Deanna's brother had made, spread bets and options.

"It is necessary, however, that we send a signal that this kind of behavior is completely unacceptable, however it may have come about. It destroys investors' confidence in the honest movement in markets, and it weakens the whole structure of our financial system. For that reason I am bound to ensure that the level of punishment is still a clear deterrent to anyone who may believe this to be a 'victimless' crime."

Ed stood in the dock trying to work out what to do with his face and was fined £750,000 and costs, and sentenced to six months' imprisonment, suspended for twelve months.

It was over.

Gemma let out a long, shuddering breath and dropped her head into her hands. Ed felt curiously numb. "That's it?" he said quietly, and she looked up at him in disbelief. A clerk opened the door of the dock and ushered him out. Paul Wilkes clapped him on the back as they emerged into the corridor.

"Thank you," Ed said. It seemed like the right thing to say.

He caught sight of Deanna Lewis in the corridor, in animated conversation with a redheaded man. He looked like he was trying to explain something to her and she kept shaking her head, cutting him off. Ed stood staring for a moment, and then, almost without thinking, walked through the throng of people and straight up to her. "I wanted to say I'm sorry," he said. "If I had thought for one minute —"

She spun round, her eyes widening. "Oh, fuck off," she said, her face puce with fury, and pushed past him. "You fucking loser."

The faces that had swiveled at the sound of her voice took notice of Ed, then turned away in embarrassment. Somebody sniggered. As Ed stood there, his hand still half lifted as if to make a point, he heard a voice in his ear.

"She's not stupid, you know. She would have known she shouldn't have told her brother."

Ed turned, and there, behind him, stood Ronan. He took in his checked shirt and his thick black glasses, the computer bag slung over his shoulder, and something in him deflated with relief. "You . . . you were here all morning?"

"Bit bored at the office. I thought I'd come and see what a real-life court case was like."

Ed couldn't stop looking at him. "Over-rated."

"Yeah. That's what I thought."

His sister had been shaking hands with Paul Wilkes. She appeared at his side, straightening her jacket. "Right. Shall we go and ring Mum, give her the good news? She said she'd leave her mobile on. If we're lucky, she'll have remembered to charge it.

Hey, Ronan."

He leaned forward and kissed her cheek. "Nice to see you, Gemma. Been a long time."

"Too long! Let's go to mine," she said, turning to Ed. "It's ages since you saw the kids. I've got Spag Bol in the freezer we can have tonight. Hey, Ronan. You can come, too, if you like. I'm sure we could add some extra pasta to the pot."

Ronan's gaze slid away, as it had when he and Ed were eighteen. He kicked at something on the floor. Ed turned to his sister. "Um . . . Gem . . . would you mind if I left it? Just for today?" He tried not to register the way her smile fell. "I'll definitely come another time. I just . . . there's a few things I'd really like to talk to Ronan about. It's been . . ."

Her gaze flickered between them. "Sure," she said brightly, pushing her fringe from her eyes. "Well. Call me." She hoisted her bag onto her shoulder, and began to make her way toward the stairs.

He yelled across the busy corridor, so that several people looked up from their papers. "Hey! Gem!"

She turned, her bag under her arm.

"Thanks. For everything."

She stood there, half facing him.

"Really. I appreciate it."

She nodded, a ghost of a smile. And then she was gone, lost in the crowds on the stairwell.

"So. Um. Fancy a drink?" Ed tried not to sound pleading. He wasn't sure he was entirely successful. "I'm buying."

Ronan let it hang there. Just for a second. The bastard. "Well, in that case . . ."

It was Ed's mother who had once told him that real friends were the kind where you pick up where you'd left off, whether it be a week since you'd seen each other or two years. He'd never had enough friends to test it. He and Ronan nursed pints of beer across a wobbling wooden table in the busy pub, a little awkwardly at first, and then increasingly freely, the familiar jokes popping up between them like Whac-a-Moles, targets to be hit, with discreet pleasure. Ed felt as if he had been untethered for months and someone had finally tugged him in to land. He found himself watching his friend surreptitiously: his laugh, his enormous feet, the way he slumped over, even at a pub table, as if peering into a screen. And those things he hadn't seen about him before: how he laughed more easily; his new, designer-framed glasses; a kind of quiet confidence.

When he opened his wallet to pull out some cash, Ed caught a glimpse of a photograph of a girl, beaming into his credit cards.

"So . . . how's Soup Girl?"

"Karen? She's good." He smiled. "She's good. Actually, we're moving in together."

"Wow. Already?"

He looked up almost defiantly. "It's been six months. And with rental prices as they are in London, those not-for-profit soup charities don't exactly make a fortune."

"That's great," Ed stuttered. "Fantastic news."

"Yeah. Well. It's good. She's great. I'm really happy."

They sat there, silent for a moment. He'd had his hair cut, Ed noticed. And that was a new jacket. "I'm really pleased for you, Ronan. I always thought you two were great together."

"Thanks."

He smiled at him, and Ronan smiled back, pulling a face, like all this happiness stuff was a bit embarrassing.

Ed stared at his pint, trying not to feel left behind while his oldest friend was sailing on to a happier, brighter future. Around them the pub was filling up with end-of-the-day office workers. He had a sudden sense of limited time, of the importance of laying things out, straight, in front of him.

"I'm sorry," Ed said.

"What?"

"About everything. About Deanna Lewis. I don't know why I did it." His voice emerged as a croak. "I hate how I've messed things up. I mean, I'm sad about the job, yes, but mostly I'm just gutted that I messed us up." He couldn't look at Ronan, yet he felt lighter having said it.

Ronan took a swig of his drink. "Don't worry. I've thought about it a lot these past months and, while I kind of don't want to admit it, there's a good chance that if Deanna Lewis had come on to me I would have done the same." A rueful smile. "It was Deanna Lewis."

They sat in silence. Ronan leaned back in his chair. He bent a beer mat into two, and then into four. "You know . . . it's been kind of interesting with you not being there anymore," he said finally. "It made me understand something. I don't much like working at Mayfly. I liked it better when it was just you and me. All the Suits, the profit-and-loss stuff, shareholders, it's not me. It's not what I liked about it. It's not why we started it."

"Me, too."

"I mean the endless meetings . . . having

to run ideas past marketing people even to proceed with basic code. Having to justify every hour's activity. You know they want to bring in time sheets for everyone? Actual time sheets?"

Ed waited.

"You're not missing much, I tell you." Ronan shook his head, as if he had something more to say but felt he shouldn't.

"Ronan?

"Yeah?"

"I had this idea. This last week or two. About a new piece of software. I've been fiddling around, working on a piece of predictive software — really simple stuff — that will help people plan their finances. A sort of spreadsheet for people who don't like spreadsheets. For people who don't know how to handle money. It would have alerts that pop up whenever the user was about to incur a charge from their bank. It would have an option calculation to show how much different interest charges would add up to over a set period of time. Nothing too complicated. I was thinking it's the kind of thing they could give away at a Citizens' Advice Bureau."

"Interesting."

"It would need to be able to fit cheap computers. Software that might be a few years old. And cheaper mobile phones. I'm not sure it would make much money, but it's just something that I've been thinking about. I've outlined it. But . . ."

Ronan was thinking. Ed could see his mind working away, already chewing over the parameters.

"The thing is, it would need someone who is really good at coding. To build it."

Ronan kept his eyes on his pint, his face neutral. "You know you can't come back to Mayfly, right?"

Ed nodded. His best friend since college. "Yeah. I know."

Ronan met his eyes and suddenly they were both grinning.

Chapter Thirty-Nine:
Ed

All these years, and he didn't know his own sister's number by heart. She had been living in the same house for twelve years, and he still had to look up her address. Ed seemed to have an ever-growing list of things to feel bad about.

He had stood outside the King's Head as Ronan left for the Tube station and a nice girl who made soup, whose presence in his life had given him a whole extra dimension. Ed knew he could not go home to an empty flat, surrounded by boxes.

It took six rings for her to pick up the phone. And then he heard someone screaming in the background before she actually answered.

"Gem?"

"Yes?" she said breathlessly. "Leo, don't you throw that down the stairs!"

"Does that offer of Spaghetti Bolognese still stand?"

They were embarrassingly pleased to see him. The door of the little house in Finsbury Park opened and he walked in through the bikes and the piles of shoes and the overloaded coatrack that seemed to extend the entire way along the hall. Upstairs, the relentless beat of pop thumped through the connecting walls. It competed with the cinematic sounds of a war game on some kind of games console.

"Hey, you!" Her sister pulled him to her and hugged tight. She was out of her suit, wearing jeans and a jumper. "I can't even remember the last time you came here. When was the last time he was here, Phil?"

"With Lara," came the voice from down the corridor.

"Two years ago?"

"Where's the corkscrew, love?"

The kitchen was filled with steam and the smell of garlic. At its far end two clothes horses sagged under several loads of washing. Every surface, mostly stripped pine, was covered with books, piles of paper, or children's drawings. Phil stood and shook his hand, then excused himself. "Got a few e-mails to answer before supper. You don't mind?"

"You must be appalled," his sister said, plunking a glass in front of him. "You'll have to excuse the mess. I've been on late shifts, Phil has been flat out, and we haven't had a cleaner since Rosario left. All the others are a bit pricey."

He had missed this chaos. He missed the feeling of being embedded in a noisy, thumping heart. "I love it," he said, and her eyes scanned his swiftly for sarcasm. "No. Seriously. I love it. It feels —"

"Messy."

"That, too. It's good." He sat back in his chair at the kitchen table and let out a long breath.

"Hey, Uncle Ed."

Ed blinked. "Who are you?"

A teenage girl with burnished gold hair and several thick layers of mascara on each eye grinned at him. "Funny."

He looked at his sister for help. She raised her hands. "It's been a while, Ed. They grow. Leo! Come and say hello to Uncle Ed."

"I thought Uncle Ed was going to prison," came the cry from the other room.

"Excuse me for a minute."

His sister left the pan of sauce and disappeared into the hall. Ed tried not to hear the distant yelp.

"Mum says you lost all your money," said Justine, sitting down opposite and peeling the crust from a piece of French bread.

Ed's brain was desperately trying to marry the awkward, reed-thin child he had last seen with this tawny miracle who stared at him with faint amusement, as if he were a museum curio. "Pretty much."

"Did you lose your swanky flat?"

"Any minute now."

"Damn. I was going to ask you if I could have my sixteenth birthday party there."

"Well, you saved me the trouble of a refusal."

"That's exactly what Dad said. So are you happy that you didn't get locked up?"

"Oh, I think I'm still going to be the family cautionary tale for a while."

She smiled. "Don't be like naughty Uncle Edward."

"Is that how it's being pitched?"

"Oh, you know Mum. No moral lesson left unlearned in this house. 'You see how easy it is to end up on the wrong path? He had absolutely everything and now —' "

"I'm begging for meals and driving a seven-year-old car."

"Nice try. But ours still beats yours by three years." She glanced toward the hall, where her mother was speaking to her brother in low tones. "Actually, you mustn't be mean about Mum. You know she spent all of yesterday on the phone working on how to get you into an open prison?"

"Really?"

"She was properly stressed about it. I heard her telling someone you wouldn't last five minutes in Pentonville."

He felt a pang of something he couldn't quite identify. So deep in self-pity had he been that he hadn't considered how others would be affected if he was sent to prison. "She's probably right."

Justine pulled a lock of hair into her mouth. She seemed to be enjoying herself. "So what are you going to do now that you're a family disgrace with no job and possibly no home?"

"No idea. Should I take up a drug habit? Just to round it off?"

"Ugh. No. Stoners are so boring." She peeled her long legs off the chair. "And Mum's busy enough as it is. Although, actually, I should say yes. Because you've totally taken the heat off me and Leo. We now have so little to live up to."

"Glad to be of help."

"Seriously. Nice to see you, though." She leaned forward and whispered, "You've actually made Mum's day. She even cleaned the downstairs loo in case you turned up."

"Yeah. Well. I'm going to make sure I do

it more often."

She narrowed her eyes, as if she were trying to work out whether he was being serious, then turned and disappeared back up the stairs.

"So what's going on?" Gemma helped herself to green salad. "What happened to the girl at the hospital? Joss? Jess? I thought she'd be there today."

It was the first home-cooked meal he had eaten in ages, and it was delicious. The others had finished and left, but Ed was on his third helping, having suddenly reacquired the appetite that had disappeared for the last few weeks. His last mouthful had subsequently been a little overambitious and he sat there chewing for some time before he could answer. "I don't want to talk about it."

"You never want to talk about anything. C'mon. Price of a home-cooked meal."

"We split up."

"What? Why?" Three glasses of wine had made her garrulous, opinionated. "You seemed really happy. Happier than you were with Lara, anyway."

"I was."

"So? God, you're an idiot sometimes, Ed. There is a woman who actually seems normal, who seemed to have a handle on you, and you run a mile."

"I really don't want to talk about it, Gem."

"What was it? Too frightened to commit? Too soon after the divorce? You're not still hankering after Lara, are you?"

He took a bit of bread and wiped it around some sauce on the plate. He chewed longer than he needed to. "She stole from me."

"She what?"

It felt like a trump card, laying it down like that. Upstairs the children were arguing. Ed found himself thinking of Nicky and Tanzie, placing bets in the backseat. If he didn't tell somebody the truth, he might actually explode. So he told her.

Ed's sister pushed her plate across the table. She leaned forward, her chin resting in her hand, a faint frown bisecting her brow as she listened. He told the tale of the CCTV, how he had pulled out the drawers of the chest to move it across the room, and how there it had been, sitting on some neatly folded blue socks: his own laminated face.

I was going to tell you.

It's not how it looks. The hand to the mouth.

I mean, it is how it looks but, oh, God, oh, God —

"I thought she was different. I thought she was the greatest thing, this brave, principled, amazing . . . But fuck it, she was just like Lara. Just like Deanna. Only interested in what she could get out of me. How could she do that, Gem? Why can't I spot these women a mile off?" He finished, leaned back in his chair, and waited.

She didn't speak.

"What? You're not going to say anything? About my poor judge of character? About the fact that yet again I've let a woman screw me out of what's mine? About how I'm an idiot on yet another count?"

"I certainly wasn't going to say that."

"What were you going to say?"

"I don't know." She sat staring at her plate. She registered no surprise whatsoever. He wondered if ten years of social work did that, whether it was now ingrained in her to appear visibly neutral whatever shocking thing she heard. "That I see worse?"

He stared at her. "Than stealing from me?"

"Oh, Ed. You have no idea what it is to be truly desperate."

"It doesn't make it okay to steal."

"No, it doesn't. But . . . um . . . one of us

561

has just spent the day in court pleading guilty to insider trading. I'm not entirely sure that you're the greatest moral arbiter around here. Stuff happens. People make mistakes." She pushed herself upright and began to clear the plates. "Coffee?"

He was still staring at her.

"I'll take that as a yes. And while I'm clearing up, you can tell me a little more about her." She moved with a graceful economy around the little kitchen while he talked, never meeting his eye.

When he finally stopped talking, she pushed a drying-up cloth toward him. "So here's how I see it. She's in trouble, right? Her kids are being bullied. Her son gets his head kicked in. She's afraid it'll happen to the little girl next. She finds a wad of notes at the pub or wherever. She takes them."

"But she knew they were mine, Gem."

"But she didn't know you."

"And that makes a difference?"

His sister shrugged. "A nation of insurance fraudsters would say so."

Before he could protest again, she said, "Honestly? I can't tell you what she thought. But I can tell you that people in tight spots do things that are stupid and impulsive and ill thought out. I see it every day. They do crazy things for what they think are the right reasons, and some people get away with it and others don't."

When he didn't reply, she said, "Okay, so you never took a ballpoint home from work?"

"It was five hundred pounds."

"You never 'forgot' to pay a parking meter and cheered when you got away with it?"

"That isn't the same."

"You've never exceeded the speed limit? Never done a job for cash? Never bounced off someone else's Wi-Fi?" She leaned forward. "Never exaggerated your expenses for the tax man?"

"That isn't the same thing at all, Gem."

"I'm just pointing out that quite often how you see a crime depends on where you're standing. And you, my little brother, were a fine example of that today. I'm not saying she wasn't wrong to do it. I'm just saying maybe that one moment shouldn't be the whole thing that defines her. Or your relationship with her."

She finished the washing up, peeled off the rubber gloves, and laid them neatly across the draining board. Then she poured them both a mug of coffee and stood there, leaning against the sink. "I don't know. Maybe I just believe in second chances. Maybe if you had the litany of human misery trudging through your working day that I do, you would, too." She straightened up and looked at him. "Maybe if it were me, I'd at least want to hear what she had to say."

She handed him a mug.

"Do you miss her?"

Did he miss her? Ed missed her like a limb. He spent every day trying to avoid thoughts of her, running from the direction of his own mind. Trying to dodge the fact that everything he came across — food, cars, bed — reminded him of her. He had a dozen arguments with her before breakfast, and a thousand passionate reconciliations before he went to sleep.

Upstairs in a bedroom, a thumping beat broke the silence. "I don't know if I can trust her," he said.

Gemma gave him the same look she had always given him when he told her he couldn't do something. "I think you do, Ed. Somewhere. I think you probably do."

He finished the rest of the wine alone, then drank the bottle he had brought with him, crashing on his sister's sofa. He woke sweaty and disheveled at a quarter past five in the morning, left his sister a thank-you note, let himself out, and drove down to Beachfront to settle up with the managing agents. The Audi had gone to a dealer the previous week, along with the BMW he had kept in London, and he was now driving a third-hand Mini with a dented rear bumper. He had thought he'd mind more than he did.

It was a balmy morning, the roads were clear, and even at ten thirty, when he arrived, the holiday park was alive with visitors, the main stretch of bars and restaurants filled with people making the most of rare sunlight, walking, laden with bags of towels and umbrellas, to the beach. He drove slowly, feeling irrationally furious at this sterile semblance of a community, one in which everyone was in the same income bracket and nothing as messy as real life ever intruded beyond the perfectly aligned flowering borders.

He pulled into the immaculate drive at number two, pausing to listen to the sound of the waves as he stepped out of the car. He let himself in and realized he didn't care that this would be the last time he came here. There was just a week left until he completed the sale of his London flat. The vague plan was that he would spend the remaining time with his father. He had no plans beyond that.

The hallway was lined with boxes bearing

the name of the storage company that had packed them. He closed the door behind him, hearing the sound of his footsteps echo through the empty space. He walked upstairs slowly, making his way past the bare rooms. Next Tuesday the van would come, load the boxes, and take them away, until Ed could work out what to do with his stuff.

Right up until then, he supposed, he had plowed resolutely through what had been the worst few weeks of his life. Looked at from the outside, he seemed to be someone grimly determined, sucking up his punishment. He had put his head down and kept moving. Perhaps drinking a little too much, but hey, considering he'd lost a job, a home, a wife, and was about to lose a parent, all in a little more than twelve months, he could have argued that he was doing okay.

And then he spotted the four buff envelopes propped up on the kitchen work surface, his name scribbled on them in ballpoint pen. At first he assumed they were administrative letters, left by the managing agents, but then he opened one and was confronted by the filigree purple print of a twenty-pound note. He extracted it, then pulled out the accompanying note, which said, simply, THIRD INSTALLMENT.

He opened the others, tearing the envelope

carefully when he reached the first. As he read her note, an image of her sprang to mind and he was shocked by her sudden proximity, by the way she had been waiting there all along. Her expression, tense and awkward while writing, perhaps crossing out the words and reworking them. Here she would pull her ponytail from its band and retie it.

I'm sorry.

Her voice in his head. *I'm sorry.* And it was then that something started to crack. Ed held the money in his hand and didn't know what to do with it. He didn't want her apology. He didn't want any of it.

He walked out of the kitchen and back down the hall, the crumpled notes clutched in his hand. He wanted to throw it all away. He wanted never to let it go. He walked from one end of the house to the other, backward and forward. He gazed around him at the walls he'd never had a chance to scuff, and the sea view that no guests had ever enjoyed. The thought that he might never feel at ease anywhere, belong anywhere, was overwhelming. He paced the length of the hallway again, exhausted and restless. He opened a window, hoping to be calmed by the sound of the sea, but the shouts of the happy families outside felt like a rebuke.

A free newspaper sat folded on one of the boxes, obscuring something beneath. Exhausted by the relentless circling of his thoughts, he stopped and absentmindedly lifted it. Underneath sat a laptop and a mobile phone. He had to think for a minute to work out why they might be there. Ed hesitated, then picked up the phone and turned it over. It was the handset he had given Nicky back in Aberdeen, carefully hidden from the casual view of passersby.

For weeks he had been fueled by the anger of betrayal. When that initial heat dissipated, a whole part of him had simply iced over. He had been secure in his outrage, safe in his sense of injustice. Now Ed held a mobile phone that a teenage boy who possessed next to nothing had felt obliged to return to him. He heard his sister's words and something began to open up inside him. What the hell did he know about anything? Who was he to judge anyone?

Fuck it, he told himself. I can't go and see her. I just can't.

Why should I?

What would I even say?

He walked from one end of his empty house to the other, his footsteps echoing on the wooden floors, his fist tight around the notes.

He stared out of the window at the sea and wished, suddenly, that he had gone to jail. He wished that his mind had been filled with the immediate physical problems of safety, logistics, survival.

He didn't want to think about her.

He didn't want to see her face every time he closed his eyes.

He would go. He would leave here and get a new place, and a new job, and he would start again. And he would leave all this behind. And things would be easier.

A shrill noise — a ringtone he didn't recognize — shattered the silence. His old phone, recalibrated with Nicky's preferences. He stared at it, at the rhythmically glowing screen. Caller unknown. After five rings, when the sound became unbearable, he finally snatched it up.

"Is Mrs. Thomas there?"

Ed held the phone briefly away, as if it were radioactive. "Is this a joke?"

A nasal voice, sneezing: "Sorry. Awful hay fever. Have I got the right number? Parents of Costanza Thomas?"

"What — who is this?"

"My name's Andrew Prentiss. I'm calling from the Olympiad."

It took him a moment to collect his thoughts. He sat down on the stairs.

"The Olympiad? I'm sorry — how did you get this number?"

"It was on our contacts list. You left it during the exam. I have got the right number?"

Ed remembered Jess's phone being out of credit. She must have given the number of the phone he'd given to Nicky instead. His head dropped into his free hand. Someone up there had quite a sense of humor.

"Yes."

"Oh, thank goodness. We've been trying you for days. Did you not pick up any of my messages? I'm calling about the exam . . . The thing is, we discovered an anomaly when we were marking the papers. The first question contained a misprint, which made the algorithm impossible to solve."

"What?"

He spoke as if reciting a well-worn series of statements. "We noticed it after the final results were collated. The fact that every single student failed the first question was a giveaway. It wasn't picked up on initially, as we had several different people marking. Anyway, we're very sorry — and we'd like to offer your daughter the chance to resit. We're doing the whole thing again."

"Resit the Olympiad? When?"

"Well, that's the thing. It's this afternoon. It had to be a weekend as we couldn't expect students to miss school to do it. We've actually been trying to reach you all week on this number, but we got no response. I only tried you the one last time on the off chance."

"You're expecting her to get to Scotland in . . . four hours?"

Mr. Prentiss paused to sneeze again. "No, not Scotland this time. We had to take the space available to us. But looking at your details, I see this might work out better for you, seeing as you live on the south coast. The event is scheduled to take place in Basingstoke. Are you happy to pass the message on to Costanza?"

"Uh . . ."

"Thanks so much. I suppose these things are only to be expected in our first year. Still, one more down! I only have one more entrant to reach! The rest of the info is on the Web site if you need it."

An almighty sneeze. And the phone went dead.

And Ed was left in his empty house, staring at the handset.

CHAPTER FORTY:
JESS

Jess had been trying to persuade Tanzie to open the door. The school counselor had told her it would be a good way to start rebuilding her confidence in the outside world, as long as she was in the house. She would answer the door, safe in the knowledge that Jess was behind her. That confidence would slowly stretch to other people, to being in the garden. It would be a stepping-stone. These things were incremental.

It was a nice theory. If Tanzie would only agree to do it.

"Door. Mum."

Her voice carried over the sound of the cartoons. Jess was wondering when to get tough with her on the television watching. She had calculated last week that Tanzie now spent upward of five hours a day lying on the sofa. "She has had a shock," the counselor had said. "But I think she'd feel better sooner if she was doing something a little more constructive."

"I can't answer it, Tanze," she called down. "I'm standing here with my hands in a bowlful of bleach."

Her voice, a whine, a new development these last days: "Can't you get Nicky to open it?"

"Nicky's gone to the shop."

Silence.

The sound of canned laughter echoed up the stairs. Jess could feel, if not see, the presence of whoever was waiting at the door, the shadow behind the glass. She wondered if it was Aileen Trent. She had arrived uninvited four times over the last two weeks with "unmissable bargains" for the children. She wondered if she'd heard about Nicky's blog money. Everyone in the neighborhood seemed to know about it.

Jess yelled down, "Look, I'll stand at the top of the stairs. All you have to do is open it."

The doorbell rang again, twice.

"Come on, Tanze. It's not going to be anything bad. Look, put Norman on the lead and bring him with you."

Silence.

Out of sight, she let her head drop down and wiped her eyes in the crook of her arm.

She couldn't ignore it: Tanzie was getting worse, not better. In the last fortnight she had taken to sleeping in Jess's bed. She no longer woke crying, but crept across the hallway in the small hours and simply climbed in, so that Jess woke beside her with no idea of how long she had been there. She hadn't had the heart to tell her not to, but the counselor said pointedly that she was a little old to do that indefinitely.

"Tanze?"

Nothing. The doorbell rang a third time, impatient now.

Jess waited. She was going to have to go down and do it herself.

"Hold on," she called wearily. She began to peel off her rubber gloves, and then she stopped as she heard the footfall in the hallway. The lumbering, wheezing sound of Norman being tugged along. Tanzie's sweet voice entreating him to come with her, a tone she used only with him these days.

And then the front door opening. Her satisfaction at the sound was tempered by the sudden realization that she should have told Tanzie to tell Aileen to go away. Given half a chance she would be in with her black bag on wheels and straight past her, settling herself on the sofa and her sequined "bargains" spread out on the living-room floor,

tailored to Tanzie's weakness so that it
would be impossible for Jess to say no.

But it wasn't Aileen's voice she heard.

"Hey, Norman."

Jess froze.

"Whoa. What happened to his face?"

"He only has one eye now." Tanzie's voice.

Jess tiptoed to the top of the stairs. She
could see his feet. His Converse trainers.
Her heart began to thump.

"Did he have some kind of accident?"

"He saved me. From the Fishers."

"He what?"

And then Tanzie's voice — her mouth
opening and the words coming out in a
rush. "The Fishers tried to get me in a car
and Norman bust through the fence to save
me but he got hit by a car and we had no
money and then —"

Her daughter. Talking as if she wouldn't
stop.

Jess took one step down, and then another.

"He nearly died," Tanzie said. "He nearly
died and the vet didn't even want to give
him an operation because he was so sick
with infernal injuries, and he thought we
should just let him go. But Mum said she
didn't want to and that we should give him
a chance. And then Nicky wrote this blog
about how everything had gone wrong, and

some people just sent him money. And we had enough to save him. So Norman saved me and people we don't even know saved him, which is sort of cool. But he only has one eye now and he gets really tired because he's still in recovery and he doesn't do very much."

She could see him now. He had crouched down, and was stroking Norman's head. And she couldn't tear her eyes away — the dark hair, the way his shoulders fit in his T-shirt. That gray T-shirt. Something rose up in her and a muffled half sob came out so that she had to press her arm against her mouth. And then he looked up at her daughter from his low position, and his face was deadly serious. "Are you okay, Tanzie?"

She lifted a hand and twisted a lock of her hair, as if deciding how much to tell him. "Sort of."

"Oh, sweetheart."

Tanzie hesitated, her toe rotating on the floor behind her, and then she simply stepped forward and walked into his arms. He closed them around her, as if he had been waiting for just that thing, letting her rest her head against his shoulder, and they just stayed there. Jess watched him close his eyes, and she had to take one step back up to where she couldn't be seen because she was afraid if he saw her, she wouldn't be able to stop crying.

"Well, you know, I knew," he said finally, when he pulled back, and his voice was oddly determined. "I knew there was something special about this dog. I could see it."

"Really?"

"Oh yes. You and him. A team. Anyone with any sense could see it. And you know what? He looks pretty cool with one eye. He looks kind of tough. Nobody's going to mess with Norman."

Jess didn't know what to do. She didn't want to go downstairs because she couldn't bear him to look at her the way he did before. She couldn't move. She couldn't go down and she couldn't move.

"Mum told us why you don't come round anymore."

"She did?"

"It was because she took your money."

A painfully long silence.

"She said she made a big mistake and she didn't want us to do the same thing." Another silence. "Have you come to get it back?"

"No. That's not why I've come at all." He looked behind him. "Is she here?"

There was no avoiding it. Jess took one step down. And then another, her hand on the banister. She stood on the stairs with her rubber gloves on and waited as his eyes lifted to hers. And what he said next was the last thing she had expected him to say.

"We need to get Tanzie to Basingstoke."

"What?"

"The Olympiad. There was a mistake with the paper last time. And they're resitting it. Today."

Tanzie turned and looked up the stairs at her, frowning, as confused as Jess was. And then, as if a lightbulb had just gone on in her head, she said: "Was it question one?"

He nodded.

"I knew it!" And she smiled, an abrupt, brilliant smile. "I knew there was something wrong with it!"

"They want her to resit the whole paper?"

"This afternoon."

"But that's impossible."

"Not in Scotland. Basingstoke. It's doable."

She didn't know what to say. She thought of all the ways in which she had destroyed her daughter's confidence by pushing her to the Olympiad the previous time. She thought of her mad schemes, of how much hurt and damage their single trip had caused. "I don't know . . ."

He was still balanced on his haunches. He

reached out a hand and touched Tanzie's arm. "You want to give it a go?"

Jess could see her uncertainty. Tanzie's grip on Norman's collar tightened. She shifted her weight from one foot to the other. "You don't have to, Tanze," she said. "It doesn't matter one bit if you'd rather not."

"But you need to know that nobody got it right." Ed's voice was calm and certain. "The man told me it was impossible. Not a single person in that examination room got question one correct."

Nicky had appeared behind him, holding a plastic bag full of stationery from his shopping trip. It was hard to tell how long he'd been there.

"So, yes, your mum is quite right, and you absolutely don't have to go," Ed said. "But I have to admit that, personally, I would quite like to see you whup those boys at maths. And I know you can do it."

"Go on, Titch," Nicky said. "Go and show them what you're really made of."

She looked round at Jess. And then she turned back and pushed her repaired glasses up her nose.

It's possible that all four people held their breath.

"Okay," she said. "But only if we can bring

Norman."

Jess's hand went to her mouth. "You really want to do this?"

"Yes. I could do all the other questions, Mum. I just panicked when I couldn't get the first one to work. And then it all went a bit wrong from there."

Jess took two more steps down the stairs, her heart racing. Her hands had started to sweat in her rubber gloves. "But how will we get there in time?"

Ed Nicholls straightened up and looked her in the eye. "I'll take you."

It's not easy driving four people and a large dog in a Mini, especially not on a hot day and in a car with no air-conditioning. Especially if the dog's intestinal system is even more challenged than it once was, and you have to go at speeds of more than forty miles an hour with all the inevitable consequences that brings. They drove with all of the windows open, in near silence, Tanzie murmuring to herself as she tried to remember all the things she'd become convinced she'd forgotten, and occasionally pausing to bury her face in a strategically placed bag.

Jess read the map, as Ed's new car had no built-in GPS, and using his phone, tried to steer a route away from motorway traffic jams and clogged shopping centers. Within an hour and three quarters, all conducted in a peculiar near silence, they were there: a 1970s glass and concrete block with a piece of paper marked OLYMPIAD flapping in the wind, taped to a sign that read KEEP OFF THE GRASS.

This time they were prepared. Jess signed Tanzie in, handed her a spare pair of spectacles ("She never goes anywhere without a spare pair, now," Nicky told Ed), a pen, a pencil, and an eraser. Then they all hugged her and reassured her that this didn't matter, not one bit, and stood in silence as Tanzie walked in to do battle with a bunch of abstract numbers, and possibly the demons in her own head.

Jess hovered at the desk and finished signing the paperwork, acutely conscious of Nicky and Ed chatting on the grass verge through the open door. She watched them with surreptitious sideways looks. Nicky was showing Mr. Nicholls something on Mr. Nicholls's old phone. Occasionally Mr. Nicholls would shake his head. She wondered if it was the blog.

"She'll be cool, Mum," said Nicky, cheerfully, as Jess emerged. "Don't stress." He was holding Norman's lead. He had promised Tanzie they would not go more than five hundred feet from the building so that she could feel their special bond even through the walls of the examination hall.

"Yeah. She'll be great," said Ed, his hands thrust deep in his pockets.

Nicky's gaze flicked between the two of them, then down at the dog. "Well. We're going to take a comfort break. The dog's. Not mine," he said. "I'll be back in a while." Jess watched him wander slowly along the quadrant and fought the urge to say that she would go with him.

And then it was just the two of them.

"So," she said. She picked at a bit of paint on her jeans. She wished she had had the chance to change into something smarter.

"So."

"Yet again you save us."

"You seem to have done a pretty good job of saving yourselves."

They stood in silence. Across the car park a car skidded in, a mother and a young boy hurling themselves from the backseat and running toward the door.

"How's the foot?"

"Getting there."

"No flip-flops."

She gazed down at her white tennis shoes. "No. Not anymore."

He ran his hand over his head and stared

at the sky. "I got your envelopes."

She couldn't speak.

"I got them this morning. I wasn't ignoring you. If I'd known . . . everything . . . I wouldn't have left you to deal with all that alone."

"It's fine," she said briskly. "You'd done enough." A large piece of flint was embedded in the ground in front of her. She kicked at some dirt with her good foot, trying to dislodge it. "And it was very kind of you to bring us to the Olympiad. Whatever happens I'll always be —"

"Will you stop?"

"What?"

"Stop kicking stuff. And stop talking like . . ." He turned to her. "Come on. Let's go sit in the car."

"What?"

"And talk."

"No . . . thank you."

"What?"

"I just . . . Can't we talk out here?"

"Why can't we sit in the car?"

"I'd rather not."

"I don't understand. Why can't we sit in the car?"

"Don't pretend you don't know." Tears sprang to her eyes. And she wiped at them furiously with the palm of her hand.

"I don't know, Jess."

"Then I can't tell you."

"Oh, this is ridiculous. Just come and sit in the car."

"No."

"Why? I'm not going to stand out here unless you give me a good reason."

"Because . . ." Her voice broke. "Because that's where we were happy. That's where I was happy. Happier than I've been for years. And I can't do it. I can't sit in there, just you and me, now that . . ."

Her voice failed. She turned away from him, not wanting him to see what she felt. Not wanting him to see her tears. She heard him come and stand close behind her. The closer he got, the more she couldn't breathe. She wanted to tell him to go, but she knew she couldn't bear it if he did.

His voice was low in her ear. "I'm trying to tell you something."

She stared at the ground.

"I want to be with you. I know we've made an unholy mess of it, but I still feel more right with you doing wrong than I usually feel when everything's supposedly right and you're not there." A pause. "Fuck. I'm no good at this stuff."

Jess turned slowly. He was gazing at his feet, but looked up suddenly.

"They told me what Tanzie's wrong question was."

"What?"

"It was about the theory of emergence. Strong emergence says that the sum of a number can be more than its constituent parts. You know what I'm saying?"

"No. I'm crap at maths."

"It means I don't want to go back over it all. What you did. What we both did. But I just . . . I want to try. You and me. It might prove to be a huge fuckup. But I'll take that chance."

He reached out then and gently took hold of the belt loop of her jeans. He pulled her toward him. She couldn't tear her eyes from his hands. And then, when she finally did lift her face to his, he was gazing straight at her and Jess found she was crying and smiling.

"I want to see what we can add up to, Jessica Rae Thomas. All of us. What do you say?"

CHAPTER FORTY-ONE:
TANZIE

So the uniform for St. Anne's is royal blue with yellow piping. You can't hide in a St. Anne's blazer. Some girls in my class take them off when they're going home, but it doesn't bother me. When you work hard to get somewhere, it's quite nice to show people where you belong. The funny thing is that when you see another St. Anne's student outside school, it's the custom to wave to each other. Sometimes it's a big wave, like Sriti's. She's my best friend, and she always looks like she's on a desert island trying to attract a passing plane, and sometimes it's just a tiny lifting of your fingers down by your school bag, like Dylan Carter, who gets embarrassed about talking to anyone, even his own brother. But everyone does it. You might not know the person waving, but you wave at the person in the uniform. It's what the school's always done. It shows that we're all a family, apparently.

I always wave, especially if I'm on the bus.

Ed picks me up on Tuesdays and Thursdays because that's when I have maths club and Mum works late at her handyperson thing. She has three people working for her now. She says they work "with" her, but she's always showing them how to do stuff and telling them which jobs to go to and Ed says she's still a bit uncomfortable with the idea of being a boss. He says she's getting used to it. He pulls a face when he says it, like Mum's the boss of him, but you can tell he likes it.

Since the start of school in September, Mum has taken Friday afternoons off, and she meets me at school and we make biscuits together, just me and her. It's been nice, but I'm going to have to tell her I'd rather stay late at school, especially now I'm going to do my A level in the spring. Dad hasn't had a chance to come down yet, but we Skype every week and he says he's definitely going to. He sold the Rolls to a man at the police pound. He's got two job interviews next week, and lots of irons in the fire.

Nicky is at sixth-form college in Southampton. He wants to go to art school. He has a girlfriend called Lila, which Mum said was a surprise on all sorts of counts. He still wears lots of eyeliner, but he's letting his hair grow out to its natural color, which is sort of a dark brown. He's now a whole head taller than Mum and sometimes when they're in the kitchen he thinks it's funny to rest his elbow on her shoulder, like she's a bar or something. He still writes in his blog sometimes, but mostly he says he's too busy and he prefers Twitter these days, so it would be okay if I take it over for a bit. Next week it will be less personal stuff and more about maths. I'm really hoping lots of you like maths.

We paid back seventy-seven percent of the people who sent us money for Norman. Fourteen percent said they would rather we just gave the money to charity, and we were never able to trace the other nine percent. Mum says it's fine, because the important thing was that we tried, and that sometimes it's okay just to accept people's generosity as long as you say thank you. She said to say thank you to you, if you're one of them, and she'll never forget the kindness of strangers.

Ed is here literally *all* the time. He sold his house at Beachfront and he now owns a really small flat in London, where Nicky and I have to sleep on put-you-up beds when we're there, but most of the time he stays with us. He works in the kitchen on his laptop and talks to his friend in London on this really cool set of headphones, and he goes up and down for meetings in the Mini. He keeps meaning to get a new car, as it's really hard to fit all of us in when we want to go somewhere, but in a weird way none of us really wants him to. It's kind of nice in the little car, all squashed together, and in that car I don't feel so guilty about the drool.

Norman is happy. He does all the things the vet said he'd be able to do, and Mum says that's enough for us. The law of probability combined with the law of large numbers states that to beat the odds, sometimes you have to repeat an event an increasing number of times in order to get you to the outcome you desire. The more you do, the closer you get. Or, as I explain it to Mum, basically, sometimes you just have to keep going.

I've taken Norman into the garden and thrown the ball for him eighty-six times this week. He still never brings it back.

But I think we'll get there.

ABOUT THE AUTHOR

JoJo Moyes is the *New York Times* bestselling author of *The Girl You Left Behind, Me Before You, Honeymoon in Paris,* and *The Last Letter from Your Lover*. Moyes writes for a variety of newspapers and magazines, and is married to Charles Arthur, technology editor of *The Guardian*. They live with their three children on a farm in Essex, England.